Praise for the Novels of Thomas E. Kennedy

"An elegantly written and wise work." —THE TIMES

"IN THE COMPANY OF ANGELS possesses an integrity, force and dignity that can only serve as a moral purpose... In its wisdom and empathy, in its understanding of the supreme importance of love, in its portrait of a strong man and its knowledge of the human soul in all its suffering, this is indeed a profound and exceptional work." —Joanna Briscoe, GUARDIAN

"A moving love story woven from a delicate web of emotions... remarkable." —TIME OUT

"The essay, the guide book, the comforting exchange of facts in a bewildering—all are to be found in KERRIGAN IN COPENHAGEN ... Stunning prose that twirls with the impovisations of the jazz musicians Kerrigan admires..." —NEW TORK TIMES BOOK REVIEW, chosen as an EDITORS CHOICE

"FALLING SIDEWAYS is that rarest of commodities in American, a novel about men and women at work; it is part satire and part drama, and it is very smart." —THE WASHINGTON POST

"[An] eloquent satire on corporate life and the pursuit of happiness." —GUARDIAN

"[KENNEDY] has an ear and eye for modern life." —STAR TRIBUNE (Minneapolis-St. Paul)

MY LIFE WITH WOMEN
Or, The Consolation of Jazz

Volume 1

Thomas E. Kennedy

SERVING
HOUSE
SHB BOOKS

My Life with Women

Or, The Consolation of Jazz

Volume 1

Copyright © Thomas E. Kennedy, 2020

Published by Serving House Books

Copenhagen, Denmark and South Orange, NJ

www.servinghousebooks.com

ISBN: 978-1-947175-40-2

Library of Congress Control Number: 2020944341

Member of The Independent Book Publishers Association

First Serving House Books Edition 2020

Cover Design: Peter Selgin

Proofreading: Louise Stahl

Serving House Books Logo: Barry Lereng Wilmont

Always for Daniel and Isabel, Søren & Leo
For all my friends and colleagues
and for my friend of friends,
Walter Cummins

"And if the soul
is ever to know itself
it must gaze
into the soul…"

—George Seferis

"…it is said that those who see will find something captured that escapes explanation. This conviction that direct deed is the most meaningful reflection, I believe, has prompted the evolution of the extremely severe and unique discplines of the jazz or improvising musician."

—Bill Evans, pianist
From liner notes of the 1959 LP
Release of Miles Davis' *Kind of Blue*

SOME OF THIS REALLY HAPPENED,
as memory serves me.

PART ONE

Jazz on a Summer's Day

WHEN I WAS SIXTEEN, Bert Stern's full-length documentary film made me heady with dreams of the adult life I was awaiting. The film focused on the Newport Jazz Festival. It played at the Earle Theater in Jackson Heights on a side street to a side street to Roosevelt Avenue, where the Elevated train ran from the East River to Main Street, Flushing.

The train began as the subway in Grand Central Station in Manhattan and snaked under the East River to Queensborough Plaza and Long Island City (where my father James Ryan Fitzgerald, Sr. was vice president of a small chain of banks which doesn't exist anymore), proceeded just past the border of Astoria (where my sister Jenny lived when I was eight with her husband and her infant son in the projects), hooked south through Sunnyside (where my oldest brother James, Jr. battled with his fists in the Golden Gloves at Sunnyside Gardens), screeching north through Woodside (where my older brother Joseph, a.k.a. Jos., blew the horn of his early twenties) and ran straight as a crooked arrow through Jackson Heights and Elmhurst (where we lived in a house my father bought on Gleane Street beneath the Roosevelt Avenue El for ten thousand dollars in 1940 while my mother was in Flushing Hospital birthing my older brother Jos.), through Corona and East Elmhurst (where Louis Armstrong lived and LaGuardia Airport lay) and proceeded to Flushing (a bastardization of the Dutch, Vlissingen—an area in Zeeland—where the World's Fair 1939-40 and 1964-65 and Shea Stadium were, home to the NY Mets and Jets, and the site where the Beatles would play to the euphoria and mass hystera of fifty-five thousand fans in 1965) and ended in Main Street, a host to a row of men's clothing stores. The side street to a side street was known vulgarly back then as "Fag

Alley," and the Earle showed indies and European "films" (as opposed to "movies"). The concept of anything European reeked of socialism and permissiveness and made our lower middle-class minds spin back to the other side of the Atlantic where our great-grandparents had come from, and we wanted distance from that, except when my father was in his cups and played his John McCormack records: *And the tears will surely blind me/For the friends I leave behind me,/But I'm bound for Philadelphia in the morning....*

Indie and European films and permissiveness had an overwhelming attraction to me. I had seen and would see Bergman, Bo Widerberg, Henning Carlsen, Fellini, and de Sica films. In 1960, I also saw the documentary of the July '58 Newport Jazz Festival, my eyes wide and blue in the dark: Jimmie Giuffre blew staccato tenor sax, "The Train and the River," hopping to the rhythm of the imaginary train, and the film switched from impressionistic images of the sea and the yacht races and the public and the musicians, all decked out in suits and slim neckties mounted to the throat. The 39-year-old Anita O'Day (it was said that she was high on heroin), in white gloves and an elegantly tailored black summer dress and wide-brimmed black hat adorned with a long white feather, looking beautiful and smiling playfully from the audience to the band, sang scat, impossibly fast on "Tea for Two" without missing an enunciated note, and made room for Hank Jones by uttering two words, "Mr. Jones?" and there followed a cascade of notes on the ivory-and-ebony piano keys.

There were more wonders in the film: A couple let themselves out the window of a second story bar and danced Lindy hop—which originated in Harlem but was named for Charles Lindbergh when he landed in Paris—on a slanted roof, the guy clapping his hands, a cigarette jutting from his smile while the woman wore a cardigan, unbuttoning it promisingly. The couple looked mature and adult and normal as they danced because it was an adult, normal, mature way to behave!

Sax-man Sonny Stitt and Sal Salvador, eyes closed on cool, icy electric guitar notes got a black woman in a blue dress, dancing, smiling and bopping, making all things possible. The sea was glistening and choppy, and as the sun disappeared, coloring the water red, Dinah Washington, in her prime, sang "All of Me," to the ringing, shimmering vibes, as women in the audience smiled knowingly, and that knowingness was so

14

innocent and reflected back on me, heating my blood. Looking serious, almost pained with concentration, Chico Hamilton was beating with padded sticks on a number of kettle drums, while a tall dark man blew a silver fluteful of mysterious music.

Redheaded crewcut Gerry Mulligan in a red blazer blew his young lungs out on "Catch as Catch Can," while a magic woman closed her eyes to the music and rhythmically bit her lip to his baritone, her smile, bathed in night, of sheer appreciation and lust, and Art Farmer blew trumpet, and a trombone said BRMMPP. Big Maybelle, 34-years-old, looking so modest in her hugeness, with her big throaty voice belted out, "I ain't mad at you, pretty baby, don't you be mad at me," and a long slender grown-up woman in a red cashmere sweater, smiling with all her long teeth, danced demurely; she surely is dead now, but captured on film for the rest of my life as an old friend....

I came out of the Earle, blinking in the sunlight, a changed boy.

The Outlaw Safari

LATER IN 1960: At the Times Record Shop in the subway at Times Square & Forty-Deuce Street, kids like me stood flipping through the bins of used 45s in new blank paper jackets. You could get the vinyl disks for a nickel, a dime, a quarter, minus a 10-percent discount if you had a card from "The Voice in the Night" on WHOM radio.

On one of my forage visits, I came upon a sparkling new 45 on the Blue Note label, titled on one side "The Outlaw," on the other "Safari." Those words were elixirs to my teenage imagination. I would learn, much later, they had been recorded in January 1958 in Hackensack, New Jersey, two rivers over—the East and the Hudson—only two months before my fourteenth birthday, but at the moment of discovery, the record might have been an antique in mint condition.

The name on the label was the Horace Silver Quintet, but what arrested my attention was the indication of the playing time: The one side ran for six minutes and seven seconds, the other five minutes and ten seconds. In those days, most rock 'n' roll sides played for three minutes or less, and their brevity was tantalizing. My Webcor portable record player stacked half a dozen 45s, and a side played for, like, two minutes and forty seconds, then the mechanism whirred sluggishly, the pick-up bearing armature lifted and swung away from the turntable and hovered there while the next record plopped down the spindle and settled on top of the one that had just finished. There would be a crackling silence before the next number began. The whirring, crackling, music-less silence returned you to your self-consciousness.

But 6:07 plus 5:10 was more than eleven minutes. For a 16-year-old, eleven minutes was a fat slice of eternity. The record, apparently remaindered, cost ten cents (minus my discount). I bought *two* copies and rode the subway and the El back to the place where I played records—the basement of our home in Elmhurst, Queens, bordering on Jackson Heights and Roosevelt, not ten blocks from the side street to the side street where I had first discovered jazz.

My gray portable Webcor played records that were 33-1/3, 45, and 78 revolutions per minute with a sapphire needle. In the big hole at the center of a 45 (manufactured because American jukeboxes had difficulty coping with small-holed records), you fitted a yellow plastic insert, called a spider, that made the 45 amenable to the thin spindle of a phonograph. I positioned both copies on the spindle, "The Outlaw" first and "Safari" second. *Jazz on a Summer's Day* was a potpourri of jazz—cool, bebop, Dixieland, Blues, R&B, R 'n'R, spiritual…. This was to be my first taste of pure, hard bop, but I wasn't aware of it. The hard bop might have been my first tumbler of whiskey or that first unexpected burgeoning and shock of orgasm four years before when I prayed to a picture of Brigitte Bardot on the cover of a *Modern Photography* magazine.

I didn't suspect what was going to happen—I didn't know a modal implication if it be-bopped me on the skull, and polytonality might be the name of an island in the South Pacific, though I knew what moved me. On came Art Farmer's trumpet, Clifford Jordan's tenor, and Horace Silver, tickling and banging ebonies and ivories melodiously—time shifts, starts, stops, thirteen bars, ten bars, a two-bar break, and Farmer's trumpet melding with Jordan's horn, Silver's meticulously wild notes. The pounding, lilting, screaming lyrical streams of sound-feeling led you ontoa thin ice of emotions that might at any second crack and break and let your ego drop.

At that time, on that first encounter, all I knew was what was happening to me—no, I didn't *know* what was happening I *felt* it, as surprise, amazement. As I listened again and again and again, the amazement began to transform to infusion.

I listened to those two records repeatedly, so it wore grooves in my brain that corresponded to the vinyl—and they let other jazz in, the improvisations of live jazz grooved on wax. It surprised me every time, the way that Quintet got from here to there, but it did—they did it with a stop for a breath of a second, then took off in a new direction, in a new time figure.

I didn't know music. I knew what Dixieland and swing and big band were, and I was starting to learn that the big bands had been decimated by the war and led to trios and quartets and quintets and all the way up to nonets and decets, shifting from the big band arrangements to improvisation and the musicians interacting and extemporizing.

Talk of diatonics and chromatics and metronomics and polytonality and bitonality and multiphonics quickly made my eyes glaze over, and if I tried to define bop, rebop, hard bop, neobop, modern jazz, mainstream jazz, progressive jazz, avant-garde jazz, cool jazz, modal jazz,and and free jazz too exclusively, it all began to writhe together.

Hard bop—hell, *jazz!*—had come and found me.

The World According to Bernard Herrmann

I HAD A GIRLFRIEND THAT SUMMEr when I was sixteen. Anne Suffier was the first girl I met entirely on my own, with no introduction. Sunday was the only day I was free from my after-school job, and I used to go to the white sands of Rockaway Beach, Beach 108. I saw her lying on an enormous towel all alone. I looked up from my reading a fat book, *The Possesed*. I had just got to the long-suppressed chapter, preserved by Dostoyevsky's wife, when Stavrogin is at Bishop Tihon's monastery and confesses that he had dallied while a 14-year-old girl, whom he had seduced, hung herself in the next room when Stavrogin is engaged in observing a red spider, fully cognizant that the girl is hanging herself.

But Anne arrested me from reading. She was slender and tan and pretty. I marked my page, waited until I was sure she was alone, I went over to her, the electric feeling fluttering in my stomach when you're about to do something dangerous.

She made it easy for me. "Summer reading? That should keep you engaged all summer. It's thick enough."

She had some kind of an accent. I said that it was something for school rather than say it was a book I was reading on my own, not to think I was weird. Her slender body hypnotized me. Her legs were long and tan, her hands little and sculpted, and her mouth, when she smiled, one eye sun-squinting, had one tooth that overlapped cutely, beautifully, and her accent was sexy. I made small talk and learned that she was fifteen and from Montreal. She pronounced it in the French way.

I asked if she minded if I sit with her and tried some of the phrases I had learned in my two years of high school French. She told me that her father had been "transplanted"—she pronounced it in her accent, with the stress on the last syllable—by his American company from Montreal to New York City. I asked if she wanted to go in "*la mer*," and guided her by the hand beyond the breakers where the water was smooth and the swells concealed something that swelled in my trunks.

The softness of her palm where it clung trustingly to mine, her tan slender body, buoyed by the waves, floated into mine. She was a little afraid of the water; I could see that. We dove into the swells and came up, our faces close, and I looked into her hazel eyes. I was smitten. Her gaze met mine unashamedly—she might have been afraid of the water, but she wasn't afraid of boys, of me. We dived in again and again. We swam until we were famished, and we walked out of the ocean, plodding against the pull of the breakers.

On Rockaway Boulevard, I exchanged silver and nickel coins for two corn on the cobs from a steaming pot. "With extra butter." We salted and peppered them, and she gobbled the corn kernels with her white teeth. The melted butter smeared across her lips. We fixed our gazes.

"You have blue eyes," she said.

I made a date to take her the next night to the Forest Hills Theatre, adjacent to Middle Village where she lived on Dry Harbor Road, a leafy street, just twenty minutes by bus from my neighborhood in Elmhurst.

Alfred Hitchcock's *Psycho* was playing, and we made the eight o'clock show. We sat in the back row of the balcony, where you could smoke, but we didn't. We were—at least, I was—saving our mouths. Anne was delicately eating a box of chocolate-covered icecream bon bons which I had bought her at the candy counter: Nothing but the best. She fed me one, fitting it through my lips with her fingers.

I couldn't concentrate on the movie. Its opening scene featured a white-brassiered, white-slipped, beautiful-faced Janet Leigh and the bare-chested John Gavin in bed together, exchanging post-coital kisses to the romantic music of Bernard Herrmann. Slender Anne, whose slender finger tips had just touched my lips, in tight white short-shorts and an off-the-shoulder blouse was so close to me. I had my arm around her shoulders, and she reciprocated with her sweet tan one pressing against me, as far as the chair arm would allow.

In the film, the lunch time tryst was over, and Marion Crane reported to her real estate office with old-man oilman Tom Cassidy flirting, a fat stack of rubber-banded hundred dollar bills in his mitts, saying, "Know what I do with unhappiness? I buy it off."

I launched my lips at Anne's mouth, and she let her box of bon bons fall.

She surrendered her mouth to me. I kissed her lips and neck and bare shoulder. Her blouse was not only off-the-shoulders, but had a plunging neckline—as far as the times would permit it to plunge, and I kissed the line between her slight breasts, as far as her neckline would allow, and I could see she wore a lacy blue bra. Was she wearing it for me? We intertwined our fingers and our tongues, and I tasted her chocolate-covered icecream mouth in the first French kiss I ever had.

We kissed through the scene where Marion decides to steal the money, wearing a black bra and slip, and through the highway scene and then the one where she changes cars and the Bates Motel scene, where Norman Bates spies through a peephole in his motel office, filled with taxidermied birds, at Marion Crane of the black bra, and through the shower scene where Bates, in his mother's clothes, repeatedly butcher-knifes Marion as Herrmann's shrill bursts of violin music burgeon and climax and lead to quieter cello notes as a shot of the tub drain, water mixed with black-and-white blood whirlpooling down it dissolves to a shot of Janet Leigh's staring eye which is dead, but still beautiful. We kissed through the screams and gasps of the audience and, afterward, the did-you-see-*that* buzzing.

Granted, I read Robert Bloch's novel earlier in the year—borrowed it from my sister, who had it from the lending library—and had guessed the telegraphed plot halfway through the book—you could see that the mother was Norman Bates in drag from the moment he ripped open the shower curtain as you could surmise from the clumsy foreshadowing of Bloch's novel. After all, I had been reading fat Russian novels since my fifteenth birthday; that was the summer I refrained from reading.

I was compelled to see the movie once again, later, to see if I had missed something, but I didn't miss anything. It was more thrilling entertainment as Anne and I smooched, swapping icecream bon bon spits.

In a tangle of arms, we walked all the way back to Anne's house in Middle Village and proceeded to kiss full-bodied kisses in her darkened hallway, fronts fused together, my palms on her tight white-shorted rump, grasping desperately. She reached her hands back out of our embrace and slid my grasp up to her lower back. I didn't care as long as I could Frenchkiss her mouth and slide my tongue against hers and feel my front grinding against her formidable mystery.

We kissed—no, "made out" was what we were calling it then—for three or four weeks in the evenings. As soon as my shoemaker assistant job let out at seven p.m., I would take the bus to Dry Harbor Road and call on her. I got to know the bus driver, a young guy, who chatted with me and automatically, without my pulling the stop cord, let me off at Dry Harbor Road.

After polite greetings to her parents, we made out in her finished basement, she sitting on my lap in an overstuffed chair. That presented another problem; the blood rushed to my center beneath her bottom. Then, we made out in the dim light of her front door hallway while her parents watched television. I could hear the Perry Mason theme or the *Gone with the Wind* music they always played for the *Million Dollar Movie*, while full frontally, we made out, pressing together, my palms inching down to her bottom, she letting them a moment, then reaching down to slide the hands up to her back.

She let them a moment more every night, and she let me traverse her bare thighs in short shorts, but she didn't allow me to go to her sweet mystery which was getting sweeter and my hands more urgent every night. She had a method of scooping my hands away decisively when they got within inches of that mystery. Indefatigable, my palms would move up to her chest and then position themselves to allow the fingers of one hand move into her bra and feel up the little globes of her breasts, but she scooped the fingers away before they met the nipple. I knew—not from experience, but from hearsay—that the nipple was key to her passion. But this was love, passionate love; this was not like Suzie Bluelips by the LIRR tracks where I had her once, groping for her breasts. This was reverence.

Then she would walk me to the bus stop, and we would make out against the bus stop pole until the bus came with a wheezing of brakes. She waved from dark Dry Harbor Road, and I waved from inside the lighted bus, feeling the pain of abandoning her to the dark street, desiring just one more taste of her lips.

On Sundays, I had the whole day free from the shoemaker shop, and we would bus the long way to Rockaway Beach or walk over to Forest Park or subway to Central Park and find a good spot to make out— against a tree, on a deserted bench, by the lake, supine on top of some boulders. When our bellies grumbled, we lunched on Sabrett's hot dogs with plenty of fried onions and boiled sauerkraut and shared a Mission orange soda. At Rockaway, we ate buttered and salt-and-peppered sweet corn cobs and paper cones of French fries with plenty of salt and ketchup.

After lunch, we resumed making out, the tang of the fried onions or the ketchup or the sweet melted butter on our tongues. I kissed the butter from her lips, and we camped under the boardwalk in the shade. The sand was cool beneath our bodies. There, we had a view of the ocean with dapples of black and blue and green and the white crashing of the breakers, but we didn't gaze at it long. We lay down and continued to make out in the prone position, so hungry for our bodies were we, but she wouldn't let me to her sanctum.

We seldom spoke. We were too busy making out, doing the essential. I explored her neck and her shoulders and her breasts, as far as she would allow—no nipples—and those fleeting feels of her bottom in my palms was ecstasy in the making. One time she let me get an inch from her mystery. I walked my fingers up her thigh and forked my legs around her leg, with my blood-hard cock, but she clamped her thighs shut.

She sat up, and my erection was so painful that I lay on my stomach on the hard, cool sand. It didn't help.

She asked if I'd ever "done it."

"Came as close to it as if." *Like, now!*

I eased my face on her lap and glided my lips along the inside of her thigh, up to the hem of her short shorts. And I was tasting it! Tasting and smelling the sweet-pungent mystery! Ocean and salt. All that was between her mystery and my mouth was the white cotton of her panties and damp shorts. At first, I thought she peed in her pants, but this was heavier, mixed with the cotton, and she was crying out and moaning and gasping, "*Edward, Edward....*" Abruptly, I realized that girls got wet, and I was harder than I'd ever been, and I found with my mouth the place that was soft and damp, the warm source of all the wetness, and I breathed mightily into it and of it, and she clasped her hands at the back of my head, holding me to her, forcing me to continue, but I didn't want to stop—ever.

She let out a scream like a jungle bird, and with a heavy gasp, I came in my jeans. I slumped. Everything I ever wanted. She played her fingers through my hair.

My high school ring with the amethyst stone was on the ring finger of my right hand. It had been available for purchase at the end of our junior year, name engraved on the inner band with the projected year of my graduation, 1961. I worked it off my ring finger and asked if she would go steady with me.

It was the most precious thing I had. Ring from a Roman Catholic high school, Bishop Loughlin, Diocesan scholarship. Three years ago, I had to take an examination to qualify. A plot commenced to form in my brain— no, it was lower than my brain, and my brain didn't have to know it.

"Your *Loughlin* ring?" Anne might have come here recently, but she had heard of the second best Catholic high school in the Brooklyn Diocese. She was Catholic, too, but she was French. I had already read Joyce's *A Portrait of the Artist as Young Man,* and was delivered from that hell-promoting creed to which my father and mother ascribed. Only I had not told my parents about it, and I didn't inform Anne. About my religion or my plot.

The World According to Leonard Bernstein

I HAD A PLAN. TO DO IT WITH HER. I didn't know how or where. I drew some money out of my savings and subwayed early on Saturday into Manhattan to the Broadway Theatre at 53rd and Broadway. I bought expensive orchestra tickets for *West Side Story.* That play had been on Broadway for three years—based in a modern setting in upper Manhattan, between the White and Puerto Rican immigrants, like the Montagues and Capulets in Shakespeare's *Romeo and Juliet.* It was an ingenious idea, and what a setting—*Romeo and Juliet!* The eponymous names of love!

22

I walked down Fifth Avenue to the Rainbow Room in the RCA Building and took the elevator up to the 65th floor and reserved a late table for two for the night in question. Why the Rainbow Room? It was the only restaurant I knew in Manhattan, a place frequented by my older brother Jos., who worked at Pan American on Park and 45rd Street; Jos. and a Pan Am Stewardess used to catch Stan Getz there. He always referred to her as "the Stew." I thought they would serve me alcohol with the assistance of Jos.'s tank driver's license. He had been in the National Guard.

Then I took the IRT Elevated train all the way to Flushing Main Street and from a Puerto Rican sales clerk in Joseph's Men's Clothing I purchased, for thirty dollars of my own money, a suit—a khaki green one, double-breasted with brass buttons and shiny red paisley lining. It was a beautiful thing. I bought a striped green-on-green necktie at Tie City for a buck and a gold-plated tie bar. There was a tobacco shop next to Tie City, and I bought a whole carton of Pall Malls because I was attracted to the motto on every pack of cigarettes and on the carton: *In hoc signo vinces per aspera ad astra.* Brother Anselm had not taught me Latin in vain; I could translate that: In this sign you will conquer through suffering toward the stars. I wasn't thinking of conquering, but I was suffering from my attempts to get closer to the mystery.

A cigarette case caught my eye from the glass display case—a gold plated one with a spring-top. I also bought a Zippo lighter, brushed chrome.

As a last measure, as though it was part of my plan—and I was devious enough to keep that from myself—I rented a room at the Sunchester Transient Rooms on a side street off Roosevelt Avenue. The Sunchester was known to all the boys as the place when you were hot for a piece of tail, and you didn't have a room. Of course, it wouldn't be like that with Anne. It was the first time I would use the Sunchester, and I just wanted to have a room—just in case. It cost, like, five bucks a night, and check-in was at a side office so you could rent a room, get the key, and skip the check-in. I had only to tell Anne about it. I couldn't be as devious as that, could I? It was fusion of passionate love and falsity. I told myself that she wanted it as much as I did; she only had to know it. The time to tell her would show itself.

I modelled my new double-breasted khaki-green suit for the family later that Saturday afternoon, complete with tie and tie bar. My sister said, "Elegant." Jos., who had done it with "the Stew" (he had his own apartment in Woodside then and still came home for dinner) said, "Sharp, Edward!" My mother said nothing, and my father said, "Every man buys a green suit once in his life."

I was just in time to go into Tony's shoemaker shop on 83rd Street where I worked a 15-hour week as a cobbler's assistant. Anthony A. Antoniou paid me a dollar-twenty-five an hour off the books.

On the appointed night, dressed in my khaki-green suit, I picked up Anne in a Checker Cab. She wore a linen, pearl-gray skirt with matching, waist-length jacket and black high heels borrowed from her mother, so she was as tall as me. She was perfect. She wore on a gold chain around her neck my Loughlin ring.

Driving across the 59th Street Bridge, flanked by the glistening blue of the East River, lighted windows of Manhattan buildings reflected impressionistically in the dark water, I produced my plated-gold cigarette case from my inner jacket pocket. I pressed the catch on the lid and offered her a Pall Mall. She accepted, and I lit her cigarette with the spiraling flame of my brushed chrome Zippo, hand on her sheer-stockinged knee. I leaned over to taste the smoke on her lips. She exhaled in my mouth, and I inhaled the smoke and felt giddy, with the bulge in my khaki-green trousers. I eased back in the seat, my hand on her knee, fingers playing under the hem, enjoying the reflections on the river.

How to tell her about the Sunchester? It looked like an apartment building; I could tell her we were invited to party there, but what would she say when there were no guests? Anyway, that didn't seem copacetic. I would have to think of something else. Something suave and true. Something like, level with her. Why not? *Just tell her.* But I held off.

At the theatre, we collected two programs and took our seats in the fifth row center and perused the Playbills. I had not realized that the orchestra had a place for, like, a fifty-piece, live orchestra, tuning up right there before us with violins and cellos and contrabasses and flutes and oboes. The cacophony produced ecstasy to my ears.

When Leonard Bernstein in person came out to applause, bowing his mop of gray-shot hair, I burst out with, "That's Leonard Bernstein!"

Anne murmured, "So it is." I didn't register the lemony flavor of it until later.

Bernstein tapped his baton on the conductor's stand and with a gesture of his arms set the orchestra playing the Overture. I sat forward in my seat.

When the Scene One cast emerged on the stage, which was arranged to look like a drug-store soda fountain and an upper west side street, and began to speak and sing, I was speechless. Shakespeare had begun his play with a street fight between the Montagues and Capulets, and *West Side Story* pretty quickly began with a rumble between the Whites and Puerto Ricans.

But I was not speechless for long. I could not find the words to express it, but I could not stop talking about it: the songs, dancing, the spectacle, the actors, singers, music, scenery, orchestra. It was a play, a ballet, practically an *opera* with believable characters. They weren't singing in some foreign language; they were singing English, and not some shrieking notes. Overwhelmed, I could not stop my mouth moving, forming words, talking—not during the pause, not in the taxi to the Rainbow Room, not through the dinner, not through the cab ride across the 59th Street Bridge. The Sunchester didn't even exist in the same world as that play.

As we crossed the bridge, it was suddenly as though an entire world, one that I did not suspect existed, was open to me. Ceaseless wonders were opening to me—jazz, Anne, reading big fat books, now *this*: I asked, "What play do you want to see next week? In fact, let's see *West Side Story* again."

"Let's not overdo it now." She added under her breath. "A bunch of men dancing ballet! And *cursing*!"

She spoke quietly—whether to stop me from gushing or that she was not as impressed as I was. It stopped me talking. The hypnotic spell was shattered. I only wanted to be free of her and think about the play. I didn't resume speaking all the way to Dry Harbor Road.

At the front of her house, I said, "Goodnight." I think I hugged her in parting. Or maybe I shook her hand.

So much for the mystery of her. I was interested in a greater mystery now.

La Musique dans le Jardin Public

THE PROSPECT OF READING a thick Russian book of characters with unpronounceable names was forbidding. I was fifteen, and some whim—

it might have been because I had celebrated my fifteenth birthday by drinking a full bottle of Seagram's Seven, and after puking up my guts, I was ready for more sedate pleasures—had inspired me to ask my father, who sat in the living room, absorbed in a book, to recommend one for me. After consulting some of his shelves, he provided a fat red one. The thick book looked boring.

In my room, lounging on my bed, pillow plumped beneath my head, I thought I might need the introduction to ease into it. I read the first sentence. It was by someone called Clifton Fadiman. *Clifton*! "Unless he has been thoroughly briefed, the English-speaking reader who enters *Crime and Punishment*, for the first time may well believe he has strayed into a lunatic asylum."

That sounded promising. I scanned ahead, read another sentence: "The attentive reader at last admits that the world of this book is no mere creation of an overheated brain. We recognize the author's intuitive knowledge of the night side of human beings, of their unconscious drive, of those furious capacities for emotion which are ordinarily inhibited by the universal censor we call society."

Now I could feel something stirring in me—*the night side of human beings! The universal censor we call society!* I had never heard something like that. It was completely foreign from anything I had ever been exposed to, but just those two sentences seemed to promise a revelation that might change my life.

Eagerly, I flipped to the first chapter and began to read. I was breathless with fascination. This was a window to another world, escape from the life that I suddenly realized had been oppressing me for years, the life of hypocrisy and lies. Raskalnikov entertained thoughts I did not even know were in my mind. Not that I wanted to kill anybody, no. But when he tore into the greedy pawnbroker with an axe, and the gentle sister appeared by chance, Raskalnikov had to kill her. He made me understand that the strange private world of my own mind was perhaps a place I might enter and explore, that I might discover and learn to understand the hidden world inside me by carefully observing the world depicted in words between the covers of this century-old novel.

Often, I had enjoyed reading a book, liked to read, but this was an entirely new experience—as Fadiman had predicted in the introduction, it was like wandering into a lunatic asylum, but the lunatics made more sense than the people around me who were supposed to be sane and normal. This was fiction, a novel, but it was more real than anything I had experienced in my life, more true.

Fiction had come for me. The real world would never be enough again.

Fiction became my constant companion. I always had a novel or a short story collection or anthology with me. I read on the subway to and from school, forty-five minutes between Queens and Brooklyn. I read during breaks in my afterschool job. I read in the evenings, in the mornings over breakfast, on the jakes, in the bathtub. Hard as it may be to believe, I even read sometimes at parties and hanging around with friends in the schoolyard.

Some acquaintances viewed my absorption as an affectation. In those days, it was uncool to carry your schoolbooks in any kind of bag or briefcase; you carried them in a stack beneath your arm. I remember a guy in my class named Richard Degnan, eyeing the thick spine of a Dostoyevsky novel, nestled between my history and math texts. He snorted. "Figure it looks good around campus, huh, Fitzgerald?" I had no idea what he was talking about.

Another time, a beautiful Ecuadorian girl named Rebecca Merino, who hung around with us in the neighborhood schoolyard, saw me lugging around a Heritage Club hardback of *The Brothers Karamazov* and squinted with disbelief. "What is that you carry there? A book for school?"

"No, it's a novel I'm reading."

"You are reading that thing for yourself? How many page?"

I slipped to the back and said, "Seven hundred fifty-two."

She crossed herself. "*A que no!*"

But I wasn't reading to get girls. Partly, maybe, I was reading because I didn't have a girl, or because when I did have a girl, it was never enough. Nothing was enough to make up for the insufficiency of life. Only books came close.

For my seventeenth birthday, early in March 1961, my sister gave me a biography of Dostoyevsky by Robert Payne. When he was only eighteen in 1839, Dostoyevsky had written in in his journal, "Man is a mystery. I occupy myself with this mystery because I want to be a man."

Later, one evening in my room with a fat anthology of short stories, I happened to read a story by someone named Katherine Mansfield. It was titled "Miss Brill" and was very short, only five-and-a-half pages. Miss Brill is an old woman whose main pleasure in life is dressing up to go out to the public gardens on Sundays and hear the music of the public orchestra from the bandshell. The people in the gardens are like her family, although she doesn't really know or speak to any of them. But she listens to the music from the orchestra and to snatches of conversation around her and feels as though she is involved, and the light is beautiful and makes her feel she wants to sing, as though everyone is about to sing, as though she is part of a beautiful theatrical performance with all the people in the gardens and she becomes an actress as she sits on her special bench, discreetly, smilingly observing all the people around her. Then a beautifully dressed boy and girl sit down nearby. Miss Brill overhears them muttering devastatingly unkind things about her, about her appearance, about why she even bothers to come to the gardens. Miss Brill returns home to her cupboard of a room and sits for a long time and thinks she hears something crying.

Furiously hurt, I flung the book across my little room and sat there for a long time on the edge of my bed, furious that I was unable to do anything to help or comfort this poor, lonely, old woman or to reprimand the young couple who had been so thoughtless, who had, with a few cruel, careless words, snatched away her only joy in life.

It seemed to me that I was responsible for it. No, Katherine Mansfield was responsible for this, placed the young couple just on the bench with her so that she could overhear them, saying their cruelties about her, destroying her pleasant Sundays. At least I could contact her. I could muster whatever power of words was available to me and write her a letter, scolding her, telling her off for creating this lamentable situation. I retrieved the book from where it had landed beneath my rickety writing table, flipped it open to find out where I could get ahold of this brutish writer and learned that Katherine Mansfield had died in 1923. She had been dead for thirty-eight years.

All at once, it seemed that this writer had reached out from her grave to grab my heart and squeeze a profound, hidden sorrow from it.

There was no one to blame, no one to scold or tell off. There was only me and the story, the injured old woman, the thoughtless young boy and girl. Then I began to understand. This story was an illumination of life, had been crafted to go beneath the surface and made it possible for us to see, to comprehend the meaning of things, the meaning of this isolated event one Sunday afternoon in the public gardens, how we hurt one another without a thought and how Miss Brill was an instrument of Mansfield's pain. It had made that moment of pain eternal; an eternal reminder, an eternal understanding.

And I realized that this what I wanted, the only thing I wanted to do.

Immediately I sat down at my wobbly little desk with a notebook and pen, and I began to write. It was a story about an old woman, Constance, who lived in a dilapidated mansion in Brooklyn. She and her sister, Edith, had never married, but had stayed home with their father, who had assured the sisters they would never want for anything and would never have to work, for work was beneath their station as ladies. They were not educated to any profession, could do nothing practical. It was unnecessary for them. In time, their father died, but they inherited what was left of his fortune. It was not a great deal, but by being frugal, they could manage. They closed off much of the great house in which they had been born and lived all their lives. They could not afford to heat all those rooms. But in the kitchen was a woodstove, and they broke up the furniture in the other rooms and burned it for heat and to cook. They collected newspapers, which they stored in great piles throughout the house to use as fuel when the furniture was gone. They lived in the kitchen and slept in the scullery, where they set up cots, and it was warmer. They hoarded canned food on sale and watched the last of their money dwindle and wondered what they would do.

Then, one morning, Edith did not get up. It was a bitter, cold February day. Constance was convinced that Edith had influenza and needed to rest beneath the covers so she did not disturb her. She went about her day as usual, went out collecting newspapers, bought yesterday's leftover bread from the bakery with her last few pennies, returned to the house through the cold streets. Edith was still in bed beneath the covers. It was so cold and there was so little wood for the stove and so little bread that Constance decided not to light the stove or to eat. She would save the little they had left for tomorrow to share with Edith.

29

She crawled into her cot across from her sister. She kept her fine coat on, frayed now with the years, but the details were so fine, fur on the collar and on the cuffs and around the hem. Still it was cold. Perhaps she should get up and light the stove after all. She would ask her sister's advice. "Edith," she whispered, but her sister did not answer. It was so late, so dark, so cold, that she could not face the task of getting up, breaking wood, finding matches. So she closed her eyes and waited for sleep to come.

Basically, it was an account of what had happened to my mother's two old maiden aunts, who had been found three years before, frozen to death in their dead father's big house in Brooklyn. I never met the sisters, the maiden grand-aunts of my mother, but the story was family lore fitted out with a few details. So I had not made up the story, but I was vaguely aware that with a little help and inspiration from Katherine Mansfield, I had imagined the last day in the life of the last sister. It was not really a story, rather a vignette, a slice of life. Still, I felt I had discovered a power within myself. Yet what would anyone else think of it?

Next day, when my father was at work, and I was "sick" home from school, I helped myself to his Remington manual typewriter, and using the touch typing skills that Brother Charles had taught us in school the year before, I put the story into typescript at the breathtaking speed of thirty-five words per minute. It scarcely filled four pages, double-spaced. I gave it a title, too, a simple one, "Constance." This was pure fiction, for my mother's aunt's name was Florence.

After dinner that night, when my father had stationed himself in his armchair with ginger ale and Camels and an historical novel, I looked in on him and said, "Dad, I wrote something."

"You did? What?"

"A short story."

"Well, let's see it."

I couldn't bear to sit there and watch him read it so I crept back up to my room and shut the door, sat on the bed, sat on the chair, paced, thought, Who am I trying to kid? But then I remembered the way I'd felt when I was writing those pages. It was as though I had entered another dimension, as though the world had disappeared, as though *I* had disappeared, as though as long as my pen was on the page scratching across the lines, recording the words that arose from somewhere inside me, I had entered another place, a weightless place, and that when I was finished, when I came back to the real, quotidian world, something new existed there, something I myself had created.

There was a tap on the door.

I knew it was my father. I didn't want to hear what he would say. I didn't want to hear him say, "Not bad, kiddo." Or, "Keep at it, sonny boy." Because without being fully aware of it, somehow I knew that what he saw on those four sheets of paper I'd given him was only half the story. That was only the product. The other half was the writing of it—what I would decades later come to know as the process, the moment of creation.

I opened the door.

My father looked in at me, his brown eyes, his big belly and big warm face, his thinning silver-chestnut hair, his dentures smiling beneath his red-grey moustache. He was fifty-five years old. No age. How could I have ever guessed that in three years he would be dead, his dream of writing unsatisfied, that when our family doctor told him, *Quit drinking, James, or it'll kill you, fast*, he would choose death.

All I knew at that moment as we stood looking at each other across the threshold of my room was what I hoped he might say to me.

He smacked the pages in his hand and said, "This is terrific!"

Later that day, or perhaps the next, I overheard him from the next room saying to my sister, "Did you read Edward's story? That kid has really *got* it!"

That September I started at the City College of New York, even joined the Reserve Officer's Training Corps—what was I thinking!—and had a course load that included economics, calculus, physics, Latin, PT, and composition—all basic, required courses at that time. I'd had four years of Latin in high school, but needed a fifth, and I needed another year of science. The only course I had that interested me at all was composition. Then I found out I could switch Latin for Greek Literature in English Translation. So at least I would have one lit course. Physics could as well have been Greek for me, so I switched to astronomy, which was a little more bearable (and flunked—so I still had astronomy to do).

And I dropped out of the R.O.T.C. via a note from my family doctor that I had low iron and was border-line anemic.

Basically, all I wanted to do was read and write, and basically that was all I did. I read most of Dostoyevsky, most of John Steinbeck and Aldous Huxley and Sinclair Lewis, some of Hemingway, Tolstoy, Turgenev, Camus, Gide, Jack London, *Gilgamesh,* Dylan Thomas, hundreds of short stories and poems. I had little guidance. My reading was what you might call eclectic—or, rather, coincidental. What I happened upon, I read.

My composition professor, an old guy named Professor Lefferts, with a little tubular wart on one eyelid, took an interest in me because I'd had four years of Latin in high school and he found out in conference that I wanted to be a writer and was well into my apostasy. He urged me to write an essay on Divine Providence and to read Graham Greene and James Joyce. I had already read Joyce's *A Portrait of the Artist as a Young Man,* so I read it again. It had been written about early 20th century Dublin, published nearly fifty years before I read it, but as far as I was concerned it might as well have been written yesterday about Irish Catholic, barely post-McCarthy Queens.

Then I was reading the closing discourse between Stephen Dedalus and Cranley, and I must have been a very weird 17-year-old because I was enthralled by it: "Look here, Cranly, Stephen said. You have asked me what I would do and what I would not do. I will tell you what I will do and what I will not do. I will not serve that in which I no longer believe, whether it call itself my home, my fatherland or my church; and I will try to express myself in some mode of life or art as freely as I can and as wholly as I can, using for my defence the only arms I allow myself to use—silence, exile and cunning."

And Stephen continued: "I will tell you also what I do not fear. I do not fear to be alone or to be spurned for another or to leave whatever I have to leave. And I am not afraid to make a mistake, even a great mistake, a lifelong mistake, and perhaps as long as eternity, too."

Professor Lefferts had urged me to keep a journal and to write in it every day, even if only a single sentence. "It will loosen up your style. And who knows? Perhaps in a year or two it might even become a book."

And I did that. I filled many thick spiral notebooks with thoughts, quotes, stories, ponderings, doubts, ecstasies, descriptions, dialogues with imaginary people (including an old black man who would calm me at my moments of worst despair and fears).

My primary question, then, became the question of what I feared.

How bizarre it seems now to think of myself in a regulation Class-A U.S. Army uniform and spit-shined low quarters marching around Lewisohn Stadium like some Hitler youth with a bunch of pimply officer candidates pondering, while I tried to keep in step, whether I feared making a lifelong mistake, or even one as long as eternity.

Then I met Jack. Kerouac, that is. I came at him obliquely, happening upon a copy of *Maggie Cassidy* with a lurid cover in some drugstore rack, and it made my heart break royally. And led me to *On the Road* and *The Subterraneans* and *Tristessa* and beyond.

And then I knew what I had to do. I had to write books because we're all going to die, because nobody—*nobody*—knows what's going to happen to anybody. I wanted to emulate Jack, to be "a great rememberer struggling in the dark with the enormity of my soul." I had to get away, just like Jack Kerouac had done, and write the books. Go west and write the books. It was so clear. What could be more clear?

That night I told my father I needed to speak to him. I told him that the only thing I wanted to do in the world was to write, that school was driving me crazy, that I had to get away. To get away and write.

He looked at me and his strong brown eyes were brimming with sorrow. He said, "You know, son. I always wanted to write. Maybe you should take the chance and do it. Okay."

"Okay?"

He nodded. "Okay."

Now I was really scared. Now I had permission. Sometimes permission is the scariest thing in the world.

That was the end of 1961. My plan was to get a job, save my money and get out on the road.

Like Stephen, I no longer feared making a mistake—at first. Years would pass. Decades. And I began to understand that I might have made a mistake, a great mistake, a lifelong one.

33

Coltrane's Favorite Things

SOMETIME BEFORE, IN THE '50s my parents had gone to the Lunt-Fontanne Theater at West 46th Street in Manhattan to see Rodgers & Hammerstein's *The Sound of Music* with Mary Martin and Theodore Bikel. They purchased the LP afterward. They never played it, had it as a mere souvenir with the Playbill shoved into the LP jacket. But I was interested in the record because I picked up the LP *My Favorite Things* by John Coltrane when I was in the Army. I did a comparison of Mary Martin's and John Coltrane's versions of the song and the Rodgers tune. The melody was always informed by the lyrics. As Lester Young—known as the greatest tenor saxman of his time, died in 1959 at fifty, nicknamed "Pres" by Lady Day—as "Pres" advised: "You have to absorb the meaning of the tune's lyric." I didn't know what the lyrics were, but the melody is built of them—you can hear the words, foggily accompanying the music beneath the surface.

I listened to each version perhaps five times, and I could not understand why Coltrane had chosen it to record with his quartet, with himself on soprano sax, McCoy Tyner on piano, Steve Davis on bass, and Elvin Jones on drums. I could not understand why he had named the entire LP *My Favorite Things*—except for the recognition value of the tune and its commercial success.

The jacket to Coltrane's album informed me that the title waltz crystalized "his modal approach" to standards, forcing the improviser to play in a horizontal rather than a vertical manner. The improviser could create the interest of the audience in another way—melody, rhythm, timbre, emotion and, always, the lyrics subconsciously informing that melody. That was too analytical for me, too removed from the music— and didn't give me a clue: What did playing horizontally even mean?

So, I decided to descend to the basement, which was where I listened to music (lest my parents go .round heavily sighing) and listen to the Coltrane once more. I was obsessional by nature—probably that meant several or even scores of times. With Mary Jane enhancement. I had a—what were we calling it then?—a reefer. I was home alone, the desolation of the Army behind me, about to begin again at C.C.N,Y. next month. I had already done a semester when I was seventeen, before I went into the Army. I had quit my job of six months at Triborough

Bridge & Tunnel Authority on Randall's Island, beneath the George Washington Bridge, to take a break from it all. I was twenty years old. I had a girlfriend named Darlene—a green-eyed Italian—whom I was laying low from; she had told her best friend, Dee-Dee, that I had kissed her "all over." Dee-Dee, who was also one of my friends, promptly told me, creating a problem. Which was damning. You didn't go down on a girl unless you loved her, and I was not certain that I loved Darlene, and I didn't want my friends to know that I had.

At a party, Dee-Dee (an Italian girl, too—I was partial to Italian girls) said, "I heard you kissed Darlene 'all over'. " She made a disparaging face. "Even the *you-know*. Did you like it? Don't boys do that just to make their girlfriends feel good?"

"No, it's beautiful," I said. She was pretty and sexy, and I was more than lit. "I would eat your pussy, too!"

"*Ick!*" she said and made an excuse to get away from me.

Now I was not lit and was feeling the repercussions of my kissing Darlene "all over" and offering to kiss Dee-Dee's "all over." I was humiliated.

I hadn't been able to follow my plan and work my way across the country because I was a "dangling man" with the draft. That was what you had to do back then, do two years in the Army when you didn't have college to go to, so I volunteered for the draft when I was eighteen. At first, it was okay, but then I underwent a top-secret security clearance because I was selected to work in the White House—as a typist, I was really good at typing, could do a hundred w.p.m.—and got stuck in the process. I had not gone all the way with a girl and the FBI found out. They flagged my file and interrogated me again. With a lie detector. With the thing on my diaphragm and clip on my finger, the FBI man asked me four questions:

"Have you ever had normal sexual relations with a woman—that is, penetration?

I blushed and said no.

"Have you ever engaged in abnormal sexual relations with a woman?"

I didn't know what abnormal sexual relations with a woman were. I wondered whether that's what I did with Anne Suffier. But that word, "abnormal," seemed like poison to me, and I answered no. The FBI man must have known I was lying.

"Have you ever engaged in sexual relations with a man?"

"No!"

"Have you ever engaged in sexual relations with an animal?"

"NO!"

They asked me these four questions every two weeks for four months, even though they assigned me to the White House, until I became obsessed by the four questions, became paranoid, thought people were watching me, spying on me. I had what we used to call a nervous breakdown, now called PTSD. I was having my nervous breakdown when JFK got assassinated. I didn't feel much about the assassination. I didn't cry or anything. I guess I was focused on my paranoia. The assassination seemed distant, like it wasn't happening to real people—JFK and Jackie and Governor Connally, and a couple of days later Oswald, was shot and killed by Jack Ruby. I saw these things on TV in the hospital dayroom among people who seemed more real than the television images: the farmer guy from upstate New York who said that there were worms squiggling under the skin of his arms, and the black guy from Philly when you came near him, without moving a muscle in his face, he would say, "All I know is somebody's trying to kill me," and the enormous guy who suddenly stood up and began to bang his head against the wall.

I got out after a year with an honorable discharge. They said that it was a medical condition existing prior to service. I was discharged because I didn't want to admit to "abnormality" of a sexual nature—which exacerbated the "kissing all over" of Darlene and that drunken offer to do the same to Dee-Dee. These were other reasons I wanted to steep myself in the problems of why Trane had chosen to record "My Favorite Things"—that and to disappear for a while down my basement.

I descended into the cellar. I sat at my grandmother's old, battered solid-walnut dining table, lit a candle stoppered in a bottle of wine, put the LP on my Webcor, torched the reefer and toked.

The record began with McCoy Tyner playing piano notes and chords for about fifteen seconds, after which Trane's soprano took the melody line, started with the song intact, only Tyner intimated something else was in store. At about a minute, Trane took off with the soprano; he improvised for half a minute, then came back to the melody, but took off again, and again dropped back to the melody.

Trane restrained himself, while McCoy Tyner took about three and a half minutes on piano, by turns melodic and improvising. It became maddening at one point, several points, the way he kept playing the same chord, but at just the right moment went off improvising on the notes of the melody—then, again, maddening with the chords, burgeoning, and he returned to the melody; suddenly he was improvising scales, repeating the same note many times. At about seven minutes, Trane kicked in with the melody, which he played for about half a minute, and with that, he took off in wild soprano-sax notes, alternating with scales played at lightning speed, which just about popped your brain; then he returned to the melody, but immediately went off on scales.

I took another toke, and the hair lifted on my arms.

Coltrane was showing me his favorite things—acceptance of spiritual pain, alternating with wild harmolodic lines of joy—for thirteen minutes and forty seconds. Plaintive notes signaled the end, melding into notes of somber resolution, then a rush of flourishes of all the instruments—to provide resolution and to remind you what is inherent in that melody.

The album sleeve told that the number was recorded in October 1960, released in March '61, that it was Coltrane's first recording on soprano sax, bought for him by Miles Davis earlier in 1960 when they were on a European tour, that the first pre-echoes of modal jazz with free-jazz—unplanned improvisation—were created on it.

I played it again, taking another toke and holding it down deep in my lungs and waving the sparked, smoking end of the reefer under my nostrils, hearing the familiar lyrical melody devolve, spiraling away from that melody, becoming more melodious then, when the soprano seemed to reach a place of pure formless sound, working back down and into the melody again. As I listened to the soprano move back again out of the melody, feeling a chill of recognition over my body, the soprano broke free of one structure to find a purer one, music without harmony, the supreme structure of the unstructured, pure sound. Or was it destruction, self-destruction, the obliteration of structure—or perhaps what is obliterated is recognized structure—sameness, the same-old tune and melody?

It occurred to me that all of these improvisations had been etched into my own brain already, just as they were pressed into vinyl and, therefore, were no longer really improvisations. They were only improvisations when Coltrane created them and, to me, when I heard them. Then they became something else, in my head, fascinated and colonized by the notes as I was, drawn into the rapid flow of them, but no longer surprised and yet surprised. I was a prisoner of the sound now—because it kept going inside my brain and no way to turn it off until I forgot about it. Or I played it again.

I suddenly realized that these guys, these master musicians, had to be responsive to the music constantly, whose players might do something that all had to react to. It was what Miles Davis referred to when he said that he didn't like musicians who were too comfortable—"They don't react to anything."

The thought was so heady; I had to take another toke, and I realized that I was infinitely high but was making sense, and I thought, *Write it down.* I would *never* remember this!

But I did remember.

Next day, I wrote all that down in my journal, listening to Coltrane and Tyner, the whole quartet. I could *never* escape that understanding.

Blue Rondo À La Turk & Here's That Rainy Day

IN SEPTEMBER, MY FATHER SANK into the easy chair where he was always reading. He made a face and spouted blood. In the ICU at Elmhurst General, he continued losing blood, but they could not find the place where he was losing it from. After three days, the doctor greeted us with, "I'm sorry. He's gone." It was sudden, but not unexpected. He was only fifty-eight years old.

I returned to C.C.N.Y. and took a part-time office job. For a year I saved every dollar. I didn't have a girlfriend to spend my money on. I was incapable of having a girlfriend. Guilt about Anne Suffier and Darlene and Dee-Dee beset me. I told myself that I hadn't "talked" to them, that they couldn't share my thoughts, my enthusiasms, and I theirs. To *fall* in love seemed an irony. I jerked off a lot. There was a girl named Sandy Guldbrand in my Romantics class, a good-looking girl with a red T-Bird sports convertible—she liked me, too—but I told myself she was too good for me.

Then, in September '65, I took another leave of absence, sold my '53 Olds and began to hitchhike around the country, and I felt free of all things. Back and forth across the country, back and forth from L.A. to San Francisco, staying for a month in Long Beach and a month in San Francisco, trying to write. But mostly I hitchhiked.

Thumbing around the States in January, 1966, I was heading from San Francisco on Route 1 to Mexico, and it led to Route 101, which led to the San Diego freeway, near the Marine and Navy base, just across from a gas station. At that moment fifty cents was the money I had in my pocket, and I thought about investing part of that fortune on a phone call to my mother to have her send me part of the rest of my savings.

Those were the days before self-service gas stations, and the gas pumps here, I saw, as I came closer, were manned by young women wearing pink hot pants, white cowboy boots, and cowgirl hats. A cute, short-haired blonde looked at me and asked, "Forget the way to the barbershop?" Her vowels were twangy as a cowgirl's—made me smile.

"I was hoping you'd give me a trim." By now the length of my hair had been insulted and commented on so many times that I had learned not to let it annoy me. A red Corvette convertible pulled in between us, a black naval officer behind the wheel, double silver bars of a Lieutenant on one collar, medical corps insignia on the other.

"Don't hold your breath," the blonde girl said to me and yanked the gas hose nozzle from its mooring on the pump and into the tank of the Corvette.

"Howdy, captain," the blonde girl said, although being in the Navy he was better called a looey, but he didn't correct her.

I stepped off to the side, listening with one ear to their flirting banter as she topped off the lieutenant's Corvette, feeling the envy and resentment of a wheel-less single-striped ex-enlisted man for an officer in a sports car. When he paid and got his change, he slipped her a note, which she opened and read as he drove off.

"Love letter?" I asked.

"None a your business. He just wants into my pants," she said. "Where he's not gonna get. Would you believe he's a psychiatrist? Keeps givin' me love letters and little presents." She told me he had given her books, and she said the last one was amazing. "About this teacher on a Greek island and this Greek guy sort of stages these plays that kind of turn real and get him involved in these strange situations."

"John Fowles," I said. "*The Magus*. You read it?"

"Couldn't put it down."

Wow! A cute cowgirl who not only read but had an astounding butt beneath her pink hot pants. Instead of squandering money on a Coke, I filled my canteen with water from the men's room sink, and decided to wait on calling my mother in New York. I sat on a cement curb in the shade and broke out my journal from my duffel. She glanced over as she swabbed dead flies from the windshield of a pick-up. "You writin' or posin'?" she called over.

"Posin', " I said. "Hopin' to impress you."

"Better luck next time, buddy."

A few cars and half-backs later, she sauntered over, rolling her hips with each stride of her cowboy-booted feet, and handed me a cold, opened bottle of Coke. "Here you go," she said. "What're you writin' there anyway?"

Actually I was writing about her—or trying to. How sweet her mouth and little nose were, how blue as bleached denim her eyes, how cutely bottle-blond her short hair, how her legs looked curving down into her white cowboy boots. Her little breasts, like halves of oranges. But all I said was, "I'm just a beginner. Trying to learn how to write. See if I can get the hang of it."

She smoked a Newport while I drank my Coke—this was before the connection had been made between gas station accidents and smoking. It was easily the most delicious Coke I'd ever had. One of those green, ribbed bottles, thick cold glass against my lip and the sweet-rough feel of the soda running down my dry throat.

By late afternoon, I'd filled a lot of pages, and another girl—not nearly so cute—reported for duty, and the cowboy hat passed to her. Blondie stood in front of me, one knee cocked at a heartbreaking angle, her belly pushed forward. I knew enough not to try to win this girl by flattery.

"You need a ride somewheres?" she asked.

Her '54 Buick needed a muffler bad. It sounded like a Mack truck. It also needed power steering fluid; the steering whined at every sharp turn.

"Where you want to go?" she asked.

"Why don't we go to the beach?"

"I got a baby to pick up at daycare."

"So let's go there. I like kids."

The baby was two, Lori May, a blond little angel every bit as pretty as her gas-pump mommy, Toni June. The "daycare" turned out to be a woman married to a Navy E4 stationed temporarily in San Diego. She was a sweet, plump redhead from Fort Worth, named Angi, with a gap between her two front teeth. Angi came over to the Buick to check me out, then she whispered something to Toni June and giggled raunchily while Toni June slapped her on the arm.

Toni June invited me to dinner at her Ocean Beach duplex—her "famous chili mac"—and after she put Lori May to sleep in her crib, we took a walk along the sand cliffs over the crashing waves of the Pacific, about a hundred feet from her backyard. That's what you could get in Southern California back then—a three-room furnished duplex right by the water for fifty bucks a month. They had overbuilt.

"God, I love the ocean," I said.

"I'm scared of it."

"You know what Freud said about that?"

"I didn't say I was scared of sex, just the ocean."

When we got back to her place, before she inserted the key in the lock of the door, she turned to me and said, "If I invited you to sleep on my sofa, could I trust you to be a gentleman?"

"Of course."

"No funny business?"

"Never."

Turned out we both slept on the sofa, the radio tuned softly to a rock station. I slid into her, and I looked into her blue eyes which were frightened, and I fell in love. The sofa was made of splintery rattan, so we transferred onto her double box spring in the middle of the night. I woke again, later, to find her performing upon me what back then was an illegal form of abnormal sexual relations—which seemed the most natural thing I had ever experienced in my nearly two and twenty years.

Next day on her way to work, Toni June dropped me in downtown San Diego at the Western Union, where I hung around until I figured my mother was out of bed in New York and phoned her collect to send half the remainder of my savings, which I had within the hour. Instant gratification. With all that dough in my pocket, I felt expansive. I went on a shopping spree, picked up two John Barth novels and a record by

Dave Brubeck. I had heard "Time Out" on various of the car radios I hitched a ride from and wanted to hear the rest of the album. Then I remembered that Toni June didn't have a record player. I was dying to hear the Brubeck, so I bought a stereo console on credit—$8.95 a month for two and a half years.

I figured I'd just fill out the application and see if they bought it, and to my amazement, they did. I gave Toni June's address in Ocean Beach as a c/o—luckily I'd seen her last name on the bell—Holland. I ordered the stereo for immediate delivery, the show-room model, and rode out in the delivery van to Ocean Beach. I sat on the front step to read Barth while waiting for her to get home from the gas tanks, pausing occasionally to wonder about my motives, having put myself in debt for two and a half years. But to hear the piano of Brubeck and Paul Desmond on alto!

The thundering tail pipe of her Buick could be heard all the way down Cable, all through the little bungalow-lined allies. Then she was out of the car with Lori May balanced on her hip. Her lips were pressed together in what I soon came to recognize as her way of showing disapproval that might erupt into a hail of stinging sarcasms.

"What in the *hell* is that?!"

"A present," I said. "For you."

"You think that's gonna pay for another blow job?"

"Honey, please, don't use trashy words about something I consider sacred. And I don't expect a thing from you…"

"Good. 'Cause that's exactly just what you're gonna get. And I'm gonna be real interested to see how you get that monstrosity out of my yard without no wheels!" Whereupon she kicked it with the toe of her cowboy boot.

"Hey! Easy on the walnut," I said. It was—or seemed to me—a beautiful cabinet, walnut, Danish modern, with a bin behind a rolling door to store LPs in and an AM-FM stereo radio, too. All I had in the record bin, of course, was the one Brubeck.

From the corner of my eye, I saw little Lori May watching me through the screen door. I waved at her and she lowered her face, then peeked up shyly again. The smell of macaroni stew coiled through the screen door right into my nostrils, and the water in my mouth started to run. I washed it back with canteen water and turned another page of Barth.

"It'd be a shame if the weather ruined your brand new stereo," I called in to Toni June.

She positioned herself behind the screen door. "You think I'm in love with you or something just cuz you're a writer?"

"I'm only trying to be a writer."

"Right. So, you're not *even* a writer yet."

"I did sell three songs," I said. "To Bill Graham in San Francisco." Which made me feel like a braggart. "And I'm already crazy about you."

"Tell it to the moon," she said and disappeared into the house again, only to come back to the door a few minutes later. "You gonna eat, or what?"

"Yes, ma'am. But could you help me carry this stereo in first, please."

She'd made a huge wrought iron potful of her famous chili mac, and I did my best not to wolf. It had been a while since my last taste of home-cooking, only last night, but I was hungry. As she was shoveling thirds onto my plate, she said, "You know you're too young for me anyway. I'll be twenty-two in three months."

"I just look young. I turn twenty-two early in March."

After a while she said, "I like your hair."

"I thought you thought it was unpatriotic."

"You think I'm for Vietnam? I ain't no redneck hawk." A few minutes later, she said, "Know what Angi said when I picked up the baby today? She said we'd make a cute couple."

After dinner, Lori May sat on my lap on the rattan sofa. She sat facing me and, twisting around, pointed at things for me to name for her: Lamp, chair, table... Already she had my heart locked inside the baby blue of her eyes. "Where's her father?" I asked.

"Back in Hot Springs. He told me if I tried to slap him with paternity, he'd slap me with a dozen depositions from friends swearing they slept with me, too."

It seemed clear to me that both she and the little girl were a lot better off without him.

It was Friday. After Lori May was asleep, by way of celebrating the weekend, I walked up the road to Paloma Joe's Groceries and bought a gallon of mountain red for seventy-nine cents, and we listened to the new Brubeck, she cross-legged on a shag throw-rug, me on the splintery rattan sofa.

It had been half a year since I heard jazz in my basement, and I really absorbed myself in it. Toni June wanted to hear the familiar one first, "Time Out," which had been recorded in 1959, but was still getting radio play. It was the third cut on the record, and after it was over, she wanted me to play it once again. She liked the drum solo best, which came on about the middle of the cut and lasted for a couple of minutes, backed up by Brubeck's repeatedly playing piano chords, the same ones over and over, but I particularly admired Paul Desmond's alto sax.

The liner notes said that the cut was a Desmond composition, all others were by Brubeck. Desmond wrote it in 5/4, "one of the most defiant time signatures in all music," Steve Race wrote on the album sleeve. He went on to say that the piano play figure throughout was 5/4, even under the drum solo, but Morello gradually released himself from the tempo and played "counter patterns" over the piano figure.

I was enamored of Desmond's alto improvisations, especially on "Blue Rondo À La Turk," which is the first cut on the album and begins with a 9/8 time signature, and it haunted me with its Turkish rhythm, combined with jazz improvisation.

However, I was more enamored of Toni June, who seemed to get restless or bored. She got up from the floor and sat sideways next to me on the sofa and started playing with my hair. "It sure is cute. Can I comb it?" And she sat cross-legged beside me lavishing attention on my hair. Then she started popping the blackheads I didn't even know I had, searching intently for them, running her fingertips over my face in her hunt, finding one, popping it, moving on.

She asked what my middle name was—Francis—and decided that she would call me Eddie Frank.

I had always hated the names "Eddie" and "Frank" (sounded to me like beans & franks), but from her sweet mouth both suited me fine.

In my duffel bag, wrapped carefully in tin foil and a tied-off clear plastic baggie, I had two sugar cubes that had been eye dropped with LSD-25. I'd heard you got the best trip if you were with a woman. She was willing so we popped them, crunching the sugar between our teeth. We took a walk on the sand cliffs, and the waves that crashed on them flung up a fan of droplets of electric color, pooled in amoebas of purple and red and yellow and green, sliding off the cliff slopes. At one point, we lay on the floor of her duplex, staring up at the stucco ceiling, and I was seeing figures there—sand-beige figures from some temple art in India or Thailand or someplace, something from the *Kama Sutra*. They were copulating. Many of them. Vigorously. Coupling in every manner imaginable, and it occurred to me that everything imaginable either entered or was entered, was either an opening or something with which to fill it.

I asked Toni June, "Do you see that? On the ceiling?"

"Yes."

"What do you see?"

"They're all just—doin' it. Every which way."

Then, in a few moments, or maybe after many moments, we were naked as those sand-beige *Kama Sutra* figures on the ceiling, only we were on the floor, and mirroring what they were doing on the ceiling. Everything in this world either entered or was entered. Everything in this world of enterers and enterees, everything I had that could enter was entering and everything she had that could be entered was being entered, and everything I had that could be entered was also being entered. Never before in my life—and rarely since—was I quite so happy. Brubeck was pounding, tinkling keys, and Desmond was blowing his breath into cool, fluid figures and eating the reed, and Wright was plucking the thick coiled wires of the bass with his fingers and Morello was sticking the snares and cymbals and oomphing the bass drum, and I was on and under and in and over and through Toni June, and I was smiling. I could not stop smiling.

When it was over, I lay on my hip, a reclining Buddha, cheek propped in my palm, as I smoked—no, *relished*, no, *ravished*, one of my Pall Malls and gazed at her naked body—her little citrus breasts and the magnificent golden fleece at the fork of her gorgeous thighs, the triumphant conclusion of Jason's pelagic voyage, those golden strands between my fingers, and I smiled and I smiled.

It has been said that the mind of a young man is like the display window of a cheap porn shop, so rich is he with the urge to procreate the human race. Nothing could be truer of my mind at that moment, although the procreation part was something my urge did not deem I had a need to know, only the cheap porn part—but it wasn't cheap. It was as only pure passion can be: cheap and rich, sordid and sacred all at once.

Her lips were purple from the wine, and I wanted to lick them pink, but her blue eyes, pale as faded denim in the sunlight, were clouded now like the wine-dark sea, peering back at me.

Slowly, she whispered, "You have the smile of the devil."

I said, "No, I..."

"Smile... of... the... devil," she whispered again, eyes stiff with horror. "I don't want you here. Don't want you with my baby girl. Stay away from me..." She was crawling now, naked, toward the bedroom, looking over her shoulder at me with those staring eyes, crawling fast, her knees striking the floor with hard rapid thumps, and she slammed and locked the bedroom door behind her. I heard Lori May start to whimper, and Toni June crooned, "Don't worry, honey-baby, he ain't gonna get you, I'll *stick* him if he tries, I *will*, I'll *stick* him right in the heart!"

I crashed like a shot and the hair all over my body bristled at her words, her tone. Did she have a knife? From experience I knew the dose we'd taken lasted for twelve hours, and we were maybe five hours into it. I didn't dare risk leaving the house to wander the night with seven solid psychedelic hours ahead of me. I pictured myself being found at the foot of a sand cliff, my neck broken from a fall. But if I slept here, would she come out and stab me in my sleep? Had the dose turned her psychotic?

I put an end table in front of the bedroom door and stood a floor lamp on it so she'd knock them over if she came out and wake me with the noise. (I'd forgotten that the door opened inward.) I turned off the music and the lights and curled up in a ball on the sofa, surfing my way through wave after wave of images as I lifted again and settled down, lifted and settled in paisley scraps of color and patches of dream, broken visions of a paddleboat on a river, fixed to a wharf, carved wooden heads of carousel horses fixed to each paddle, turning again and again, their wooden eyes painted with dread...

When the sky began to lighten, I went under completely into sleep, deep under.

Then I opened my eyes, and sunlight dappled the beige walls. I glanced up at the ceiling. The *Kama Sutra* players had packed up and gone. And I could smell coffee. Over the arm of the sofa, I saw Toni

June in the kitchen, which opened on one end of the living room. She was barefoot in a pair of cut-off jeans—her pale knees bruised pink and purple—and a pink T-shirt. The baby sat on two telephone books and spooned cereal into her mouth.

"Hi," Toni June said softly. "Want some eggs and fried baloney?"

That day she drove me downtown again to rent a typewriter, and we bought a lot of groceries and a ream of very fine Pyramid bond typing paper (a penny a sheet!) and beer and the *Getz Au Go Go* album, and when we got home, she gave me a gift-wrapped package and said she hoped it wasn't too early for a birthday present.

It was a copy of *The Prophet* by Kahlil Gibran, on the flyleaf of which she had written, "To Eddie Frank—this is not actually a birthday gift but more a long note of thanks for the gift you have shown to me—patience, acceptance, and friendship. Toni June." Was this love? I wondered. Or mere contrition?

We spent the rest of Saturday sipping Mountain Red, our senses still aprickle from the acid. We put on the Getz, featuring Astrud Gilberto. It was mostly easy listening with Astrud, but Getz and Gary Burton laced tenor and vibes impressively throughout, and on the last cut, the standard "Here's That Rainy Day," Getz positively unfolded, and his tenor blew lyrically and screamed, improvising so it would break your heart.

I read aloud to her from Gibran, the music in the background, and we didn't turn on the overhead lights when it began to get dark. Every time Lori May napped, we put on Getz or Brubeck and helped ourselves to each other to a background of "Corcovado" or "Blue Rondo À La Turk" or "Rainy Day." When Getz's tenor screamed, as her eyes grew wide and she put her hand over her mouth and whimpered, I felt that our love-making became love.

I remember being inside her and pausing to stare into her eyes, reading the layers of emotion on her face—fear and pain and ecstasy, and I wondered if I had run away from my life only to find the unlikely place I was truly meant to be.

At sunset, we walked on the sand cliffs, Lori May sitting up on my shoulders, arms around my head, while her mother and I held hands. The little girl felt as though she had been born to ride my shoulders, and Toni June's small hand fitted perfectly in mine.

Rexroth & Ferlinghetti & the Jazz Cellar Quintet

ONE DAY, WHEN THE BUICK was with the mechanic in the station overnight, Toni June had to take a bus home, and she telephoned Angi to ask her to take Lori May overnight.

Toni June said that it was a long wait for the bus, and she chatted with a woman, Shari, who asked us over after-dinner for coffee. She lived a couple of blocks from us, further from the cliffs and the sea.

I asked what kind of woman she was, how old was she?

"She's sort of beatnik," Toni June said. "Round about forty, but good-looking, She wore a turtle neck and jeans and sandals. She has a fifteen-year-old daughter. She started the conversation by saying I looked interesting."

I made a face. Toni June had told me when she was sixteen, she had an affair with another girl. That was okay with me in the past, but not in the present. It was not all right for a woman to lust after my girl.

"It wasn't like *that*," she quickly added.

We went.

The house was in a duplex, like ours, but bigger, wider, the front door taller, had an nice plant garden, like ours. "Shari said to go in the side door," Toni June told me. We followed around down the alley, and the house had a messy strip beside it—an old rusty refrigerator with the door taken off and other rusty things and two big truck tires.

Shari brightened when she saw Toni June and exclaimed, "You came!"

Toni June introduced me to her. "Evening," I said, and she took a long look at my face, then turned away without a word. She must have decided I wasn't interesting because she didn't look at me the entire evening. Her daughter and the daughter's boyfriend were just leaving for a walk on the beach. Shari referred to the boyfriend as "Monkey Boy." (I guessed she didn't find him interesting either.)

Shari served us coffee in metal enameled mugs of different chipped colors, and she and Toni June chatted, and I noticed that Shari had on tight, faded jeans which fitted over her butt and her crotch quite nicely. Then she asked Toni June if she liked jazz...

"I *love* jazz!" I said.

"...and poetry," Shari said and put on an LP.

I was hurt because I thought she was cool-looking and, well, cool, and I am not accustomed to people being disinterested in me. From my seat on the corner of the sofa, I looked around the room: There were pictures on the walls that I took in in a blurring glance, some kind of geometrical shapes, and I recognized a photograph of Walt Whitman, and three naked women, backs forward, standing before a lake with arms around one another's shoulders, and some kind of patch of Indian blanket hung over an old battered sideboard, and a small painting of a bright red ostrich against a dark blue and black sky, books across the top of the side board and on the shelves of a wide bookcase with multi-colored spines. I wanted to look at the titles of the books, I wanted to look at everything, but I didn't dare, she was so formidably cool.

The record came on, a man's voice with an enunciated New York accent, "This is called 'Autobiography,' and immediately bebop came on for about half a minute, then the same man's voice said drily, "I am leading a quiet life in Mike's place every day...," and he said more but only a few lines before the bebop trumpet and tenor sax and piano and bass and drums punctuated the lines again. It continued that way for a long time, and I thought it would continue, but then there was a break, and that New York accent said, "This is called, 'The Statue of St. Francis,'" and simple piano notes played, then a thin line of a tenor sax or sometimes a trumpet. The voice was ironically lyrical, but suddenly after a minute or two it was over with a line of something about a naked young woman dressed only with a bird's nest in a very existential place....

Then another began. I didn't catch the title, but the music began with a drum roll and the voice yelling, "Let's go! Come on, let's go!" and I *knew* after a few seconds it was a parody of Eliot's "The Love Song of J. Alfred Prufrock." T. S. Eliot had published that something like fifty years ago, and this was an update and an underscoring of it for contemporary American civilization.

I didn't want to ask because I thought Shari would refuse to let me see the LP jacket so I walked over to the chair where she sat, the album case on her knees, and I took it from her lap, saying, "This is *fantastic!*"

The cardboard jacket had only sketches of two faces—I recognized them from a framed picture on the wall—and under the one, Kenneth Rexroth and, the other, Lawrence Ferlinghetti. And over the both, *Poetry Reading in the Cellar with the Cellar Jazz Quintet* and on the other

49

side, *Recorded at the Cellar, San Francisco, 1957*. Nine years ago, I was thirteen! I didn't recognize any of the names of the jazz men. They had a tenor sax, a trumpet, a piano, a bass and drums, and I saw the bass player was Negro, and I memorized the names of the poets and reminded myself to buy a little notepad and always carry it with a pen.

Then the record was over and Shari was fluttering her fingers at me, like *gimme!*

"Please," I said. "Play the other side!"

With the only words she addressed to me that evening and even those, she was looking at Toni June, she said, "No, it could get too much."

"Where did you hear them, how did you get the album?"

"Heard them in the Cellar. In San Francisco," she said, replacing the album in the bookcase. "In North Beach." She made scissors of her fingers. "I snipped off some of Ferlinghetti's hair!"

When we were walking home, after a silence, Toni June said, "That was an exciting evening."

"The poetry record was exciting and the jazz was exciting, and the place was exciting, but I don't think your friend was interested in me."

She shrugged her lips. "Maybe because she didn't know you were coming."

"Didn't know?"

She was speaking quickly, "I forgot to tell her. And I didn't have her phone number. Anyway, maybe she didn't think you were interesting."

"But you're interesting—to her?"

"What are you saying?"

"I think I'm saying it: That Shari is interested in you."

She glanced at me and away, as though she was weighing not saying something. "She thinks you're queer. She told me when you went to the bathroom."

I was about to explode—that Toni June, of all people, would know I wasn't queer—but took a breath and didn't let it get my "agot," as my father used to say. I used to think it was an acronym for "goat," but now I started thinking how close it was to the word "faggot."

"And what did you say?"

"I didn't say anything."

"Because you agree?"

She shrugged her lips again—that was getting to be an annoying habit of hers—and said nothing, and I didn't speak the rest of the way home. I went directly to the phonograph and put on "Blue Rondo À La Turk," because I liked it—and suspected that she hated it. Then I remembered to write the names of the poets in my journal. Couldn't recall other than their last names. I wrote about the evening and the conversation on the way home. It felt better to write it down. I got over my sulk and started thinking about Toni June's body.

She went to bed and, in a while, peeked out of the bedroom and asked if I was coming in.

"In a minute. When I finish writing." I listened to "Blue Rondo À La Turk" once more, admiring Brubeck's piano pounding and Desmond's improvisations, but hoped she was still awake and would let me go down on her. I wanted to eat her with enormous juicy gusto, but she closed her knees the one time I got my face into position with an embarrassed, apologetic smile. "No," she moaned. "Please. I don't like it. Because it's dirty. The vagina is dirty. Everything with a woman's inside. You can't clean it. With a man it's all outside. It's cleaner."

Which made me want to all the more. "Of course, it's dirty. The act. That's why it's so satisfyingly messy."

She was awake when I came into bed that night and romantic, but she didn't allow me to go down. However, she did make love. With abandon, she got on top of me and fucked my brains out, and in the morning, too. Lori May not being there helped. I slept in, while she washed and dressed. And I started thinking about Shari's *interest* in her. And her interest in making love with me after Shari suggested I was queer. I drifted off to sleep, dreaming sweet fragments from which I awoke when she leaned over to kiss my mouth goodbye for work.

What did it matter what she imagined when we fucked? I imagined every sort of thing.

I had a mission that day. At the bookstore. I took the bus downtown to go to the friendly middle-aged woman with the long gray braid and hear if she had any titles by either Rexroth or Ferlinghetti or maybe an LP from 1957 with them reading. "It's got a jazz background."

"You should stick to the American classics," she said. "Melville and Whitman and like that."

"Whitman was a beatnik in his day." Was also gay, I didn't say.

"Whitman was proven by time," she said riffling the pages of the Books in Print catalogue. "There's *A Coney Island of the Mind* by Lawrence Ferlinghetti. I think I have a copy here. But we don't carry spoken word."

Toni June came home to complain about the book I bought.

"I will buy any books I want."

"You're squandering money on jazz records and books and a stereo. What's next? You

don't even have a job!"

I said that I saved up for this, to learn to write. Writing was my work. And she started in on a job again. When she got like that, I left the house and walked on the cliffs or the beach.

In fact, I got on better with the baby than I did with the cowgirl. I never knew what to expect from her. One minute she adored me, the next she was cussing me out with no cusses pulled. Then came the physicality.

One morning in the kitchen while she was melting margarine in a pan to fry our breakfast, I sneaked up behind her and reached around and cupped her breasts in my palms. Snatching the carton of eggs from the counter, she spun and started whacking me over the head with it.

I was stunned. "You little bitch!" I hollered, egg goo drooling from my hair, and she came at me with a pot of boiling water. "Put that down!" I snapped, and she hesitated, seemed to remember herself, placed the pot back on the stove. "You fucking idiot," I said and turned to the sink to clean myself up, but she jumped on my back and hammered her fist into my shoulder and I twisted away and smacked her in the face.

I couldn't believe I'd done it. Short of breath, I glowered at her, close to tears, expecting her to retaliate, slug me back, start what she referred to as a "knock-down, drag-out," but instead her shoulders slumped and she caressed with her own palm the cheek I'd slapped. She looked in the mirror over the sink. "You can still see the imprint of your palm," she said, as if amazed. "All four fingers."

"And I still got egg goo in my hair!"

"I deserved it, Eddie Frank. You should put me in my place more often."

What in the world was she saying? I felt miserable enough over what had happened. I'd never even *thought* of hitting a woman, and now I'd *done* it. Was this going to be part of our life together now? And exactly what kind of life had she come from? A boyfriend who knocked her up and threatened to get his friends to swear in court they'd slept with her as well. Did he beat her, too? Did she beat him? What kind of life was this? It wasn't for me. But I had no idea what do about it.

We were okay in bed. More than okay. I tried to get Toni June to experiment with a couple of things from a pornographic book her babysitter, Angi, had loaned her—some positions that involved placing an end table at the foot of the bed—but she grew indignant: "There will be *no* props in my bedroom!"

But then she asked me once, holding my belt, if I had ever wanted to use this kind of thing on a girl's butt—or have one used on mine. And another time, when I asked her where *precisely* the urine came out of a woman, a question that had been nagging at me—so deficient in human biology was a Catholic-school education then—she demonstrated for me in the bathtub.

I was excited by the look and the smell and sound of it, and she asked, "Would you like me to piss on you?"

It occurred to me that this sort of thing might be what the FBI man who had grilled me for a top-secret clearance in the Army was referring to when he asked me if I ever engaged in abnormal sexual relations with a woman. To do this might entail the crossing of some line on the other side of which lay incurable perversion. Voltaire, on the other hand, had declined a second invitation to an orgy, but not the first: "Once a philosopher, twice a pervert," he quipped. Maybe I could give it a single try?

It made me nervous, though—the thought of doing something like that. I asked Toni June why she thought I would be interested in such things.

"Just seems like it could maybe be a part of your personality," she said, with a nonchalant shrug, as if it was all the same to her either way. Deciding I did not want her estimation of me to be correct in that direction, I declined.

A few hours a day I read and tried to write, tried to rewrite the manuscripts that had been stolen from a Ford in which I had hitched a ride in Oakland the year before, but I suspected they hadn't been very good to begin with and were just getting worse in the reconstruction. The pieces always wound up being about Toni June and how she had locked herself in her bedroom that night, saying I had the smile of the devil, and I didn't feel easy writing about that. Then I started writing about her anyway, her and her daughter and what she had told me about her life. Her mother had been a dancer—I wasn't sure what that meant and wondered if she had been a prostitute—who had died driving drunk when Toni June was sixteen. Her father, who drifted away earlier in her childhood, had been a wino; Toni June tried to give him a home, the house she inherited when her mother died, but he died homeless a few years later. Her mother, she said, had written her autobiography, but the manuscript must have been thrown out one time when she moved. The only thing Toni June could remember from it was that her mother had written that she always took a bath after sex because it made her feel dirty.

Toni June had no real family to speak of, an "uncle" in downtown San Diego who, I surmised, had been one of her mother's longer-term boyfriends but was now in his seventies. I went with her to visit him, briefly, expecting it to be a little like the meeting between Lolita and Humbert Humbert after she married and wrote to him for help. But her "Uncle" Marty was no Humbert. He lived in a tiny downtown apartment stockpiled with discount soap and toothpaste and cans of soup. He served us iced tea and talked in clichés about the weather and seemed the furthest thing I could imagine from an intellectual or a pedophile.

Writing about her family made me uneasy, though, too. I needed more details than I could ask her for. And what would she think if she found out I was writing about her?

I thought about the scene in *Lolita* where the girl's mother discovers Humbert Humbert's secret diary which had terrified me. *Charlotte, that's just notes for a novel, and I used yours and Dolores' names.* Of course, I wasn't lusting after Lori May or writing scornful things about Toni June. But I began to worry that the only safe place for my thoughts was in the lock-box of my skull. I was no longer alone, and the distance between what I thought and what I wrote suddenly took on new meaning.

I tried writing about the day that Toni June, without warning, suddenly took a full swing with her right and smacked the little toddler so she staggered across the room and fell on her bottom, blue eyes huge with shock before they filled with water and she started to wail pitifully, gasping, breathless, her terror so complete.

"How could you do that?!" I shouted. "Don't you hit her! You want me to smack *you* like that?"

"Don't you tell me how to raise my baby! Big writer! You're so full of shit! It's just an excuse not to get a job."

She claimed she was the only one earning money around here, and I pointed out that I paid for things, too. Yeah, she said, with your mama's money! I told her I'd earned that money, but then she wanted to know how much I was earning now.

Writing about these scenes, however, didn't seem like writing at all. That was just copying down the stuff that happened. It embarrassed me, embarrassed me all the more that I wouldn't even crumple it up and throw it out. I saved even that, saved every worthless word I wrote down.

What I wanted was to write fiction, serious fiction, like the stuff that I had read, that moved me, that made me feel the life within my own head was not…*wrong*. That it made sense. That I was not alone with the strangeness of life.

I flipped through the front pages of Barth's *Floating Opera* and read a sentence: "I never wrote a novel before but I've read a few to try to get the hang of it." Was he serious? Was it a joke? I went back to the shelf to try to get another idea of what good writing was and took down Toni June's copy of Fowles' *The Magus* and a piece of paper came floating out. It was from the navy psychiatrist. *You are so fine*, it said. *Please call me. Any time. For a drink for lunch, for…?* And his first name and number. Clyde: So, I knew his name.

I wondered why she had saved it. I even wondered if she was seeing Clyde, but we were together all the time except when she was working. I thought about Clyde being a Negro. A Negro and a doctor and an officer. He had money, he had to have money with a car like that. I hadn't even finished college, and he was an actual doctor. Why would she want to be with me when she could have Clyde, a doctor with a sports car—a doctor, an officer? But then he was a Negro. How would she feel about that? Did that make a difference? Did it make a difference to me? It shouldn't. My parents always taught me that Negroes were as good as anybody else. When I thought about the Negro jazz players—most of them were black, jazz had originated with them—I understood that if there was any difference, the difference was they were *better* than whites, and maybe somehow that jealousy explained some of the ugliness of segregation.

But why did the Lt. Clyde have to want my girlfriend? Just to go to bed with her? Did I want more than that from her myself?

I got the idea of trying to write about these thoughts, and turned the page of my spiral notebook to a fresh sheet and sat there looking at it, but I couldn't even find a word to start with.

Toni June would come home from the gas station, sour and sweaty— it was summer and the Santa Annas were blowing in from the desert— and I would dig into my pocket and go out for tacos and tell her meantime to take a shower. When I got home, I mixed her a tall 7-Up and Gin and a slice of lime from the provisions I had bought and produced a carton of Newports for her. We sat drinking cool cocktails and eating tacos, and after the baby was asleep, we wound up in the sack with her on top, smiling that beautiful cunt-ful smile she had, and I knew everything would be fine.

But soon we were fighting again. She accused me of getting it on with the baby sitter, Angi. I might have *wanted to*, but I wasn't. Toni June stepped up close to me—half a head shorter, but she was always ready to take me on. "If you *ever* sleep with that dirty whore, I will kick you so hard right in your *balls* that you can forget any hope you might have of making a family."

I grew sick of her and even sicker of myself. What the hell was I doing here? Playing at being a writer, playing at being Jack Kerouac? I should have finished college by now, but all I'd done was a year with mostly C grades at City College of New York. I had an A in British Romantic Poetry and a Survey of English Lit. At least I had the army out of the way, and worked in a part-time job for six months at Epic, Inc. for two Czechoslavakian partners on Nassau Street and Triborough Bridge & Tunnel Authority on Randall's Island—that was in '64 and '65, when they were building the Verrazano Narrows Bridge, from Brooklyn to Staten Island. But what had I accomplished other than wasting a couple of years of my life? It was time to leave. Next day was Friday, and I decided to tell her when she got home from work. I would be sad to leave Lori May, but it was time.

What's That Got to Do with Me

NEXT DAY, LATE, SHE CAME HOME with a pizza and a tall, thin brown paper bag in which she had a bottle of Smirnoff. She turned on the radio and found some Frank Sinatra music, then sat at the kitchen table with her pack of Newports and a glass of ice and poured herself about ten fingers of vodka, filled the rest of the glass with 7-Up, while the baby munched a slice of deep pan. She didn't speak to me. Sinatra was singing some romantic crap about only the lonely.

I asked what she was doing.

Without looking at me, she said, "I'm drinking myself under the table." She had told me her mother used to do that periodically. I also remembered that her mother had killed herself driving drunk. It occurred to me that I might have to wrestle the car keys away from her.

"May I ask why?"

She pressed her lips together and turned her eyes on me, darker blue than usual, and lifted her chin. "'Cause I'm not gonna do it again."

"Do what?"

She lit a cigarette and dragged on it in that way she had of shoving half the filter between her lips and sucking in the smoke so the filter made a wet popping sound when she jerked it from her lips again. I recognized for the first time how much this habit annoyed me, as did the way she held the cigarette between her first two fingers with the others splayed out, and the way she tilted up her chin and pressed her lips together, and numerous other things—the way she said "excape" and "axed" and "expecially." And the way she had of getting this self-loving smile on her face when certain songs came on the radio—"Wild Thing" by the Troggs and "Little Red Riding Hood" by Sam the Sham & the Pharaohs—smiling all to herself with her eyes turned down to the side and twitching her hip to the beat, and all the unexpressed annoyance reared up in me at that moment. And her constant, pointless, never-ending chatter about the two "cute" teenage boys she worked with in the gas station, how they looked with adoring eyes at her, about the "cute" chief who came in to be tanked up while he serviced her with little compliments, about the "captain" in the Corvette who wanted to get in her pants, and about every other goddamned thing in her world, talking and talking and talking and talking until I was about to go insane from her unstructured, incessant, never-ending flow of pointless words about utterly inconsequential people and things.

"I *axed* you a question," I said.

She pouted up her lips—another annoying habit—and said, "I will *not* have another bastard."

So, I was even stupider than I'd realized. I had managed not to concern myself with the fact that she was not one of the, later calculated, 6.5 million American women on The Pill that year. Nor had I used condoms, as they'd seemed an unnecessary expense. The general, unvoiced agreement had been that I would withdraw at the crucial moment of our love-making but I far from always managed it, almost never in fact, and then somehow we just stopped worrying. I didn't remember Jack Kerouac ever worrying about it. Maybe he just never stayed around long enough to have to worry.

This was in 1966, seven years before the Roe v. Wade decision in the U.S. Supreme Court. In 1966, not only were abortions illegal, they were expensive, and abortionists—even of the rusty coat-hanger ilk—were hard to come by. The question now was whether Toni June was going to be one of the 3.5 million American women who would give birth that year or one of the, later estimated, 100,000 to 200,000 who underwent illegal abortions and, if the latter, one of the approximately 10,000 who died in the process. As if to underscore the possibilities of that outcome, I had just finished reading Barth's *End of the Road*, in which the abortionist forgets to tell the woman not to eat before she is put to sleep, causing her to vomit under anesthesia and inhale her own vomit, dying on the table.

But this was not a novel; this was nonfiction in progress, and it seemed as though the way it would end was not an option of my choosing.

Toni June's "Uncle Marty" had helped her through the birth of Lori May and was willing to help her through this one, too, but he would not pay for an abortion, and Toni June was adamant about not having "another bastard."

As for me, I couldn't help but think of the potential child growing in her. It would be my child, too. I'd been raised Catholic and though, with the help of James Joyce, I had left the church behind me, some aspects of it died hard, and this was definitely one of them: Thou shalt not kill. In those days, both the legal and moral opinion prevailing was that abortion was murder. Would I participate in a murder? Or be a passive observer of one? I spent a lot of time worrying about it, doing internal battle, moralist versus pragmatist. But it was not only a question of morals against practicality, it was also the unknown factor of the law. How would I feel to be guilty of aiding and abetting a murder? I could be arrested. I could go to jail. What was the right thing to do here? The best thing? The safest? I could run, of course. Just pack my things while she was at work and head back to New York, or somewhere else. Could I really do that?

I brought it up after dinner one night, after the baby was asleep. She said, "Why don't you ask your momma what's right?"

I said nothing.

She lit a Newport. "Maybe *I* should ask your momma. How would that be?"

Still silent, I tried to remember if she had my address in New York, my mother's phone number. The personal information we give to our lovers when we still trust them—mother's first name, bank account number…

"After all, she's the grandmother. Don't you think she has a right to know about it?"

She was goading me, I knew that, but it was not having the effect she aimed for. Instead of making me nervous, it was making me see things in a moral perspective, as a question of family and doing the right thing. I was trapped.

A few days later as the three of us sat at the breakfast table, before Toni June left for work, I opened my mouth and heard myself say, "We could get married."

Her chin tilted up, lips compressed. "You plan to support four of us on what you earn writing?"

"I could get a job."

"Sure. As what? What can you do? A file clerk. And what'd you earn anyways?"

"I worked in the army," I said. "I worked in New York. I'm perfectly capable of getting a job. When I was in the army I worked in the White House! With a top secret security clearance! I worked for the Triborough Bridge & Tunnel Authority! They told me they'd hire me back anytime."

"Sure. In New York. You gonna commute?"

"I sold song lyrics! To Bill Graham in San Francisco! Three songs for a thousand dollars!"

"Sold any lately?"

"Let's calm down and talk about this calmly, can't you?"

"I will *not* have another bastard."

"Well if we got married the baby wouldn't be..."

"You are so full of *shit!*" she said and slammed down her cup so coffee sloshed out onto the table. Lori May's blue eyes widened and watched me as her mother grabbed her wrist and dragged her out to the car.

I stayed home for another day, worrying about it. I *was* full of shit. Was I really willing to marry her, or did I just want to cover my back, to be able to say, "I asked her to marry me, but she wouldn't." Once again, I thought of just packing up and taking off, but I was incapable of doing that either. I was incapable of doing anything.

I had laid my forehead down on my typewriter late that afternoon to soothe myself for a moment and had drifted off. The thunder of Toni June's Buick crashed in on me. The screen door squeaked open, and she plopped Lori May on the sofa and said, "Stay there!" She stepped around me without saying a word, and went into the bedroom. I heard the sound of the shower. Then she came out, wearing her one good skirt and a white blouse and a string of river pearls she had from her mother. She poured half a tumbler of vodka, not bothering with ice or 7-Up and drank it down straight, standing by the kitchen counter.

"Would you please watch Lori May while I'm gone?" she asked. Her words were suspiciously polite but her tone was not.

I asked where she was going.

"Will you watch her or not?"

A horn beeped out front. "I'll be back tomorrow night," she said. Through the window, I saw a red Corvette, a black face behind the wheel—Clyde.

And still I hadn't figured it out.

60

I made a baloney sandwich for Lori May, and after she ate, we took a nighttime walk on the cliffs, the two of us. I looked up at the Big Dipper and a crescent moon.

"See, Lori May?" I said, pointing. "Can you see those stars?" I traced them with my finger. "It's the Big Dipper. See? Those are so far away that no one will ever be able to go there."

"Tars," she said.

"The Big Dipper."

"Bippa."

"Stars, darling. Thousands and thousands of light years away."

"Tars."

"See the handle, honey?" I asked, making an ironic joke she couldn't understand and which was no comfort to me. There was no handle for this situation.

She caressed my cheek, that little person, and the stars blurred in the sky, and I knew I would be abandoning her, this precious little girl, and I knew there was nothing to do about it. This was the first substantial piece of me that would die, and I didn't even have the right to mourn because I was the executioner.

The lieutenant dropped Toni June off the next evening after the baby was asleep. She went straight for the vodka bottle and ice. I was on the sofa, listening to "Blue Rondo À La Turk," reading Ferlinghetti.

"Would you turn that noise off."

I did as she asked. "Where you been?"

She sat at the table, her shoulder to me, chin tipped up. "Are you really so stupid?" she said. "Where you think I been, baby?" She did not look at me.

"What were you doing with that lieutenant?"

Now she turned to me. "Are you really so stupid?" she said again.

I thought about that for a while. Then it occurred to me: He was a doctor. Incredulously, I asked, "Did *he* do it for you?"

"He only started it so I could go to the hospital with it already happening, then his doctor friend could finish it. *After*," she added and the expression in her eyes was one I had not seen there before, a look of vulnerability that worried me.

"After what?"

"What do you think after *what*, stupid?"

I did feel stupid, very stupid, but I had never been good at guessing things, and still I could not figure it out. "How much did it cost? How did you pay?"

Now the smirk was back, the vulnerability gone, her chin tilted up, her lips pressed so tight they were bloodless. "How do you *think* I paid?"

Then I got it. I still couldn't believe it, but it was the only answer. "Both of them?" I whispered.

Slowly and distinctly, she said, "*Fuck. You.*" She refilled her drink and carried it into the bedroom and locked the door.

I turned in the typewriter and got my deposit back. Toni June allowed me to leave the stereo instead of asking them to repossess it. My duffel bag was packed, but I didn't want to leave without saying goodbye so I waited in the living room, feet propped on the bag, until I heard Toni June's un-muffled Buick thundering down the back alley. I got up to greet them.

Little Lori May came in through the screen door first. She seemed not to see me. She turned her back to me and asked her mother, "Where Eddie Frank, Mommy? Where Eddie Frank?"

It was the first complete sentence I'd heard her speak.

Toni June's parting words to me were spoken the night before. I was knocking off the remains of a bottle of Mountain Red and she was into the vodka. She said, "I can see your life. You'll go home to your mother and back to college and have a normal life. You'll probably even publish a couple of books. But they won't be very good."

The words, rather than angry, were sad. We both knew that our time together was finished.

I left the Getz and Brubeck albums—what was I going to do with them?—and hitchhiked back east, along the southern route. Through Arizona, New Mexico, Texas, Louisiana, Mississippi, the panhandle of Florida, and up through Georgia, the Carolinas, Virginia, Maryland, Pennsylvania, and finally New York.

The first ride I had was from a couple in an Impala hardback convertible. They shared a joint with me while driving me toward the

California-Arizona line. I said to the couple, "This is good shit!" and they chuckled. I was transfixed by the radio and the music that sounded *good*—Jim and Jean singing harmony, "What's That Got to Do with Me?" over and over, it seemed all the way to the Arizona line.

I made it to New York in ten days.

You Can't Catch Me

1967, AUGUST 20TH: Across the George Washington Bridge, on the west side of the Hudson, with sweaty hands, Nick and I lifted our bicycles from the back of the pick-up truck, securing the baggage strapped to the carriers. Late afternoon humidity and temperature ran neck and dripping neck in the high 80s. I was tight on farewell suds, shirt stuck to my back and beer belly, and this year-long discussed trip, now beginning, felt unreal. Was I really doing this? Big Nick's jock-grey, sawed-off St. John's sweatshirt blurred dark beneath the arms, and from the grin on his ruddy puss, I guessed he was tight, too. The driver, Jimmy, a short, chesty ex-marine, twenty-three years old, my age, ceremoniously shook our hands.

A dozen friends from the Friendly Tavern on Corona Avenue, where we'd been held captive since noon Sunday opening time, stood outside their cars in the dusty cut-off of the old two-lane Lincoln Highway, established in 1913 to span the continent, 3,389 miles from Times Square in New York City to Lincoln Park in San Francisco. We were cheating, skipping the Times Square part, taking it from the other side of the GW Bridge.

I reminded myself to lift my leg high as I swung up onto the bike, to clear my deep-packed carrier baggage and avoid the humiliation of starting the journey with a flop, leave them with that image as we set off, their laughter chasing us.

Someone tooted his car horn from among our entourage, and a cheer went up. The young women in hip-hugger bell-bottomed jeans, long flowing, late '60s hair, middie blouses, waved, navels winking as we put feet to pedals and began to pump. We lifted an arm in heroic Roman salute as beer churned in my belly, our rear carriers weighted down each with nearly half a hundred pounds of gear—shelter halves, sleeping bags, ground mats, tent poles, pegs and ropes, powdered and canned food, a sterno-stove, and in my case, a fat Webster's which I never traveled without, just in case, in Nick's a 30/30 lever action rifle and box of ammo—Nick supported the NRA and the constitutional right to bear arms.

As we rounded a curve in the narrow highway, I heard the motors of our escort revving up behind us to head back to Queens and the lazy pleasures of the air-conditioned Friendly Tavern. I am leaving Queens behind. Leaving behind my dead father.

Bye-bye, New York. Howdy, East Orange.

This was 1967. I had decided to ride by bicycle from New York to San Francisco. The bike was a three-speed Schwinn, as banged up as my life. This symbolic journey was meant to trim the beer fat off my body, tighten my muscles, give me a tan. More important, to make of me a young man who had bicycled across the American continent. Already I had become a young man who was going to bicycle across the American continent. Now I only had to do it.

Then I would return in triumph to the C.C.N.Y. from which I had taken numerous leaves of absence in the beginning of 1962, at the age of seventeen, after my first semester and two semesters in '64-'65, to become a writer. Who needed a degree? John Steinbeck didn't have a degree. Ernest Hemingway didn't have a degree. William Faulkner, J. D. Salinger, Jack Kerouac didn't have degrees. During the 5½ years since dropping out, and three years since my father had died, a fact still alien to me, I had lived in a variety of crummy apartments in a variety of cities, surviving on onions, tomatoes, rice, and generic beer and wine. I left my father, Toni June and Lori May behind, in the land of the dead and forgotten. But I didn't forget them; I remembered them at three o'clock in the morning of many nights. I had also filled a lot of spiral notebooks describing my journeys around the U.S. on Greyhound and Trailways buses and in various cars which had stopped on various roads in various states at the request of my thumb—as well as other, inner journeys, fueled by alcohol and psychedelics and my hated, nervous-breakdown time in the army, pre-Vietnam. But nothing I wrote had earned more than a printed, impersonal rejection slip.

In fact, a year-and-a-half before, my collected writings to date, locked in an attaché case, had been stolen from a locked '66 Ford on Fillmore Street in San Francisco. I could still imagine the incredulous, disappointed scowl on the face of the poor junky when he jimmied the attaché case locks to find nothing inside but a mass of scribble. Not even a junkie wanted to read me.

Clearly, I needed to find my way back to some kind of normal, sane life—the life I used to have, before my father's drinking turned fatal. So, I cut my long hair, shaved my burns and 'stache, and enlisted Nick to accompany me on this crossing. Nick seemed a model of normal American youth. He had played football for St. John's University where he majored in German; he stood half a foot taller than me, had a powerful body, pugnose, a broad, underslung jaw, and a crewcut, which he constantly ruffled to see if it was getting longish. Though a football injury had prevented him from serving, he supported the Vietnam War. As long as we didn't talk politics, we got on fine. For some reason, I've always hit it off with jocks, despite that I never once in my life, apart from a mandatory semester of soccer, boxing, lacrosse and swimming at City College, had had a thing to do with balls or bats or hoops.

Our plan was to cross the continent on the less trafficked Lincoln Highway rather than the other, more contemporary Route 66 of Nat King Cole and Rolling Stones fame. The Lincoln passed from New York and New Jersey through southern Pennsylvania, a sliver of West Virginia, the northernly parts of Ohio and Indiana, slashing down to central Illinois, Iowa and Nebraska, through Nevada to Reno and on across northern California to end in San Francisco—where we hoped to arrive on November 1st. Our journey had been lined out for us by a white-shirted, bow-tied Esso PR man in mercurochrome-colored highlighter on a series of promotional road maps. We would ride idyllic farm roads, see the real country, coast through small-town America, where smiling families would wave from white wooden porches, farmer's daughters would offer drinks of body-temperature-hot creamy milk from aluminum buckets, gazing at us with shy, admiring eyes. We would meet the real people. (And—I would find out—their real dogs, too.)

Despite Nick's history as a German-speaking jock I was, at least initially, better prepared for the trip than he because I had been biking a few hours a day for months. Nick had only purchased his bike—a brand-new five-speed—two weeks before. Now we were on the road, me and Nick, sweating, our seat heights adjusted just so for the full thrust of leg, thigh muscles flexing as we pumped pedals, turning sprocket and chain and wheels along some back road through a Jersey swamp, headed toward the sun as it flattened red as a bruise along the blue horizon.

Before long we were coasting up to a camp ground, eerily misted in the gloamy dusk, paid fifty cents and hunted through the marshy trails for a spot to pitch our pup tent. I rolled my bike behind Nick, in short pants and sawed-off sweat shirt, and watched his thick, mossy arms and legs quickly cover with red welts from the stinging, whining mosquitoes; I thanked the gods of chance that had me wearing long sleeves and jeans. Actually, though, it was the gods of poverty—I didn't even own a pair of shorts—or a decent set of clothes for that matter. I was an impoverished artist trying to get back into the mainstream. I wore two-dollar Army-Navy jeans and my old Class-A khaki Army blouse, white spaces where the PFC stripes and rifleman's badge had been, lapels tugging at the button over my beer belly. My only luxury in life had been the 15-cent eight-ounce glasses of tap beer I drank at the Friendly.

Nick never uttered a complaint about all the bites. Soon he was snoring in our steamy pup tent while I lay awake, smacking my ears to silence the mosquitoes, thinking.

In a sense this was the overnight trip my father once had promised me I could take when I turned fourteen. I was eleven then and he thought I'd forget, but on my fourteenth birthday, when I reminded him, he reneged. Then, however, it was only to have been an overnight camping trip by bike. Now he was no longer around to stop me, and I was setting off for months of nights, thousands of miles. Not that he could stop me anymore anyway, even if he'd been still alive. Even when he was around, he had been unable to stop me from dropping out of college—he didn't even try. He let me do what I wanted—which I didn't fully want him to do. Now a gap lengthened from my due course of education, and I had to fit back in.

In the morning, we sat on twin rocks, waiting for coffee water to boil on the slowly crawling blue flame of our little collapsible sterno stove, but the cool night air more quickly heated and turned sodden.

Nick asked me, "Are you stiff?"

"No."

His blue eyes were incredulous in his freckled, pug-nosed, square-jawed face, and he ruffled his crew cut. "You're not stiff?"

"No."

He looked away, shaking freeze-dried coffee grains into the curved tin cup that fitted onto the bottom of his army surplus canteen and said nothing more. But it was enough to tell me that his muscles were lumped with pain, shot through with lactic acid. In but a day or two, he would be in better biking shape than I, and every time we took a break, if I showed signs of wishing to stretch it out or knock off for the day and find a place to drink beer—which was virtually constantly—he would suggest in a brisk tone, "Come on, Eddie. Let's push on. Couple more hours." He called me Eddie, a name my mother had with success prohibited anyone from calling me—except for Toni June and Lori May who called me Eddie Frank, but I didn't want to think about them now. Nick could not be induced to take a break unless for a skinny dip in a pond, lake, stream or river. He seemed to consider it his natural obligation to strip and swim in any body of water which entered his field of vision—would even insist we pedal miles out of our way when he spotted a glint of water far off the road.

Soon we had traversed the swamps of the Garden State and were onto the rising, dipping roads of Pennsylvania, pumping up hills as far as we could, our ascent slowing as our grunts increased until, often as not, I had to dismount and push the bike up the last fifty yards of baking, black tarmac. Then I was on the crest and zooming downward, cool breeze rushing across my cheeks as my face split the air, hoping to maintain speed to carry me up to the top of the next hill. Nick had the weight on me, thus a constant advance of twenty or thirty yards. He flew further past farm gates with a milk-curdling whoop, alerting the dogs inside to race out to the road just in time for my appearance—barking and snarling as they sprinted along on either side of me, trying in vain to catch my ragged jean cuffs in their snapping jaws as I prayed to maintain momentum, not to have to dismount.

I had to swing off my cycle anyway and was surrounded by four or five snarling mutts of all mixes—flat-faced, long-snouted, low-legged, short-haired, shaggy, kinky-furred, broad-backed, half-breed huskies, all wanting nothing more than an excuse to jaw my butt as I humped my back-heavy bike up toward the hilltop, doing my best to ignore the growling curs, fearing fear itself as I wondered whether it was true that dogs could smell fear and instinctively attacked the smell. But then I was on the bike again, pumping like mad and the dogs launched after me in frenzy until I looped over the top and picked up enough speed to leave them behind, only to repeat the process halfway up the next hill.

Our first Pennsylvania night, after dragging our loads up a long, steep piece of highway to the top of a plateau, we found a wooden lodge with a two-bed room for fifty cents a bed. We were the only guests and, after meat loaf and mashed potatoes at the local diner, sat on the porch sipping bottles of Yuengling beer while polka music played softly from a radio inside. The porch looked out from the edge of the plateau, and we looked out over the landscape which would confront us next day—more hilly woods, red barns, fields, farm yards, as far as the distant horizon. It looked gentle now, washed in the soft red light of late sunset. The lodge owner had joined us, a man of fifty or so, craggy-faced, barrel-bellied. His gray eyes grew wistful when he heard we meant to cross the country.

"Always wanted to do that myself," he said softly, gravel-voiced. "In a horse wagon. Camp by rivers. Cook meals on a wood fire."

I was still thinking about dogs and managed to drag them into the conversation. "I guess they're just playful," I suggested hopefully.

He turned his eyes to me, sharp now, drawn from their dream. "Oh, I don't think so. They ain't playin'. They want a piece of you."

Which reminded me of a sign I saw in a diner where we stopped for lunch; a thick-backed short-snouted brown mutt strained at its chain outside beneath a hand-painted sign that said, *Mean Dogs Make Good Neighbors.*

That night I lay awake in my bed listening to Nick snore from across the room. Tired as I was I couldn't sleep. Outside our window screen, the air was country night cool, cicadas chirping among the green darkness of leafy trees, a sliver of shining moon behind in the navy sky, asparkle with stars. And I was thinking about my father.

At the end of the summer of 1964—three years before, when I was twenty—he died. The reasons for his death were complex, and I have spent the decades since thinking and writing about it, and in the process have learned how ignorant I was and still am about my father. But that ignorance now was an informed ignorance—an ignorance that occupies a lot of rooms with a lot of doors in an edifice of memory where a boy could lose himself, looking for answers.

That is now. Back then, as I lay in that metal bed in a wooden lodge on a south-east Pennsylvania plateau, hands behind my head, gazing out the screened window into the summer darkness, his life and his death were still as new to me as the night was mysterious and ancient. And my thoughts about him—about how he had just given up—haunted the night and frightened me. In those first years after his death, I felt I was adrift on a vast, boundless ocean.

That I was adrift was not only due to my father's death. There were other factors as well, but many of them were bound intimately to the reasons for his death. If, today, one of my writing students had written the above sentences, I would likely tell him or her, "Too abstract and general. Be more concrete." But perhaps sometimes abstraction and generalization were the quickest way to the heart of a matter.

A few months before my father died, I had been discharged from the army, a confused young man, and my response to his death was to buy a Greyhound bus ticket from New York to Los Angeles, the first of many continental crossings, east to west, west to east, across the south, across the north, north to south... Some Roman poet—Horace perhaps—said something like, "You may cross the land but your soul will follow you."

One thing about my father's death, one important central thing, was that it seemed to me he gave up, he despaired. As a young Catholic I learned that the only unforgiveable sin was despair, but in my father's case, I didn't believe the despair was fully voluntary. I think he had been driven to it by several factors—his job, his childhood, his wife (who, in turn, was driven by him to quiet desperation, despite their love for one another), the failures of his children. I will not go into detail, but I will add that to some degree, I think, he was responsible for his own early destruction. He let life happen to him rather than acting. He was a perfect Prufrock, content with tea and cakes and ices, with a few lines of verse and shots of Wild Turkey and a whiff of perfume from a dress, forever turning back to descend the stair. Prufrock was a pale Hamlet, and perhaps I myself am a pale Prufrock. Son of Prufrock, pondering his demise.

He was a kind man for the most. He read to me, told me stories, never struck me—even in his cups, was usually patient, if too often distant. I remembered his story of shipping out of New York Harbor as a cabin boy on a freighter in 1921 when he was fifteen, a summer voyage to Mexico.

69

There were open cans of condensed milk in the galley for the coffee—when you shook them you could hear the cockroaches rattle around inside. The captain was a hard man, used to pinch Dad hard to emphasize orders. Dad jumped ship at the first port, in the Carolinas. And I recall his telling me once how in high school he played baseball and just before the season started the coach began to make cuts. He knew that he would be dropped, so he quit first. Months later, on the street, he ran into the coach who asked him, "How come you quit? I wanted you for the team." Maybe that was a parable for my edification—but maybe it was true, a key to his character. He did not have the life he wanted, yet took no steps to change it. Unlike his sister he had not gone to college. He worked in a bank instead of working with the poetry he loved. He tried to be happy at home, but he was not—I remember my mother's sad face as she quietly washed dishes, him trying to come up behind and embrace her for a boozy kiss, her trying to make a joke of it: "Hold off! Unhand me, grey-beard loon!" Which made me laugh. But it wasn't funny. His four children were not doing well either— including the youngest, me, a scholarship boy whom he had expected to be the first college graduate, now a drop-out. Dad's response to these things was to drink, then when things got worse to drink even more, and when he was warned by his doctor that he was killing himself with drink, when the president of the bank told him he was fired unless he joined AA, he drank double as much until finally one day he spouted blood like a fountain and died.

My response was to flee, to dive off the side of a ship whose captain's mind was hurt, who had hastened his own destruction.

Finally, I slept and woke to a raucous choir of birds, each singing in its own distinct voice—chirps, twitters, squawks, quacks, whistles, cooing. I pictured them in a group, tall and short, small-beaked and long, puff-breasted, multi-colored feathers, as I listened from the warmth of my sleeping bag on the metal bed in the chilly Pennsylvania mountain air. Nick and I ate big American breakfasts in the local diner—eggs and back bacon and sausage patties, a mess of home fries, and pancakes with butter and Log Cabin syrup, toast and juice and lots of black scalding coffee (I drank black coffee for the crossing)—fuel for the hills to come. Since we stopped the day before on a rise, we could start today coasting down before the first contingent of dogs surrounded me.

How like a whining snot-nose I felt, whimpering in my heart about a bunch of dogs, and I turned that loathful image of myself into a dynamo that fueled my courage—*Move your butt, you sniveler!* I commanded myself, and that got me through the remaining days of the farm dogs. At last I grew indifferent to their snarling, began to fling shouts and curses at them and was delighted to see confusion shiver in their wet, black noses. *Hey,* they seemed suddenly to be thinking, *Maybe that guy is strong or something.*

Pennsylvania was perhaps 400 miles wide where we crossed it—as the crow flew. As the bike rose and fell, however, I wouldn't venture to estimate the distance we covered. We were twelve days getting to the West Virginia line, but we lost two days to an accident.

Outside McConnelsburg, descending a long, steep, curving decline in south central Pennsylvania, Nick kept gaining in his lead until he was so far ahead I lost sight of him. Which was fine with me. By then, I was one with my bike, took my hands off the handlebars and laced them behind my skull, felt the air stream along my cheeks, ruffling my hair. I steered by leaning, could move my body as I wished without losing balance, and had no fear of losing balance because I could sense the first instant of imbalance and correct it. I sang as I coasted round the curves, picking up speed—how fast? Who knew? 15, 20, 25 miles an hour? More? I loved it. Not a dog in sight, and I felt fit for fight, the occasional pick-up flying past with a beeping salute as I sang Dylan's "Rolling Stone," Simon & Garfunkel's "America," Chuck Berry:

> You can't catch me.
> No, ba-bee, you can't catch me.
> Cuz if you get too close, you know I'm gone
> Like a cool breeze...

Around one sharp curve I saw Nick sitting on the edge of the road, and I laughed aloud. What a great joke! But rounding the next curve down the mountain, I suddenly registered the stunned expression that showed in his eyes as I flew past. I took hold of the hot rubber handgrips and eased on my brakes.

Nick had crashed, and his arms and legs were brush-burned and peppered with gravel. He'd hit his head, too, and was bleeding and dazed.

Whatever the politics of that region might have been, there was nothing wrong with their humanity. The next pick-up stopped and, without hesitation, drove us, bikes and all, to the nearest medical center, in a town called McConnelsburg, just about midway across the state. There, a dark-haired, sweet-faced young nurse tweezed the gravel from Nick's wounds, cleaned and disinfected and bandaged them. Nothing was broken and his head was okay, too, but we would have to spend a couple of days in a motel. We had been on the road for about seven days.

Nick had been working all year as a claims adjustor and could afford to foot the bill. I couldn't be happier, having two days off the road while he recuperated and a bent rim was re-spoked. We ate steaks for dinner and sat on the porch of our tiny motel discussing matters of deeper philosophy, swigging bottles of beer. Nick knew I was incapable of talking sports with him, and his potentially fatal spill had him thinking. He told me that Goethe claimed that he wrote to achieve immortality and asked if the reason I wanted to write was to try to immortalize myself.

It seemed important to him that that be the reason, so I said, "Not in the least. I write because words are more fun than a football. And if I publish a book, I might get laid more often." I knew that was churlish of me, but Nick was unflappable anyway. I was still pissed off that the nurse in the little medical center seemed to treat him with more TLC than necessary. Especially when the beer began to creep up on us there on the motel porch and he told me that nurse was ugly. She was gorgeous, but she only had eyes for him. I thought cave-men had gone out of style. It seemed to me the age of the gentle, peaceful, compassionate man should have arrived about then, but women still took to the brute. I even once—I swear it—saw a girl cross the floor of Nellie Keough's Rose of Trallee and genuflect to Nick. In my case, they always seemed to be interested in matters of the intellect, the spirit. I guessed some basic animal truths of human nature were always valid. Anyway, I probably would have been a brute if I were able.

During our hiatus, Nick changed his own bandages a couple of times (I couldn't do it), and he was the one who, two mornings later, woke me to say, "What do you say, Eddie? Let's push on."

"Please, don't call me Eddie."

"Why? That's your name."

"Okay, *Nickie*. Let's push on then."

Rested and strong after nine days on the road, the last two in a cozy motel, we embarked under a blue sky, determined that this would be our last day of Pennsylvania. But the blue sky whitened, then went dark, and the gods began to pelt us with stinging pebbles of hail. Right in the face. The earlobes, too, and the naked hands on the handlebar grips. It felt personal. We reconnoitered under a tree as spears of lightning flew across the sky. I counted seconds to the thunder—flash-to-bang time. The lightning was close.

"Let's push on, Eddie. With the rubber tires beneath us, we'll be insulated."

I would have argued but what use was there in huddling wet under a tree? So, we donned our ponchos and on we pushed in the rain. (Which made the girls in the Friendly Tavern giggle, because the ponchos had spouts where our dicks would be.) How gray and wet and chill it was in late August in a mid-afternoon rain, biking up and down the hills of southwestern Pa.! It was no doubt a gorgeous region with many interesting topographical features, but I saw nothing that day. Gray rain. Dark sky. Even the dogs had lost interest in us.

We pitched our tent that night in a muddy place near a small body of water with a misty rain still wrapped about us. As I crawled into my damp sleeping bag, a bodacious green insect was perched where my head wanted to be; it appeared to have a toothpick-sized lance on its snout.

"Fuck you," I muttered and crawled in alongside it.

We woke, ravenous, to sunlight and opened cans of Warhol beans in tomato sauce which we wolfed from the can with our Swiss army forks. Munching beans, I considered the fact that everything I had—jacket, sleeping bag, shirt, jeans, underwear, socks, sneakers (this was before we called them running shoes)—was wet. Not damp, but soaked. It was our eleventh day on the road, the last day of August, and I tried to remember some beautiful sight I had seen. I knew that I had seen things, experienced idyllic moments, swimming in a stream in a green valley, say, while sunlight glinted off the water and willow branches hung lushly down, but at the moment I could remember none of it. I forked up the last of the little red beans and sighed.

Without discussing it, we crumpled up our gear and made our way to the high ground, out of the mud and the wet, and on a stony slope, we stripped to our damp swimsuits and stretched out all our things on the grey rockface in the sunlight. The sun was lovely, but we were wet, and I could feel depression seeking to descend upon me. How I yearned for a Twinkie and a beer! A White Castle hamburger and a Mission orange soda. A baloney hero with lettuce and mustard. Words of advice and comfort from my father.

Then I recalled once, in 1963, when I was in the army. I had received orders to fly from Indianapolis to Washington, DC, arrived at Dulles at one in the morning with all my belongings packed into my duffel bag and a dodgy cardboard suitcase. I was to report for duty at some gate of the Executive Office Building but not before 8:30 the next day, and I had no idea where to sleep. Then my suitcase split its seams, and everything in it spilled out onto the pink linoleum floor of the terminal. I gazed down at my belongings—shaving cream and safety razors, hairbrush, toothbrush, toothpaste (my ditty bag had been stolen), a package of 7-day deodorant pads (for spit-shining my boots and low quarters), blousing garters, church-key, badges, brass, pens, and whatever—skittering across the floor... I was nineteen years old and wondered if someone would do something for me.

Call Dad, *I thought then.* He'll tell me what to do.

Fishing into my pocket for a dime, I left my gutted suitcase where it was and headed for a phone booth, composing what I would say to my father. And then it occurred to me that no matter what I said, he couldn't help me. He was hundreds of miles away. It was one a.m. He was asleep. I would have to call collect. He hated it when I called collect—remembered that blue, lonely evening when I called collect from the Post, desperate to hear the family's voices, and Dad snapped, "This is costing money, son. What do you want?"

What could he tell me anyway?

I spotted a sundries shop where I bought a roll of masking tape, repacked and taped shut my suitcase, looked in the yellow pages under "hotel," found a listing for a Soldier's & Sailor's hostel and slept that night in one of a four-high stack of bunks with about a foot of stale air between my face and the next bed, wrapped in the snores and farts of the others, feeling I had just crossed over to manhood. Of course, I hadn't. I was still a confused kid. But at least I'd dealt with one situation without calling my father for help he couldn't give.

Now he was dead. And I was twenty-three. Old enough to be over it. And I was sitting in my bathing suit on a rocky slope, hoping that the sun would dry my wet gear before dark. I glanced at Nick, marveling that he had not yet said, "Let's push on, Eddie." He said nothing. His underslung jaw was set, and he plucked at his lower lip as his blue eyes gazed off at nothing.

In the buttoned pocket of my wet army shirt, spread out on the rock, I found a damp pack of Pall Malls and laid them out to dry. Two of them were not soaked through. I offered one to Nick and lit us up with my Zippo. He rummaged in his bag and found two cans of warm beer and punched them open with his oversized brazened church-key. The beer sprayed up from the can. He looked silly, sitting on the rockface, beer foam dripping from his nose, wearing his checkered swim trunks, surrounded by his spread-out T-shirts and boxer shorts and tube socks. But no sillier than I did. I began to laugh, and he laughed, too. We sputtered to a stop, began to laugh again, giggle, in paroxysoms of deep, belly laughter.

The beer was warm and frothy and bitter. There was nothing else to do but smoke and drink warm beer, while we waited for our stuff to dry.

I said, "What the fuck are we doing here?"

Nick looked surprised. "We're going to San Francisco."

But I was not so sure.

Our stuff was dry enough that night that we could camp there—down on a wide grassy divider on the highway. And next day, August 31st, we stopped off in Bentleyville, Pennsylvania, so Nick could cash some traveler's checks at the Peoples Union Bank.

Thursday, September 7, 1967.
The Courier, Bentleyville, Pennsylvania. Vol XXI, No. 29
CROSS-COUNTRY CYCLISTS *Nick Slovak, left, and Ed Fitzgerald stopped in Bentleyville last Thursday afternoon, August 31st, long enough to cash some travelers checks, replenish their napsacks and explain their stunt to Courier Editor Guy Paul, right. The pair left New York City August 20 with the idea of arriving in San Francisco about the first of November. If their bikes and their legs hold. "We're doing it just as a lark," said 22-year-old Slovak who received his Bachelor of Arts Degree in Modern*

Languages from St. John's University last June. Fitzgerald, 23, will return as a sophomore to City College Of New York after the trip. "If they'll have me," he commented. They reported the only mishap thus far was a slight spill in McConnelsburg where Slovak received scratches and brushburns to an elbow. Accepting their checks for cashing is Peoples Union Bank Manager Clyde O. Finney as Stanley Beck and Anthony Jurik look on.

In the photograph accompanying the little news piece, Nick looks healthy and happy and strong. Leaning over my bike, I look like Renfield crawling up out of the hold of Count Dracula's ship, crooning, "Spiders, master! Spiders!" It would take more than our legs and our bikes for me to hold out for the remainder of this stunt, Guy! Hark, hark the lark's gone dark!

But at least I'd lost my beer belly and had a suntan.

In West Virginia, on Friday, September 9th, we wheeled past the outskirts of Wheeling, stayed that evening in a youth hostel with a big group of kids. Across a campfire, I fell for a young woman with a sweet face though not the world's greatest complexion. But she rendered me the kindness of gazing longingly at me. Men and women's quarters were strictly separated in the hostel, though, so we only had time for a walk under the starry night sky and a quick, chaste kiss before the ten p.m. curfew. I asked her for another, and she said no but gave it to me anyway and touched my cheek, looking into my eyes for one beseeching instant before disappearing into the women's quarters.

What was your name? I miss you.

The Letter

NICK AND I ROLLED INTO BEAUTIFUL OHIO, the smoothest part of the journey because we crossed on a band of level lowland that ran across the state to the northwestern corner. "Ohio" was from a Seneca word that meant "beautiful" or "beautiful river," and it felt mightily beautiful as we achieved our first of two "century" days—100 miles, biking a 12-hour day. But it was also the beginning of my undoing as we pumped across the flat country between waving, golden wheat fields.

Wheat. Wheat. More wheat. Wheat. It didn't matter if it was rapeseed or some other produce: I saw *wheat!* The wheat raped and seeded my vision until I could see nothing else.

This is not fun, I thought, pushing pedals in September heat, around the fourth hour of the thirteenth day. *Why am I doing this? Just because I said I would? There is no shame in quitting a dumb stunt like this.* I had already quit so many things—school, jobs, Anne Suffier, Toni June—that shame hardly seemed an issue anymore. Then I remembered when I went back to college last time, very briefly, the year after I dropped out, then dropped out again after a semester, a friend at the Friendly Tavern turned his back to me and muttered, "No guts."

No guts. Sum of the total of a young man's character. Or guts. *What did he know anyway?*

That first day of Ohio we ran out of water in the middle of nowhere, and I inhaled a floating wheat seed and had to stop short on the highway, coughing, dying for breath. First farm we came to, we ventured through the big gate and in along the entry road, expecting at any moment to be attacked by a pack of dogs or geese, but we got all the way to the well where two extremely large men, brothers—wearing peaked caps at a time when no one but baseball players wore peaked caps—came out to greet us in their overalls. We asked if we might take some water, and they brought us icy bottles of coke, sit in the shade with us and asked about our trip. They must have weighed 700 pounds between them, gentle-mannered men living, ostensibly, without women or children or anyone else, expressing wonder at what we were doing. Their farmyard might have been the Garden of the Finzi-Continis, so isolated did they seem.

I think of those brothers now, wonder if they are still alive, if their farm has survived. Their act of kindness, giving a bottle of Coke to each of us and asking about our trip. Such a tiny, enormous thing.

Canteens sloshing-full of water, we pushed on, camped alongside the wheat fields, and I dreamed that the wheat seed I inhaled was planted in my heart and growing. We woke next day alongside the wheat fields, began biking again along the road between the wheat fields. Wheat. More wheat. I found myself wondering increasingly how to get out of this. It was my idea in the first place. How could I quit on Nick?

Then, on a side road through a little town, we heard music. A song I hadn't heard before but one that instantly spoke to me:

Get me a ticket for a air-o-plane
Ain't got time to take no fast train
Ain't got time to take a fast train
Baby wrote me letter

We followed the music through side-roads and came to a public swimming pool—the only thing that could inspire Nick to stop and take a break during this second potential century day. We locked our bikes, dug into our packs for swimsuits, paid a quarter, and were in the pool amidst splashing, giggling Ohio girls in two piece swimsuits, the Box Tops booming from the loudspeaker. It seemed to be the only song they played that day which suited me fine. I could listen to it until sundown, eyeballing the muscle tone of Beautiful Ohio's beautiful girls.

My body had already responded to the long days of exercise and sun. I could sense the young ladies returning my appreciative glances, and I thought, *Here!* Let's stay *here!* Forever! Let's drop the lark, jettison the stunt, and make a new life right here forever. Maybe those two fat farm brothers would give us work—notwithstanding the novel by Larry Wodwode *What I'm Going to Do, I Think*, where the greedy farmer enlists the protagonist for a day's work and doesn't even offer him dinner, drinks a whole gallon of juice out of a damaged can in front of him in the parching sun, exclaiming, "Good juice! Cheap!"

One young woman was smiling with apparent appreciation at my unabashed appreciation of her. She was tall, long-limbed, with looong red hair, a little pouch of belly above the bottom of her suit where tiny red hairs glinted like copper in the sunlight.

I said to Nick, "She will be the mother of my children."

Nick laughed, stubbed out his Marlboro. "Come on, Eddie. Let's push on. We can still do another century today."

And we did that.

In Indiana: Wheat. Wheat fields. Wheat fields. Rape Fields. Rape Fields. Wheat and Rape and Cornfields.

That is the story of the remainder of the trip. Day after 12-hour day. Wheat fields. Rape fields. Cornfields. No more dogs. No more hills to speak of. Just flat roads through endless wheat and rape and corn fields. And it was like the stultifying sameness of all the days of high school, of college, of jobs I couldn't hold, wouldn't hold, of everything I had quit over the past few years. It was too much. *Same thing everyday gettin' up goin' t' school...* And just as the wish to quit college had slowly grown in me, so too the wish to bail out on this journey grew as from a wheat seed in my heart until it was a flourishing stalk that bloomed in my mind, leaving room for nothing else.

Laying in the pup tent one evening, head filled with a vision of endless wheat fields, it occurred to me that perhaps my father's life was like this trip. Day after day after day of sameness, no hope for change. Until there was only one way out for him. At the bottom of a bottle of Four Roses. And I was thinking about my father again.

Saturday mornings my father and I sometimes spent time together, he in his armchair in the living room, reading, while I played on the floor with my toy soldiers or sat on the sofa and read or daydreamed. This one particular day I recalled looking at him—his big, strong face, big nose, his red-grey moustache and clean-trimmed brown-silver hair, his clear brown eyes and strong jaw, his manly smell of whiskey and tobacco and whiskers. I watched him take a pack of Camels from his pocket and tap one out, strike a match and light it, one eye squinted against the smoke, and I felt a radiance in my heart gazing at this man who knelt by his bed most nights to pray and rose every morning to put on his suit and tie and go out into the world and do what men do so that their families can live. And he was even more than that, it seemed to me then, that morning, as I watched him from the corner of my eye, because in addition to just doing the job he had, he wrote poems, too. He was an important man, he was a leader in a big organization where people called him "Mr. Fitzgerald." He was a vice president, respected—and in addition he was poet, and his picture was sometimes in the newspapers, the Long Island Star Journal, when he got another promotion or chaired some fund-raising committee of the Red Cross or Cancer Federation or the Grand Jury. And I looked at this man this one particular day, my hero, and my heart opened with love, and I wanted to tell him what I felt for him, and the words that came into my mouth were, "Dad, when I grow up if I am just half the man that you are, I will feel I've done well."

I was maybe ten, which meant that he was forty-eight and only had ten years left to live—only the length of time I had lived to that point, ten

79

years. But it must have been a good period for him—or the end of a good period—because as I recall he was sober, the nightmare of the DTs he had over two years before seemed more like a dream left behind in the misty past, a nightmare. I was full of admiration for him, my father, my Dad, who went out into the world and did things and was not afraid.

He heard my words and looked up from his book and one nostril puckered as though he had smelled something bad, and he muttered, "Sure! Butter up the old man." He put down his book and stubbed out his cigarette and walked out of the room, and I heard him out in the pantry, taking down a bottle from the top shelf, getting a glass out of the cupboard, heard the cap being screwed off, the chuckle of liquid into the glass.

Stunned, feeling unworthy to be the boy of this man, I searched in my heart to try to see if he had seen something I was not aware of, some insincerity. Was I just trying to flatter him? No, I meant it. Why then? I wondered. Why did he say that?

It would take decades for me to understand what he was expressing to me with that reaction: His own sense of unworthiness. He could not accept my love and admiration because he did not love or admire himself, and ultimately, that must have been at the heart of what made him give up, what killed him. His own hatred of himself—for whatever reasons.

Morning again, pack the shelter halves, roll the sleeping bags, on the bike for another day like so many days before: hour after hour of flat fields, yellow hair growing upon it. And then we were out of Indiana, too, entering Illinois, and perhaps my memory is tainted but all I could remember seeing there, throughout all those days, was wheat fields.

On the outskirts of Peoria on Tuesday, September 13th, we pulled into a diner for breakfast. By my calculation, we had been on the road for twenty-three days, had covered 1,250 miles—approximately a third of the way to San Francisco.

That would make three times twenty-three days. Forty-six more days. At least. I'd had it. And I had decided this was the day to bail out, jump ship, quit. We ordered eggs and mashed potatoes. An enormous, big-bellied cook carrying an enormous pot of mashed potatoes came out from behind the counter to look through the front window at our bikes, locked against a pole outside.

"Whachoo boys up to?" he asked.

Nick said, "We're biking across the country."

"Across the country? Across this whole country of the United States? Well, gimme them plates." He began to dollop mashed potatoes until our plates were huge snowy mounds, and he said, "Har har, feeds ya like I feeds myself!"

I had twenty dollars left from the hundred-fifty I started with. I could wire my mother to send some of my savings, but that was not the point. I'd had it. I was bailing out, and this was the day.

"I can't take any more wheat fields. I'm done," I told Nick. "I don't want to use up all my money on *this*."

"Eddie," he said. His eyes were sad. "No. Don't quit. Let's push on."

Nick was such a capable guy. He set out for something, and he followed through with it. He could do so many things, but there was one thing I could do that he couldn't: Quit. Jump ship. My father taught me how.

How not to be a poet, how to be a writer.

If You're Going to San Francisco

IN PEORIA, I SOLD MY BIKE for twenty dollars and continued on thumb to San Francisco. Nick sold his bicycle, too, and hitchhiked south toward Mexico. I never regretted my decision.

Six days later, I arrived in Haight-Ashbury. I was headed for San Francisco to meet Ray York, who had written me that we could stay with him. York was a buddy from Elmhurst who had just been discharged from four years in the Navy in San Francisco and rented an apartment on Haight Street. Turned out, he had moved to Joshua Tree. The hippie who was sharing rent with York said I could stay if I paid half the rent. I stayed for one night, but his apartment had roaches and rats. I could take roaches, but the rats were too much.

Besides, I didn't like Haight-Ashbury which was mostly stoned people sitting on the curbs and streets, people filthy as the street. On the second day, I saw a man squatting and taking a dump in the middle of Ashbury Street. "It's natural," he explained.

It was the summer of love, but the summer of fucking love had ended before it even got a name. In truth, though we couldn't have known it then, the summer of 1967 was the end of the innocent '60s—if the '60s had ever been innocent at all. End of the illusion then. We were about to enter ugly '68 where another couple of assassinations would demonstrate that the ones which came before were no fluke; this was America now, this stuff *did and does* happen here.

But it was still '67, and Scott McKenzie was still singing in his smarmy voice about going to San Francisco and wearing flowers in your hair to meet all the gentle people there. Sure. Tell it to the Zodiac Killer. Tell it to Vietnam. I got out of San Francisco.

I got a ride in a Volkswagen that had the heater stuck on full. It was all the way to Los Angeles, so I sat in the passenger seat in the unnatural heat, sweating. I arrived in downtown L.A. with a fever. I holed up in the Optic Theater on South Main St. for a quarter. It was a triple feature of Yul Brynner-Steve McQueen-Charles Bronson movies non-stop. It was crowded, but I got two seats in the first row, one for my duffel, one for me. You could stretch out if you didn't mind the cinemascope screen right in front of your eyes. I minded. I napped on and off, while I sweated out the fever. A big, uniformed usher came around at dawn, clapping the backs of the seats with a ping-pong paddle, droning, "Time to get out, gentlemens."

Alone and sick on the streets of downtown L.A., I ate a poisoned taco and got the runs, so I found a Western Union office and called my mother to ask her to send part of my savings. After staying in a buck-a-night hotel for two days, I took a Greyhound for seventy-two hours, straight through to New York. I arrived at Port Authority and took the El train to Elmhurst. I planned to sleep for at least three days in my old room in my mother's house.

Two days my mother allowed me to sleep, but she woke me with breakfast and asked me what I was going to do. Her manner was kindly, but I could tell by the way she moved her hand on the table, flexing the fingers against her paper napkin—that she had made up her mind to keep moving me toward the door until I was out of her house. Amazing the way that one person can without even speaking telepathize her message. But anyway, it was time. I showered and shaved, put on my old woolen suit and necktie. The suit was baggy on me, I had lost so much weight. I took the subway into Lexington Avenue, midtown, to the Manhattan branch of the New York State Employment Agency—which didn't charge a fee—and got a part-time job as a typist for a non-governmental organization in Columbus Circle.

After that, I took the A train to Harlem and cancelled my leave of absence from C.C.N.Y. for the beginning of 1968. It was free then, the poor man's Harvard. Then I rode the IND subway down to the East Village, bought a copy of *The Village Voice* and read the classifieds for rentals and looked at two studios. The one was on East 4th between Avenues C and D. I favored that because it had a runty bath tub in the kitchen, and it was larger and cheaper by ten bucks a month; when I peeled up the edge of the linoleum by the refrigerator, a mass of insects was beneath it. I took the one on East 3rd between A and B in a modern building with an elevator for a hundred a month. I was determined to live in the East Village.

You could do that back then in Manhattan—get a job and enroll in college and rent an apartment in the same day.

The apartment was just down the street from Slug's jazz house where Lee Morgan, a hard-bop trombonist, one snowy night in February 1972, at thirty-three, was shot dead by his wife. I was long out of there by then.

The NGO's Secretary General—Miss Brown—took to me like the son she did not have, and she was like Toni June, quick with quips and opinions, but was essentially insecure. I was essentially insecure also, so we made a good pair. I was hired as a temporary typist for two weeks, but jobs in New York were growing like dandelions in a lot in the late '60s. Within two weeks, Miss Brown found out I could write and had me writing the newsletter and working-papers and speeches and typing them as well.

The years 1968 and '69 were horrible ones. Aside from Charles Manson and his cult of women having murdered Sharon Tate and nine others at four locations in July and August, there was mass racial violence in the USA. On the east coast, right in the East Village, we had the heiress with the hippie Groovy who met two black guys in a basement to score some speed, and the black guys crushed their heads with a cinder block. The article in the *East Village Other* ran under a two-inch headline, GROOVY IS DEAD. Subway-pushers would push an unsuspecting passenger who stood too near the edge of the platform in front of a train, and chain-snatchers would rip the necklaces and religious medals off the the necks of pedestrians.

Not only had JFK and Malcolm X been assassinated in 1963 and '64, Martin Luther King and Bobby Kennedy got offed in '68. Fred Hampton was killed the same year by two shots in the head at point blank range while he slept beside his pregnant fiancé, and Mark Clark was shot and killed, and seven other members of the Black Panther Party were beaten by the FBI and the Chicago Police. Clark was the only one of the Panthers to fire a shot while the FBI and the Chicago police fired eighty bullets. The Chicago police were already tainted to the public with the Police Riot of 1968 at the Democratic National Convention; Hubert H. Humphrey was nominated. Other candidates were Eugene McCarthy ("Get Clean for Gene"), George McGovern, and Pigasus (a 145-pound domestic pig) was nominated by the Youth International Party—the YIPpies—as a mock candidate. Pigasus was seized by the Chicago police, and several YIPpie backers were arrested for disorderly conduct. Worse, the anti-war protestors were clubbed down in Grant Park, across from the Hilton Hotel where the Democratic National Convention was held. Humphey was the Demoractic nominee, but Richard M. Nixon, "hero" of the Alger Hiss case, was elected U.S. president on the "Law and Order" ticket.

Vietnam was blazing then—a couple of my friends were always in the Nam—the first official battle having been staged in November 1965, "Landing Zone X-Ray." It started out low key, but soon it was raging, and more and more American troops were being shipped out. By March 1968, Lt. Calley and Charlie Company had raped and murdered the whole village of My Lai, defenseless women, many of them pregnant, and children and old men.

Every day the newspapers were filled with items like those, and the TV news showed the Vietnam war battles. People were frightened. At least I was. You didn't know when you saw a solitary black man walking on an isolated street whether he had infused in his heart that a white man was his enemy—whether he thought that *I* was his enemy. You didn't know whether a short-hair was the enemy of a long-hair. I wore my hair mid-length. You did not know where to stand on the subway platform, whether to stand in the center, where most people stood, or on the fringes, where the vulnerable stragglers were.

I was disgruntled by the national anthem being played before the movie in theaters, and those who were pro-war would stand and those who were anti-war would remain seated. Even when they played a re-run of *Dr. Strangelove*, the scattered people would be standing up amid the persons seated. It was about fifty-fifty.

There were good things, too. I watched the announcer on television saying two times, "A man's standing on the moon," as Niel Armstrong and Buzz Aldrin landed on the moon on July 20th, 1969, at 2:46 a.m. at Susie's Bar & Grill, right across from my apartment building. It was a Sunday, but Susie's stayed open two hours longer. I was torn between pride and regret—that the government was using so much on the space program instead of deploying it on the poor people—but when I saw Armstrong step down the ladder onto the moon's surface, I felt only pride. My eyes got wet, probably as did the eyes of all the other rednecks along the bar.

I didn't start back at C.C.N.Y. until September '68. Scrapegoat Gate, in Barthian parlance. Wonder if anyone would understand *Giles Goat Boy* anymore? I was twenty-four. I felt embarrassed to be so old compared to the other students, felt I should have been finished, my B.A. framed on my wall. But I told myself I was just there to learn. I had hit the wall of my ignorance. I was like Socrates: I knew nothing but the fact of my ignorance. I remember other classmates making sounds of disgust at my stupid questions, but I was determined to learn.

My classes at City included Composition II, Introduction to Philo, British Literature I, Introduction to Art, and the flunked Astronomy. I had another semester of science, having got an F in Astronomy last time and thrown out of the chemistry lab in high school by Brother Stephen for clowning. Astronomy was just like physics, which I couldn't understand. I pulled a C in it this time.

The Composition II class was just what I was looking for, though I didn't think it at first. It was taught by Edward Hoagland, who had a stutter. At the first class, he said it was sometimes worse than others. As if to demonstrate, he twisted his mouth around to the side of his cheek, and he was helpless against paroxysmal shudders that lasted a full five seconds; his mouth remained there while he resembled a man whose face was being run through with electricity. Eventually, he regained his mouth and face and began to speak naturally.

I admired his courage. In fact, later, a review appeared in the *New York Post* by Jimmy Breslin or Pete Hammil, one of the new journalists, on his book *The Courage of Turtles*, which was titled, "The Courage of Hoagland." It detailed how he had three novels out, and the one had sold more abysmally than the other, in reverse order.

85

Hoagland announced that he was a professional writer, and despite this being a comp class, we could write anything for this course but poetry. He was not an expert in poetry writing, but he managed compositions, essays, personal essays, short stories, articles, or any prose. He figured out what the proportion of study would be to forty-hour work week; he calculated that Comp II was 2 credits of about 16 so that was an eighth of a forty-hour week: "You have five hours that you are expected to devote to your writing. In the Army they specify that a person needs ten minutes per hour. That means b-b-b-bathroom b-b-breaks and snack b-b-breaks have to be f-f-fitted into ten minutes per hour." He wrote the titles of his novels on the blackboard: *Cat Man*, *The Circle Home*, *The Peacock's Tale*, and currently he was writing nonfiction, *Notes from the Century Before: A Journal from British Columbia*.

I went to my local public library and withdrew his three novels. I had never read a novel by someone I knew. I liked all three, but in descending order, the first book best. It had been written while he was an undergraduate at Harvard and published before he graduated in 1954. A chart was published in *Esquire* that month and among a list of serious literary writers, his name was on it, along with Norman Mailer, John Cheever, Robert Coover, Donald Barthelme, and John Barth.

With my first assignment, Hoagland called me to the front of the room to read, then he expounded on something called "purple prose," of which my manuscript was apparently an example. I sat at the front of the room, blushing through my ordeal. Then, when he had finished, he invited questions. My only friend in class, Donald Kelly, had gone to Regis High School, a Jesuit school, the only Catholic school which was "better" than my high school, a Christian Brothers institution. I had taken the entrance exam to Regis, nine years before, and failed to be admitted. Kelly's hand shot up and he asked, "Why did you make the piece so flowery?" So much for friends. After all, I had been writing for seven years then, from the time that I read "Miss Brill" and decided to be a writer. I felt that I had some expertise. I had a public library copy of *The Peacock's Tail*, and I marked it, under the library card, "B-."

We were given a twenty-minute conference per week with Hoagland, and he let me stand behind him while he took a red pen to my manuscripts, crossing out words, lines, paragraphs. At one point, he looked over his shoulder, clutching his hands in air, and shouted, "You are including every fucking detail!" But I learned. I guessed I was ready, having admitted I was ignorant.

The next manuscript I submitted was a full-fledged short story, based on my time with Toni June. It was titled, "The Gas-pump Cowgirl," a title which was inspired by the novel *Midnight Cowboy* by James Leo Herlihy, who taught at C.C.N.Y. I hadn't had him, had only read his book and would later see the movie. The movie, I thought, was better than the novel, but the title was splendid.

In my fourth conference, Hoagland said, "You have a sense of argument and relationship. I never saw or heard of a student like you. I don't give A's, but I'm giving you an A. This is publishable."

I wrote another story for his class, "Flies," based on my experiences in the Army of the slow-moving flies in Indianapolis, which floated through the sodden air while soldiers—particularly black soldiers—were being sent for the first forces in Vietnam.

Hoagland said in the last class of the semester, "Let's end this semester with drums and bugles and ask Fitzgerald to read his latest story."

The Secrets of the Sun

MEANWHILE, THE BEAUTIFUL BLOND in apartment 3A in my 3rd street building was greeting me most days with a fleeting smile and a glance out of the corner of her eyes. Her oh-so-tight, black leather jeans which showed the outlines of her long legs and exhibited a triangle of air and light at the tops of her thighs.

I looked at the bell of 3A: M. Kennedy. No help. I could always call her Miss Kennedy. Next time I saw her in the hall, we were waiting to take the elevator down. She had said, "Hi," with her fleeting smile and looked away immediately. She had thin lips and bright, white, flawless teeth. I would never forgive myself not talking to her. "What's the M. stand for, Miss Kennedy."

"Mary," she said with a faint brogue, which seemed second generation to me.

"Good morning, Mary."

"Good morning, Edward."

That she knew my first name was potent liquor to me. I was on the way to the Intro to Philosophy course with Dr. Beard at City, an exciting lecturer who would be talking about René Descartes today, but her saying my name was like a caress that made me think a missed class in the interests of beauty would be totally okay. "I'm going for breakfast. Like to join me? My treat." She said she had to go to the doctor. I said, "Hopefully, for nothing." She didn't answer for a moment; then, she said, "Just a check-up."

All during my philosophy class, I was elated by her long, straight, blond, impeccable hair, but I quickly got caught up in the lecture with just a feel-good backdrop of Mary Kennedy's hair and leather jeans. It was a lecture hall, with a stage on which Dr. Beard stood. There must have been a hundred-fifty students. Dr. Beard had just got his doctoral degree in philosophy, and he was young—not a year or two older than me—and he always wore a dark suit with white shirt and no tie and had a full auburn beard. The beard was in place of the tie. He was an exciting lecturer. He was speaking today on Descartes' "The Sphere of the Doubtful." It was like poetry, Descartes' writing, even the title. Dr. Beard was on the part where Descartes supposed not that God, who is supremely good and the fountain of truth, but some evil genius not less powerful than deceitful. "I shall consider that all external things are nothing but the illusions of which this evil genius has made use of to lay traps for my mind, and I shall consider my senses all extinguished, and I shall have firm purpose to avoid giving belief to any false thing. I shall persuade myself there is nothing in all the world, no minds, no bodies: was I not likewise persuaded that I did not exist? Not at all! Of a certainty I myself did exist merely because I thought of something. Then without doubt I exist. The Evil Genius shall not cause me to be nothing as long as I think I am something. I *am*! I *exist*! is necessarily true each time I pronounce it or *think* it. There are two certainties: One, I think therefore I am. And two, I seem to sense external phenomena."

It sounded better in Latin: *Cogito ergo sum.*

Timed precisely that the last word was at the bell, Dr. Beard said, "Read St. Anselm for next week, 'There Exists Something Than Which a Greater Cannot Be Thought.' Edwards and Pape, page 390, and Thomas Aquinas 'The Five Ways' and Coppleston's and Paley's commentary on it and Darrow's 'The Delusion of Design and Purpose.' "

At that moment, I loved Dr. Beard and I loved Mary Kennedy. The one was feeding my mind and the other was feeding my heart with her long, straight, blond hair, which she must have blowed dry, and light blue eyes and tight leather pants and the triangle of light between her thighs. And Hoagland, who'd said at the last conference of the last semester that I should be publishing soon. Mose Schwartz, who sat beside me in philosophy and passed the class register to me, printing his name out clearly so that I could discern it, invited me to have coffee with him afterward.

"What do you think of the eponymous Dr. Beard," I asked. Eponymous was a word I had just learned, eagerly used it. He said, "I don't like him. He reads too much instead of sharing his thoughts." Mose was a young guy, only nineteen, and he seemed shallow and a bullshitter, but soon I would admire him and think otherwise. But mostly I loved Mary Kennedy.

Mose and I had a class with Irving Malin on critical writing, where we were assigned one novel per week—Hammett's *The Maltese Falcon*, Salinger's *Franny and Zooey*, John Hawke's *The Cannibal*, Robert Coover's *Pricksongs and Descants*, Donald Barthelme's *Snow White*, Russel Edson's *The Very Thing that Happens*, and William Golding's *The Inheritors*.

Every Monday we were to write a thousand-word paper for Malin on the book that was to be discussed that week. I always wrote four or five thousand words—all except for Barthelme's *Snow White* which I considered fatuous. I liked Barthelme's stories in *The New Yorker* and *New American Review* and in his collection, *Unspeakable Practices, Unnatural Acts*, but *Snow White* didn't say a thing to me that was other than fatuous.

Malin would always ask me to read my paper. I went up to the front of the classroom and began to read. Malin interrupted me every Monday after a paragraph or a sentence or a half page and launched into his exegesis on the book. I would be sitting at the desk-chair, which I'd pulled up screechingly to the front of the room, and he never let me finish, would speak until the bell rang. He sat at the corner of the lectern, near the door, asking every time he made an esoteric point on the novel, "Am I insane?" Like he meant it sincerely, a nervous man with tics, as though he would bolt out of the door.

After class, Mose Schwartz got incensed. He implored me to refuse to read unless Malin would let me finish my paper, but I had too much respect for Malin—after all, I was his student, he the teacher. He had co-edited an anthology with my creative writing teacher, Irwin Stark, called something like *Jewish Writers in the Sixties*, which included all good stories by Phillip Roth, Bernard Malamud, Saul Bellow, Isaac Bashevis Singer. I was impressed. I also wanted to figure out the game he was playing with me. Besides, he always gave me an A on each paper, and the last time—though he interrupted me, as always, until the bell rang—he called me to his lectern and offered to be my mentor. I told him I was majoring in creative writing rather than critical writing, but I would think about it. I didn't want to be a critic.

One March day, late in the afternoon, I was standing with Mose preparatory to going into Malin's class. It was just dusk. A black guy had obviously wandered onto the campus looking for easy pickings—I remember he had on a yellow houndstooth suit. He snatched a purse from an unsuspecting student. The girl screamed, like the purse-snatcher had done something to her.

Mose took off running after him. He clearly could move. The man soon knew it. He was gaining on him within half a block, and the black man threw the purse down behind him and continued running. Mose picked up the purse and looked at the guy. The guy stopped after another fifty yards and shouted, "You mother-fuckin' faggot!" but he kept backing away and disappeared into the dusk of St. Nicholas Terrace.

No one else moved. I would not have done that. The dazed girl didn't even thank him when he handed her purse back, but I declared him a hero. Mose shrugged his shoulders and said, "Nah…" I couldn't get over it. Who would think that Mose would do that?

We went into Malin's class. I had written a fourteen-page paper on Salinger's *Franny and Zooey,* and as always, Malin invited me to read it and, as always, he interrupted me after one paragraph. As always, Mose was incensed and demonstratively left the room.

Another course in creative writing was taught by Irwin Stark, who challenged the class first day, "Don't look! What's the picture on the back wall of the room?"

There was no picture on the back wall, but no one got it, and Stark said, "You have to be observant about everything and yourself, too, and honest. I used to think I was the only one who masturbated until I found out that my father masturbated, too."

That relieved me because the first story I submitted had a scene of a boy's masturbation. I had just read a story in *New American Review* by Philip Roth called "The Jewish Blues" which began, "Sometime during my ninth year one of my testicles apparently decided it had had enough of life down in the scrotum and began to make its way north," and was about an epic onanist and would later in the year find its way into *Portnoy's Complaint*.

Next class, Stark came in and, without identifying the author, read my story. I sweated and writhed in my chair. He read a sentence about a girl wincing when she stepped on a shell on the beach; he interjected, "It takes a writer to put that shell just there where she'll step on it!" When the bell rang, many students in the room groaned with disappointment that he wasn't finished reading the story, and Stark said, "Only a page left. Do you want to be late for your next class?"

One girl hollered, "Yes!" and the students remained seated, grumbling approval. He read the last page and said, "Ladies and gentlemen, we have a writer in this class. Fitzgerald, will you come up here and see me?"

Stark wanted to introduce me to his agent, Theron Raines, who had just sold the paperback rights to Stark's novel *A Room in Hell*—it had been retitled that from *Subpoena*, it was pretty good in a tough-guy manner—and had negotiated a quarter of a million advance for Rod Thorpe's *The Detective* that was soon to be made into a "major motion picture," starring Frank Sinatra and Lee Remmick. Stark said that Thorpe was another student of his, years back.

Theron submitted my story to *Playboy*; it won a personal letter from Robie Macauley, saying, inter alia, *no*. As all the thirty magazines he submitted it to did.

The irony was that for a decade in the nineties I taught with Robie Macauley every summer for ten days. He told about the negotiations among the editors and executives of his publishing house for a book titled *Nora* by Brenda Maddox, and the executive accountant objected. "You want to give fifty grand to some biography about some writer's wife!"

At that point, Robie interrupted the negotiations. "Stan, we have to go out for lunch—now!—and I will explain something to you."

I interviewed Robie about when he was fiction editor of *Kenyon Review*, and he was invited to Chicago by Hugh Heffner, to be fiction editor of *Playboy*. Yevtushenko was in the mansion, and he waited until Heff went to bed, and the Russian poet proclaimed to Robie, "He is a *beasant!*"

"But Heff let me put a Christmas present of a thousand-dollar check in an envelope—and that was when a grand was a grand—to certain writers of my choosing: Cheever, Irwin Shaw, O'Faolain, etc."

Such money was in fiction writing then, and I only got a letter in the "Playboy Forum" in all the years when *Playboy* still existed—and a personal note from Robie Macauley.

At another class with Stark, he said in discussion of some student story, "The characters aren't changed here. The characters have to be changed in the course of the story."

I raised my hand and asked, "Isn't the change in the reader more important?" It was a sincere question, the answer to which I wanted to know, but Stark said, "That was a slap in the face! Yes, the change in the reader is more important!"

Afterward, another student, Woody Allen (no relation), came up to me and said, hypberbolically, "You should be teaching this class."

"It was an honest question."

Woody and I walked and talked from the south to the north campus while we went over to the cafeteria. Woody had chocolate milk, and I bought coffee. Woody was addicted to chocolate milk. He was a math genius, had gone to the Bronx High School of Science. He said that he was twenty, hadn't made a discovery yet in numbers theory, which was his focus, and it was too late in his life to be a child prodigy, so he decided to minor in literature and creative writing. I surmised he was equally good at both. He showed me a twenty-page manuscript, called "Bellman." It was derivative of Ginsberg's "Howl," but it was fantastic. I sat marveling over the manuscript, when Mose Schwartz happened past. I introduced them, and they soon discovered that they had a mutual acquaintance, Hiram Schwartz. Woody wasn't friends with him, but he was acquainted with him from afar. Mose was his cousin. Woody sang the praises of Hiram Schwartz, math genius, and Mose talked Hiram slightly down: "Hiram is a bright guy, but he's also a questionable guy."

Strolling home from the subway that night, I thought I smelled snow in the air. I got off at W. 4ᵗʰ St. and walked along 3ʳᵈ St., crossed the street not to pass the Men's Welfare Shelter, guys in putrid clothes looking like they were walking underwater, picking their feet up carefully, slowly, and setting them down again. I recrossed the street, coming up on the Hell's Angels headquarters.

I was feeling good, *discovered,* with my own agent, but the thing with Mose was niggling at me, that he would just give chase to that purse-snatcher. I didn't have the guts. At least, I could write about it. Honestly. That *Lord Jim* kind of thing. Just write about it. No matter where it's going.

The snow was falling now, gathering on windowsills and fences and parked cars. So why didn't I go up to 3A and see Mary Kennedy? That was the real reason I was feeling good about myself. Invite her over to Slug's.

I tapped at the door of 3A. Seemed a more intimate thing to tap than to ring the bell. Could control your tapping.

There came what seemed like a frightened voice. "Who is it?" Something in the manner of her voice attracted me. "It's Edward, Mary. Edward Fitzgerald? Your neighbor from 3G."

I could hear her opening two locks and the police chain. The door opened a little crack, then swung wide. I asked her if she liked jazz, if she wanted to go to Slug's. She had her leather pants on and a white turtle neck, fluffy sweater and was more beautiful than I'd ever seen her. The sweater fitted her very nicely. With her long, blow-dried blond hair falling over her shoulders and blue eyes and white, perfect teeth.

"Please," she said. "Come in."

Her apartment was a studio, same as mine, but her floor was covered by an immaculate white wall-to-wall and her double brass bed was spread with a white bedspread. Her sofa was white, and her walls were freshly painted white. I was ashamed of my apartment with its mismatched furniture—my grandmother's battered dining table from our basement in Elmhurst, and the bare wood floor and my cot and the kitchen table. Which had been picked up from the street. The two folding beach chairs had been picked out of the garbage. My cinder-block-and-board bookshelf was the only thing in which I was proud of, with its hundred or so books. The Remington typewriter, my father's, positioned on my grandmother's table. The window was covered by a cracked, yellowed pull-shade. Hers was adorned with white lace curtains, looking out over the backyards with the same chain-link fencing as I saw from my window.

"Wow! This is beautiful!"

"Would you like some tea or coffee? I only have instant."

"I only drink tea when I'm sick." *Why did I say that?* "Instant would be fine. I was going to invite you out to Slug's. They're having Sun Ra and his Solar Arkestra tonight."

We skipped the tea and coffee and went down in the elevator. It was still snowing, steady white flakes on dirty E. 3rd. We crossed Avenue C—which looked nice in the snow blowing along the avenue, gathering on parked cars. I put my palm in the small of her back, on her long camel's hair overcoat. I reminded myself not to rush things. But the snowflakes were sticking to her camel's hair shoulders and headscarf, and it was difficult.

"What kind is that scarf?"

"Givenchy."

"Looks like silk."

"It is."

In Slug's, the music was already playing in the back. A bunch of weirdly dressed musicians playing weird music with red and gold metallic overalls. Sun Ra had a metal hat and played "Take the A Train" on his piano; in the beginning, some notes resembled "A Train," but as it progressed, it didn't sound like anything similar. The piano and an electric Fender bass were playing a naked strip of notes and chords, but a trumpet sounded masterful. Then what sounded like a baritone clarinet playing spacy notes. It was like no other music I'd heard. Jazz with a touch of outer space.

The bartender was white and squat and smiled sweetly beneath his broken nose. All the other patrons, as far as I could see, were black. I caught some glances at Mary. She untied her scarf from beneath her chin, and her blond hair cascaded out. The bartender said, with a trace of a brogue, "You have a fine head of hair on you, girl."

I bought two bottles of beer, and we took a seat at the tables in front. I shouted over the music, "What do you do?" She cupped her hand behind her ear and shook her head. I began to listen to the music, trusting that there would be a pause in which we could talk. I had heard of Sun Ra, and the music of *Secrets of the Sun*, but I hadn't heard him either on record or live. It sounded *avant garde*, but it was further out than *avant garde*, though I heard a trumpet, a piano, an alto sax, an acoustic bass which were beginning to make sense.

I gestured to her beer. We were drinking from the bottles of Schaeffer. She nodded. She was keeping up with me. After three or four beers, the musicians broke, and customers rushed the bar. I said, "Want to get out of here?"

A black guy was looking at Mary hungrily and was getting on my nerves. I remembered that once Mose told me he was in Shea Stadium with a girl, and she told him that a guy walking through the crowd grabbed her pussy. Mose shrugged it off. What could you do?

It was still snowing on 3rd St. I put my arm around her shoulder, and she melted into me. I kissed her in the elevator to the 3rd floor. The one kiss led to another, and they became make-out kisses. I braced her against the wall of the elevator and pressed my belly against her. We went into her apartment and resumed making out, shucking our clothes.

But she wouldn't let me mount her, and she wouldn't mount me, and she wouldn't allow me to go down on her. She was a natural blond, and I wanted to go down—very badly; she was so beautiful—but she pressed her thighs together and that triangle of light vanished. It was extraordinary, the muscle power in her thighs. I couldn't get her thighs separated with persuasion and a helping nudge from my hand. Soon, I gave up trying.

Instead, she reached to me and started pumping. She held it in her thumb and tip of her index finger, holding her curtain of blond hair back with the other hand. She had a determined look on her mouth, at her teeth, and I closed my eyes and let the sensation take me. I opened my eyes again in preparation. Still the determined look, her lips and teeth, and when I came, she made a sound in her throat of surprise, almost disgust—but she kept moving her hand, her fingers.

It occurred to me that she had never seen a guy come. We slept that night in her bed. In the morning, we had coffee, and I asked everything about her, but the one obvious thing: Was she saving herself for marriage? Did she have vaginismus? But I couldn't ask these things; there was a foreboding in me that it was graver than that.

95

She was two years younger than I, went to Fordham Lincoln Center, the Bachelor of Arts program, came from Sunnyside, which was where her father had found his way to from Northern Ireland more than twenty years before. Her mother died when she was ten—she owed her husband some money and had to work as a cleaning lady. "For Jewish people."

Ignoring the last comment, I asked, confused, "Did your mother owe your father money? Surely, she didn't owe her husband money?"

"Do you think that's wrong?" she asked. "It was a forbidden thing—mental disease. My mother was beholden to my father for. She had to have…"—she whispered—"…*shock treatments*." She owed more money than she could earn. She would have been paying still, had she not died. "*Death was the only luxury she could afford,*" Mary said Her father died three years ago. She was an only child; and she had inherited her father's fortune. She had been raised a Roman Catholic, and her father wouldn't permit her to go out with boys. "I had my first date with a boy three years ago."

"But you're *beautiful*! Weren't the boys breaking your doors down?"

"I'm not beautiful. I'm too thin, and my face is plain." She looked down as she said this.

"You *are* beautiful. Astonishingly so!"

"*Astonishingly so,*" she murmured with a faint, mocking smile. Then she said, "I'm not."

"You are!" I kissed her. I had only my T-shirt and shorts on, she her nightgown, which she had put on during the night when I slept. My penis began to stiffen.

She was obviously fascinated by a soft limb changing nature. "How," she whispered, "how big does it get?"

I thought she was being facetious. "One time, it got three feet long."

"*Three feet!*" Apparently, she was serious; she had never seen a boy's erection.

"Haven't you ever been with a boy?"

"Not since I was a little girl. My father caught us, and he made me go to the priest, the *Irish* priest. Ever since then, I have… *S*."

"*S?*"

She didn't answer.

"*Syphilis?*"

"You can catch it from plant lice," she whispered. "My father used to hang the mattresses out the window—in freezing weather. The eye can't see the monsters that people the dust." That was what Mary Kennedy told me. Tiny gray creatures with claws that affix themselves inside your nose and *other* organs. "You can get S from it."

"You *can't* catch syphilis from plant lice. Or dust. You can only catch it from intercourse—and only from someone who has it. And you can't catch it from a toilet seat. *Or* from plant lice or dust. Go to a doctor."

"I've been."

"And...?"

With an odd kind of confidence in her smile, she said, "He was lying. To spare me."

I stayed with her for a couple of hours, trying to argue with her. She should see another doctor, just to be sure—but she needed to see a psychiatrist. She needed medicine. Her thoughts were twisted. Medication was necessary. I could not reason with her.

There was no question about the beauty, but the beautiful girl was only on the outside; her spirit was festering within. I looked at her, trying to keep these thoughts from my face. Meanwhile, I had to take the subway up to City for an economics class. I had cut so many economics classes that it would affect my grade. They had a formula by which so many cuts would make it that you could get a maximum grade of B, and I was working on a C—if I weren't careful, I would get a D or even an F. I had a mental block against Economics. Dean Morse was the teacher; he wrote his name on the blackboard the first day, and I thought his first name was a title. I didn't know what a "Dean" was, but it was pretty high up on the cadre. Then I figured out it was his first name.

That day, I listened to "Dean" Morse talking about supply and demand and the law of diminishing returns, but I could think of nothing else but Mary: How she looked naked, how the sight of her bottom could make me happy and her natural blond bird's nest and small breasts. But she has a festering wound inside, in her spirit. I thought I was involved with her, how she was my neighbor, how I should never have tapped on her door, how her beauty was a trap.

She was an unhappy creature trapped in her beauty. Now I was trapped, too. I couldn't abandon her to her misery. I thought of quitting

C.C.N.Y., taking off on a bus, but I had a job that I liked, friends, classes, an agent that would soon get me published.

I took the A train down to Columbus Circle. It always made Duke Ellington's "Take the A Train" play in my mind from 125th to 59th, an unbroken string of sixty-six streets. I transferred to the F train (which made me worry about what I wanted to do to every sexy girl) and took that to W. 4th Street and went to the Lion's Head on Christopher Street to think further about Mary and have a couple of beers.

Norman Mailer, who was running for Mayor of New York City, and Jimmy Breslin, for City Council President, were at a back table, along with a slew of hangers on, and they were very loud, so I sat at the bar. Normally, a Mailer and Breslin sighting would make the stars shine in my eyes, but I was considering Mary, her beauty and her misery and how to proceed.

After three draft beers, I decided to confront her once again and insist she go to another doctor, with *me*, and manipulate the doctor into recommending a psychiatrist. Maybe I would not have to manipulate him. Maybe the first doctor had recommended a psychiatrist when he saw how fucked up she was.

I set off—after a fourth draft—down 3rd St. resolutely. I crossed the street to avoid the Men's Welfare Shelter in the dark, and then recrossed it past the Hell's Angels Headquarters, with the American flag adorning the front of the building. I became less resolute. By the time I reached Susie's Bar & Grill, I crossed the street again and took a table and ordered a pitcher of Schaeffer and perfunctorily caressed Susie, a white and black mutt bitch, on her fat stomach with the two rows of beady nipples all along her distended belly. The dog had rolled over on her back and splayed out her stumpy legs, and I thought—god curse me—how a woman like Mary could be so beautiful and a mutt like Susie so distasteful. I thought of the FBI man who was subjecting me to the top-secret clearance: *Have you ever had sex with an animal?*

I shooed Susie away and ordered another pitcher.

Next morning, I woke to a ring at the door. It was a Western Union messenger with a telegram: EDWARD Stop DID YOU SEE THE MOON LAST NIGHT Stop REGARDS MARY. I made a mug of instant coffee, took a sip, scalded my mouth, and left the apartment, mug in fist, padded across to 3A, and tapped.

She didn't answer, but I could hear her behind the door. I waited a moment. I could still hear her. I knocked again. "Mary. I hear you in there."

A door further down the hall opened, a brown face looked out of a crack. I knocked again. "Mary, I still hear you in there." Another knock. I whispered, "Mary, you've got to go to a doctor." I waited, though what that could mean to the brown ears listening confounded me.

Days passed. I heard a bell ring somewhere down the hall and a knock at a door that was not mine. I looked out. It was a pizza delivery man at her door. She—or someone within—opened the door, just a crack, and handed the money through. "You want change, ma'am?" the pizza man asked. "Hey! Thanks!"

I thought of his seeing her beauty without a clue what lay underneath. The flat cardboard box changed hands, and I rushed for her door in my sock feet, but it shut just when I got there. I hammered dead center and pressed the bell. Two or three doors opened a crack. I looked, and they shut with clicks. I could feel the pizza man's eyes on me, trying to determine whether he could take me or not. He threw his hands up in the air and took the stairs down.

What if someone called the cops?

That woman is sick mentally and driving me nuts with her passive aggression! Best way to get locked up. Me, in my sock feet. Reluctantly, I retreated to my own apartment. Sat in the beach chair. Meantime, I had bought the Sun Ra album, and I sought consolation from that and the fact that Bird had lived from 1950-54 at 151 Avenue B, just around the corner. Lived with Chan Berg, the mother of his son, Bird and his daughter Pree, who died as an infant of cystic fibrosis, a year before Parker died on March 12th, 1955, at thirty-five, watching the Dorsey Brothers Stage Show on television. Two weeks later (or was it two months?), Chan married Phil Woods, nick-named the New Bird, but other alto sax players were named that for taking up with Chan.

It helped you when you're feeling sorry for yourself—and for someone else—to consider the lives of the Jazz men.

Life went on as before I met Mary Kennedy—after a few heart pangs. I didn't see her again, though, and as time passed I became inured to her presence behind 3A, but my apartment was tainted.

I went on reading papers—or parts of papers—before Malin interrupted me until the bell rang, and Mose would get incensed every time he interrupted. Mose and Woody would gather in my apartment for six-packs. Mose always brought a gift of two bottles of Mateus Rosé; it was good wine, and I appreciated it. I went to Slug's to hear Sun Ra and his Arkestra, sometimes with Mose and Woody and I listened to *Secrets of the Sun* on my stereo. There was talk of a T. B. Goodman Award for me and Woody, championed by Stark. The winners would be announced in June.

Mose used to leave his house in Boro Park, Brooklyn and, when he got a block away, put his yarmulke in his back pocket. Some Fridays, he would call his mother in Boro Park from my apartment and say he could not make the subway before sundown, and according to the Jewish faith and tradition (I was confused about whether it was faith or tradition), you could not handle money or ride on public conveyances between sundown Friday and sundown Saturday, which was the Sabbath. We—Woody, Mose, and me—would go to Chumley's or The Lion's Head or the White Horse or Slug's or Susie's and get drunk, all except for Woody, who would drink chocolate milk with rum, a Lumumba, only one or sometimes two, because he was concerned about destroying brain cells. Woody was a Jew, too, but he was not orthodox, so he wouldn't call his mother. He had gone to Chicago for the DNC and braved the police riot, camping out in Grant Park, but he didn't get his head bashed. I didn't go to Chicago. Didn't have the guts.

We would end the night in my apartment, Mose and Woody and me. At some point, Mose started taking his girlfriend Carol over to my place. He had been dating her since high school. She was very beautiful and sexy, and Woody and I used to dance with her competing for her touches, but she only had eyes for Mose. She was now in Bennington and was editor of the school's literary journal, and she said she would publish Woody's short story "Bellman." Mose said that she should also publish something by me, but she didn't like anything I showed her, said, "Maybe boys feel like that about girls, but it doesn't feel credible." I didn't question her about what boys felt about girls; I was too proud. Credibility was all, reality was nothing.

One night we all got drunk—I don't know where Woody was—and

Mose got into my bed with Carol. I was sitting in one of my beach chairs, listening to Sun Ra and his Arkestra, drinking Mateus.

Carol said, "I'm so *hot* and bothered!" and I slurred, "May I kiss Carol on her pussy, Mose?"

I was expecting him to say no or "You're drunk, Fitzgerald," but he said, "Yes, you may. We got to share the wealth." I got up from the beach chair and crossed to the bed. Carol was naked, but for her panties. While I was deciding what to do, I edged near her pussy, and she opened her thighs, and I was down there between her white, slender thighs, but decided no. Carol's pussy was so appealing that I would be lost in it rather than giving a peck. Carol asked, "Well? Do it!"

But then I thought Mose was always trying to fob Carol off on one of us, like he could see in the future, his dread of the inevitable; the family would expect him to marry Carol—both his and her families.

I might have been the *shegetz* (the detested thing) to get him off the hook. I didn't do it. I didn't kiss it.

I was disappointed, and she must have been disappointed, too, because a week later, a Sunday, we let ourselves into my alcove office with the keys Miss Brown had provided to me. My girlfriend Sarah was with me, Mose and Carol.

Carol asked, "Do you have any jobs available?"

"None that you would be interested in," I said, and Carol said, "I wasn't speaking to you. God knows, you wouldn't have any interesting jobs. I was speaking to Claire. At her furniture design place."

I wondered what the motivation for the slight was—if it was a slight—whether she held a grudge because I didn't kiss her pussy. I deeply regretted it, but things might have got out of hand.

A little later, Mose came over to my apartment, and he was weeping. Carol had been seduced by the faculty-adviser of the literary journal, and he was planning to leave his wife and family.

"They're only six months and three years. What kind of man leaves his babies?"

Woody turned twenty-one, and Mose turned twenty. I was the elder. I became twenty-five in March 1969, which seemed like a mature age, but I didn't feel like the elder. These were two very bright guys, and they only had to catch up with me in experience, and they were catching up by leaps. I had no doubt they would surpass me.

I met Sarah in the MoMA. In connection with my term paper for Intro to Art. I saw this pale-haired girl, her eyebrows and eyelashes were pale, too—that was part of her attractiveness. Short and cute, but not excessively cute, not so that I was afraid to approach. The business with Mary Kennedy had left its mark on me, and I thought I was not so great-looking anymore. I was putting on some weight from beer. Sarah was looking at a canvas painted purely white, titled *Voices* by Alfred Newman, and I came up to her and asked what that "meant."

"What do you *mean* by *mean*?" she said. "Oh, of course, it does *mean* something. It's ripe for meaning. The fact that it's all white may correlate with the title—*Voices*—to mean that every color is voices. You are aware, that white is the presence of every color? Black is the absence of color. But do you see those tiny black pinpricks there—I've counted two—that's the absence of color and might mean that the absence of color is getting through in the voice. Or it might mean death, the presence of death. Do you see that faintly marbleized pigment to the white? It might mean the voices are nuanced. Bright and less bright. But urgent and juxtaposed. Like the urgency is blending together against death."

"It makes me furious."

"Well, fury is a good start for a reaction to a painting. If it can cause you fury, it achieved something."

"It makes me furious because I don't understand it. I don't think the painter means anything by it."

"I don't understand it either. But when you asked me what it means, I stitched that meaning together. Maybe the *Voices* are ours, conversing about meaning." I was attraced by her method of explaining; she was like a mother explaining to her kids, the same good-humored way. How her little, white teeth were cute, I thought. And her smile enchanting. And her lips were full, meaty. I had underestimated this girl, but the underestimation conquered my fear to talk to her. I asked if I could buy her a coffee.

The cafeteria was enclosed, out in the sculpture garden, right across from a bronze statue of Balzac. I wanted to impress her that I was not a know-nothing. "You know Rodin said when he made that sculpture that he had taken a man's soul and put it on his face."

She looked at my eyes, duly impressed. I was glad that I had not added that the poet Rilke, Rodin's secretary, had chosen his studio that was the Rodin Museum now. That would have been showing off. Anyway, I only knew it from the Intro to Art professor, Spiegelmann.

The cafeteria had bottles of Tuborg beer, and I said that I was just going to have one of these Danish beers. We conversed as we sat in the cafeteria, facing through the glass Rodin's *Balzac*, not a dozen yards from us. Neither of us had been to Europe but were hoping to go. I told her I had hitch-hiked out west—even rode a bicycle across, hoping to get to San Francisco. "I got to Peoria, Illinois and quit, sold my bike, continued on my thumb."

Her name was Sarah, and I felt comfortable in her presence. She was an artist, a painter. I said I had thought that she was, the expansive way she'd answered my question. Or an art critic. She said she'd gone to M&A—Music and Arts. "The Castle on the Hill," she said.

That was near C.C.N.Y. in Harlem. "City is where I go." There were more coincidences. She lived near Columbus Circle, I worked on the Circle. We began to walk west and north from the MoMA. It had been raining, and Sarah said, "Oh, it's a blue day." She showed me that the puddles and the cars and all the wet surfaces of the streets reflected the blue of the sky. I had never noticed it before. I looked at all wet surfaces; they reflected blue. It was remarkable!

We strolled toward Columbus Circle. It was mid-April, and the trees and the vines and the bushes were stippled with furry buds, and they were a shade of blue, too, and the wet branches.

"Why don't we go up to my apartment?"

"Okay," I said, and the tone of my voice must have revealed surprise, for she added, "My mother is home. I share with my mother. A three-room." Her mother and she had one bedroom, and the third was divided into a common living room and a studio for Claire. "The kitchen is large, and we have a dining table in it with six places. Come see."

Her studio was a genuine studio, with three tall windows that looked out on Eighth Avenue, and easel and pallet and tubes of paint and bristling brushes in a mug. There was a rainbow of every color dripped on the floor beneath the easel but the canvas was covered with a cloth.

"Wow! Its *light*! May I?" Questioningly, I lifted the edge of the cloth, but she said, "No. It may be coquettish of me, but I don't like anyone to see it before it's done." It was a big canvas—maybe two by three yards. I let my curiosity alone.

Her mother didn't come out of her room, but I could hear her moving around in there.

Then, Sarah adjusted her sandal from behind, picking her leg up by the sandal strap so her calf bent back at the knee, and her gray and white dress hiked up at mid-thigh. It was an astonishingly natural movement and beautiful.

We ended necking at the kitchen table. Sarah sat lightly as a feather on my lap. I tried all the moves I knew to get to her, but she asked me didn't I like just kissing. Chastened, I surrendered to kissing her fleshy lips and neck, and urgently French-kissing until my erection started to get painful. "My balls will be blue as the day."

"I'm sorry."

The manner in which she said that somehow inspired me to to ask her if she was a virgin.

"Yes," she whispered and the blood ran into her cheeks. She was twenty-three and hadn't found anyone she'd like to try it with. "I mean— until now. I mean, if you want to try it. I mean, later. Much later. I mean…" She was blushing fiercely, but I liked it, knowing that a girl would be available—in time. I thought of my recent encounter, and I was grateful to Sarah for saving me from my dick.

Her full name was Sarah Little (I had a lot of fun with this), but we were not destined to fulfill our love. I was soon to have my moment of satori. In my apartment, I was writing a story, another story that I knew would not be published, a story I had to care about with more or less every cell in my body even if I knew it was not to be published, even if I knew it was yet another in a Beckettian row of fail-betters. The agent recommended to me by Stark, Theron Raines, kept sending out my stories and collecting notes of the ilk of "Better not" or "I found something to admire in this, but in the end, no." Theron was to do good for Stark, even better for Rod Thorpe and his other customers, but he would do no good for me. I was confused: What was I doing wrong? Did I have to learn something else?

I was in my East 3rd St. apartment, writing at my grandmother's battered dining table, and I looked up from my ecstatic absorption to gaze out the dusty window at the messy, chain-linked back lots below and understood suddenly that what I was feeling right then was and had to be the most important part of it: the moment of creation. I no longer remember what I was working on, but the process of creating it was engaging everything within me, and I understood then that was and is quintessential. Not money, publication, reputation, not even the possibility of getting near to a literature-loving lass—but the process, the moment of creation. Climbing down into the darkness to bring up what I could discover and cast into language about my existence.

I was twenty-five years old. I had an agent and soon to have a grant for a novel-in-progress, part-time writing an NGO newsletter on Columbus Circle. I had a girlfriend who was an artist and with an apartment just around the corner from Columbus Circle. I had encouraging letters from editors, hyperbolic rejections, and had been trying to write for eight years but nothing published.

"So, *quit!*" Sarah told me. She had then completed the painting, ultimately entitled *Straining Man* and let me look at it—a picture that astonished me, the minimalist figure of a man straining all the muscles of his body as he grimaces challengingly upward. The figure was painted in thick, rich pigments of oil, multi-colored lines delineating muscle and sinew, abstract face with anguished eyes, but I had an immediate recognition that the figure represented human endeavor straining to overcome the opposing forces of circumstance. It was, in my opinion, a very good picture. I would even call it a masterpiece. I loved her for painting it, wanted to consummate our love in an appropriately romantic setting.

But as soon as the oils were dry, she threw a cloth over it and reorganized her midtown apartment, threw away all her oils and acrylics and brushes and rags, vacuumed and mopped and painted the walls. She even enlisted me to paint the walls, while she painted the details. She bought an architect's desk on which she mounted a blue architect's lamp and started designing sofas. I asked why, when she had clearly just made an artistic breakthrough, she would go commercial, and she replied that those categories had no meaning, that I was trying to validate elitism, that all art was equal, that basically all art was either entertainment or pragmatic, and that this was what she wanted to do now.

"What, sell out?" I teased.

Her pale eyes flashed within their pale-haired frame, she said, "If you got anything to sell, why not? Got anything?"

I ducked my chin, but I was unrockable. I'd already had my satori, and my choices were clear now for the time; I knew what was important to me.

I got an A on my term paper for art from Professor Spiegelman, the artist. What was more, he called out, when he was handing the papers back, "Who is Fitzgerald?" I had written a thirty-page paper, complete with postcards bought from the MoMA shop of Hopper, Newman, Picasso, Appel, De Chirico, Dali, Giacometti, Van Gogh, Gaughin, Klee, Magritte, Manet, Miro. Modigliani, Munch, Pisanello, Pollack, Rothko, Seurat, and Balthus. I put many questions in the text on the meaning of art—of text and painting—and made some leaps into understanding. It was just like when the Horace Silver Quintet paused for a breath of a second and took off in a new time signature.

Identifying me, Professor Spiegelman said, "Your questions, Fitzgerald, are cunning and artful."

Last I heard, Sarah Little had an interior decoration firm called "Little Interiors." Probably rich and highly respected among those who were satisfied with the esthetics of a beautiful, entertaining, pragmatic sofa.

And, hey, who's putting it down?

PART TWO

Spinning Wheel

AT THE END OF '69, I submitted to the Goodman Fund. It was to be decided in January 1970, the announcement of the winners on an unseasonally warm day, bright with sun. Stark said, "Let's have barbecue!" and sent out for two six packs and bags of chips. Two journalists came from the *New York Amsterdam News*, but I think they only came for the beer.

Another guy who nobody knew—Anthony Keyes—knocked Woody out of first place. The winning story was titled "Swim," and it was about a guy who swims the Mississippi River, just on a whim, and he is arrested on the opposite bank, having completed his swim and thrown in a police car, wrapped in a blanket. It was not better than Woody's, which was linguistically more exciting, but "Swim" had control instead of linguistic fireworks. Woody's story won second place of fifty dollars but, more important, Carol was going to publish "Bellman" in *Bennington Review*.

Rather than entering the short story contest, I had applied for a Goodman grant, which was a thousand dollars, renewable for three years. I submitted the first chapter of the novel which dealt with my father's death, five years before. The judge wrote a note to Stark, which he shared with me, "If more people are going to compete on Fitzgerald's level of skill, we're going to have to petition the Foundation for more money."

A week later, I got a letter from Theodore Solotaroff, editor of *New American Review*, in response to a story that I'd sent him. *N.A.R.* was issued as a hardback from New American Library, then issued in paperback. Its circulation was around 100,000. It was then one of the prime markets. Solotaroff said that he couldn't use the story, but he thought it could be expanded into a novel; if I was interested, I should contact Nancy Hardin of New American Library at 1301 Avenue of the Americas.

My story was an imitation of a short fiction by a writer who was making a reputation for himself—Raymond Carver—"Would You Please Be Quiet, Please?" printed in *Best American Short Stories* in 1964. I didn't want to expand that imitation-Carver story into a novel. I sent another story to Nancy Hardin at NAL. She wrote back that everyone in the office was excited about it, and could she buy me lunch?

At the lunch, which was fancier than any meal I'd ever had, Nancy—who was the girl of my dreams, older by four or five years and trim and *so* collegiate. She knew Hoagland, too, on a personal level. The Goodman money was intact, but I wanted *more* cash. You never outgrow your need for cash, when it's cash for your fiction. I asked if I could get an advance. She said, "Were this a lunch to celebrate your contract, you couldn't even get money for many months. You have to write the novel first. But with this story, I'm confident that you can write it." Novel publishers must have different tastes than editors who publish short stories. No short story editor was interested in that story. Hyperbolic rejections, but no cigar.

She had asked me as starters if I wanted something to drink. I ordered a vodka martini, which came in a chilled cocktail glass. My cocktail was soon quaffed, and by the end of the lunch, she hadn't touched hers. I asked, "You going to drink that martini?"

An Army buddy, who had been in Fort Dix and Fort Benjamin Harrison, was living now in Stockton, California. Farrar, Straus & Giroux had published a 1969 novel called *Fat City* by Leonard Gardner set in Stockton. Gardner was a first novelist, but it was written like he'd inherited the ghost of Hemingway. John Huston made a movie of it with Stacey Keach, which was before he'd gone all Mike Hammer—he'd starred in the film of one of Barth's novels, and now this. It made Stockton look good, in a gritty way.

His name was Ben Flaherty. I had visited him in Berkeley a couple of times. He had a master's degree in sociology from Berkeley and since had married and was living with his wife and children on a commune in Stockton with a couple of musicians. He was always after me to come out to the commune and stay. It would only cost me fifty bucks a month for room and board. Liquor and cigarettes were excluded, but it included all I could eat.

My East Village apartment had been tainted by the presence of Mary Kennedy. Sometimes I would get to thinking about her in there, wretched. I didn't want to think of her like that. But then she would gang up with the memory of Toni June and Lori May and Darlene and DeeDee and Claire and all the way back to Anne Suffier. Sometimes, this gang of women would mug me in the dark hours, and I had to get out.

My thousand dollars from the Goodman was still safe in the bank. A thousand divided by fifty was twenty months. Let's get reasonable: You have to live—cigarettes and booze. Let's say a hundred a month for the commune. That would go into a thousand by ten months, and my separate savings would be to rent an apartment when I got back and while I got a job—and maybe the novel would be finished after ten months and saleable and the advance would be permissible by then. I wasn't keen on poverty; I just wanted to make money writing something I wanted.

I planned to give a month's notice for my NGO job, but Miss Brown said I could still write the lead article for the newsletter for fifty a month and still have my job to come back to. "Unless you're making a living as a writer! Maybe you can send me some of it sometime." I knew what Miss Brown was expecting; she probably thought I was a neat and tidy writer, but my fiction was as messy as my life. She wouldn't like my fiction. She had an idealized expectation of it. I had to keep her from reading it, so long as I was dependent on her fifty a month.

Ben was a few years older than me. Over a couple bottles of port wine in the fields behind the barracks in Indiana, he told me he had been in jail once. He wanted to tell me what for, but he would likely despise me afterward if he told me. He was a lean, ruddy-faced Irishman who looked like a hobo with his five o'clock shadow and black eyebrows and chipped front tooth and deep voice. He scowled at me, passing the second bottle of port. I thought, *Murder? Rape? Armed robbery?*

Ben was the only real friend I had made in the Army. We would discuss things. When I read a book, if he hadn't read it, he'd read it, and vice versa. He explained things to me, things that should have been obvious to me, but I missed them. Like he explained that the pistol that Shatov sold in Dostoyevsky's *The Possessed* to provide for his pregnant friend was the instrument of death versus the instrument of life.

He laughed ironically when he read that novel. I remember him reading on his bed stripped down to the bare springs, in full field gear, folded poncho over his pistol belt, boots bloused, and his M1 beside him.

"What's so funny?" I asked. Dostoyevsky was a serious writer.

"Don't you find the way he describes the mayor, saying he won't be led by the nose—figuratively, of course—and Stavrogin literally leading him by the nose around the reception?" Ben asked this in his deep, resonant voice, bursting out with laughter so tears bubbled out of his perennially-bloodshot eyes. I laughed, too. I had read most of Dostoyevsky when I was fifteen, sixteen. Now I was nineteen. *I needed to read his books again—with a sense of humor.*

In answer to his question, I answered, "No. If you're going to despise me, I don't want to know."

A week before I left for Stockton, twenty-nine Ohio National Guardsmen fired sixty-seven shots killing four students and wounding nine others during an unarmed protest against the Vietnam War at Kent State University. I thought of my days hitchhiking through Ohio, riding my bike through the state. I had marched in demonstrations against Vietnam on Fifth Ave., had been called a "commie punk" by a boy not older than I who was looking for a fight, but I didn't know he wanted to *shoot* me! I had sheltered a deserter for three weeks until he could be smuggled into Canada, but I didn't know it was life or death.

I was glad to get away to a small city in northeast California. I took a Trailway seventy-two hours to San Francisco, then doubled back three hours to Stockton.

There was merriment when I arrived in the commune, which was a ten-room house on the southside of Stockton's suburbs. The other members of the commune were a Fillipino man named Sam and a Negro named Malcolm and a sometimes member who was sixteen and paid ten bucks a week to sleep on the sofa, sporadically. He was having trouble with his parents; they were nudists and made him go to the nudist colony.

"Are young girls there?" I asked. "What if you get an erection?"

And Zeke, the 16-year-old, said, "Believe me, it doesn't happen."

I was disappointed that there were no women in the commune, other than Ben's wife, Peg. It didn't seem like a real commune without any women.

Malcolm and Sam were playing the second album by Blood, Sweat & Tears which was a jazz-fusion record that I liked. Also, I liked that they were of other races, felt like some modern strife had not reached Stockton.

While they were listening, Sam played his trombone, and Malcom banged his sticks on a practice pad, playing their parts, obviously a number they would do with the whole makeshift band. Obviously, too, Ben didn't like them. But I did. They'd brought for my welcome party a gallon of mountain red, but I was weary from my days on the bus. After one glass of wine, I needed to sleep. I had a front room. The dog, a moppy little thing named Daffy, crawled under my bed. "She doesn't do that with everybody," Ben said, wonder in his deep voice. "In fact with no one. You must have good vibes."

I lay in my bed, Daffy underneath, listening to David Clayton-Thomas singing Laura Nyro's "And When I Die." It was a positive view of death which appealed to me—before Kent State. I vaguely heard Billie Holiday's "God Bless the Child" with a full jazz-fusion band behind it, in David Clayton-Thomas' belting, bluesy voice, then "Spinning Wheel" by Clayton-Thomas, and I dropped off somewhere during it.

I slept for twenty hours, woke when it was about six—lay, in fact, in bed for hours, bemoaning my fate. Time and again, I used to do these things, uproot my life when I had it relatively good because…because…I didn't know the reason for it. I should get up out of bed and go through the motions, then it would get real, then it would get tolerable.

I got up, prepared a face to meet the faces, then joined the others on the porch, manufactured some enthusiasms and slipped into life habits. Dinner awaited me: two breaded pork chops and applesauce and boiled potatoes, salad mixed with shredded radishes, carrots, quartered tomatoes, and a jelly glass of wine. The kids awaited me, too: Ben, Jr. four years old, and Sarah, two. They were cute. Ben sang for me, "Ed, Ed, the Edder!" and Sarah was blond and didn't have to be anything other than cute. She sat right on my lap and looked steadily at me with the same blue eyes as her mother's. In some sense, I felt like I was filling a role of saviour.

The wife was handsome, too, tall and slim and big-breasted and a perennial blush on her high cheekbones. She wore a wrinkled plaid shirt and wrinkled jeans; obviously, she didn't bother with ironing her unisex clothes. Her name was Peg, and she was bright and articulate. Frankly, I was surprised that Ben could win such a wife, but she told me when he was out of the room that she knew the first time she looked at him that he was the man for her. He came into the Berkeley cafeteria, sort of scowling in a humorous way, with his rugged face and his lean body, and when he spoke to her, she got wet. When she said that, the blush in her cheeks heightened, but I saw something else in her blue eyes, a sadness. *Oh, no, you're not going to fall for her!* Another thing she said to me was, "Must be nice. Move to a place, and then when things get too hot for you, move on." I felt that I was being aggressed against, regardless of the gentleness of how she said that.

When the kids were put to bed, Ben and Peg and I sat over the remnants of the jug of mountain red. Sam and Malcolm were off to a concert at the local college, some blues group, and Zeke was god knew where. Ben and Peg had something on the agenda.

Ben asked me, "Remember when I told you I'd been in jail?"

"Who wouldn't?" I was confused that he asked that when Peg was there. Maybe she knew.

He said that he had asked the same thing of her the night before they married, and she had told him the same as me: she did not want to know if the result would be his despising her. "But when she was pregnant with Sarah, she woke me up one night and said she had to know." It was after they'd moved to Stockton, said that she had to know, with his being the father of her children, what he could do. So, he told her.

"That night I wanted *one* thing," Ben said. "and *only* one thing. I was seventeen."

He had been arrested in a parked car on a dark street wearing his sister's underwear. The cops didn't even let him change into his regular clothes, locked him up with two car thieves in his sister's underwear. They thought they would have fun with him until Ben became ferocious.

When his father came to pick him up in the morning; he'd said, "Your own sister's clothes!"

"He'd been really troubled by that. That it was my sister's clothes."

The law was such then that the judge had to decide whether he would release Ben's name and picture to the local papers. He decided to, said that people had a right to know. It was a small town. News got around fast. He had no choice but to leave town.

Peg was horrified when Ben told her. "He seemed so *masculine*. I would have preferred that it was even a violent crime."

"You asked so I told you."

Did that mean he liked *men*? She was even more horrified when she learned that he still did it. With her clothes!

"What do you make of that?" Ben asked me.

I said the first thing that came to my mouth. "Well, it's pretty weird, but it doesn't make me want to puke with revulsion." I was pretty drunk on mountain red. I thought for a couple of moments, tried to make it okay. I said, "There was a hamper in my bathroom, a laundry hamper, and once when I was about fourteen, I rummaged through it, found a pair of my sister's panties. They excited me, and I tried them on." That was a lie, but I wanted to make it okay.

In bed that night, I attempted to get the image of Ben with his skinny hairy chest wearing a bra and his hobo's face wearing lipstick. *Why did he have to tell me?* And *after* I'd come out to the commune? Some things were best kept secret. Anything but that. As long as he didn't wear women's clothes in front of me. Did he wear panties beneath his clothes? I thought of women wearing men's clothes. Quite cute—if they were feminine. I remembered when I was just a little kid, an older girl in an MC jacket with zippers all over it, Duck's Ass haircut, and she was manly in the face. I asked her—I had to know the answer, "Are you a boy or a girl?" And she put her face close to mine and whispered, "I'll cut your little cock off for you." Thoughts like that kept me from sleep, but I finally did go under.

Next morning, Ben took me in his car to rent a typewriter and buy a ream of bond paper, some onion skin, carbon paper, and a little bottle of Wite-Out. In those days, you would correct the original and just strike over the copy—at least I did.

Afterward, he invited me to a bar where there was cheap whiskey. The barman was black and a bunch of silent men of varying colors, just sitting around at noon, a drink in front of them. It reminded me of Fort Ben Harrison in Indianapolis when Ben used to ask, "Want to take a walk on the wild side?" The wild side was the black district.

When he drank one shot of whiskey, neat, and ordered another, I was still half-way through my beer, and he said, "You know, Ben, Jr. shouldn't have been born. He was an accident." I'd had enough of truth-telling, but he went on. "I *had* to marry Peg. She should have had an abortion, but we couldn't come up with the money for a decent guy, a doctor."

I said that I experienced a similar situation in San Diego, but that I didn't know if it had been a good idea—which was a lie. But I didn't like that he was saying Ben, Jr., a person who was already alive, shouldn't have been born. If he'd heard it, he wouldn't understand, and I didn't know if Ben talked like this all the time. I ordered another beer, and Ben another shot glass of whiskey. The bottle had a label on it, something like Paddy's Irish Rose.

"Peg is a nice girl. She'll understand this thing—you were arrested for. The circumstances."

Ben scowled into his whiskey, then drank it, a half shot. "I think that was her plan all along. To have the kid. And marry me. She's a purposeful woman. Sam is fucking her. Or she's fucking him. I guess it will be a matter of time before Malcolm does, too. She's already planning it. I can see it on her face. She doesn't know yet, but it's in her plan. I would rather have you sleep with her than Sam or Malcolm. At least, I like you. Like Peg, too." He drank off the other half of his whiskey and ordered another.

"Why are you drinking so much? It's not like you. You want to have an accident?" I thought that was a bad choice of words. "With the car."

"You were always more rational than me," he said with a good-natured scowl. "I think Peg will get around to you, too. I just want you to know that it's okay."

"I couldn't."

"She's a purposeful woman. Just want you to know that it's okay."

After that, I was almost exclusively in my room, writing my novel, Daffy beneath the bed or my desk. She was always quiet, never barked. She would pad over to me periodically to be scratched and to have her long ears fussed with, but she knew I was working; she would leave me alone when I was typing, Blood, Sweat & Tears seeping through the wall.

I only came out for meals and when it became too much for me to be alone, to chat with Ben or Peg and the kids, Sam or Malcolm or Zeke when they were there. Sam liked me, but for obvious reasons, he didn't seem to like Ben. Sam was afraid of Ben. He only came out of his room to practice by the phonograph.

Sometimes I worked through lunch. Breakfast was filling—eggs and potatoes and sausage. After dinner, I sat out on the porch with my gallon jug of mountain red which cost $1.29 in the supermarket and chatted with Ben—and Peg when she was there. Ben had bought a motorcycle and told me he would drive through the hills and high desert at night and sometimes in the afternoons. But often they were there, sitting with me on the porch, rolling filter cigarettes with their machine, mostly silent. That silence got on my nerves.

I was careful when I was alone with Peg, not to sit on the sofa with her. Sometimes Sam had his door closed, and I could hear there was something going on in there. Once, I saw Peg stepping out of the bathroom. She was naked. She looked at me for a moment. My blood moved to my center. Then she shrugged and stepped into Sam's room.

One morning when Ben was out on his motorcycle on a camping trip, Peg came into my room while I was still in bed. She locked the door behind her. She was wearing a wrinkled mumu, and she said, "I don't have anything on under this. Want to?"

I didn't think. Or it was all preordained, from the moment Ben gave me permission. I lifted the covers up.

After, she asked me, "Do you want to tell Ben? Or should I?"

The first thing that entered my mind was that Ben said it was okay, but I was too proud to say that. *I couldn't tell.* "You tell him."

Peg snorted. "I'll tell him."

Then she said, "You know, you can bring a woman in here. I always thought there would be women here. I don't want to be the queen bee."

Usually there was the Blood, Sweat & Tears album playing, Sam practicing the trombone parts to "Spinning Wheel." I tried to abstract from the situation, what I'd done by sleeping with Peg. I was ashamed. The least I could have done was honor my friendship with Ben. I was determined to get my novel finished. At least I could do that. After a couple of false starts, beginning from the characters in the story I had showed to Nancy Hardin, it changed into what was going on in the house, Ben and Peg and Sam and Malcolm and Zeke and the kids. And me. Slowly, it became clear that I was just waiting to finish my book and get out of there.

Next night or two nights later, I came out on the porch. I hadn't spoken to Ben since Peg had told him. I could hear he was alone on the porch, and it seemed an opportunity. My writing was done for the day. Ben was sitting there with a 30.30 lever action rifle. The stock was walnut, and there was a rubberized butt, soft-recoil. He began to unload it, ejecting bullets with the lever action, then reloaded it. I counted six bullets that went in, plus one in the chamber. He aimed the thing across the street, at the house where the middle-aged Mexican husband Hector lived with the "white" woman, Doris. He did odd jobs for Ben in exchange for wine and beer, and Doris had a buzzer set up which rang when she wanted him home.

"Pick off Hector and Doris, too," Ben said.

I cleared my throat. "Seriously. What's that for?"

He thought for a moment. "To hunt whitetails and black bears."

About a week later, I was in my room, typing—about halfway through my novel, Blood, Sweat & Tears playing and Sam practicing on his trombone. He used to stand by the one speaker. It was a component stereophonic player that had the turntable and tape deck with the amplifier under them, the speakers spaced out to the sides on a board that the components were stacked on. The board was beneath the front windows. Sam stood by the one speaker near the front door, working the trombone slide. It was an expensive trombone—a Superbone—but he was not very good on it, used to play only the few notes of Jimmy Hyman's part and, disembodied, the notes sounded silly.

I heard the shot, and the music stopped. There was a lot of static, and ringing in my ears. Daffy whined under the bed. I sat at my desk, fingers poised over the typewriter keys. I had just got to the part where Richard had brought the rifle home—Ben was called Richard in the novel.

Then I heard Sam say in a falsetto, "You fucking nincompoop!" Then he said, "Don't point that thing at me!"

I listened for shot number two. When it didn't sound out, I thought

I ought to go in there. Still, a long time passed—maybe it was only seconds—before I stood up over my typewriter and looked down at the sheet rolled onto the platen. It was half a page, a half sentence was typed of the new line. The lines were just black squiggles across the white page, the ribbon half red and half black. I saw through the window out into the street, the house across the way. I remembered Doris complaining that Sarah toddled out without her diaper. "It doesn't look right to the little boys," and Ben said in his deep voice, "Looks all right to me."

I opened the door just as Sam was going into his room. He slammed the door behind him. Ben was standing across from the phonograph, the butt of his rifle down beside his shoe. I didn't know where Peg and the kids were. Ben leaned forward to study the bullet hole in the amplifier. It was not symmetrical, a star burst shatter. He looked from the hole to me with his bloodshot eyes.

"Guess you got tired of B, S & T," I said.

His laughter was slow and clicking like a bicycle wheel with a stick in its spokes.

Sam moved out that day. Malcolm stayed, took over Sam's room, and soon, Peg was going into Malcolm's room. In two weeks, I finished my novel and took a plane back to New York. It was a short novel.

You Made Me So Very Happy

NANCY HARDIN WAS NOT at New American Library anymore. When I wrote to Nancy, I got a letter back from her replacement Cathleen Reilly, who invited me to send the novel. I titled the draft *The Stockton Split*, and it was just a hundred and seventy-eight pages, including the front pages and the bio note. The book had an epigraph from George Seferis, "And if the soul/is ever to know itself/it must gaze/into the soul…"

She acknowledged receipt, saying, "Give me six weeks to read the ms. Swamped with work." Six weeks later I called her, and she said to come in, and I took the subway to Avenue of the Americas. I told the receptionist that I had an appointment with Cathleen Reilly, and the receptionist said that Miss Reilly would come out, take a seat.

When I saw the manuscript on the arm of Miss Reilly, I thought, *Why do I waste my time*? She said, "It was very talented, and there was so much to admire there, but it's slight and we won't be offering a contract." She didn't even sit down, held the ms out to me in the self-addressed envelope I had sent. Didn't want to waste postage.

I saved the Seferis epigraph but stored the remainder of *The Stockton Split* in a box in my mother's basement, after I had sat down in the chair I listened to jazz in and read at random through the treacherous thing to see what I could learn. I had written it too quickly. It would have made a short story, but a short story that I could not write. I started drinking, put on B, S & T on just the blank spot for the grooves of "And When I Die." That song was written by Laura Nyro when she was fifteen; I was twenty-six. I had a letter from Ted Solotaroff. And blew it.

Next day, I went back to my part-time NGO position and told Miss Brown I would be in Monday, if she would have me (she would), and I looked for an apartment in Queens: there were too many pan-handlers and Vietnam vets on the southwest corner of Central Park, too many homeless huddling in the subway stations to get warm and dry, too many blacks and Latinos wandering the streets alone, looking over their shoulders, looking at me. I was a Queens boy. I found a ground-floor studio on Ithaca Street in Elmhurst.

I fell for a Norwegian who had a charming accent, the shortest skirts and longest legs, and a freckled, wholesome face. Her name was Signe Blomenstenberg. She was working for the NGO as typist. She used to leave on her lunch hour, and one day I followed her, feeling like a stalker. I saw her sitting on a bench in Central Park, having finished a sandwich from a crumple of tin foil in her lap, long thighs spread to catch the October sunshine, miniskirt hitched up, head back, eyes closed, smiling into the sunny, blue sky. *That is one healthy, handsome woman*, I thought, eyes closed to possible danger. New York was going down in the "70s'. There were any number of druggies, grifters, scam-artists looking for a scam, and she sat in the sun like that, eyes closed, smiling, her skirt revealing her thighs, practically up to her panties. *Wonder what color she's got on?*

One morning, she walked through the office door. She didn't say anything, good morning or hi. Her face was twitching, and she sat at her desk without taking her coat off. I asked what was the matter.

"My next door neighbor fired a rifle through my door last night." She laughed a little, but both eyes were twitching. *Her wholesome, trust-*

ing face!

"Jesus! Are you all right?"

In her sexy accent, she told me that the other day, her faucet was dripping, and her neighbor came to complain, said he would kill her if she didn't stop that faucet.

"I said that he should complain to the superintendent, and he came back last night and said, 'Open the door, Miss, I'm going to kill you.'" She opened the door. Apparently, Norwegians were not afraid of anything. He had a rifle, and she told him to go down and point the rifle at the superintendent to make him fix the faucet, and closed the door. And he fired five shots through it.

"Jesus! Where do you live?"

"On East 2nd Street between Avenues A and B."

"Damn! I used to live down there. On East 3rd Street. It's changing. When I moved in, it was safe. But it's extremely dangerous now. Were you hurt?"

"No. My five-years nephew was there. Miraculous, he didn't get hit. My sister was out with her boyfriend." Her twitching eased, and the receptionist and a staff member from the Spanish Department came over, and I returned to my desk. I pretended to be working, but I was having a debate with myself: Where could she stay? And her sister and her nephew. And the sister's boyfriend. My mother was in the process of selling her house, buying a co-op. I could stay with my sister, move out and house Signe and her whole family. As a temporary measure.

I telephoned my sister, Jenny, at work at the Ford Foundation. She was still separated, thirty-six, and was going out with an actor and didn't see her husband, who had become homeless. She had a 3½-room apartment which she shared with her 17-year-old son, a rock musician.

In her easy way, Jenny said, "Sure. You could stay with me. We'll have fun!"

I asked Signe to lunch at Childe's, across the Circle, and asked some questions. She was living with her sister and her sister's five-year-old son. Wictor, her sister's boyfriend, lived in Jamaica, Queens and had only a room in boarding house. She pronounced it "Ya-ma-ica."

Would she like to stay with me? Her whole family. I had just a studio, but I would move out, stay with my sister. "It's a safe neighborhood. In Queens."

She protested—a bit feebly—but I easily prevailed.

The remaining thing was to accompany her to E. 2ⁿᵈ Street. I saw the bullet holes in the door, felt them with my fingers. Wictor was there, too. He introduced himself as "Victor." He was tall and black and spoke with a Jamaican accent. We carried their six suitcases on the subway to Elmhurst. I had bought some roller skates for the little boy.

Victor had to go to work. He worked as a security guard at a construction site in Manhattan. Kirsten kissed him on the mouth at the door of my little apartment, and I showed how the fold-out sofa could be made into two beds, and the other "sofa" served as a bed with the big cushions taken off. Suddenly I was ashamed of the littleness of my apartment, the metal book case, the cinderblock and board coffee table with their six suitcases ranged around the living room amidst the furniture.

"It's small, but it's only temporary," I said.

They offered me coffee, and I refused. They insisted. Kent was asleep on the "sofa" that served as his bed. I still had my coat on, but Signe slipped it off. "You have coffee. It's still your apartment." Kirsten was pretty, delicate-featured, but she wasn't as wholesome as Signe. I sat down and had coffee which Signe made strong and black. It tasted good, the bitter flavor of coffee, and we chatted like we never did in the office

I left after an hour. In the lobby, the Super's apartment door opened. I had taken the girls there and said that they were staying for a while. "With their little son." I indicated Victor. "He's just helping. And I'm staying with my sister while they're here."

Sweeney was a little, wiry guy who seemed to be always drunk. "It's your apartment," he blurted.

"I just wanted you to know."

This time it was Mrs. Sweeney who looked out. "What is he, black?"

The voice of Mr. Sweeney sounded from inside the apartment. "Mind your own business. Let the man be. *His* apartment."

The wife asked again, "What is he, black?" Her tone was matter of fact, but I couldn't believe what she'd said. "He's not staying here. He works as a security guard. He's a gentleman," I added. I'd just met him, didn't know if he was a gentleman, but gave him the benefit—especially with the racist assumption Mrs. Sweeney made.

"Does he sleep in bed with her?"

"Why don't you ask her?" I said and let myself out the lobby door.

A week later, Kirsten moved down to Baltimore with her little boy. Apparently, she abandoned "Wiktor," moved in with a teacher. I met the teacher when he drove up to take them down. He was a history teacher. He was black, too.

After they had gone, Signe confided in me, "Kirsten only goes out with black men. I went out on a date with a black man once, and she got the idea to do that. Now she only goes out with black men. She's my younger sister. She's only twenty-five. I'm thirty."

Jenny was right. I had fun with her and her son, Jack. Jenny was my favorite person. Jack and I resumed writing songs. Jenny and Jack and I used to sit in the living room and smoke and drink beer, and Jack and I wrote songs. It was one of the best times of my life.

We had started composing songs when he was fourteen, and we were living in our mother's house. Jack was a talented guitarist, jammed in Café à Go Go in Greenwich Village with Jeff Beck and B. B. King and Jimi Hendrix, opened for Miles Davis and Jethro Tull in the Village East.

It was a pleasure working on songs instead of fiction. We would sit in Jenny's apartment and write long into the night, Jack strumming an acoustic. He also had a Gibson electric and a Gretsch, and he stood them in a holder frame in his bedroom, but he always composed on acoustic. In fact, I had given him his first guitar when he was little, an acoustic my father had bought me for twenty bucks when I was a teenager. I used to take lessons from Mr. Mungo on 82nd St. up over the stores in Jackson Heights, playing "The Carnival of Venice" and "Down in the Valley." Bling, bling. I would fit my hand awkwardly to the neck and strum chords with my other hand—G and C and D and F—D7 and A7, too, which was essential to Rick Nelson's "Lonely Town." I was just developing calluses on my fingers when Jack took up my guitar—he was about six—and picked out some Broadway show tunes that we had on LPs—*Fiorella* and *The Sound of Music* and *Tenderloin*. He had a natural talent, and I told my mother I was ashamed of my paltry lessons and wanted to give Jack the guitar. My mother said, "You never learn something which cannot benefit you in time. Give him the guitar, and you'll see."

Meanwhile, when I was staying at my sister's, Mose Schwartz had come back with a full beard and a mop of natural curls, looking like an

Egyptian prince. He first came back to his Boro Park house in Brooklyn from the Hippie Highway and wowing me and my friend Woody and Jenny and Jack and Jack's girlfriend, Darria, and Signe with tales of his life in England, Germany, Switzerland, Spain, Morocco. He'd hitchhiked across Northern Africa to Egypt, to Israel, moving from there to Afghanistan, India, Nepal, and Thailand.

He told stories about the Muslim farm in Morocco where he stayed, and he became increasingly guilty about the fact that he was a Jew and staying with Muslims. He worked up his nerve to tell Mohammed, the owner of the farm, and after weeks, he finally told him, "Mohammed; I have to tell you something. I'm a Jew."

Mohammed looked at him quizzically. "So?" he asked. "I knew you was Jew."

Stories about the most erotic moment he'd ever experienced: the moment a woman in a burka, covered head to foot in black so only her eyes showed, and she gazed at him, in the eyes, with her brown tea-colored gaze, and he instantly had an erection.

About the woman he had seen in New Delhi, who had no nose. "No nose!" he repeated. "I don't know if somebody had cut it off, or she lost it from some disease!"

About the French girl he stayed with in her van, and he was dabbling in poetry. One day, he confessed he was a poet. Immediately, she said, "You are *not* a poet!"

Woody had turned to writing fiction from math, kept switching to one and the other, and never quite flourished at either. Me, Mose, Woody and Signe used to hang around in The Lion's Head on Christopher Street and used to eat clams and drink beer and hope for a glimpse of Norman Mailer or Jimmy Breslin or Pete Hammill, but other than the one sighting in '68, there were no more. We did once get more than a glimpse of Gregory Corso, who tried to sell me the world's "most valuable postage stamp printed ever." He had it in a samples strip, and he thrust it under my nose.

"That doesn't look like a British Guiana one-penny Magenta to me," I said. I had collected stamps when I was a kid.

"You're a very smart man," he said and put the stamp in his field jacket pocket. But he had only eyes for Signe, though she would not pour him a glance, not knowing who he was. I was glad she didn't know.

Since the day I saw her sitting on the bench in Central Park in the sunshine, I had loved her from afar.

I was meeting Signe every morning at the subway on Broadway (Queens) to ride the train into Columbus Circle which took about twenty minutes if we caught an express. I invited her out to dinner once or twice and up to Jenny's in Jackson Heights and walked her home to my apartment on Ithaca to check the mail. One night, she asked, "Vould you like to come in for coffee?"

"It's too much trouble," I said, aware of her having lived in my apartment for three or four weeks and not wanting her to think I was making assumptions.

"No trouble. I vould like you to come in."

When she was pouring coffee, she touched my hand. I looked at her, and her eyes said yes. I kissed her. With a cryptic smile, she raised her arms lazily, coquettishly, indicating that I should remove her pullover, and that seemed the most natural, wholesome thing she could do, seemed like something from *Jazz on a Summer's Day*.

Under her implicit tutelage, I made my journey to health and normalcy. She seemed so wholesome and fresh and healthy. We shopped at the local supermarket where she lingered over the cauliflowers and broccoli and celery and three kinds of lettuce and two kinds of tomatoes and small bulbs of radishes and long carrots in a bunch with green leafs on top and cucumbers and Walla Walla onions, potatoes—baking and new, inspecting them to see that they were ripe, no brown spots. Same thing with the fruit—apples, oranges, mangos, even a pineapple. She inspected them, one by one, and weighed them in her palm and later on the scale.

She bought things I would never consider—cress, parsley, chives, dill, chopped horse radish, avocado. Sword fish and steaks and meat which she would broil, roast in the oven, liver and kidneys and cow hearts she would sauté.

I stood back with the cart, eyed her fingers, her inspection, her concentrated gaze, eyes, her freckles—she even had them on her arms and high on her chest and fine-fine blond down that would show in a certain light over her arms and belly, even her face, the span of her upper lip. Once in a while, I smiled at her in her concentration, and she slowly looked up at me and asked, "Vhat?" But that was my secret. How she was healing me, making me healthy with her examining the texture, the skin of each vegetable and fruit and the meat to see that it was lean. Something so natural to her with her freckles—and alien to me.

I'd been in the habit of frying chopped meat in diced onions and rice with a can of tomato puré, buying a pizza, two fried hamburgers. For the first time since childhood, I ate three meals a day: Dinner with two kinds of vegetables—*and* a salad with lettuce, tomatoes, radishes, celery—meat and potatoes. Lunch she fixed, sandwiches in tin foil— no white bread, dark rye bread—with sliced cucumber, ham or sliced roast beef from the roast she would fix for dinner the night before or hand-cut salami, and a blade of lettuce (which she pronounced "let-yuce") with a sprinkle of chives and cress. Breakfast of a soft-boiled egg and toasted, buttered rye or whole wheat bread, just half a slice, and cheese sawed off a block with a slice of green pepper on it—no individual slices of "American," wrapped in plastic. A small glass of orange or grapefruit juice, freshly squeezed, including the pulp, and a cup of strong black coffee. Afterward, an apple—"To cleanse our mouths," as she said.

In the mornings, we walked briskly, arm-in-arm, to Broadway and take the IND subway to Columbus Circle. Sometimes we kissed, people packed around us, to the horror of middle-aged women in frumpy coats. I could not help myself; her lips were so raspberry sweet. She could not contain herself either, helped herself to the kisses, an infinite supply provided—or so it seemed.

For Christmas, which we celebrated at my sister's, Signe gave me a Konica 35 mm camera for my "sweetness" in saving her from East 2nd Street. It was the first real camera I had. I took black-and-white pictures of her by Jenny's Christmas tree or Forest Hill Park or Central Park, and the snow-strewn pathways—or she climbed up on a rock and an equestrian statue; she was so athletic.

I photographed her in my apartment in various states of undress. I shot a roll of her in her slip and bra and nude. She was so natural with her blond pubic hair and her small, uptilted breasts, lying on our sofa bed. The guy in the camera store said, "Those are *some* pictures!"

"They're art! They're European! Do you look at our prints?"

"I gotta look at 'em to develop 'em, don't I?"

The pictures excited us. We made love, and it seemed to be the first real act of love I had engaged in.

Once, she asked me to tell her the most memorable act of sex I'd ever had.

I said, "You tell first."

She had been on a Norwegian ocean liner, working as a cabin maid, and there was a Ceyloni sailor on board, and he asked her to go ashore with him in Valpairaiso.

"Where's that?"

"Chile."

They rented motor scooters and went up in the mountains. "The day was wery hot, and I felt so free, experiencing the breeze all around me on my body." (Bo-dy, she prounced it—with a foreign quality to the vowel, which suited my ear.) At one point they stopped, and she sat on a rock with her legs stretched out, and he knelt before her. He started rubbing her feet, first the one, then the other. "He worked up to my legs so slow-ly, and I thought he would never get there, but he worked so slowly, deliber-a-te-ly. And I became vild!"

The story excited me and made me jealous. That faceless Ceyloni sailor—where was Ceylon, anyway?—massaging her feet and legs so that she thought he would never get *there*. To her pussy? To her *cunt*! Trying to control my breathing, I said, "That makes me jealous."

Quickly, she said that she came with me almost every time. (*Almost*!) "It doesn't mean anything. A moment from the past."

Was I being unreasonable? I was embarrassed. Then, I got the idea that she was telling me something. I started to massage her feet slowly. Her feet were delicate and long-boned, long-toed. Blood, Sweat & Tears was on, the brass of "You've Made Me So Very Happy," Clayton-Thomas singing sweetly about losing in love before, then rough and quick about thrilling his very soul and the bracing brass. I was up to her lower legs, caressing and massaging, kissing, trying not to think about her center because then I would dive right there. Over the knees to her thighs and tracing my fingers, almost *there*, but inching back to the inner thighs.

After, I was—we were both—satisfisfied and we lay back separately, hands touching, catching our breaths. *Was this a demonstration of love-making? Was she showing me how I should do it?*

Suddenly, she told me, "You know, I had a boyfriend on 2nd St. Raymond. I think he arranged for the neighbor to shoot the rifle through the door. He could only be the one."

"You didn't tell me you had a boyfriend, Signe."

"I met him that same time that Kirsten met Wictor." (She pronounced Kirsten like "Shersten," and I first thought she had a speech impediment, but realized that it was the Norwegian pronunciation.) "They were pretending to not know each other, but I could see they did. They were both black."

"Not every black man knows every other black man."

"No, but I could see. Raymond was playing in a Reggae band, and Wictor was vatching the musicians. This was in that park? Thompkins? When Wiktor started flirting with Shersten, Raymond had a break and came over and started flirting with me."

"Don't you think that they were attracted to two Norwegian sisters?"

"I used to go with one black man in Oslo. That's where Shersten got the idea. She only dates black men now. She was married to a white man, Norvegian. That was where she got Kent. Now she is divorced and only goes out with black men. Raymond was in prison before. I don't know, but think when I broke up with Raymond, he got the neighbor to shoot the rifle through the door. Wiktor might be inwolved, too."

The hair on my arms lifted. Victor knew the address of this apartment, and Raymond must know it, too. "Do you think we should move from here? Get a bigger place in another neighborhood?"

"Yes."

"We'll start looking next week."

It was January, and I wanted to re-enroll in college. My oldest brother had started in Fordham, Lincoln Center, right around the corner from Columbus Circle, night classes in the Excel program, which had a "Life Experience" component that could earn up to forty credits. They would transfer credit from C.C.N.Y., too, and I could do my B.A. in two and a half years at night. I had started full time at the NGO and was making a hundred-seventy a week. Somehow, we didn't follow through with the new apartment—until it was too late.

FLC was just around the corner. I would get off at 4:30, and my first course was at six. I would eat in an Irish bar, the Blarney Stone. They had a cheap meal if you bought a glass of beer. Mashed potatoes and some kind of roast and vegetable. I would have time to stop at O'Neal's Baloon happy hour for a double Dewar's on the rocks before my class. O'Neal's Saloon was originally called O'Neal's Saloon until New York City passed an ordinance that you couldn't have a saloon when there was a church within some blocks. So, they solved that problem by painting over the sign with the "S" turned to a "B"; this is why the "Baloon" doesn't have two l's and *has* two O's.

O'Neal's was just across from the fountain at Lincoln Center and the two Chagal murals in the glass-fronted Metropolitan Opera, and I gazed over at the fountain and Chagal over my Dewar's for half an hour before I went to my first class, which was Milton with Professor Grace, followed by Professor Jay's Victorian Poetry and Professor Elizabeth Beacon's Chaucer.

I was happy, after, to go home on the IND subway to meet Signe at 9:30 p.m. Signe had a salad for me with all the good things she put in— three kinds of lettuce (Iceberg, Romaine, and leaf). Sliced radishes and celery and raw red onions and crutons and quartered tomatoes with a dressing of Balsamico vinegar and Virgin olive oil with a dash of Dijon mustard and salt and pepper, both from a mill. She would sit with me at the kitchen table while we listened to B, S & Ts, and I would tell her about the poets. Literally, we were so very happy. I almost asked her to marry me several times, but it was too soon. It might have made her doubt my seriousness. I *was* serious, and just waiting for time to convince her that I was sincere.

One night, she said to me that Raymond was here.

"Where? In this apartment?"

"He rang the doorbell, and I used the microphone to ask who it was. I didn't let him in. I didn't answer."

"We've got to start looking for another apartment."

At the beginning of March, she stopped talking to me—for three days. It was my twenty-seventh birthday on the 9th of March. I didn't know whether the fact that she was already thirty made her feel strange. My mother had had an issue with the fact that my father was one year younger than she; she thought people would think she was "robbing the cradle." She told me so.

Four years would really be an issue, but I wouldn't let it.

By the third evening, I had been assuring her that I loved her, that there was no one else for me, that I wanted to marry her. There—I said it. I remember that I was sitting at the table, and she was standing with her back to me at the sink, when she spun around and crouched.

"*Nawsty!*"

I was startled. She looked like a crazy woman, crouching there, her eyes twitching, hands clutched. "Do you think I do not recognize the fake postman? Poking around! Employed by whom? To spy on me! And god knows what else!"

She began to list her complaints about my failings. She said that I always showed her the lead article in the NGO newsletter. "It's not even a *newspaper!*" She explained angrily that she was going out with a journalist in Oslo who had real articles in a real newspaper and he wouldn't brag about them. She said that I thought she was kissing me on the subway (*subvay*) out of love—she was only kissing to take the piss out of the oh-so-fine ladies in the crowd. "And you thought it was out of *love for you!*" And there was the fake postman. "Who was he hired by?"

We hadn't even got a chance to move to a new neighborhood. I didn't know whether she was unbalanced by the neighbor firing the rifle through her door, or that was a fiction. But I had felt the bullet holes. Kirsten or Victor hadn't talked about it, however, and I didn't mention it for the sake of delicacy. Didn't want to tramp around in it. Maybe the bullet holes were already there when she moved in. Kirsten was already planning to move to Baltimore with that American guy she had met in Oslo. He was leading a group of junior high school students on a tour group. Apparently, Kirsten had just used Victor to spice up her month in New York. Maybe Victor knew, just was using her to get laid. Benefits all around. Whether Victor and Raymond knew each other, or whether Raymond had been her boyfriend and worked *Gaslight* on Signe, or whether Raymond didn't exist at all—these were all questions.

Signe stayed home from the office next day and was gone by night when I returned. She left me a note: "Under the situation, I am going to Baltimore." Unsigned. Next morning, I asked Miss Brown whether she had heard from Signe, and Miss Brown asked me if I didn't know. It was common knowledge that Signe and I were involved. Signe had called early yesterday morning and said her sister was seriously ill, and she was going down to Washington. She was sorry that she couldn't give notice, but her sister was *really* ill.

My work occupied my days and my studies occupied me evenings. However, when I lay in bed at night, I had my phantoms of Signe. I found a pair of her panties in the basket we used for a hamper. She had worn them. The panties had her aroma on them. Of her pussy. They were a pink pair. I jerked off to those panties, imagining her here in the flesh, in my bed, in the dark.

I tried to write about her, but quickly saw that all the unanswered question would have to wait a little longer. Maybe forever. The questions that were unanswered about Signe—and about me. I did not know what to do about them.

I decided to move. My older brother, Jos., found me an apartment on 86th St. in Jackson Heights, between Roosevelt and Polk Avenue. I left the furnishings in the apartment I had been living in. Even my grandmother's dining table. Leave them to Mr. and Mrs. Sweeney. Clean start. Jos. was married now, to a Colombian woman, and had an apartment on the same floor as me. I wondered if my brothers and sister considered me a zero.

The new apartment was a three-room for a hundred-seventy a month; that was a forth of my salary. It was a mezzanine, three steps up from the ground-floor. It had a very small dining room with a larger living room connected and a bedroom. My brother Jos. told me I had to slip a hundred under the table to the super. Jos., who managed a rental car firm, got a new car—a cherry Vega—cheap.

I visited the Catholic Charities wedged between Polk Ave. and 88th St. and measured with a yard stick what furniture I needed and could fit in. The first night in my new place, it occurred to me that Signe wouldn't know my new address. I worried about that for a moment. B, S & T was on. "You Make Me So Very Happy." I took it off. I put on the Horace Silver Quintet. *Further Explorations.* Sitting at my kitchen table by the double window, looking at the budding trees on the street, a bottle of export Heineken and a Pall Mall, I began to be glad that Signe wouldn't know my new address. The panties I threw down the incinerator.

When it got too lonely for me, I visited Jos. and Beatriz for a late dinner, which always started with empanadas and always finished with coffee, a lot of sugar and cream—it was like a dessert. One night she had another Colombian girl to dinner, Olga. After dinner, Olga moved over to the love seat and said, "I like that shirt on Edward: *Flaco, flaco, flaco!* Come sit with me?"

But I wasn't ready.

Standinavia

COPENHAGEN: I FELL IN LOVE with the dark, winding, narrow streets, the cobblestones, the architecture, the sculpture on the street and in the green parks, the værtshuse (the serving houses—pubs) which when one of them closed, another opened—around the clock. I fell in love with the beer, the quiet manner of the people (friendly but not too friendly—they could let you alone, too, to enjoy yourself). The women were great looking, the jazz was hot and cool.

I purchased a LP beforehand that Jos. had—*Stan Getz in Denmark*, recorded in 1959. Getz had been in Copenhagen multiple times, particularly in Café Montmartre, where he played tenor with Danish musicians (particularly Niels Ørsted Henning Pedersen—NØHP for short—then only a fifteen-year-old bass player, and John Tchicai, born of a Danish mother and a Congolese father. Tchicai played all manner of sax—alto, tenor, soprano and a baritone clarinet). And the American expats here (Ben Webster, Dexter Gordon, who both play tenor, Oscar Pettiford) and the visiting musicians. Getz had played in the little hours jam sessions with Gerry Mulligan, switch-hitting, Stan blowing baritone sax and Gerry playing tenor.

At the end of August 1972, I was sent by the NGO on the Circle to Copenhagen for a four-day conference in the Falkoner Center in Frederiksberg. I took two weeks of vacation afterward. I stayed in the Imperial Hotel, where Jos. had stayed at the end of the '50s' and early '60s. When Jos. was twenty, he worked for Pan Am and got flights for ten percent of the fare. He loved jazz and Copenhagen. I listened to his dazzling stories when I was sixteen. Jos. hadn't lied.

First, I went into Monmartre, which was still open then—a little club with long tables. I was disappointed that Getz was not there. Some African music with lots of drums. Reminded me of Chico Hamilton playing kettle drums. Afterward, I went into Long Johns (rhythm & blues) and the White Lamb (Dixieland), Andy's Bar (rock), the Drop

Inn (cool & hardbop), Laurens Betjent (which opened at midnight), and the Evergreen (which was open at four in the morning when they served Gulasch soup for free). I drank bottled beer in green bottles, drank myself sober, bought a pack of ten Prince cigarettes, stepped from behind the dark curtain which ket the light from getting in the door.

It was light, and people were walking briskly and cycling to work. The bartender had opened the pack, but didn't provide matches when you bought a pack, and my Zippo was out of fluid. I stumbled into the walking street—drunk, but not too drunk, which was a nice place to be. I loved getting drunk but hated being drunk. I stopped a person on the street to ask for a match. It was drizzling, and the person wore a woolen French policeman's cape and pulled down the hood at my approach. I saw twin blue eyes and delicate features which transfixed me. The woman in the French cape took out a box of stick-matches, tried unsuccessfully to light my cigarette—two, three matches. Unused to a woman lighting my cigarettes, I said, "Let me try."

"*Nej*, I want to get this right."

She managed to get it lit on the fourth match. By that time, we were chatting. She asked me why I was here, in this little kingdom. I told her I was from New York and was here for a conference and decided to take two weeks' vacation. She said that she had just been in Crete for holiday. I asked where that was.

"Greece, a Greek island. It's fantastic."

She was a psychology student at Copenhagen University. Did I want to see how a Danish university student lived? I said why sure, thinking I was getting lucky. I thought I would do the dirty with Grethe, the woman in the French cape. Boys' minds were like porn shop windows—girls' minds, too—and pornography was free since the sixties in Denmark, a sign.

Grethe led me down the walking street and through some other streets and a square and crossed a bridge across a street lake to the northside. I was lost, would just flag down a cab when it came to that.

"This is the *Sorte Firkant*," she said. "The Black Square. I live in an apartment in the third backyard."

She led me through the port and to the third courtyard, the light getting dimmer with each courtyard and into an outside door and up three flights into a two-room apartment.

Several pairs of panties were suspended from a drying rack in the front room. "I'm dying them purple. The color is very popular. Would you like some coffee?"

Then, when we were seated at a table, drinking black coffee out of metal mugs, she started talking about "William."

"Is he your boyfriend?"

"No, but I'm crazy about him. Do you want to meet him? I'm having a party tomorrow night. Can you find the way to my apartment? I'll write down the address. I want someone to meet you."

A loud knock at my door in the Imperial woke me. I looked at my watch on the night table. It was two a.m.

"*Politi!*"

The first thing I could think of was Grethe. I opened the door a bit to a cop in uniform. The policeman started speaking Danish, then corrected himself at my mystified expression, and tried English. There had been a bomb threat by telephone in connection with the situation in Munich. "Please go down to the lobby and await further instructions."

The situation in Munich? "Can I put my pants on at least?"

"Quickly."

I slipped into my pants, sockless feet into shoes, into my corduroy sports jacket over the T-shirt I'd been sleeping in and entered the hall. People were moving in the corridor, walking toward the bank of elevators.

Munich? Did that cop say Munich?

The police were directing us to the stairs. My room was on the fourth floor. A cop pointed out a direction to some woman with his night stick and almost cracked me in the nose. The policeman laughed self-effacingly. I noted how my nose would be broken, and laughed.

About fifty other hotel guests and I were sitting on the sofas or standing in the lobby. The bar wasn't open. A woman desk clerk told us about Munich. The PLO had taken hostages from the Israeli team at the Munich Olympics, demanding the release of 234 Palestinian prisoners and non-Arabas from Israeli jails, plus West German Andreas Baader and Ulrike Meinhoff from the German prison system. Initial reports were that the terrorists from the Black September faction of the PLO were killed, but the eleven Israeli athletes and coaches survived. However, an hour later the factual report came out: five of the terrorists and all eleven Israelis were killed as well as one German policeman. Three PLO terrorists had survived. The desk clerk was filling us in, and one woman asked, "Why do you automatically say they are terrorists. Change the point of view, and they become patriots."

The five Black September members had fired Kalishnikov assault rifles at point-blank range into the bound Israelis. All were dead. The surviving terrorists were arrested. Tears filmed the eyes of the desk clerk. I thought it was good to be American; the Vietnam War was still being fought, though I was against the war.

The bomb scare was a hoax. I returned to my room and slept behind the drawn dark curtains. When I awoke at a little past one p.m., it was light out and drizzling. I had just one thought in my mind: breakfast and a glass of cold milk.

After I ate in the hotel restaurant, I walked over Vesterport Station and past the Circus building, strolled along the street. *Fat City* was playing at the Dagmar. Just what I needed. To sit in the dark for two hours. Ben Flaherty flashed into my mind wearing a bra and panties with his skinny, ruddy face and hairy arms and deep voice. It was not a good couple of hours.

I got out of the film at six o'clock and discovered the slip of paper in my pocket with Grethe's address on it. I hailed a cab.

There were only five people at the party: Grethe and William, who sported a blond beard and was arrogant; "Red" Susanne, who was communist and had red hair and just visited China; and Finn whose face was covered in black hair almost from beneath his eyes and wore short pants which were tattered in the crotch; and Vibeke who had big breasts beneath a rough cotton Greek blouse and wore no bra. She also had oversized eyeglasses.

At first, they spoke English about the referendum that was just about to be held for joining or not joining the European Economic Community. I made the mistake of voicing the opinion that it was good to be in the E.E.C.—Europe had been torn by wars for hundreds of years. William asked if I was also for Vietnam and against China.

"Not Vietnam."

I was left, but apparently, all university students were far left—against the E.E.C. and pro-P.L.O. and Mao's *Little Red Book* was a best-seller here.

Fortunately, they lapsed into Danish then and ignored me, and I sat on the corner of the sofa, wondering how to slip away. Vibeke came along to me. She stood over me, large red-framed eyeglasses dwarfing her face, big breasts straining against the Greek cotton blouse. I tried to look away from her big brown nipples which were visible through the rough white cotton, but it was difficult. Apparently, this was the someone Grethe wanted me to meet.

"Can you fight, Edward?"

I thought she was inviting me to fight with her. Whether I just attracted nutty people I did not know. Maybe I was nutty myself.

I said, "When I have to."

"If you can fight, I'll ask you to take me home." She was smiling with all her teeth, but her smile looked fake. Something about her wavering lips and her oversized glasses made me uncomfortable.

"Are you inviting me to fight with you?"

"No," she said without losing the smile. She had a British accent, but it was clear she was a Dane. She said that she had a Bulgarian boyfriend. "He might have broken into my place." The relationship was over, but he wanted her moped, her motor bike. "We have had an—how do you say it?—an adversarial relationship, and he's a bit violent."

Too proud to say I didn't want to fight her Bulgarian boyfriend, I agreed to go with her. At least, it was an excuse to exit the party.

She told me she was a medical student in her fourth year, and I was impressed. Before we left, she kissed Grethe at the door on the mouth.

On the stairs, she asked me if I was interested in women kissing on the lips.

"Under the right circumstances," I said, though I had never experienced two women kissing on the lips before. But I was interested. Every experience added to the sum total.

She lived in Vesterbro, on Istedgade. We took a cab. There was a porn shop on the corner, and right across the street from her building a shop advertising live shows. People who were obviously junkies and street walkers loitered on the sidewalk outside her building. The street walkers were nothing that interested me, but apparently recognized her, made small talk, seemingly friendly comments in Danish to her.

"My father bought me this place, but I picked the location, and he wasn't happy about it. He said, 'I got out of Vesterbro, and you, a medical student, go back to it.' That addict there said, 'I see you brought your purse with you.'" She smiled, but I frowned. "You should not take it so serious. It is only the Danish humor."

I was uneasy, thought of going back to the hotel. It was on the west side, but not *this* west. The Bulgarian was not there. The apartment was small with high ceilings, until you looked out the window to the street. I looked for a way I could get out of there. Lately I was in places I had to get out of. The European vacation seemed to be turning sour. She took off her jacket and opened the refrigerator and picked out two bottles of beer and capped them. She invited me to sit. She sat on the sofa. After two beers, I relaxed and focused on her nipples beneath the white cotton and moved to the sofa.

She woke me the next morning. She was already dressed. "As Henry Miller said, now comes the dirty part: Do you have any money?"

Groggily, I looked at her. We had had a bunch of beers and a half bottle of Export Aquavite the night before, and I didn´t remember when we started undressing each other.

"Do you have money for morning bread and coffee and cheese?"

I gave her a hundred kroner and went back to sleep, but a few minutes later, she was calling me for breakfast. She'd made coffee in a fancy thermos can and sawed the bread with a knife and sliced the cheese with a wire slicer. She had apricot marmalade, too. I had never had a better breakfast, knowing I had stayed the night in the apartment of a Danish girl, a medical student.

There were benefits to her being a medical student, too: she explained how my sperm was discharged. Her handling my apparatus made me hard, and she manipulated me. Then, when I came on her thigh, she said, "Lick it up!" It might have been ill-humoured of me, but I refused.

She said that she was just testing me. Then, she asked me if I wanted to stay for the rest of my holiday and save the money from a hotel. She said she would show me the sights. I figured she wanted me to pay the hundred-twenty kroner for a night; and twenty dollars a night was a lot of money. For seven nights! I would have less freedom, too, and I didn't know if she meant sleep with her or sleep on the sofa. And I didn't know if I liked her and her fresh mouth.

When we were naked the night before, she pinched the skin over my kidneys and said, "You're fat."

"I just lost thirty pounds." Which I had, preparatory to coming to Copenhagen.

"You must have been *very* fat," she'd said, smiling with her teeth, framed by the wavering lips. She wasn't a flyweight. Still, the morning coffee and bread and cheese and jam were charming, and the demonstration of how I ejaculated.

"For now," I said, "Let's play it by ear." I saw she was hurt. Was she insecure beneath her bravado?

Toward the late afternoon, we were eating in Galatea Kro: a cut of pork I had never eaten, smothered in soft, fried onions and boiled potatoes and brown gravy and drinking Carlsberg and Jubilæum aquavite, served by a waiter who called me, "Old chap!" because he thought I was British. There were masks on the wall from some Kontiki-like expedition and hard bop playing from a tape deck. She obviously liked me, which made me like her. The way she was kissing me, she didn't intend for me to sleep on the sofa. I said, "I regret not taking you up on your offer this morning."

We had seven days to sightsee (we saw mostly the serving houses, of which there were 1,525 in the city) and seven nights together to fuck. She was the only woman I had met who matched my sexual appetite: we made love one day and night four times. The amount of friction debilitated us for the next day, but on the second day we were okay.

Still, seven days and nights are not a whole lot when you've just met someone. She saw me off in Kastrup, and we had a beer and a big open sandwich at the one cafeteria in Terminal 2 outside security. The security was lax still, but on May 30, 1972 three members of the Japanese Red Army attacked Lod Airport in Tel Aviv and massacred twenty-four people. But that was in Israel, and Tel Aviv seemed far away, but this incident at the Munich Olympics was closer. I was grateful for what security there was. Non-passengers were not allowed beyond the security gates. Vibeke was getting surprisingly emotional. She couldn't eat her sandwich and was sighing a lot and looking like she would start crying. I told her she could visit me in New York.

"When?"

"Christmas-time. That's only three or four months away." I was still not sure about her.

At the security gates, which were upstairs, she kissed me. The kiss was like she actually meant it, and it softened me. "Christmas?" I said, pulling away from her. Anyway, what did she know about my life in the U.S.? She must have thought I was rich or something.

I was relieved to be away from her and bought an *International Herald Tribune* once I was through security and got on the plane. I was looking forward to the meal and the American Scandinavian Foundation charter flight. It had an open bar in the galley, and you could smoke in the rear of the plane then.

There was a lot of reportage in the paper about the Munich terrorist action. On September 8th, Israeli bombers hit ten PLO training camps in Syria and Lebanon in response to the Munich massacre. Two hundred were killed. The five dead Palestinean attackers from Munich were delivered to Libya where they were given hero's funerals and buried with full military honors.

The XXth Munich Summer Olympics were allowed to continue. On September 6th, a memorial service was held with the Olympics flag flown at half-mast, and the flags of most of the 121 nations participating lowered. Ten Arab nations objected to their flags being lowered to honor massacred Israelis. Their flags were restored to full-mast.

After the meal of cold sandwiches and cake with a four-pack of cigarettes, included Viceroys, I went back to the galley and poured a generous scotch on half a glass of rocks and began to flirt with the stewardess. She was a student, just working for the summer, June to mid-September, but she was a stewardess and had a cute face, and I had a fine time.

On October 2nd, Denmark voted yes, to join the E.E.C. Of 90.1% of the Danish population voting, 63.3% were in favor of joining. As a result of the vote in three countries, the six became the nine of the E.E.C.; Denmark, Ireland, and the U.K. joined on January 1st, 1973.

I got an airmail letter—on flimsy paper—from Vibeke, detailing how the population of Copenhagen made a silent procession to the Parliament. All of the Jutland farmers had voted *yes*. I was glad. Warfare was no longer possible between the nine E.E.C. Member States. The thing was to attract all the countries in Europe to join.

On the 29th of October 1972, a Lufthansa flight was seized with passengers, and the hijackers threatened to blow it up unless the three surviving hostage-takers from the Munich Olympics be released from prison.

They received a hero's welcome in Libya.

Vibeke wrote me almost every day and sent the letters special delivery. She flew over for three weeks at Christmas time, and I introduced Vibeke to Mose and Woody and my sister and Jack and Jos. At one point, when she was out of the room, Mose said, "I approve." Woody didn't say anything, but that note of approval from Mose meant a lot to me. It surprised me, but I was relieved, as though literally a burden had been lifted from me.

A Horse with No Name

"THE DRIFT OF CIRCUMSTANCES" was a term I had read somewhere that year, 1974, in *Your Stars Today.* Astrology was nonsense, but I was an inveterate reader of my horoscope—at least when I had a tabloid. I wrote it down in my journal, thinking the phrase explained everything that was happening to me.

At the end of December 1974, I was due to marry in Copenhagen, living in Ferney-Voltaire, France, a town whose population was about ten thousand, just across the *douane* from Genève. Voltaire, who was still referred to as *Le Patron* in Ferney-Voltaire, relocated there from Paris in 1759, when he published *Candide,* to be close to the border to escape to *La Suisse,* the novel having disavowed the King and the Church and God. Voltaire had said that the world would not be free until the last king was strangled in the entrails of the last priest. I relocated there from New York at the end of the summer.

The Bellevue Hôtel was my home on the Grand Rue, and I rued my life grandly. I was staying in a *pension* run by two middle-aged sisters who spoke only French. I had taken three years of high-school French and a fourth year at Fordham and polished it off with eight weeks of conversational at Berlitz in Manhattan, the bill footed by the company that was relocating me, but I discovered that I could not speak French.

140

Rather, I could not understand the French spoken by the two sisters or by anyone in my new home in France, although my accent was *très charmant,* according to everyone with whom I spoke French ("Êtes-*vous Canadien?*").

In Ferney-Voltaire, I began to realize that I was a New York City boy, a Queens boy, and more accustomed to hamburgers than cows. There were cows wandering in the streets in Ferney. In fact, I poked my finger in the first cow pod I'd seen, not even knowing what it was, and the crust on top of it gave way to a liquidy beige paste. I'd had to go back to the hotel to wash the cowshit from my finger. I didn't like shit in the streets, either turds of dogs or pods of cows.

My Danish fiancé spent three months of the summer before with me in my Jackson Heights three-room apartment, which I was closing up in preparation of sending my goods to France—mostly books and records and precious few clothes. I had bought two suits, one navy blue to get married in and one tweed suit to work in and a sports jacket for weekends, and five shirts and a pair of Florsheim's shoes in addition to the shoes on my feet, which happened to be Flagg Bros., also disco style. I was happy to add two inches on my height due to the elevated disco heels.

To keep her from getting bored, I had arranged with my company for her to work at Cornell Medical Center's OB-GYN department as a supernumerary, which would be credited as her course work in gynecology at the University of Copenhagen. She was a fifth-year medical student. That impressed me. I was to have a B.A. I told myself that, after all, it was *summa cum laude* (Fordham didn't count grades for transfer students, only credits), but still: She would merit the prefix "Dr."

My fiancé became my fiancé—Vibeke—in the summer of 1973, when we were staying in her parent's summer home in north Zealand on the cliffs over the Kattegat. I had said that I didn't know whether I should marry Vibeke, but Mose reassured me, "You would be a fool not to marry Vibeke." I didn't know what he meant—whether she was pretty enough, whether it would be a long-term investment, whether we would be happy together, or whether he just didn't know, whether he was just flapping his lips, but Mose usually meant it when he said something. I was dangling: Would I regret it if I let Vibeke go, slip away in the world, or would I regret it if I married her? Mose meant a lot to me me, and he said I would be crazy to let her go.

He was together with an older Japanese woman, then on Jane Street, who was a wealthy photographer. Mose was a student, among other things, of photography and finagled a Nikon from her. I was impressed with his journey on the Hippie Highway and his girlfriend and his hero status and his judgment that I was crazy not to marry. One of the things that made sense to me, when he told me: "You know when Vibeke tells you you got bad taste, she just means that she don't like your tie." And, "With a woman like Vibeke, you think you ought to take down your defences. *Don't!* Strengthen them!"

I had one ulterior motive for marrying Vibeke, albeit semi-conscious. She had a completely open attitude to sex: She kissed girls on the mouth. She seemed like a sex dream come true. All the secret things I had fantasized about seemed possible with her. I thought that I could nullify my Roman-Catholic, bourgeois "niceness" under her influence; I had read Joyce's *Portrait of the Artist* two times, and been freed from the hell-fire of that faith. I was not adverse to her being a medical student either, in two years to be a doctor, or her parents being comfortable economically; those things were dim to my mind, semi-conscious. I was twenty-nine, old enough, and I was looking at the big 3-0, on the other side of which, things indeterminant would happen.

So, alone in her parent's summer house with Vibeke, I popped the question. After all, I was twenty-nine, she twenty-five, and I had fallen in love with Copenhagen and thought I was in love with her, whatever love was. The sex was more than good. We made love in her parent's home over the beach or in her west-side two-room to the shrill sounds of the factory, across the courtyard, cutting the carcasses of pigs. I had a diamond I bought, in Schiphol, the Amsterdam airport, on my layover there, for three hundred dollars, bought to assuage my uncertainty about moving to the next step. The diamond was in a black velour-covered box with a push-button top. "It will have to wait to be set in a ring."

She said, "Well I'm of child-bearing age, so, Yes!"

I glossed over her response—I hadn't thought about having children—and only heard the "Yes!" We could discuss the question of children when it came to that.

We had been visiting each other for two or three weeks at a time in Copenhagen and New York intermittently since we met in September 1972. But the summer of '74, we were together for three months, and we

argued virtully every day: Both because the New York summer was un-
usually cloudy and hot and humid (I'd imagined us going to the beach in
my '71 Vega at every chance, but we didn't get there once) and because
my apartment didn't have air-conditioning (I *liked* the heat, but Vibeke's
complaint was, "It's bad enough not to have an air-cooled home, but I
have to walk the boiling hot streets and feel the air-conditioners of other
apartments *pissing* on me!")

I played jazz records for her on hot summer nights—sweat and bebop seemed to me to combine positively. I put on an LP of Rexroth and
Ferlinghetti with the Cellar Jazz Quintet, and I tried to read Ginsberg's
Howl, once, aloud to her to a low background of Bird, but she interrupted after a few pages. She found it "un-delicious" with all that ass-fucking
and "the holy cock and asshole in a man's mouth." She asked if I was
queer, too. "Or at least bisexual."

"No, I think you know better than that. The poetry transcends sexual preference."

She displayed her teeth in that non-smile of her. "Is that why you
have that big glass of Vaseline in your medicine cabinet?"

Granted I was always forcing poems upon people—I liked inordi-
nately reading poems aloud, and that must have been annoying—but
she had a stormy, sarcastic temperament, whereas I had a—depending
on your definition—phlegmatic nature (her definition was "passive,
stolid"; mine was "self-composed"). I began to doubt Mose's assessment
of being "crazy not to marry Vibeke." In fact, she seemed to gravitate to
Mose and obey him when he said, "Sit down and be quiet!" The same
order from me (I tried it) produced a storm of Vibeke's invective. Anyway, Mose was in Oregon now and living with a woman, cutting trees.

Still, as much as I was put off by her sarcasm and her outrageous
way of saying things, I was fascinated by it. It seemed that I could super-
sede my bourgeois manner, my "niceness," if I could adopt her attitude.
I didn't want to be a "good Catholic boy" in manner all my life.

It didn't help that she didn't help me pack and was cranky about my
making noise while she was reading her OB-GYN texts. She shouted, "I
have to take a fucking exam!"

I was getting sick of her impatience and her constant arguments.
Why didn't she read in the library? Becaus she chain-smoked while she
studied. I packed my stuff in three suitcases and a large wooden trunk

which the super's wife had given me for free from a wealth of suitcases and trunks in a locked room in the basement. It had a label on it that read "Mrs. Vesterberg," and it looked like it was very old, but still sturdy. I imagined Mrs. Vesterberg coming from snowy north Sweden where it was dark half the year and the midnight sun came out in late June.

"Look at this," I told Vibeke, hunched over her texts. "This says Mrs. Vesterberg on it."

"Will you *shut! The fuck! UP!*"

I shut up, but I held a grudge. She didn't give me time to say what I had intended to say. It was a ceaseless procession where I didn't say things.

The day came when she took her test. She was to meet me at O'Neal's Saloon around the corner from Columbus Circle. It was late August. I got there first and took a table for two. I ordered a double Dewars on the rocks, preparing myself. This was technically a celebration— of her taking the test and my graduating from Fordham. But the B.A. was so less than her M.D. If she hadn't passed the OB-GYN test, I was prepared to say that she could take the course again and not mention my B.A. The B.A. was the lowest of the low, and I had got forty credits in life experience. They were debating whether I should get thirty-eight credits but then I wouldn't graduate, so by administrative dispensation they gave me forty. After all, I had got straight A's other than the transfer credits from C.C.N.Y., and they printed *summa cum laude* on my degree. I showed my displeasure by not going to the ceremony.

Finally, she showed up, sweaty from the subway, found my table, and said, "Can I have a drink?" That was the summer with "A Horse with No Name" by America, and it was playing over the sound system. "What do you want?"

"A drink! A strong one!"

I ordered her the same as me and waited until it came and she drank until I asked, "How did you do?"

"No thanks to you, I passed."

On the first of September, which was a Sunday, I had to route through Stockholm for a five-day company conference, then Vibeke and I were to take a week's vacation in her west-side apartment in Copenhagen before I relocated to Ferney-Voltaire. I had already visited Ferney and was not impressed.

But I was glad to get away from Vibeke—at least for respite—on the plane and for five days in Stockholm. I thought about Mrs. Vesterburg. I had a big chill since that *No thanks to you…*

The Stockholm conference planners initiated it with a banquet, at which my table lady was a young, blonde, pretty Norwegian sociology doctor, who opened the conversation by asking, "Excuse me, do you like sex?" That got me flirting with her and, though I did not follow through, neither did I phone Vibeke a single time during the Conference. I spent my evenings, when there wasn't a social event, with Jack Blackwell, my counterpart from D.C., and Dr. Boohene, the delegate from Ghana, peeling and gobbling crayfish, all you could eat for 10 Swedish kroner, and quaffing draft in Viktoria Garden, eyeing the blonde, pale, sexy Swedish girls.

Vibeke called me on the last night and asked urgently, "Are you all right?"

"Just busy," I said, with chill.

She said her parents wanted to have dinner with me on the first Saturday I was in Copenhagen. "Okay?"

Her parents threw generous dinners. "Okay," I said decisively, although I was not certain of anything.

The dinner was attended by not only her parents and her brother and sister-in-law and their infant son, but her mother's brother and wife—Uncle Alfred and Aunt Anna—and their two teenage children. After the three-course dinner—which started with lobster tails and an Alsatian Riesling, the main course was T-bone steak (in my honor—they thought Americans only ate steak) and a Pinot Noir, and concluded with crepe-suzettes and sparkling Moscato. We adjourned to the sofas for coffee and pralines and an *avec:* VSOP cognac for the men and crème de menthe for the women.

Her father could only speak Danish and German—Vibeke's mother interpreted for him in English. He said that we had to set a date for the church, the banquet hall, and the guests. "What date would suit you?"

Sensing that I was being railroaded, I said, "There's no rush."

"But we have to set a date!" Vibeke's mother exclaimed, and her father said something sotto voce to her. "For the church," she continued, "the banquet, and the guests. Would December 28th suit you?"

"1974?"

"*Ja,*" the father answered directly.

I didn't see any way out of it, with three generations of her family listening to what I would say and all eyes fixed on me. I thought, that's three and a half months away. Time for my doubts to resolve themselves or to call off the wedding.

"Okay," I said under the eyes and ears of her entire family.

"Okay?" her father asked.

"Yes. Er, *ja.*"

"That's the date that *we* were married," her mother said. "Surty years ago."

I thought time and geography would resolve all things. Best to allow the drift of circumstances take its course.

A week later, amongst bickering (Why do you have to go? You should register with the foreign police and stay in Copenhagen!), I flew to Geneva and took a taxi across the *douane* to Ferney-Voltaire. The French border guard looked at my American passport and *Carte de Sejours* and asked officiously, "*Ou habite-tu?*"

Ignoring his slight, I said, "Ferney-Voltaire," though I was not so certain.

It's Sandy on the Beach

THE INTERNATIONAL HERALD TRIBUNE advertised that a concert in Carnegie Hall would be held on November 24th of that year—Gerry Mulligan and Chet Baker!

From the office, a Gerry-built Quonset hut on Avenue du Jura, I phoned Carnegie Hall and booked a fourth-row seat on the central aisle, then bought a business class ticket on Swiss Air, and called the Chelsea Hotel and reserved a room. I didn't tell anybody about it—neither Vibeke nor my New York family. I kept it a secret from everybody but my boss, the newly-hired president, Sir Gregory Hoare.

He raised his ponderous eyebrows. "Tell me, do you plan on coming back?"

"Of course," I said, but didn't add, *Probably.*

On the plane between glasses of champagne, I read *Either/Or* by Søren Kierkegaard, and found this "brain-picking": "If you marry or if you do not marry, you will regret both. Whether you hang yourself or you do not hang yourself, you will regret both. This, gentlemen, is the sum of all practical wisdom."

Apparently, Mr. Kierkegaard opted to cancel his engagement with Regine Olsen because he decided he would be happier in his unhappiness without her than with her.

Checking into the Chelsea, I asked the desk clerk for a smoking room.

"Sir, you can smoke anything you want in any room in this hotel."

My room was on the tenth floor, right out to 23rd Street between Seventh and Eighth Avenues. I took an hour before dinner to view the art, from the ten floors of staircases, adorned with paintings that had been apparently traded for guest bills, all the way down to the lobby with its Niki de Saint Phalle woman on a trapeze.

My first night's meal was at O. Henry's Steak House, where I was allowed to sit at the table where O. Henry had written "The Gift of the Magi," the story that made me cringe with its sentimentality, although I recognized it as well-constructed.

I spent the rest of the night in my single room, listening to *Chet Baker Sings*—"You're Driving Me Crazy" and "Dancing on the Ceiling" and "Everything Happens to Me." I had taken my battery-operated tape recorder in my cabin baggage. Listening to his eerily high voice made me feel decidedly alone in the hotel room, smoking Gitanes and peering down at the traffic and pedestrians on 23rd Street, turning their collars up and tightening their mufflers, the wind blowing refuse around. Manhattan was no place to be alone. I thought of Vibeke, her body, her wavering smile, and her sarcasm. I also thought of the way she had of greeting me at the airport with all her warmth in the kiss. I thought of the good life in Copenhagen—with a woman, with my wife.

Next night was the concert, and I don't remember what the weather was like, but I do recall that I walked up to 57th and Seventh. It was not quite two miles, and I rewarded myself with a stop at the Carnegie Tavern, around the corner from the hall, to wrestle a place at the crowded bar.

There was a bar in the lobby of Carnegie Hall but it was crowded three deep, so I took my seat. It was enough forward that I could see, when they drew the curtain, the long red hair, shot with gray, and mostly gray beard of Mulligan. I'd been expecting to see the redheaded crew-cut, beardless Gerry in *Jazz on a Summer's Day*, but that had been in 1958 when he was at Newport and he'd been only thirty-one. That was how old I'd be in four months, but there were nearly two decades between us; who knew where I would be in twenty years? By then, I'd be fifty and an old man (I thought).

Chet Baker wore a canary-yellow shirt and was thin as death—he would be dead twelve years later when he fell or jumped or was pushed out of a hotel window in Amsterdam. Bob James was on piano and electric piano and a 23-year-old John "Sco" Scofield was on electric guitar (representing parts of the fusion segments of the program), Ron Carter was on acoustic bass; Harvey Mason was the drummer, Dave Samuels the vibres man, Ed Byrne trombonist.

After the applause, Mulligan asked Baker what they should start with, and Chet said that "Line for Lyons," from 1952, was good for warm-up.

Mulligan and Baker had not worked together for ten years, but you didn't know it. A splendid night of jazz, bebop, fusion, cool, ballads, even for Chet, singing in his strange, "white voice" the 1942 Warren Gordon standard "There Will Never Be Another You." I felt a chill go across my flesh as two old masters of the baritone sax and trumpet—plus the young masters—performed, the way I did every time I heard jazz that was solid and masterful. "Line for Lyons," "For an Unfinished Woman," "My Funny Valentine" (which was Rodgers & Hart, but Chet *owned* it), "Bernie's Tune," "K-4 Pacific," and there was even a new tribute to Billy Strayhorn—author of "Take the A-Train" and "Chelsea Bridge" and "Blood Count" and so many more until he died of cancer in '67 at fifty-two—Mulligan's "Song for Strayhorn," a mournful, tender, strong ballad.

Then came a number I had never heard before, "It's Sandy at the Beach," a bebop baritone followed by a second movement of bebop trumpet, followed a minute later with Bob James' piano, followed after a little more than a minute with Sco's articulated, precise guitar, followed by vibes of Samuels, backed up with bass and drums and trombone, and the last couple of minutes of bebop baritone and trumpet harmonizing and improvising with a rousing finish and whistles and cheering. Coincidentally, the tune had suggested a personal moment for me from almost a decade before, compounded by bebop-fusion and my present quandary of what to do.

In 1965, I had tooled out to Seaside Heights in my current wheels, a '53 Oldsmobile, the cancer of rust on the quarter panels, but it had a peppy transmission. I was walking along the broad, mile-long boardwalk, just passing Funtown Amusement Pier with its 225-foot Tower of Fear and its Loop Roller Coaster and Giantwheel, strolling toward the Beach Bar that juts out into the ocean on wood pilings and where I always (at least ever since I turned twenty-one three months before) ended my day at the beach with a dozen oysters and a cold, green bottle of Heineken. A lilting feminine voice penetrated my fixated intention by calling my name—first *and* last. My brain homed into the direction of that voice which I thought must be a mistake. But a radiant woman was, no mistake, standing over a spread-out bright orange beach towel on the white sand below, waving at me, smiling. She called my name again and gestured for me to join her on the sand.

First of all, I saw her two-piece—white ruffles under her gorgeous, breasts and like whipped cream in the crossroads atop her thighs. I registered the long, tan thighs, the trim belly, the tan arm and long fingers, waving like a metronome. I saw the smiling face between two cascades of long wavy blond hair. It was Sandy Guldbrand—which in old Nordic (I looked it up in my *Dictionary of 26 Languages*) means "golden fire." Sandy Golden-fire was standing on the orange towel on the white sand in all her blazing gorgeousness, waving at me and calling my name.

Though she'd been in my Romantic Poetry class last semester at C.C.N.Y., I never exchanged words with her, other than, "Hi, Sandy," tongue-tied by her flaming, golden beauty and the fact that she drove a red 1964 T-Bird convertible. I'd been asked by Professor Rachel Brownstein to read a paper on "La Belle Dame Sans Merci," so everybody in the class knew my name, and Sandy remarked in the hall, "Your paper was *really* good, Edward," and I said something like, "*Keats* was really good," and walked away from the woman of my dreams with the T-Bird convertible. She sat next to me the day after and asked to share my Norton—"Forgot mine." I said, "Sure," and uttered not word two.

Another chance, I thought, and *direct invitation,* as I jogged down the wooden stairs to the hot sand and the even hotter Sandy. To make things more incredible, as I walked toward her, she watched my approach and she said to me when I got within conversational distance, "Anyone ever tell you, you have sexy legs?"

"No, never." Before or since. But her smile brightened, and she looked at my legs and insisted, "Well, you *do!*"

I was thinking that a plunge in the cold, salty Atlantic might get a grip, so to speak, on my speechlessness, and I asked her, "Wanna swim?"

She did and tucked her hair into a white swim cap of rubber ruffles and took my hand—so confident was her beauty—in her dry, warm fingers as the two of us stepped toward the rolling water, wincing when her bare feet encountered the belt of broken shells until the chill foam lapped at our ankles, knees, thighs, bellies.

"Shall we dive?" she asked. "But keep holding my hand, 'kay?"

The two of us, fingers still intertwined, plunged into the next wave— the salty cold rush!—and bobbed up again, grinning furiously, braced by the brisk surf. Our hands had parted with the dive, and I looked into her green eyes, noting that her irises contained gold speckles. Beads of sparkling water dotted her tan cheeks and forehead and lips, her trim shoulders.

Sandy and I swam until we were starving. I invited her to an oyster bar where a Mexican man effortlessly opened a dozen Baltimores with the blade of an oyster knife, and we carried the platter with quartered lemons and tiny paper pots of vinegar and thinly diced raw onion and two cold bottles of Heineken to a table outside on the ocean.

She had never tasted an oyster before, picked one up and smelled it with the wrinkled nostrils of her perfect nose, red with sunburn. The shell to her lips, she spilled the oyster into her mouth.

Her words thickened with the shellfish on her tongue, she asked, "What do you do next?"

"Chew."

The moment, the memory of that moment, the picture of it imprinted on my mind, was immortal, *is* immortal in a similar manner that the couple in Keats' "Grecian Urn" is immortal, reaching for one another's hands, following one another, never touching, never completing the action so that it never quite begins and never ends.

We walked to her car in the dusk—her red T-Bird convertible with white roof—and she asked, "Want a ride home?"

"I have my car." A '53 Olds, with the rust eaten into the quarter panels and around the headlights. "Parked in the other lot." It was not. It was parked in the same lot. She wouldn't drive me home to my mother's home in Elmhurst, would not be in invited into my basement. And proceed to her own Douglaston mansion. I had never seen it, but it surely must have been a mansion, with white carpets and silver objects on the sleek clean lines of Scandinavian Modern, like the one house in Douglaston I'd been in.

She rooted in her beach bag for a white leather note pad with a slender, silver pen tucked into the leather loop on its side, and she jotted something. "This is my phone number. Call me, 'kay?"

I saw Sandy once more, a few years later, in O'Neal's Baloon. I had transferred from C.C.N.Y. and was attending night classes at Fordham Lincoln Center to be closer to my job on Columbus Circle. She told me that she was waiting for someone. Her fiancé. "He's a lawyer on Wall Street." I said I was sorry to hear that.

"You had your chance," she said coolly.

That was what I thought about as I listened to the nine or ten minutes in Carnegie Hall of Mulligan and Baker blowing the bebop of "It's Sandy at the Beach." It was serendipitous. That I should find that tune just when I was struggling with the decision on "true love" and my relocation.

As Mulligan blew frenetic, plaintive baritone up and down the scales, drove his sax forward in a hammering baroque barrage of notes and made room for Chet, whose energy was stranger and cooler. Mulligan and Baker finger-fucking heaven.

Astonishment gripped me, as dumb-founded as that day in class with Sandy Guldbrand or the moment at her T-Bird. "True Love"—like Bing Crosby sang it to Grace Kelly in *High Society*, and Grace Kelly harmonized. Despite all the lyrics about true love—a dream. The improvisations were truer, rousing up something genuine in my being. You had your chance.

I couldn't get a place at the bar on the break where journalist Doug Ramsey would report later that a shabby man offered Mulligan a drink, but another man beat him to it. Suddenly, the shabby man, who had been praising Mulligan as *the* master of the baritone, rose with anger and with obscenities proclaimed Mulligan a third-rate sax player. Mulligan said that was the last time he would refuse a drink from a fan.

I wrestled with my dream of Sandy and the reality of Ferney-Voltaire and Vibeke with all her moods and hissy fits and "frankness." I wrestled for four or five days with the idea of spending the rest of my life with Vibeke in Copenhagen or in Ferney-Voltaire. In the Chelsea; in O. Henry's Steak House; in Irish bars; in a Gentlemen's Club where a topless woman, wearing only a G-string, offered to sit at my table and to drink whatever I was having—I had a double Dewars—and she drank tea on the rocks; in diners for breakfast of two fried eggs and sausage and a large glass of cold milk for a pittance.

The day came, as fate always comes, for my flight from JFK, and I decided that the drift of circumstances was drifting.

When I got back to Ferney-Voltaire, I stepped in a cow pod on the Avenue du Jura on my first day back at the office and had to go back to the Bellevue. As I was cleaning the cow shit off my shoe, I made an executive decision to relocate, once again, to Copenhagen –"true love" was a delusion.

I phoned Vibeke and said, "I'm quitting and coming home to Denmark."

"Are you sure? That's fantastic!"

"I'm sure. But there's one more thing I'm sure about. There will be *no* waltz at our wedding."

"Okay."

But Sir Gregory had another idea.

"Let's see," he said. "Do you have another job to report to in Copenhagen?" Sir Gregory was a military doctor who called "reporting to" as showing up at the office.

I told him no.

"Well, there's nowhere for you to report to? You could commute every other week or fortnight from Copenhagen. Just until you get settled, and we find someone who can take your place. You know, it's not so easy to find someone who can write as well as you. And can type."

I was flattered (except for the typing), but stipulated my terms: "Commute every other fortnight."

He told me then it would have to be half salary.

"And half cost of living allowance? It's just as expensive to live in Copenhagen as in Geneva et environs."

"All right. Then you can go to the Hong Kong conference?"

The Hong Kong Conference in October was a plum, but I didn't make it out that way while we were negotiating. "And take my wife?"

"Your wife!"

"I'm getting married the end of December."

"Poor sod. Yes, it will be a benefit for the company for your wife to come with you for the social events."

This way I would have something with which to negotiate with Vibeke.

"Stay this month, until the end of the third week in December," Sir Gregory said, "and start 1975 clean."

"Until the end of the *first* week in December."

"The third week!"

"Okay."

"Be off with you, then, and get your work done."

I had heard him describe himself on the telephone, when he was meeting someone who had not seen him before, as "a big bloke with a big nose," and decided that he was vain. He was vain in negotiation, too. It was the aggrieved expression on Sir Gregory's face, the knitted eyebrows above the large nose, that signaled me that he had won the negotiation. He had got me down to half salary and half cost of living allowance. Until the end of the third week in December! That was a negotiating stance. He probably expected me to want to leave right away and considered himself lucky to get off with my leaving the end of the third week in December. And the third week in December and the office was closed for Xmas week.

But at least I had some remuneration while I looked for a job in Copenhagen. Let's see how the negotiation went with Vibeke.

I telephoned Vibeke from the office and told her what had transpired, and before I said to her that it would mean a trip to Hong Kong and likely a vacation in Tokyo, Kyoto, and Bangkok, too, she said, "Fuck. *You!*" and broke the connection. I called her back, and she didn't pick up.

I waited two days to phone her, and she was still edgy, but she had spoken with Red Susanne and Grethe, and they said it was clear that I was flattered that the company was willing to accommodate me. Who wouldn't be? It was only a matter of time before I was moving permanently and full-time to Denmark. Then I told her about the trip to Hong Kong and the vacation in Asia.

"Do you think you can buy me off with a trip to Hong Kong?"

"Who's talking about buying you off? It's a privilege."

"Some privilege!"

"I'll see you in five days," I said curtly and hung up.

I went out to Geneva that night and got drunk in the American bar and spoke to an au pair. She was a ballerina as a child and teenager and, at my suggestion, took me home to her tiny apartment to see her feet, which she had said were malformed. The toes were certainly interesting—clubbed and flat, like she could stand on the toe knuckles of both feet.

Irate with Vibeke, I took more than the ballerina's shoes off—with her consent—and felt a combination of pride and guilt afterward.

When I got home to Vibeke, she picked me up at the airport, and we were both contrite.

Mose, clean-shaven and neatly barbered, came as my best man for the wedding with a blond girl, Sally, from Oregon where they were living, for the nonce, as tree-cutters. We found them sitting on the stoop of our building, chatting with a prostitute. Sally was a tall, pretty girl, shapely, and they stayed with us for the first night in Vibeke's Vesterbro apartment. They slept on the double inflatable mattress in their sleeping bag—they shared *one* sleeping bag. I had received from a Planned Parenthood conference that I'd had to attend in Geneva two packs of multi-colored condoms. Vibeke was on the Pill, so I gave them to Mose, and he used them all the first night to put on "a fashion show" for Sally.

Next morning, Vibeke got up first and ducked back into the sleeping niche and told me my friends were naked, and she didn't like them sitting around naked. Thinking this was truly bourgeois of her, I went out in my ratty robe. They were sitting at our table, waiting for breakfast, quite naked. I thought they wanted to show off their bodies and their attitudes about their bodies. His was chiseled from all that wood-cutting and had a big schlong, and Sally's was shapely, big-breasted, flat-bellied, and she was a natural blond. As diplomatically as I could, I told them we were not so liberal as they and to get dressed, please.

Mose said he didn't have a suit for the wedding and was it okay to come in his woodsmen's clothes. I said it was perfectly all right, but I thought he would be more comfortable if he borrowed the tweed suit I had purchased in New York from me. He was about the same size as I—notwithstanding the penile size.

"Well, I won't wear a white shirt and tie!"

I said it was all right, but I thought he would be more comfortable if he borrowed a white shirt and tie from me. Trying not to eye Sally's breasts and Mose's manhood—which were *huge*!—I said, "Get dressed, please."

Vibeke quickly mobilized an apartment which was vacated from her neighbor in the next building, Franco—they were going to Poland where his wife came from. Vibeke went to her parents' house.

Apparently, it was not good luck to see the bride the night before the wedding, and I invited Mose and Sally to Galatea for dinner.

Amid the Tiki masks on the wall of Galethea Kroen, we ate Indonesian ristafel and drank schooners of draft. When Mose found out we were not planning on taking a honeymoon, he insisted. "You're only married once. If you don't object to us tagging along, we're going to Paris the day after the wedding. Let me make you a gift of a honeymoon in Paris. We'll be there for New Year's Eve! Haven't you always wanted to be in Paris for the turn of the year?"

Like a good hen-pecked husband, I said "I'll have to check with Vibeke."

I telephoned her in her parent's house from a booth in Galatea, expecting her to disagree, but she agreed enthusiastically, and Mose, in a burst of energy, literally ran over to the Central Station and got us tickets on the same train as theirs and was back in Galatea in time for the coffee and cognac. I was reminded of the time he had run after the purse-snatcher.

We married in the west side church of St. Absalon's, which years later was desacralized. The priest voted communist and didn't like me because I was American. Before the ceremony, he said, "The sun is indeed red in the east!" and "God Bless Eugene V. Debs!"

Mose wore my borrowed tweed suit and white shirt and tie and I called him "Old Chap" (he admitted, after the wedding, that he *was* more comfortable in those clothes). Vibeke at the altar whispered to me that she didn't have any panties on, and that seemed a good sign. It was only because the line of her panties showed through the white dress, but it still seemed a good sign.

The banquet was at an inn near her parent's house, and I clumsily danced the waltz with my new bride and mother-in-law. "You can't have a wedding without a waltz," Vibeke told me. There were speeches, too: Uncle Alfred, who was a lawyer and member of the city council, made a lengthy speech about the generations. Mose tapped his glass, stood up and, his chin tucked in, said, "We're not so long-winded where I come from," and everyone laughed, even Uncle Alfred. "Good luck and a long and happy life to Edward and Vibeke." Her father made a speech in Danish, which I could not understand, though Vibeke translated it in a whisper. I still couldn't understand. I felt called upon to make comments after the dessert, and I stood up and tapped one of my glasses with a spoon—not used to making speeches, and in quavering voice I composed two or three sentences in English about how I was honored to be welcomed into the family and about my beautiful bride. Aunt Anna, also a lawyer and wife of Uncle Alfred, congratulated me on my sincere words. I was waiting for a kicker because Vibeke had told me Aunt Anna always casted the bullets, but the kicker never came.

After the formal dinner, there was a catered party for the guests who had not come to the banquet, and a pretty Danish female poet, whom Vibeke's sister-in-law knew, wore livery and served. There was smoked salmon and roast beef and shrimp salad and pâté and salt beef and diced onions and vintage wine and bottled beer of every type and whiskey and a bucket of ice, and phonograph records played on her father's Bang and Olufsen and people danced. And there were presents: an antique wooden clock that chimed the hour and silverware from her parents and beer and schnapps glasses and butter boards made of marble and three kinds of plates, enough for six people. Mose and Sally brought three wide, splashy silk ties, one with an image of a naked woman that lit up in her erogenous zones, bought from a vintage second-hand shop.

Uncle Alfred asked Mose was he of Italian descent, and Mose said he was a Jew, and Alfred made a noise in his throat. True to his Hasidic roots, Mose danced with all the women, even my mother-in-law, who put her cigar in an ashtray for the length of the dance, then said, "I'm so coffee-thirsty!" and retrieved her cigar and relit it.

It was the best party I had ever been to. I encountered Vibeke's 18-year-old Norwegian cousin, Sanne, in the hall, who smiled at me and with whom I exchanged touches in an erotic interchange, although we weren't exchanging any erotic touches. Grethe was there too, whom William had dumped, telling everyone who would listen that Vibeke has stolen me "right out of her arms." I danced slow with Vibeke, and Mose declared to my father-in-law I was "a mensch." Vibeke's father said, "I know he is a mensch." I drank many bottles of beer. Meanwhile, Mose, who tongue-kissed the poetess in the hall, had his face scratched by Sally with her long nails. I saw Finn, who was Red Susanne's husband and had a hirsute face, grab two big handfuls of Vibeke's arse, and she punched him in the face—a real punch which made his nose bleed all over his black moustache and beard. He took out his handkerchief for his nose and looked a moment at her. "You're ridiculous!" he said.

After that, Vibeke's father called a fleet of taxis, one of which Mose and Sally and Vibeke and I shared—Mose in the front seat, blotting his handkerchief borrowed from me against his scratched cheek. He said, "That smoked salmon was out of a dream!"

In the back seat with us, Sally snapped, "That was not the only thing that was out of a dream: A nightmare!"

"She was worth it!" Mose declared.

The last thing I remembered were all the young guests, ranged along the stairway, all the way up to the front door of Vibeke's apartment—*our* apartment—and me, looking down at the expressions of the guests' expectant, erotic faces. Presumably, there was a lot of copulation that night.

In the morning there were morning gifts from my bride—an expensive robe to replace the ratty robe I had worn to tell Mose and Sally to get dressed, please. I gave her a gold watch I had bought in Geneva for three-hundred dollars. Morning gifts for the bride and groom had such a hopeful, fairy-tale ring to it.

Mose and Sally had made up, though Mose had two parallel scratch marks on his left cheek. "That poetess was valuable!" he said. I never knew what went on beneath Mose's surface, but he was obviously not spoiling the day. Sally apologized to Mose repeatedly.

What went on between couples? What had gone on between this couple? Had she acted out of a sense of their seriousness as a couple? Was she jealous? Was Mose taking their devotion lightly? Had he told her in bed that he was not taking it anymore? Or had Sally said she was not taking it anymore? Or was he simply not serious? Had he told her that? Once again? Or was he holding his cards close to his chest?

It occurred to me that I was asking these questions about me and Vibeke. But it was too late now. We were hooked. Was anything ever too late? The drift of circumstance had me in its tides. Was it drowning me? Had I not taken this wedding seriously? Unlike Mose, I was not sorting things into serious and unserious—if that was what he was doing.

I capped four bottles of beer for us and poured four schnapps glasses of Gammel Dansk, a strong black Danish liquor, and I said, "Skål!"

Our train to Paris was at three p.m. We arrived in the Central Station at two-thirty and in the station's supermarket purchased bread and a block of cheese and two six-packs of Faxe Fad—a draft beer in a curious bottle that was named "an Eva Gredal," shaped like the social-democratic Social Minister, bottom heavy. We boarded the train at the 2nd class section and took up an empty couchette cabin—the seats could slide to six sleeping beds and would be that evening by the conductor. Mose took it upon himself to round up all the young people in the car for the bridal party. There were a blond-headed German, a dark Italian, a grey-skinned Spaniard, an American couple, and a red-headed Brit, spilling out of the cabin into the corridor. They had liquor, too—beers and a bottle of whiskey and the American couple had a bottle of peppermint schnapps—and they all toasted us in their languages.

The German offered a long apology for the sins of his father's generation, which moved me, and I offered him an Eva Gredal.

"Oh, yes," he said, "Danish beer," tipping up the oddly-shaped bottle. "But the Cherman beer is the *best* in the *velt!*"

We drank the inferior Danish beer and ate the bread and block of cheese, carved into wedges by my Swiss Army knife. Toward night, Mose and I were out in the corridor, while our ladies slept on the couchettes. We were hanging out the opened windows, fortunately for me upwind of Mose. He drew his head in and confessed, "I vomited." He thought for a moment. "But it was clean vomit!" he said, with the earnestness that Mose alone was capable of.

By morning, we were pulling in to Gare du Nord, and we took the Metro to Saint Michel and walked from there, Mose shouldering their duffel bag and me carrying our one suitcase, along Bd. St. Germain to Les Deux Magots, where we collapsed into the café and ordered two *pichets* of *vin rouge*. I had never been to Paris before, but Mose had, on his Hippie Highway tour. He said that he would find a hotel. "Wait here."

Sally kept talking about finding "the poor people." We were sleepy, Vibeke from sleeping on the couchettes for a couple of hours and me and Mose from not sleeping at all. Mose was the only one who had energy. I was getting tired of Sally saying "the poor people." She must have said that phrase a half dozen times.

"I want to find where the *rich* people eat!" I said.

She asked, "Your parents-in-law aren't rich enough for you?" passive-aggressively.

I could see by her expression that we had become enemies at that moment—maybe for only a moment. She must have been sleepy, too—although she must have got a bad taste from my "rich" parents-in-law. Vibeke's father hadn't gone past eighth grade and her mother did not go further than her husband, but her brothers did—they had gone on to become a lawyer and an engineer, and the brothers were doing worse economically than Vibeke's father. Her grandmother had not believed in education for women, which endeared my mother-in-law to me, made me feel protective toward her. Her husband was natively intelligent, he had educated himself in history, art, architecture; she only parroted her husband's words in a blustery manner, and she could get out on thin ice.

Mose came back in twenty minutes. He had found a Vietnamese hotel for fifty francs a night. We had a corner room overlooking the Bd. Saint Germaine and the church with a sink and bidet behind a curtain and a common shower and toilet in the hall. Mose had cajoled the desk clerk into giving "the bridal suite" to the newlyweds. Mose had also picked up a bottle of champagnoise and dashed across to their room to get toothbrush glasses. We poured bubbly. Vibeke and Sally sat on the foot of the double bed. Mose and I on the windowsill. It was an angled, three-paned bay window, looking down on the Bd. and the church. We toasted our good fortune to have such rooms so cheap and toasted Mose for finding them.

After sleep, next morning, we congregated in Vibeke's and my room and made our decisions on what we wanted to do. Sally wanted to go to "the poor streets," and Vibeke wanted to go to find a restaurant for lunch, and I wanted to find a café for breakfast. "At least coffee." Mose wanted to wash his hands. He had just gone to the bathroom, and there was no sink in the W.C. He threw back the curtains and washed his hands in our sink and began drying them.

Vibeke exclaimed, "That's my towel!"

Noting that both towels were damp, he asked her, "Which part did you use to wipe your cunt."

More harshly than intended, I said, "Don't talk to my wife that way!" It had been many months since we'd seen one another.

He looked quizzically at me sand said mildly, "I never knew anyone who had a wife," and I felt bad. Drying his hand on his woodsman's jacket, he said, "Let's get some coffee and go see Sacre Coeur. That's a must see."

After *café au lait* and baguette and jam, we walked to the Saint Michel metro. In the station, Mose studied the lighted maps of the whole Metropolitan System, which had buttons that you pressed on either the first or last station and the train line lit up. It was ingenious.

Mose said, "Okay. I got it." Unfortunately, it was a complicated route. We had to change trains three times and got off at Abesses, not at Anvers. Rather than taking a fernicular up, we had to walk up a steep, mile-long hill to Place de Tetre—which was still a walk to Sacre Couer. I didn't mind. I liked walking, but Vibeke didn't.

Mose said, "I thought you'd like to see some of Paris."

"Fine with me," I said, but it was not fine with Vibeke, who looked like she was turning sour.

Once at Tetre, we strolled around the square. Sally grumbled that the artists and caricaturists were all phony and that this square was full of tourists. "I want to go to the poor streets," and after consulting, they went down the hill to Place St.-Pierre, while we stayed there. Alone, I had a caricature done of Vibeke by a guy with a beret in front of a giant pad on an easel. He drew the caricature with a magic marker. It took about two minutes and was unflattering. It was, well, phony, and I threw it in a trash barrel and continued up to Sacre Coue. Vibeke said that she didn't want to waste our time with Mose and Sally. "After all, we are on our honeymoon." I said that we wouldn't even *be* in Paris if Mose hadn't insisted we go on this honeymoon.

All at once, with a sense of dread, I decided I had made a mistake, marrying Vibeke. What was I thinking! The only solution was to divorce her immediately. But I had planned inadequately and didn't have anywhere to go. I could always go down to Ferney-Voltaire and admit I had made a mistake. Sir Gregory had said *Poor sod* about my getting married. I was indeed a poor sod. My brothers and sister knew it; they were constantly undoing the mistakes of a little brother—getting me apartments and cars and letting me stay in their apartments while I was infatuated with Signe. I was destitute, without a clue. I'd been normal— at one time. At sixteen, when I saw *Jazz on a Summer's Day*, and my future lay before me.

Go down to Ferney-Voltaire before it was too late and eat crow. At least in Ferney I had a place at the Bellevue and half-time employment. Maybe go back to New York City. Jackson Heights was more like it. And have the siblings treat me like a little brother. Maybe go to a completely third place—where I didn't have roots in the past. Some midwestern place. Or California. Some other place than San Diego or Stockton. Maybe take an M.F.A. I could go to Iowa's creative writing program. I had applied for Iowa in 1972 and been rejected for the writing sample I sent, but I could send another sample, the ones that made Hoagland say I would soon be published or the one that I had won the Goodman with. To Iowa, I had sent a new story, carved out of *The Stockton Split*. But I would not risk another rejection, another rejection I could not take. I could apply for another program—there were about a dozen programs now, and one would surely take me. Make application to a writing program from Ferney-Voltaire. Half-time employment was better than no job. Save up.

I had decided on Ferney and Iowa or another program while we were walking to the Sacre Coeur, she ahead of me. That was another thing I didn't like about her; she was so unfeminine to walk ahead of me instead of walking beside me and saying, "Let's go there," and waiting for me to walk beside her. Instead, she just set out all alone; when you were together you had to decide things in common. And she was always taking a restaurant place where she could see the waiter, and I had to turn around to see him, making me jerk my head and practically get up to signal the waiter. It was unreasonable—you could not explain these things; she simply cramped my style. I had tried once; when we were with Mose and Sally, I said "You're always taking the man's place!"

"The *man's* place?" Vibeke enquired.

"It's difficult to be a man," Mose said.

It was impossible to explain.

It suddenly occurred to me if I was rejected by Iowa or another program, what did that Latin poet—Horace?—say about we may cross the water but our soul comes with us.

Sacre Coeur was a holy place, I thought. We stood outside the church, each one alone in his thoughts, tired of bickering, each sick of it, looking from the steps to Place de Ste. Pierre, to the levels, descending like steps from the lip of the hill, all the way down in semi-circles. We turned and looked at the tall, white domed church to its lofty tower, walked into the church.

It occurred to me at that instant, as it had occurred to me sporadically, that I was mentally ill—autistic or a psychopath. What was I doing? Married? Thinking about getting divorced? Planning for my future? Which included running off. I grappled for some wisdom, and it occurred to me in the unlikely form of a quotation by Norman Mailer, something like, It's the things you can't get out of that…What? Make you a man? Make you insane? The things that you can´t get out of that… What?

I thought of something that Peg Flaherty in Stockton had said to me, "Must be nice when things get too hot to go to another place." What was she? Married to a transvestite. Sleeping with every man in the commune. Which was just a house! What did she know!

It was dark in the interior of the church, made me feel secure in the darkness. The church seemed composed of years of prayer, and I lit a candle for my father, thought he would like to have a candle lit for him in a French church. He had never made the journey to Europe.

Vibeke and I sat in a rear pew, each to one side of the center aisle, and I formulated the question in mind: *Why does she have to be this way?* The question was clearly composed of words, and an answer to the question entered my consciousness—in a deep, calm voice—*because you have to have patience to love.*

Agitation left me. I closed my eyes and opened them again, stepped from the wooden pew, genuflected, and it was as if I wasn't genuflecting to Jesus or God or Mary, but was genuflecting to the calm voice.

I crossed the aisle to her, sitting in the pew and whispered, "I'm sorry." I didn't know what I was apologizing for. I had spoken my thoughts, my decision which I had reversed.

It was unlike Vibeke to apologize, but she whispered clearly, "I'm sorry, too."

We walked out of the dark interior of the church. It was cold but sunny. We strolled down from the hill to the steps below and streets, going down in half-concentric circles. Midway down, we came to a café. A sign outside on which was printed *Les Deux Amis*, and we went in there.

At a back table, Mose and Sally were sitting—as if it were preordained.

"Amis!" Mose said.

We sat down and had a drink and made a plan. We divided our time, two couples together and the same two couples alone. In the mornings, we all four saw the sights—the Hôtel des Invalides and the Rodin Museum and the Louvre and Notre Dame, the Cimetière du Père Lachaise, the Maison de Victor Hugo on Place des Voges, a broad square, benches all around and winter trees in the sunlight, and the Contrescarpe. I thought of "The Drunken Boat" by Rimbaud as we ate lunch at le Maison de Verlaine.

We had a glass of wine in Café Flore, which Sartre and de Beauvoir frequented, Shakespeare and Company, and the Eiffel Tower, across the Seine from which Bernard Bertolucci made *Last Tango in Paris,* just two years before. Every morning we would sightsee., and around one o'clock, Mose and Sally would stop in a boulangerie and buy baguette and pastries and buy a piece of cheese or *pâté* and sit on a bench in the cold on the bank of the Seine—they didn't seem to feel the cold—when Vibeke and I went to the Brassière Lipp or *Le Zinc* or *Les Deux Magots* and ate an expansive lunch with wines. I thought of the C.C.N.Y days back in the '60s when Mose and I were still free. But then I longed to have a woman, to be attached. Now I was. And I had to get used to being attached, to thinking of another person.

New Year's Eve we spent on the Bd. Saint-Germaine, out on the street among the revelers and drank three bottles of bubbly, and I have one recollection of it: Mose against a brick wall, smiling superiorly as though he couldn't be bothered, and Sally pressing against him, frenzied, thumping him as though she couldn't understand his blasé attitude when she was angrily thumping him as Vibeke and I, in love, looked on. I thought I should develop the fiber of his bearing, but I never did.

On January 3rd, we treated them to a meal at the Gare du Nord, and I thanked Mose and Sally—though it was only Mose—for making us take a honeymoon, and we left them, Mose in his woodsmen's clothes and Sally with her hippie skirt and hat. We took the train for sixteen hours back to *Copenhague*, snuggling in the seat.

I Am the Eggman

QUICKLY I GOT USED to my every other fortnight in Ferney. It was the kind of life that appealed to me, traveling. Except that every time my trip approached, on the day before, Vibeke would remind me I had to go to the "Foreign Police," and it would lead to an argument at the crest of which, just as I had my bag packed, my suit and overcoat on, waiting for the taxi to take me to the airport, she would be cold and angry and tell me to fuck myself, and transfer her discontent to me. During the taxi ride to the airport, I worried that she was dissatisfied with the arrangement of my work life when it was the only way I could ease into Copenhagen. I got angry at her anger, her coldness, never once saying, *Take care of yourself*, or *I'll think of you*, or *I love you*. *Fuck yourself*, she said. Then, it occurred to me that she would miss me so much, it hurt her, that she was insecure of my feelings for her. However, I concluded that she was childish; she could have been more positive, she should have been more loving, she should have kissed me, wrapped her arms around me, she should have said that she would miss me.

It ended with my dread of calling her, her flash temper tantrums. She might start out on the telephone being tender, but then a chance word would leave her cold or cursing me. I kept looking for someone to justify me against her, someone to judge her, but there was no one but myself and I felt not up to it. I should have reasoned with myself, have justified myself, but I was weak and there was no way I could have managed it. She should have been concerned with, well, my feelings more. I was having difficulties in the NGO in Ferney. A secretary-translator in the French department named Dominique was having an affair with Sir Gregory, and she was an *intrigant*. Sir Gregory's wife, Lady Susan, was in London, preparing to come to France. Dominique was married too, but her husband was in New York, at the United Nations, but he was coming as soon as his contract was up. Sir Gregory and Dominique were planning a restructuring of the whole office; they liked me, considered me their ally and their "policy" man—the man who did the work—but it was uncomfortable.

Davide, a Chilean translator in the Spanish department, was also having an affair with the former Office Manager, Bernardo, also a Chilean, both of whom favored Pinochet. Bernardo was replaced by Dominique as Office Manager, and Bernardo became the Director of Special Projects, ostensibly a promotion, but which didn't have any staff, preparatory to—Dominique told me—special projects being phased out. Meanwhile, Miss Brown in New York was in the process of being fired. She was my ally and also Bernardo's ally, which was a conflict for me. How should I respond to Sir Gregory's (and Dominique's) firing of Miss Brown and Bernardo's being fired, and still maintain my sense of the moral edge. Whether I had the moral edge I didn't know; maybe I only had the moral edge because I had been uninvolved so far—maybe the moral edge was something that disappeared into myriad shades of grey when you got involved. For example, Bernardo was a good fellow, despite that he favored Pinochet's coup and that he was homosexual—homosexuality was at the least questionable then. No one had decided then that homosexuality was okay, and I was not sure it was okay.

I tried to discuss these things with Vibeke when I made my twice weekly phone calls to her—sometimes fewer, when we were on the outs—and our phone calls went something like this:

"I miss you, Vibeke."

"Do you? You chose your life."

I didn't miss her when she was being unruly. Rather, I missed her good side. I told her that this company was going downhill and everyone was secretly at each others' throats.

"You chose to be involved in that company. You can just come home to Copenhagen and start looking for a job. And register with the Foreign Police."

"Will you *listen*?"

"You listen: *Fuck you!*"

One morning in Copenhagen, late in January, when I was eating bread and cheese and coffee, the bell rang. Because I didn't know anybody in Copenhagen except her family and friends, Vibeke answered it. I heard the murmur of a male voice and then Vibeke's. She closed the door behind her and came into the apartment to fetch her purse from the kitchen.

"Who is it?"

"Henrik."

"Who?"

I asked while Vibeke hurried out with some papers. She shut the door again and came in and joined me at the breakfast table.

"Who was it?"

"Henrik. The Bulgarian who used to be my boyfriend."

"What'd *he* want?"

"To return my key."

"Did he have a key all along?"

"Yes. And I gave him the papers for the Moped."

"Did you *give* him the Moped?"

"I promised it to him."

It was none of my business. I couldn't ride it with her anyway. And two and a half years after the fact, I didn't have to fight the Bulgarian. I pictured myself squaring off in the hall with the Bulgarian. A feckless Bulgarian. It was grotesque. What did he look like anyway? I had never seen him.

However, when her father learned she had given the Moped to the Bulgarian, he bought her a car.

The car was a '66 VW bug without a radio, heater, or gas gauge. When it ran out of gas, you pulled a switch under the dashboard and you had three more quarts. It had the engine in the back and three on the floor, which meant I couldn't drive it. I was accustomed to automatic. Anyway, Vibeke was the better driver.

When Copenhagen turned to early summer, we had Vibeke's neighbor's birthday in Svendborg, and we were mobile, so we could accept the invitation. Franco and his Polish wife, Anni, were also going, and Vibeke offered to drive them. A car was still a big deal in Copenhagen. Franco was a commercial representative; he traveled periodically to Brussels, seat of the E.E.C. He had something to do with eggs—hen eggs. Behind his back, I called him "The Egg Man," always suffixed it with, "I am the egg man—kookcatchoo."

Svendborg was on the island of Funen, one of the three or so Danish islands and the peninsula of Jutland, which extends directly north from Germany. Denmark is an archipelago. There are literally ten thousand smaller islands, some seventy of which are populated—a number of them have only a population of a handful and are only an area of a fraction of a mile or miles, ranging up to a couple of million people and thousands of miles.

The reason I knew this was I once met a couple who used to every year take a vacation on a different Danish island.

This was before the bridge was built from Zealand to Funen, and you had to take a ferry across Storebælt—Great Belt—which is the largest and most important of the three Danish straits that connect the Baltic Sea, the Skagerrak, with the North Sea.

The Great Belt took about a half hour to cross by ferry, but the loading time of the train and cars and trucks doubled it. The best thing was to get your car loaded on fast because that would let it off fast. Bow and stern were interchangeable; the ferry didn't have to turn around.

Franco and Anni and Vibeke and I went to the ferry restaurant, and I sprang for some beers and *gammel dansk* for the four of us. We *skåled* and conversed, and Franco said that I was a *gode dreng* (a good boy) because I was the only American he knew who liked *gammel dansk*. "It tastes like cough syrup to most Americans." I was deciding whether to get offended by that "*gode dreng*" crack and whether I should call him "the Egg Man" to his face or if it was only a Danish expression that was innocent. I didn't have much time to get offended though, because we were piling back to the VW preparatory to the ferry docking in Funen.

Franco held back before getting into the bug, and when the women had taken their seats front and back, Franco said, "Get in the back, get familiar with Anni." I didn't see any way to refuse, though that "get familiar with Anni" seemed an odd way of expressing it. Or was that only the way an English second-language speaker termed it? I got into the back seat.

Franco looped his arm over the back of the seat and "familiarized"

Anni and me with one another. "Did you know Edward is a writer, Anni?" I noticed something about his mouth, that he had a repaired cleft lip—just a little—but it was quite distinguished.

"Haven't published," I said.

"Yet," Franco said.

"Yet," Anni repeated.

"Still," Vibeke put in from behind the steering wheel.

When we got to the farm, the host, Kim, showed us our *room*, because the Copenhagen couples would be sharing one. Kim was a Funian in Copenhagen for university, living on Istedgade. The room was small and sparsely furnished, with no beds.

"You have sleeping bags?" Kim asked.

The seating plan for the dinner tables was decided by every male guest putting one of his shoes in an enormous burlap sack, each of the women picking one; then, the woman had to identify the shoe which remained on the man's foot. There was a good deal of hilarity—girls scrunching down to examine men's shoes, then finding it—and taking advantage of the moment to look at the man's legs and "nobler" parts. I smiled and laughed, feigning hilarity, though this was not my idea of fun.

This took place outside. It was good that it wasn't raining. I had elevated heels, disco shoes of the sort worn in New York in the mid-seventies. The woman who picked my shoe from the sack made a face. She was a slender little thing with blond, brillo hair and a delicate, pretty face. She looked from man's to man's foot, and she found me, swept her eyes up to me and smiled. At least she didn't frown when she saw my face as she did when she saw my shoe.

There was a shortage of men, and when we took our seats in the hen house—the dinner was in a huge hen house (Franco must have felt right at home)—there were women in double layers beside me, the brillo blonde named Lisbet and a brunette equally slender in a voluptuous way and pretty-faced as Lisbet. Her name was Vivi, and both she and Lisbet spoke English. I felt like I had landed in a soft place, but Vibeke looked at me from a far seat at the next table, and her eyes and lips were narrow. Usually I didn't dance at parties and she'd reprimanded me a couple of times. "You dance the first dance with the lady on your right. Then you dance with the lady on your left. That's the way things are." The tables were of eight or ten people. There were maybe fifty or sixty dancers. There was anonymity in the crowd. I resolved to dance with each of my two table ladies.

A big plastic bucket of herring was passed around the table and dark rye bread in a big basket and a bucket of fat and several bottles of aquavit. The first course was followed by a large pot of some kind of stew, light on the meat and plenty of potatoes in a brown gravy.

The only thing that there was plenty of were wooden cases of beer bottles. But no openers. This was before twist-off caps and pop-top cans. The men—and some women, too—capped bottles with combs, lighters, keys. It seemed a thing a man was required to be able to do. Fortunately, both Lisbeth and Vivi knew how to do that, and as long as I hoisted three bottles of beer from the case, they opened them. It was room temperature, but I was getting used to warm beer.

The music precluded conversation, good rock with plenty of drums and bass and electric guitars played from an endless tape with myriad speakers. There were both Danish and English lyrics, but it didn't make any difference—the volume was so high that it all blurred together. The only thing you could hear was the tympani and the occasional guitar.

I danced with Lisbeth first, who was on my right, then Vivi, then Lisbeth joined us, and we danced without holding each other, like carefree monkeys. I improvised. Touching each other without touching each other. I moved my hands along the bodies of each of them, their legs, their hips, their breasts without touching them, improvising some moves from an imaginary disco dance. They seemed to like my moves and imitated them, they touched, each in turn, my body without touching. Disco had not found Denmark. Not that I knew how to dance disco. From the few moves I knew, I imagined, and it was provocative as hell. It was maybe more thrilling to *not* touch their bodies than to touch them; it was the *not* touching them, but coming *so* close to it and the erogenous zones that was enflaming. Lisbeth turned around and let me touch her ass without touching it. It was a formidable ass. Then Vivi turned round; it was an equally formidable ass.

I was parched and hoisted three bottles from a case and took them to Lisbeth and Vivi for them to be opened, and they implored me to keep dancing. I was a dancing fool. I couldn't make any false moves with the drum beat and the bassline.

Needing a mouthful of air, I went outside with my beer bottle. There were couples making out, standing up and lying down in the bushes, standing against walls and grinding. The Danish party made sense to me. It was where men and women found each other, found strangers, danced, kissed, fucked. I stood there, gazing at the shadowy figures in the darkening summer night. It was excellent. It was the life I always wanted.

Where was Vibeke? I wanted to find out, but suddenly she found me and said, venomously, "You're in good company!" As only Vibeke could say it. I crashed down from my high point, and she disappeared into the darkness. I sat on the stoop of the main house. Our room was on the second floor, at the top of a staircase. I looked around at the necking couples and the few groups of men and women. I saw a woman making out with another woman among men making out with women. I was drunk.

Lisbeth and Vivi appeared. "Come on and dance!" one or both of them said.

"I want to find my wife."

"That's your *wife!*" It was the tone in which that was flung out, the disparaging incredulity that told me this had gone on long enough. Lisbeth grabbed my hand, and Vivi grabbed the other. "Come in and dance," Lisbeth said, but I said, "I only want to find Vibeke."

Eventually, they gave up, found another dancing or necking partner. Idly I wondered how far they would go, but I had to find Vibeke now. I sat there for a long time, asking people who passed, "Have you seen Vibeke? Have you seen my wife?" I leaned back against a solid part of the stoop and drifted off. I didn't know how long I was asleep there, but I woke up to Vibeke's kiss. "Let's go up," she said.

"I'm sorry," I whispered. "But you always said I should dance."

"Yes. You danced. Let's go up now."

We went up the stoop and the staircase slowly, supporting each other, arms around one another. Through the door of the small room: Anni was asleep in the one sleeping bag. Franco wasn't anywhere, must have been down dancing. We took our clothes off in the dark. The sky was just lightening, so it was about 3:00 a.m., and we moved our sleeping bag as far away from Anni's as we could, beside the wall, got in. Vibeke enveloped me in her arms and legs and soon we were making love. I tried to fuck as quietly as I could, but we froze as Franco came in. He stood over us and I pretended to be asleep. The wood boards squeaked, and we could hear his steps moving across the floor. Then we heard him getting into the sleeping bag with Anni and begin to kiss her, and we resumed making love.

I had never balled with another couple balling beside me. It was piquant.

One thing happened as a result of Vibeke's objecting to my dancing at the party in Funen, she never objected to my dancing again. Certain conditions were requisite to my cutting the rug, but I never figured out what they were. I could not dance with Vibeke—she wanted to lead, and I could not dance with someone who insisted on leading. Besides, she danced in a strange way, all twisty and curly, and got fed up with my dancing.

I remember once we were in the bar at the Sheraton on the west side with a professional dancer. She was a friend of Vibeke's, a nurse who made her living as a dancer, and she didn't lead, but followed my moves at my approximation of the lindy, and she was smooth. She followed my spins like she had radar, and Vibeke just sat there, not dancing, but with a largesse on her face, like she was enjoying it. I got suspicious, thought, *What's this*? I thought she would have a delayed reaction afterward, but I was having too good a time, making like I could dance, her girlfriend following my every move like she had a second sense, and Vibeke even seemed amorous as a result of my dancing with her friend. It was not like her. Go figure.

Another time we were at a party at a high school friend of Vibeke's, and I kept dancing with one woman. She was there with her husband, but I got drunk and danced slow with this woman and positioned my fingers on her nipples. After the dance we separated, but as soon as a slow number came on, I was reaching for her hand, and positioned my fingers and manipulated her nipples. I don't remember what she looked like, only remember her stiff nipples. She had her glad rags on, and she was slender and short, and my fingers found her breasts every time we danced. At some point, I thought this must be what everyone does. Warm the old lady up for the old man. But I was having too much fun to contemplate what I was doing. I had an erection, and I pressed it into her. I was intoxicated by drink and her nipples and I didn't see what anyone else was doing: Her husband or Vibeke or the high school friend or the friend's husband. I was focused on this woman. I don't even remember her name, don't know if I knew her name then or what she did or if she had children, only that every slow number that came on—and by this time they were all slow numbers—I reached for her hand and when we got on the floor, I pulled her close and my fingers positioned, my erection found its place. Maybe that was the thing—our not knowing anything about one another that made us so free.

When she and her husband called a taxi, and her husband shook my hand, and the wife kissed me—she put her tongue in my mouth. Soon after, Vibeke and I phoned for a cab and we snuggled in the back seat. She said, "You were dancing with the wife of Niels." Not in an accusatory way.

"Everyone was dancing with everyone."

Everyone must have done that. I didn't tell her about Niel's wife's nipples or my erection.

Vibeke and I went to the conference in Hong Kong, and we also met a Danish couple on the Kowloon peninsula, who owned an apartment building in Copenhagen and a house in the provinces, where they lived. We visited them in Næstved—a town in western Zealand—to show our pictures of Hong Kong and Tokyo and Kyoto and Bangkok and to see the couple's photos from Hong Kong. The woman was an art dealer, the husband a GP, and they had a lot of paintings in their house, which I admired and thought that one day my walls would be like that, with many pictures.

They offered us a 3½-room apartment for 400 kroner a month in Copenhagen, one that an old person had died in, an eighty-something lady. We accepted it sight unseen.

The apartment was worse than it sounded. In a very old cheap building, built a hundred or more years before. It had a petroleum heater in the bedroom and living room which used ten liters of petroleum every day in winter—in each heater, which made me walk down the three flights to go to the corner shop to buy two ten-liter cans of petroleum, every day. The building was a fire trap, and you couldn't, legally, store more than two ten-liter cans of petroleum at a time. The apartment was dilapidated, too. It was in need of paint; the plaster was crumbling, and we found that the paint would peel off in sheets as soon as it dried. The bathroom was narrow and had a telephone shower and a floor drain, which were at the front of the room and had to be surrounded by a plastic curtain or it sprayed the walls.

But it was 3½ rooms, and you had to know the devil's grandmother to get an apartment in Copenhagen as cheap and large as that. It was on the island of Amager, but it was "first on Amager" close to Copenhagen, of which it was part, not in the slummy part or in the farmlands, just around the corner from the SAS Hotel and Casino and *Langebro*, the Long Bridge (which was short) that led to the center of Copenhagen.

The neighborhood was like Jackson Heights with its small shops—apart from the very old Danish buildings and green copper towers and cobblestone streets—with lots of shops on Amagerboulevarden. The first time I shopped I sensed a familiar feeling, but not too familiar, with exotic Tuborg and Carlsberg and Royal signs in tavern windows and "Erik the Red," the name of one serving house I frequented, and semi-basements, with twin short bannisters that were in the form of wrought-iron griffins leading down the three steps, where there were were lamp shops and dry-cleaning and laundry establishments, fruit and vegetable shops and bakeries and butchers and fish and cheese stores, with shops windows, slivers of which were below the pavement.

On my first tour of the quarter, I strolled home with two shopping bags, having bought fruit and vegetables and meat and cheese and beer, each from a different shop. I walked three double-flights up the stairway just as Vibeke opened the front door to our first apartment.

"I love this neighborhood!" I exclaimed. I looked at the uncomfortable expression on her face.

"Franco is here."

He was sitting at the table in the bay window. "Hey!" I said. "Where's Anni?" and pumped his hand. He was a tall, lean man with that repaired hare lip.

"Franco was just going," Vibeke said.

"Why go?" I said. "Have a beer. You're our first visitor."

He shrugged on his pea-jacket and shook my hand somewhat distractedly. Vibeke was already holding the doorknob of the front door.

"See you again?" Franco asked, looking at Vibeke.

Vibeke shut the door hurriedly. In his face.

"That was rather impolite of you."

She inhaled deeply. "There's something I have to tell. I hope you will listen to the end before you react."

She reminded me about the time she and I went to the birthday party on Funen. How could I forget? "That was the night I was dancing with the two girls that were my table-ladies because you were always complaining that I didn't dance at parties, and you got sour, you got poisonous and disappeared and I couldn't find you so I sat on the stoop outside the house while people danced and ran around the farmyard."

I sat there, feeling guilty, but not feeling guilty.

"Finally, you showed up, and we made love in the sleeping bag." I didn't mention that Franco and Anni were fucking at the same time or how it excited me. "Where were you all that time?" I asked her. "I never figured that out. You must have been gone for two or three hours."

"I was with Franco," she said. "I was drunk." She looked at my face again. "I'm laying all my cards on the table and hoping you will forgive me."

"What did he want when he came by now?"

"He's called me a couple of times since that night. Wanted to see me. I told him it was out of the question. He suggested you could sleep with his wife."

"Is that what you want?"

"Of course not! I don't think it's what she wants either. I hung up on him. I was so pissed off. And he just came over."

"Why did you let him in?"

"I was surprised. I knew you would be back soon. He tried to kiss me, but I wouldn't let him. I was so jealous. At that party. I'm hoping that telling you about this, that you can forgive me. I took the chance of telling you. I hoped we could wipe the slate clean."

I had never seen Vibeke like this. Her fingers were trembling. "Just let me absorb this first, okay?"

"When a person asks for forgiveness, it's *cheap* not to give it!"

I recognized her now, could hear that she was getting mad. Which she had no grounds to. I had no grounds to be righteous either, but this had all flooded in on me, and I had to absorb it. I could not help but think that when we fucked that night in the sleeping bag, Franco's hard-on had been there first. I wondered if he came in her. If she at least washed her pussy. Had I gone down on her that night? I thought that Franco and *his* wife were fucking in the same room as Vibeke and me, what was he thinking about as he fucked his wife and I fucked mine, that he had been there first that night, that I was getting sloppy seconds?

What right did I have? I thought of the ballerina au pair that I fucked in Geneva. That had been at least *before* we were married and someone in a foreign place. She had fucked our neighbor, somebody I *knew*!

What did it matter? Who fucked who? Maybe everyone was fucking everyone—at least when they got an opportunity. Maybe she had got it on with Franco more than once, on several different occasions, trysting on *poor, stupid Edward*. What did it matter? It hurt my pride. I shielded my eyes with my palm. "It's okay. I forgive you. I just need time to absorb this."

"Come to bed," she whispered. "Make love to me."

"Please, I need a little time. You go in. I'll be in. In a while. Let me smoke a cigarette and absorb this."

"Don't be like that," she said and stubbed out her cigarette. "Let's put this behind us. Forgive and forget. Don't be *cheap*."

"I can't make love to you right this minute. I need a little time. Please, just go in. I'll be in later."

"Fuck you," she said. Her feet were hard across the floor. The bedroom door slammed after her.

I smoked a cigarette. One thing I knew: Vibeke was my spiritual discipline. I had to tend her. Then it all came rushing in on me: The uncertainty I had entered this marriage with, the "bourgeois niceness" I had brought to this marriage and thought I could overcome, that bourgeois niceness was intrinsic to my being, and I was stuck with it. I couldn't understand myself. Maybe one day I would.

We had the first Sunday in Advent afternoon at her parent's house that year, and every year, looking down from the living-room coffee table to the setting sun over the bog. Her mother had baked Christmas cakes and cookies. VSOP cognac. Sitting around the table on two sofas were her mother and father, her Uncle Alfred and Aunt Anna, and her brother and sister-in-law and their new-born son.

We had Christmas Eve dinner at her parents in Brønshøj and First Christmas Day lunch at her brother and sister-in-law's in Slagslund, and Second Christmas Day turkey at our apartment, as my mother had always made it. We all danced around all three trees. Because we hadn't reserved a table for New Year's Eve, we accepted her parents' invitation to go to their house on the hill in Brønshøj. There was only them, but her mother had bought party hats and table bombs that exploded with small paper Danish flags. Her father had purchased two hefty, three-stage rockets which we set off at midnight in the empty wine bottles we had drunk with dinner. They wooshed up in the dark sky over the bog and exploded in colors of white, red, green, and yellow light.

The wait for the taxi home to Amager was two hours, but most families had rockets, and we watched them from the living room, exploding with colors over the bog in the vault of the sky.

Vibeke was growing more bourgeois, rather than my being influenced by her Bohemianism. I was still trying to write. That January we celebrated her medical oath in the ceremonial building of the university on a small closed, cobblestoned road. The mayor of Copenhagen presented, and the Dean of the medical school presided and led the graduates through the Hippocratic Oath.

I had sliced, smoked salmon and roast beef and ham and cheese and cakes and multitude of bottles of sparkly for a reception at our apartment. Uncle Alfred and Aunt Anne came and ate one sandwich, but didn't drink any champers. Vibeke's parents were down with the flu, and her sister-in-law stayed away to watch the baby (I think she was envious), but her brother came for a half hour. He had to get home to his sick baby. He didn't drink any sec either; he had to drive. No one else showed up, so I sprang for a cab to take Vibeke over to Brønshøj to see her parents sick in bed. I took a supply of finger sandwiches and two bottles of champers. Her parents were good sports; they sat up in bed and ate a sandwich and drank a glass of champagne. It was actually Cremant d'Alsace, which we had ten bottles of, but we would drink them within five days.

The next day, a fury folded into me that virtually no one came to her reception. For a medical degree! It seemed the first in a series of moments of sadness for Vibeke. She was an unhappy person, through no fault of her own—okay, it was because of her personality. Vibeke once evaluated her mother: "You don't know what an unintelligent mother can do to an intelligent child." Like her father, Vibeke was intelligent, but his strength had not taken in her. I was starting to realize that now. For all her bad traits, she was keenly intelligent and clear-minded and insecure.

As for me, the only thing that saved me was my desire, my *need* to write, my "spiritual discipline," both for writing and Vibeke. And I wasn't getting anywhere with those.

Lipstick on Your Collar (Told a Tale on You)

VIBEKE WAS OFFERED HER INTERNSHIP shortly after that in Hillerød County Hospital with a five-room apartment on the grounds. The job I was offered in Copenhagen began on the 1st of April 1976. I only had two months in Ferney, and it was two months of bizarre happenings. Dominique's British husband claimed it was a Basque word, bizarre, with "zarre" meaning beard and the Basque men all let their beards grow, and the prefix "bi" meant without; thus, "bizarre" meant without beards and it was truly a bizarre sight when the Basque men were exposed to beardless men. I never figured out whether Dominique's husband was serious or not.

He had moved there by then, with a job in the UN in Geneva. I think he was with MI5. He discovered that the typewriters used in our office were IBM Selectrics with a one-time carbon-ribbon cartridge. Everybody but Sir Gregory did their own typing. Dominique's husband had merely to spool them out and read them. Only later, I learned that the fifth season of *Columbo* included an episode called "Now You See Him" with Jack Cassidy, produced in 1975; Columbo solved the murder with a similar feat of deduction regarding an IBM selectric typewriter with its carbon ribbon. I don't know if MI5 learned that from Columbo or vice versa.

Dominique's husband made up transcripts which revealed that Davide and Bernardo, the former Office Manager who was in charge of Special Projects without portfolio and without staff, were into water sports. The typewriter ribbon was more useful with Miss Brown who was plotting with the Secretary General and various officers of various member-association countries. There were a number of plots to launch an insurrection against Sir Gregory and Dominique.

I spoke with Dominique on the telephone a couple of times after that, but I could never ascertain whether the one side or the other was victorious. The office imploded with infighting, and a new president and secretary general were hired, so that was a moot point. I stopped returning Dominique's calls.

I finally registered with the Foreign Police in Denmark the same month. Contrary to my expectation, the Foreign Police were a bunch of smiling women whom I had to go see every six months—all except for the last time in April 1979, when a police captain in uniform appeared and took my American passport and stamped it with a permanent visa. It had been stipulated that my wife was to accompany me, and this police captain with craggy unsmiling face handed my passport back to Vibeke and said, "Your husband should be good to you because you can get him kicked out of Denmark at anytime."

Meanwhile, Vibeke and I took a five-week vacation in the States, flying into Las Vegas and driving through the southwest and Los Angeles and up the coastal highway to San Francisco. We were supposedly having our last long, distant trip before having a child.

Four years into marriage, I was still not convinced we were suited to each other. Would the bickering and her sarcasm never cease? If a child were embodied, wouldn't that preclude—or set serious hindrances to—our parting? On the other hand, a child could be just what we needed.

She was constantly hitting on my weak points that I didn't even know I had. For example, she came up behind me more than one time when I was naked and said, "A woman would be proud to have that ass," or "You know your prick is little, don't you?"

I exclaimed, "It's normal size. I measured it once. Erect, it's six inches. That's within the normal range. Henry Miller had a six-inch cock."

"It's still small. Compared to the cocks I've seen."

"Are you sure your vagina isn't abnormally large and isn't filled by a normal hard-on?"

She got hurt. I was nonplussed by her face, stricken and hurt as it was. I felt equally hurt at her hurt. I was not made for these repartees. I went around feeling guilty that she had an abnormally big pussy.

One time, as I was sitting in an armchair, she said, "Actually, you look taller—normal height—sitting down. It's just your legs that are short. And your arms. Are you certain you're not a dwarf?"

I grew immune to these slights about my body, didn't even know that they were accurate or not, but I didn't forget. They were a second "spiritual discipline" for me. At times, they would surface in my memory unexpectedly and hurt me, and I wanted to hit her with a retort, but it was no use.

I would remember when I came home from a trip to Ferney that she was doused in cheap perfume—whether that excited her or she thought it would excite me; so much did she want to create babies—or she wanted to be erotic. But they were one in the same thing, weren't they? That cheap perfume made me sad on her behalf. I was not made for this mutual cutting down of one another. I didn't have the brutality to participate in the game. I would never get over my "bourgeois, post-Catholic niceness." A couple was meant to shore each other up, to support one another, weren't they?

However, on our trip to the U.S., Vibeke and I got along perfectly. More than got along. We were in love. We swam in the Colorado River at Blythe and drove across the Mojave or swam in Lake Meade, or sat at sunset over the rim of the Grand Canyon, drinking our after-dinner cognac, feet dangling, holding hands and seeing the sunset reddening the incredible, beautiful buttes and mesas and plateaus and mountains down below as far as we could see, before retiring to our room and making love. She had stopped taking the pill then.

We had two children, nine months and two years later, a son and a daughter. We had peace, serenity, and a sense of sacredness when Vibeke was pregnant. She depended on me, and I took good care of her—as far as I could. I recall the summer midnight that Vibeke delivered our son. I was allowed to be in the delivery room with Vibeke, and I froze, aghast at the blood and the top of the baby's head appearing between my wife's thighs, appearing through a wall of flesh with a slit in it, expanding. The midwife said pointedly to Vibeke, "Perhaps your husband can wet a towel and put it on your forehead."

Astonished, awed, cowed, I did that.

179

Our son: red sparse hair, open blue eyes struck with wonder and fright at the world. The nurse rolled my wife's bed out in the corridor to allow us a half hour with the baby, and she gave us each a bottle of beer, which was most delicious. It was about 3:00 a.m., the morning was lightening and the birds twittering and squawking, and all of my doubt was stilled in those wondrous blue eyes.

Eighteen months later, our daughter made her appearance. She took longer, sixteen hours, and my wife had to be clipped with what looked like poultry scissors—I only heard the sound of the cut, and I cringed and turned my eyes away. (She told me afterward that there was so much pain that she didn't feel that particular thing, the cut.)

Our daughter came out of my wife's body, her belly, screaming, with a mess of wet, shiny auburn hair and brown eyes like Vibeke's. I recall walking back to our apartment, on the hospital grounds. It was a freezing February night, and the moon was full in the clear, cold night and so bright that it hurt my eyes to look at it. I always thought of the bright full moon on a clear, black winter night as my daughter's moon.

A month after our daughter was born, we bought a house in Hellerup, just fifteen minutes by bus or car north of central Copenhagen—a beautiful house on a quarter acre of land. My father-in-law found it for us. I remember one of the first things I did was count trees. I owned seventeen trees, among others a pear and a magnolia tree. We bought it in March and watched as the garden came up like a timed fuse: first the silver snowdrops and winter aconite and the crocus, then the tulips and the lilies, then the yellow explosions of the forsythia bushes and the lilac and blue and purple flowers of the magnolia tree in the center of the lawn. The level grass, which I kept trimmed tight and dense as a golf course, and the pear blossoms growing into fruit which my mother-in-law cut up and put in jars for us, down in the basement. Then the rose hedges—red and white and yellow all along the driveway, perhaps fifty or sixty meters of them, and the wild strawberries, just tiny things, scattered over the narrow side of the garden—Fragraria Vej, the street was called, Strawberry Way, for the genus of berries. The small yellow plums grew on the bush at the front of garden by the street (excellent for plum jam), and the dustball mushrooms which appeared in late September grew big as soccer balls, but they were better small as softballs, ready for cutting into small strips and frying in cream sauce, served on toast with a glass of chilled Riesling.

First, Vibeke's father mobilized our construction crew of painters, electricians, plumbers, and masons to ready the house for us. They owed him favors, and for the favors he wasn't owed, I paid cash—fourteen thousand to drop the ceilings, seven thousand to finish the exterior walls, ten thousand to repair the roof. I might have been more grateful for the favors that the father was owed, but when I came home from the office one evening he presented me with a paint brush and a can of white paint. The flagpole on the front lawn was down and ready for paint. He said, "You don't have time to sit on your ass and write. You're a home-owner now."

The price of the house was a way of life, where I didn't have time to write.

The wallpaper, the ceilings, where I had to break off many meters of plaster ornamental border, was dropped three feet. "It will save on your heating." The electrical fixtures were changed to plastic from wood without consulting us. I came home from the office one evening to find the whole wall of rose hedges on the left side of the house had been felled by Vibeke and her mother. Vibeke said that the garden was hers to do with what she wanted. "You have no sense of a garden!"

"But I liked those roses."

Just then, her father recruited me to lift the planks out of our basement. We lifted the planks out the basement window and brought them onto a flat-back truck and he said, with irritation, "The quicker we go, the quicker we get finished." He said that he could use the lumber. "You can't use it. You're not handy." I wasn't handy, but I wanted a say in what happened to my lumber. I had stood for the painting and raising of the flagpole and the wall of roses and the lifting of the lumber out of my basement. What would happen next?

Vibeke's parents would let themselves into our house, and I didn't like that. I told them that there was a custom in the U.S. where the visitors call first and organize a date on which one is to come over. The parents complained to Vibeke. "Your husband doesn't like us." She relayed the message to me. Through Vibeke, I said that it wasn't that I don't like them; it was only that they should get in the habit of using the telephone. I knew there was a price for everything her father and mother were doing for us in the house.

The momentousness of these events—the birth of our children, the purchase of our first house, despite the rancor with the parents—extended for months, years, but in a couple of years, my wife and I were bickering. I wasn't equipped for a life of constant skirmishes, to adapt to Vibeke's manner of quiet, cutting, sarcastic wit. In fact, I held my manner closer to me, didn't engage in argument with Vibeke. Maybe this was cowardly of me, but it represented my "dealing" with her.

When Vibeke launched into a hot argument or cold sarcasm, I learned to quickly slide a cassette into my Walkman—and, later, a CD into my Discman—and my mood was transformed to sublimity by the improvisations of Bird, Diz, Jeru, Mulligan, Trane, Baker, Webster that amplified, or softened or made ironic or wistful with the lyrics of Lady Day, Dinah Washington, Nina Simone, and the scat of Anita O'Day, Ella Fitz, et alia.

I kept writing. A tree looks dead in winter, but it's not. It's mustering the power to bloom in spring: First the little, almost invisible germinations, the shoots, then the buds, then slowly, the fruit. But when a tree is dead, it's black, and green shoots don't appear. It's black and slowly the sap running through it dries up underneath the black, dead surface. You do not know if it will bloom or not.

The irony was that some years later, I was in Saveda airport in Brussels, the capital of the European Union, in the SAS lounge, drinking champagne and eating canapés with a woman with whom I had been appointed as expert in the Danish non-governmental sector and was in Brussels two times a week for long days, from early morning to late evening. The champagne was the perfect reward for our labors: as Churchill said, champagne must be dry, it must be chill, and it must be free. In addition to the free champagne, there was a non-taxable per diem, with a part of which I would buy on the plane, a half liter of VSOP cognac and a half liter of Jack Daniels and a carton of Prince for Vibeke. (I had quit smoking when my son was born in 1979, confirmed by my daughter in '81, because I didn't want to be a bad influence on my children. I started with cigars again in 1996 when I learned my 17-year-old son and 15-year-old daughter smoked a pack of cigarettes per day and couldn't be bribed into quitting.)

The woman was Annemarie, the chairperson of our non-governmental expert group; I was a member, for ethical issues, having been involved, on loan, from the Rehabilitation Center for Torture Victims. She lived in Århus, in Jutland, and was taking a plane an hour before mine. Under the influence of the champagne, she hugged me in parting and lay her face against my breast—ours was a platonic relationship. When her boarding was called, she took both of my hands with a promising gesture—which promised nothing, it was just the champagne.

On her departure, a vaguely familiar man—perhaps he was familiar because I had seen him in the building of the European Commission—signaled me and took the tip of his collar with two fingers, with a knowing smile. I understood the gesture. He was signaling me that a lipstick smudge was on my white collar. With a nod, I thanked him, my vaguely familiar benefactor. I had packed a shirt folded into my carry-on and went into the men's room to change into it. Who knew what Vibeke would conclude, or exact retribution for, on the evidence of that innocent smudge of lipstick on my collar. I threw the damning shirt into the trash, lest it would turn up in the laundry, though I did the laundry, but I wasn't taking any chances.

My benefactor was gone by the time I returned. There was still time for another glass of champagne, which I drank, and thought about the fact that men stick together.

It was only on the plane tha it became clear to me, the repaired hare lip was distinguished: It was The Egg Man, Franco. *I am the egg man. Kookoocatchuta.*

PART THREE

Night in Tunisia

IN *LETTERS TO A YOUNG POET*, Rilke says that you have to look deep into your inner solitude to ask yourself if you can live without writing. If the answer is no, then you ought not attempt it at all.

By 1981, twenty years after I had decided all I wanted to do with my life was to write and to read fiction, I still hadn't published anything. It had been ten years since my satori about the moment of creation, and I still dedicated nearly all my free time to writing fiction. I had written about thirty stories and been collecting encouraging letters from editors—from some significant ones, still rejections, and six novels: the one for the Goodman (for a grant)—which only existed as a twenty-page chapter about the death of my father, a literary novel titled *The Stockton Split*, a novel about my life with Signe, called *Foreign Affairs*, a novel about my life with my wife (parlaying the treacherous "whole truth," let me deal with that if I get it published), a spy novel about the EEC, a detective novel, and a rock and roll novel, the latter three I didn't submit. Just wrote them to see if I could. I probably would have written a dirty book to save for special horny occasions, but I would get myself so excited in writing it that I would masturbate and lose interest in it.

I had written some songs that were recorded by Hammer, but the group broke up after the album. It was hailed as a critical success, but was a commercial flop. I had a contract for song writing from Bill Graham from whom, after I signed it, I never heard again. He didn't sign it.

My agent hadn't sold anything for me, not because he was a bad agent. I was a bad writer. No, I was not bad, I was just not good enough to get published. I had fired my agent, and I wanted to try it on my own, to try writing what I wanted. Publication was my measure. Notwith-

187

standing Whitman, who had published his own first book and even-tually revolutionized poetry, I was determined not to turn to a vanity press. Publish or perish. A cliché. But I was perishing. I could not face not getting published. I could not tolerate life as a "genius," not getting published. I was a bad writer, just a notch under getting published, and *almost* doesn't count, except in horseshoes.

When Vibeke and I had our first child, I rose at five a.m. most morn-ings, put on a pot of coffee, and drank it and wrote until my son cried or my wife got up. We were living in Hillerød then, in a five-room apart-ment that was given to my wife, a doctor, on the hospital grounds. It was a 34-minute commuter train ride from my job. I wrote on the train.

Then, we bought the house in the fashionable north Copenhagen, in Hellerup, after my daughter was born and had a relatively happy time, except that I was not publishing. Anything, but my lead articles in the NGO newsletter I wrote for my company and the occasional press re-lease which would find itself verbatim in some journal or other under another man's byline.

The celebration of my thirty-seventh birthday in March 1981, the month after our daughter was born, corresponded with my twenty-year jubilee of not getting published, the ten-year anniversary of my satori. We had just bought a house and were in debt. I felt like a failure. I had made a mess of my life. I decided to quit writing fiction. I had a decent job, which I concluded I'd better take seriously

Addicted to reading *Politiken Sunday*'s personal ads (this was before the personal computer had taken over this function) which combined sex ads—for "house friends," for lonely people and perverts—and ads for commercial and travel ventures, ads for just about anything. When Vibeke saw me turning to the back pages over Sunday breakfast, a spread of morning "French" bread, cheese, jam, and coffee in our sunny dining room, she usually said, "Any good offers?" I always forgot that she asked that question, and it always came as a surprise, with no prepared answer.

However, one Sunday, I saw an announcement from someone who wanted to buy English books, especially paperbacks, and I decided if I could not write publishable fiction, I would not *read* fiction. I possessed several hundred novels and collections and anthologies of short stories. Not the poetry; I intended to continue to read poetry—it took less effort anyway; you could just read *one* poem. I opted for the sonnets and shorter poems—except T. S. Eliot and for Patrick Kavanagh's "The Great Hunger," which was a twenty-page poem (it was *not* about the potato famine).

Vibeke applauded my decision, although she was an avid reader—both in Danish and English. Finishing a book was tantamount to her to disposing of it, and she had read all my books, but the poetry. I loved to read aloud T. S. Eliot, but she wouldn't let me read "Four Quartets" or "Prufrock" or "The Hollow Men" to her.

"It's like you're trying to *teach* me something!"

"Well, hell, the worst thing we could do is try to teach one another something."

She admitted I was right but still didn't let me read Eliot to her.

Until she apparently had a "secret" lover (I had a couple of secret lovers over the years, too), who was an Eliot addict, and she commandeered my book of Eliot's *Collected Poems* and wanted to read his poetry to me. In my thoughts, I referred to her apparent lover, whoever he was, as the "Village Eliot."

I called the telephone number in the *Politiken* ad, and the book buyer turned out to be American, and I arranged to meet him. He was a bearded man with thinning hair named David Grubb; during the Vietnam era he had disappeared in Europe and wound up running a second-hand bookshop in Amsterdam, and now was opening an antiquarian bookshop in Copenhagen.

David methodically looked through my shelves.

"Just the fiction. Not the poetry."

"I think you should keep your poetry," he said sympathetically. He put all the books he wanted on our two-meter dining table—all four or five hundred of them. After he was finished, the shelves were mostly empty in the broad, tall, beech bookcase that was the centerpiece of our living room in which I kept my fiction, and at the top of which we kept our antique chiming clock, a wedding gift from Vibeke's parents. We had the bookcase with the money we had been given from various wedding guests. Vibeke had been longing for those shelves to be freed up, at least partially, to display knick-knacks.

I thought David would offer me four or five hundred kroner, but he thought for many moments, examining the titles again, and asked, "Would you take four thousand kroner?"

To keep the startled expression off my face, I frowned and said, "Yes, okay." That would provide the bulk of our summer vacation to Malta. The only thing he had remaining was to call his partner to come with the car. His partner was a woman, a weaver, Bodil Bødker-Næss, and we invited them to stay for dinner and became friends.

David was from Indiana, until recently a resident in Amsterdam, working as an antiquarian, and he'd met Bodil at an art show in Amsterdam where she was exhibiting her weavery.

They promised us an invitation to the opening of the shop. We received it in the mail not quite three months later. It was on Skindergade in central Copenhagen, christened The Booktrader, a semi-basement, just three steps down from the street, around the corner from Gray Friars' Square. The shop was divided in two, with two front show windows for the books and one display window, just on the other side of the door and the three steps leading down to the shop, for Bodil's weavery.

David and Bodil had done a good job, painted it all white with shelves all around, a loom on the right side, and on the left a central conversation pit with easy chairs and a sofa. We spotted renowned, even famous, Danish writers and a poet and a singer and an artist, and I surmised that many of the other guests were prominent, too. David provided wine—red and white—and beer in plastic glasses and salty snacks.

I surveyed the shelves. There were many titles I recognized as my former property. Penciled on the flyleaves were figures fifteen or twenty times what he'd paid me. So, my assessment of the value of used English paperbacks in Denmark was a gross underestimation. I spied a copy of a thick soft-cover book of criticism, a "quality paperback" by William Grace, a professor I had for Milton at Fordham Lincoln Center. Feeling I should buy something, I brought it to the register: 150 kroner. That was more than I'd paid for it new, for Grace's course. I decided I needed it because of Milton's stand on divorce. More than three centuries before, he held that people united in matrimony had to be fit conversing mates, engaging in "the apt and cheerful conversations to comfort them against the evils of solitary life, lest they endanger their souls." Milton even went to prison for it. I felt that my mate wasn't a cheerful conversant.

After our July Maltese vacation, we had a barbecue in our front garden. My father-in-law and I had a few too many aquavites, and we started kicking around a soccer ball—everybody but Americans call it a "football"—and just as we were getting into it, I felt an excruciating pain in my leg which persisted. My leg would not support me. I took a cab to the emergency room. The doctor there x-rayed my leg and diagnosed it as a torn muscle in my calf. I had the choice of an operation or a cast. I decided on the cast, but not before the doctor informed me I could not walk on it for three weeks. He gave me a crutch. "Only for what's necessary," he warned. "Next time you want to play football with your father-in-law, be sure you're in shape."

I stayed home for what stretched before me as three boring weeks. I read poetry and watched the paltry daytime offerings on Danish TV, but I've always felt guilty watching daytime TV and turned it off. I listened to a cassette of Charlie Parker: "Koko" and "Billie's Bounce" and "Now's the Time" and "Chasin' the Bird." I had just read the long poem by Dan Turèll, "Charlie Parker on Istedgade," and wanted to be familiar with the Bird tunes mentioned by Turèll in his poem. I also listened to "A Night in Tunisia" by Dizzy Gillespie, which had Bird playing alto on it.

I was enraptured by that one and heard it about ten times, reading the liner notes, listened to Bird and Diz and the piano and the mysterious bass line and chorus and got so excited that I switched off the cassette player and hobbled on my crutch out our long driveway to the street. The driveway extended the whole length of the house the front garden and lawn with tall rose hedges separating our drive from the walkway of the neighbor (you will remember that the opposite wall of rose hedges was felled by my wife and mother-in-law). I would later learn that the neighbor was the daughter of the translator who had rendered Joyce's *Ulysses* into Danish—and the translator himself, a military officer, a major, lived across the street and three houses down, but I never met him or his daughter either.

It was a residential street, single-family houses with hedged-in front gardens with tall hedges. The people on the street and in the neighborhood wanted privacy. Not a bar, café, or restaurant on it. Not even a grocery store or supermarket. An empty street with the stillness and lifelessness that a suburban street emanates.

A tall, elderly gentleman turned the corner and passed on the opposite side of the street. He had a military bearing. Taking his morning constitutional. I raised my crutch in salute, and he said, "Good day," whereupon he stopped and squinted at me, then crossed the street to apologize for greeting me. He said that he thought I was someone else, but now he could see that I was rather smaller than the person he thought I was. I said there was no need to apologize because my wife and children and I had moved here a few months ago and were still saying hello to the neighbors. He had thin, purple lips and white, plastic teeth and broken veins on his narrow, long, ruddy face and said that he lived across the street just two houses down, and was a retired general. "Course, when you're a general you don't retire, you just fade away, as Ike said." He began to hum "Old Soldiers Never Die (They Just Fade Away)." He had bright blue eyes shot through with red capillaries in the whites and smiled with his plastic teeth.

So starved was I for conversation that I said something or other to keep the talk going, and he recognized my American accent and began to tell me about his experiences in the U.S. He said the day was quite hot and reminded him of one time back in the early '50s in Nevada at a bomb test site out in the desert. He and a lot of military officers, generals mostly, from various NATO lands had been invited to witness the detonation of a hydrogen bomb. They stood out on the desert at two in the morning and the temperature was almost down to freezing, but the second that flash and mushroom showed, the temperature climbed right up to over a hundred. "Terribly uncomfortable it was. All of us in our protective clothing and helmets and goggles and unable to strip down for fear of contamination. But at least the heat was dry. No humidity to speak of." The general said he couldn't stand the humidity. Bothered his sinuses.

Fascinated, I listened for perhaps half an hour. Then he told me had to be going, for it was his seventy-fifth birthday, and he wouldn't want to be late for lunch or the Queen's Guards. "Meals on wheels, you know. Another American invention. Or was it originated in the U.K.? Or Australia? Well, good day."

"Happy half-round birthday," I said.

"Why, *thank* you!"

I stumped back to the house and sat at the front window and began writing a story. I know, I quit writing fiction, but the voice of that general, if that's what he was, senile as he half was, had opened a door in my consciousness. The title was "The Sins of Generals"—the title had revealed itself to me, too—and I *knew* before I had handwritten five pages that it was going to be the first story I published. I didn't know where, but I *knew* it would see print. The voices of Robert Coover, Donald Barthelme, John Hawkes, John Cheever, John Updike, Albert Camus, Bernard Malamud, Phillip Roth, and Kurt Vonnegut, of every writer I'd read and studied, were saying to me, You are *there. Trust.*

As I was hand-writing, four horsemen were clopping past on the road, wearing red jackets with gold buttons and shoulder braids and military hats, blowing their long brass horns regally and melodiously. The general was really a general—the highest general in the Danish Army, it turned out—and he had stated a fact: that the Queen's horsemen were saluting him for his seventy-fifth birthday.

From the jazz cassettes and albums scattered around, I remembered I had been listening to Charlie Parker, and reeled the tape back and played "Night in Tunisia." Written by Dizzy Gillespie in 1942, he called it "Interlude" and recorded it under that title, but Diz had said, "Some fool at one point called it 'Night in Tunisia,'" and it was covered and recorded so many times that there was nothing to do, so Diz started calling it that. The cassette I had was a recording from Carnegie Hall in September 1947. Charlie Parker was on alto sax, Diz himself on trumpet, John Lewis on piano, Al McKibbon on bass, and Joe Harris on drums. The liner notes reported that Diz composed it, but gave Frank Paparelli, a pianist, credit for some unrelated work; Paparelli hadn't written a note, just collected royalties.

I played the track repeatedly, liked the title "Night in Tunisia" far better than "Interlude" because the name had some mystery to it—of the night and the name of a foreign country in the darkest continent that you didn't know quite where it was on the map and that smacked of turbans and kaftans and tea and hashish and lunettes. The music imparted this mystery in its beginning base line and its improvisation and harmony of alto and trumpet in the chorus. It enraptured me, and I had met the general. The music, combined with the slightly surreal voice of the general, revealed the story to me. If I just followed the path that my words were leading.

I was finished with "The Sins of Generals" five days before I had the

193

cast off my leg. I used to play "Night in Tunisia" as the kids were picked up by our au pair for the nursery and school and Vibeke left for the hospital. She was through her internship and residency now and had begun her specialty, pathology.

The music got me into the sense of mystery. When I completed and typed "The Sins of Generals," I sent it off to *The New Yorker*, an editor of which had handwritten, "Brilliantly funny!" on their form rejection. *New American Review* had ceased publication, so I sent it to Martin Tucker, editor of *Confrontation*, whose short stories I admired. In December '81, it was accepted and took two years to appear in print.

However, I had found the place from which the stories came; it didn't get easier, but at least I knew the way. I wrote six stories in the time I was awaiting "The Sins" to be published—some better than others—but they all saw print: in *North American Review, Alembic, Central Park, Crosscurrents, Writers' Forum* (alas, the last two now defunct), and "The Sins of Generals," when it appeared, was selected by Andre Dubus for an anthology he was editing.

I had a new agent, a foxy woman. She telephoned one summer day in 1989 to say my first novel, *Crossing Borders* (a.k.a, my seventh novel, but the first six I no longer had) was sold to Greenwich Village Publishers for ten thousand dollars. She only had to get a fourth signature on the contract, but it was time to open the champagne. I told Vibeke, who was sunning in the garden, and we unwired, unfoiled, and uncorked the champagne.

She wrote me the next week to say she had failed to get the fourth signature.

On my own, I sold *Crossing Borders* for fourteen hundred dollars—a two-book contract—to a small publisher in Wichita, Kansas. It was published by Watermark Press, and my publisher sent me a letter, later that year, elaborating that it could not make sufficient money off fiction and cancelled my contract for the second book, a story collection, *The Sins of Generals*, with the suggestion that I could keep the advance, sending me a copy of a semi-autobiographical novel by John O'Brien, which they had also published as their swan song of fiction, titled *Leaving Las Vegas*.

Five years later, a film was made of O'Brien's book, and it was nominated for all sorts of Academy Awards and won one. It was a good film, with sentimental tendencies, but basically a sound movie, directed by

Mike Figgis and starring Nicholas Cage and Elisabeth Shue and with background vocals by Sting doing "Angel Eyes" and "My One and Only Love," singing the two songs superbly. By this time, the 34-year-old John O'Brien, one day in April 1994, put a bullet in his head. His father said his novel was a long suicide note.

Watermark got out of the fiction game too early, and John O'Brien committed suicide prematurely.

I sent a copy of *Crossing Borders* to Irwin Stark, my first creative writing teacher, who recommended me to his agent all those years ago, and he wrote back that he he had read it three times "to find out who was doing what and to whom. Put it behind you and keep writing." It was reviewed in the NYT Book Review on my sixteenth wedding anniversary. The reviewer wrote that it was "shimmering with emotional honesty," but added it was "occasionally portentous" and "penny whistle could be heard in the background of the Irish scenes."

I kept writing.

Something Cool

IN 1972, I HAD APPLIED to the Iowa Graduate Workshop. Founded in 1936, Iowa was the grand-daddy of all creative writing MFA programs with graduates who were already accomplished and prominent and were taught by people like John Cheever, Philip Roth, Raymond Carver, Robert Coover, Kurt Vonnegut, Jr., Carolyn Kizer, Mark Strand.

My application to Iowa was rejected. I didn't tell anyone. That was a secret. I was ashamed of it. I had always had a flair for writing, was singled out by teachers, right back to grammar school when I won the religion medal for a composition I had written on matrimony. That was before puberty, before I turned apostate. What did I know about matrimony? I had a flair for writing. I had written beforehand to Iowa, and the response was encouraging: *Your writing experience is just what we're looking for*, they wrote back. But the writing sample I sent was rejected.

Nearly twenty years later, with the "success" of "The Sins of Generals," I applied for the Goddard Low Residency Program in Vermont and was accepted—mysteriously—by the Vermont College Low Residency MFA Program. An MFA was known as a "terminal degree." That meant the MFA was on par with a Ph.D., about which I had my doubts. (This was my degree phase; I got an MFA and a Ph.D. I was determined to get a doctorate. I would in 1988 from the University of Copenhagen, by which I had earned the right to call myself "Dr.," although no one with a Ph.D. called himself "Dr." Dr. Dr. Link did, my counterpart in the German organization. He happened by me and said, "This is the famous Ed Fitzgerald. I understand you haf a Ph.D., no? I haf two Ph.D's." He was soon known as "the missing Dr. Dr. Link" because he got fired shortly after that.

The answer to the mysterious acceptance by Vermont College was that Goddard dissolved and had split up into Vermont College and the Warren Wilson Program in North Carolina. I had applied to Goddard because the *fiction international* literary magazine was published there under the MFA Program. Founded in St. Lawrence College in New York in 1973 under Joe David Bellamy, (a pooh-bah at the time in creative writing academic circles), *fiction international* had since moved, with Bellamy as editor, to Goddard, and then whisked away, without Bellamy for opaque reasons, to San Diego State University, under the editorship of Larry McCaffery and Harold Jaffe. I had a hardback book of interviews with innovative writers titled *Anything Can Happen*, conducted and edited by McCaffery and Jaffe and a book titled *Super Fiction, or the American Story Transformed, An Anthology*, edited by Joe David Bellamy, with selections by illustrious famous writers. Moreover, I had been reading and admiring the short fiction of Harold Jaffe, especially, "Eat Your Grief, Cora Gilbert," on which I had modelled an unpublished story, "What Does God Care About Your Dignity, Victor Travesti," which was soon to be published—multiple times.

It was much of a toss-up whose editorship, *fiction international* was under, but it had included publications by more illustrious writers than you could shake a stick at, and the Goddard students who were promised involvement in the magazine had already moved to SDSU. An acceptance was better than a rejection; so, I accepted the acceptance by Vermont College in the beginning of 1983.

This required me to be present for a residency for ten days every August and January and in between, for one and a half years to submit a manuscript by post every three weeks and get feedback from writers of some stature, who would be my mentors. By dint of the American Library in the U.S. Embassy in Copenhagen, I researched the writers on teaching staff at Vermont, and I found that Gordon Weaver had just had a story, "Hog's Heart," in *The Best American Stories* and won the O. Hen-

ry Prize and had novels and story collections in print and had founded the *Mississippi Review*, an admirable journal. He was also a full professor and chairman of the English Department at the University of Oklahoma. I read "Hog's Heart"; it was a story about a football player who thought he was going to die and had just been made into a television film. I decided that I would ingratiate Gordon Weaver for my first mentor.

Further, I determined that Gladys Swan was on teaching staff in Vermont and had written a collection of stories titled *On the Edge of the Desert* in the Normal,Illinois famous writers series, and was a frequent contributor to *The Sewanee Review*, a fully admirable journal. I read the book and a sample story in *Sewanee* and was blown away by them.

Equipped with the names of two mentors, I congratulated myself for my research. After all, I had not known dip-shit about the names of universities and which was better when I started college—I had chosen C.C.N.Y. because it was free of tuition, and despite rumors of commie sympathies (Julius Rosenthal had gone there) it turned out to be the loser's Harvard. One college, to my mind, was as good as another college.

So, in August 1983, I began a hiatus for four years—eighteen months as a writing student in a low-residency MFA writing program, and two and a half years as MFA writing teacher. Meanwhile, I had enrolled in the Ph.D. program at the University of Copenhagen. I was set on earning that "Dr." title, even though you were pretentious to use it.

I commenced with the blessing of my company president, Erik Holst, to continue my education as a student for a master's degree in sociology. I discovered that Erik was willing for me to assume a fiction writing education, thus uniting my bifurcated career as a company man and a fiction writer (with one story publication to his credit, though it had not appeared in print yet). After all, I was writing speeches which were akin to creating a fictional character, press releases which were akin to creating a fictional situation, reports which were akin to fictional plotting, and minutes which were akin to direct and indirect fictional dialogue, and editing which was akin to polishing fictional prose and nonfictional monographs. Everybody in the company loved my editing—I was the voice of the company in the "big" world, i.e., the world which went on in English.

Erik and the CEO, who was at that time a dishy blond woman named Nina, granted me a week that was salaried and week out of my six-week vacation that was also salaried. The company would pay half of my plane fare and half my tuition. Moreover, when I achieved the MFA degree in eighteen months, they would throw a reception for me—the company receptions were famous with wine and beer and canapés catered by caterer of the Royal House of Marguerite, Queen of Denmark, who, in the person of Kurt Bagge Hansen, had recently been lured to be the caterer of our company—to which I could invite anyone I wanted (invitations were issued to Danish poets and writers of the Danish Writers Union, of which by now I was a member, as well as to the International Committee and to the Board and to the employees, all of whom it was novel to have a bonafide author, albeit a small-press author, on the staff). I would get a raise, too, of six hundred dollars per month. But only when I got my MFA degree.

I prevailed in having Weaver be my mentor for the first semester, Gladys for my second semester, and Weaver my thesis mentor for third and final semester. He was the author of a short story, "Whiskey Whiskey, Gin Gin Gin," which he used to drink—in addition to vodka and beer and cognac and aquavit, but wine gave him a headache. He was also author of some hundred stories and a dozen collections of stories and novels and literary criticism, was working on a novel titled *The Eight Corners of the World*, about an American-Japanese guy who embodied the history of the past fifty years which the main character was having tattooed on his back. Weaver asserted this novel would make him a super-star.

Gladys Swan, who just had a contract from Vintage for a novel, *Carnival for the Gods*, would write a quintet of novels about carnivals, starting with that. She was the author of numerous story collections and novels, and I used to look her and Weaver up in the annual *Short Story Criticism* and bask in their reflected glory. Eventually, I interviewed and wrote about both and Andre Dubus and Donald Barthelme and Robert Coover and William Stafford in, inter alia, *The Sewanee Review, American Book Review* and *American Poetry Review*. Interviewing them was like having a seminar with them. The editor of *The Sewanee Review*, who had sent encouraging notes to my first four submissions, posted a note to my fifth, "Dear Mr. Fitzgerald, I think it's sad for you when you keep submitting manuscripts, wasting that international postage, when I find it highly unlikely that I will ever publish anything of yours. Why don't you consider submitting to less major fora?" To which, Mark Cox, a poet in Vermont, rejoindered, "Anyone who would say, *less major fora* must wear a bow tie to bed." But I was furious, despite my practice of not saying anything to any editor who rejects my work, I had to say something to him. I blew off steam to Vibeke, and she said—focusing on the core of the matter—"Send him something else."

I did that.

He wrote back, "You are relentless, Mr. Fitzgerald! I do find this to be not without merit, if you clean up the sloppy writing!" I changed a comma and sent it back to him, and he published it, and it was republished three times, for which I got 300 dollars, in addition to the 20 dollars I got initially. I sent him another manuscript, and he published it, too, and it was reprinted, twice, in *Contemporary Authors*. I didn't send him anything else; with the help of Vibeke, I had conquered that market—no sense in trying a third time.

Among ten days of reading and writing and reading aloud to the student body, I used to get drunk with various students and faculty, who were very well-read, conversed about literature while getting drunk in Charlio's, Julio's, the Wren, the Brown Derby, and the Montpelier Hotel. Weaver used to pontificate about literature, and he was splendid about pontificating; he knew so much.

When Weaver introduced me for my graduate reading in January 1985, he made it short, sweet, and hyperbolic: "Ed Fitzgerald brought many fiction-writing skills with him when he came here. Now he is— and I mean this—my peer."

I read "The Sins of Generals" for my graduate reading—which was too long by a half, forty-five minutes, but you could read for as long as you wanted, within an hour. Andre Dubus came over to me afterward and said, "That story made me thirsty, so many martinis were mentioned in it. Want to go down to Julio's?"

Weaver made good on his claim that I was his peer by supporting my application to be a teacher until January 1988. By 1985, I enrolled in the Ph.D. program at the University of Copenhagen while maintaining my day job and my teaching job. I had such energy then—due to my quitting cigarettes and my failing marriage.

Meanwhile, I was introduced to Andre Dubus in Julio's Bar and we proceeded to drink peppered vodka. I learned that he was the author of a story which had appeared in *Best American Short Stories 1970* that had had a profound effect on me fourteen years before. He read "The Sins of the General" and professed it was so good that he wanted to include it in a short story anthology he was editing among stories by, inter alia, Leonard Gordner (author of *Fat City*) and Gina Berriault (author of "Stone Boy"). Andre Dubus wanted to introduce me to his agent and editor, and we wound up, after the bars closed, singing an old song by Julie Christie, "Something Cool," under a lamppost among a cluster of hangers on.

It didn't do me any good, being included in Andre's anthology—it was by a new imprint which went out of business in a year—or being introduced to his agent or his editor. Other than Andre Dubus, author of a story that had had a profound effect on me had admired my "The Sins of Generals" and thought it good.

Blood Count

SOMETIMES I THOUGHT OF MY LIFE as it really was—a failure, and I would gaze at it in all its horror. I was a weak man. I had ruined my chances. I had taken my potential and, unsuspected, dashed it on the floor. Liked sugar too much. Sweetness. I had not taken the challenges, had not even played sports (other than a mandatory semester of lacrosse, soccer, boxing, and swimming at C.C.N.Y.), the testing ground where a man was a man. I was not a pacifist, was nothing like that, was hiding behind a mask of pacifism, was a weak man, unable to take a challenge. This was why I wound up in this marriage—my vanity (Vibeke was a doctor and well-off, had an apartment which was convenient to stay in in Copenhagen, for a time). All that nonsense about looking for the situation where I would challenge my bourgeois side. Nonsense. Now I had children, two fates hanging on my fate, which was decided for a time, impermanent, but those were permanent fates, which would lead into other fates.

But a man cannot tolerate that for very long. He needed laughter, lightness, frivolity. A man cannot stare his real fate in the face in the long run.

However, I learned that I could not forsake my children.

The 4ᵗʰ of July 1987: We had always celebrated American Independence Day at Vibeke's parents' summer house with a Danish lunch.

Her mother made a big thing out of it: with three kinds of herring and breaded, fried plaice filets with home-made remoulade, which fish she purchased from the incoming ships at Hundested, and pork tenderloins, fresh fried onions and fresh baked lamb-liver pâté and bacon fried the way I liked it, crisp as Jack Nicholson ate it in *The Shining*, boiled cod roe, fresh smoked eel with scrambled eggs and chives, smoked salmon and parsley all ready for the pepper mill; a dozen other things—soft-boiled eggs with caviar, wild boar salami and raw onion and fried onions, breaded pork krebinetter and a hundred tiny frikadeller (Danish meatballs).

Her father had three kind of schnapps—Brøndums (which was strong but unflavored but for a bit of caraway—always translated into English on Danish menus as "carryaway" seeds), Linje (a Norwegian snaps which traveled on ships in sherry casks across the equator so it took on an amber hue) and Pørsesnaps with fresh extra pørse that was gathered green from the wild (I swear, it was psychedelic). And every kind of Danish beer—Tuborg and Carlsberg pilsner and strong beer: Elephant, Giraf, and Special Brew. Bottles were gathered in clusters on the table. A little American flag on a chrome flag pole in the center of the table was hoisted. Vibeke's father always hoisted it when I showed up. (The fact that it had forty-eight stars I ignored.)

The parents invited their son and daughter-in-law (they spoke English for my sake until I was proficient at Danish, and they never mocked my accent or my word choices—some Danes will—some Americans, too). They had two sons, and they got along with our son and daughter; Vibeke's parents had set up a table for the children with boiled red pølser and French fries and all things that three boys and one girl like.

It was a feast, and I loved it.

By 1987, I had begun to publish and had my own friends, and we decided to hold July Fourth in our own front garden. We expanded the family with the friends I made from my professional circles and expats: Hirobumi Ito, a Japanese researcher with whom I used to hang out in his Panum Institute office some Friday afternoons—he was married to a Dane also—and he had a stock of French bottles of wine and Japanese snacks in his desk which was in a large, undisturbed attic room; David Grubb and Bodil Bødkær-Ness, who had invited me to be a board member of The World Poetry Foundation, which brought William S.

Burroughs and Ken Kesey and the Fugs (Tuli Kupferberg and Ed Sanders) to Copenhagen and mingled them with Danish poets and prose writers like Bo Green Jensen, Henrik Nordbrandt, Klaus Lynggaard, Pia Tafdrup, and Dan Turèll.

Vibeke's father was not speaking to his son, and the son was not speaking to his father. The whole thing had blown up on the past Christmas Eve. We were seated at her parent's table and just eaten roast goose with apple and prune stuffing, which Vibeke's mother made to perfection, and candied browned potatoes and fresh red cabbage and new potatoes and the *gravy*—made with goose fat—and were just ready to take the dessert of ris à l'almonde with cherry sauce and vintage port wine. I excused myself to go to the bathroom (you go "on the toilet" in Danish) and, in that three or four minutes, I came out to witness the whole family standing around the table and shouting at each other—it might have been a scene from an Italian film. Abruptly the son and his wife and their two children departed, and father and son had not spoken since.

Apparently, the son's wife had requested that her oldest son, who was ten, have a half glass of the vintage ruby port which was served in a Waterford crystal port glass and the boy had dropped and shattered it. But the underlying problem was that my father-in-law's son didn't want to take over his plumbing contractor business.

Vibeke boiled corn on the cob, cut in half, and I grilled hamburgers and hot dogs on our patio. We had the long, folding table out on our lawn, underneath the magnolia tree, with masses of sliced watermelon, bowls of baked beans and potato salad—both with mayonnaise and with vinegar—and green and tomato salad and several bowls of plump strawberries.

I don't know what got into her father, but his son and family were also there—or he had taken offense that we wanted to host July 4th. He could always get to Vibeke, and she could always get to me. Her parents came in fancy dress, her father wearing a suit and white shirt and tie, and he sat on a beach chair, with his hamburger on a paper plate balanced on his knee. When he finished eating, he pronounced, "*Det var meget morsomt.*" ("That was very amusing.") And left around 7:00 pm.

The argument between Vibeke and me didn't begin, delayed reaction style, until next day and continued on Monday, when we got home from the office and the hospital at dinner time—I had made Krebenetter (a kind of breaded pork hamburger) with boiled potatoes and salad— and she said, "You *can't* cook!" and shoved her plate aside. I said, "*Det var meget morsomt*," and left the table to continue on my Ph.D. thesis, and she printed diagonally across the page of a book I was using, in felt pen, *FUCK YOU!!!* Because in my childhood home, it was the highest transgression to write, and a profanity, on the pages of a book—I snarled, "You fat, ugly *cunt!*"

She was neither fat nor ugly, but the "cunt" got to her, and she muttered, "I told you *never* to call me *that* word" (which she hadn't, but I was aiming to hurt because she had written an obscenity on my book, although the obscenity was not so bad; in Danish Danes use the eff word routinely, whereupon a "fat, ugly cunt" in Danish, "*en fedt, grim kusse*" was *very bad*, and I used it in Danish).

She proceeded slowly, deliberately, across the room, picking up a heavy glass ashtray on her way—a gift from her to me—and cracked me across the top of my skull with it. I almost blacked out and bled profusely—a scalp wound always bleeds profusely—on the beige, wall-to-wall carpet. I left her there while I went into the bathroom to tend to my wound. After I had dressed my wound, I put on my powder-blue suit with a black shirt, open at the collar, and abandoned her to cleaning the blood from the carpet with a bowl of cold water, sprinkling it on, then mopping it up with a rag.

She didn't even say I'm sorry. But that was a thing you could not say "sorry" for, like you had inadvertently bumped into someone. I took the 184 Bus from Lyngbyvej fifteen minutes into central Copenhagen. I intended to do some serious drinking. I got off at Nørreport and walked along Nørregade, where the Café Montmatre had moved from Store Regnegade under the ownership of Herluf Kamp Larsen, to Anne Linnet, a beautiful lesbian singer who was doing a performance of *Marquis de Sade*, but not at the Montmatre, which did not have capacity enough. I had seen Tom Waites there in 1978, singing in his raspy voice and spastic manner about "the pepto-bismal colored skies" of Los Angeles. This was before he got famous; he could never perform at Montmartre now—he would need a bigger venue; there would be too many people who wanted to see him.

Yet jazz, even icons, did not draw a crowd, and the Montmartre was sufficient to seat them. The club had only 120 seats on benches at rough wooden tables, but could take nearly a like number standing. This was 1987, and it was the Jazz Festival. There was a sizeable crowd outside, spilling into the dark roadway. I saw from the posters that Stan Getz was playing.

I had been listening to Getz for twenty-five years, starting with the 1962 *Jazz Samba Getz/Gilberto* (which won a grammy in '65), *Big Band Bossa Nova*, and *Getz au Go Go*. Getz was only proportianally into Bossa Nova and recorded *Sweet Rain* in 1967, in which he abandoned samba and added new material by keyboardist Chuck Corea and the title song by composer Mike Gibbs.

Trying to cheer myself up, a month after my father died, I had seen Getz in Carnegie Hall in October '64, where he introduced Gary Burton on vibes, playing an incredible solo on "Stan's Blues"—and about whom Getz said that he was enormously talented and that he was only twenty-one, adding, "The young punk!" Most memorable was Getz blowing "Here's that Rainy Day." At the Rainbow Grill on the 65th floor of the R.C.A. building in January 1972, Getz blew with Gilberto (Joao) several bossa-nova numbers, mixed with tunes by Chuck Corea and Strayhorn. It must have been a slow night because I got a table easily, despite that it was a three-week, record-breaking engagement for the Grill.

Losing track of Getz since I moved to Copenhagen, I knew he spent a lot of time in Scandinavia (*Standinavia*) and in the capital of Denmark. Anders Dyrup, paint heir and founder of Montmartre, called him "the American jazz ambassador in Copenhagen." Fellow American jazz expats in Copenhagen were bassman Oscar Pettiford, tenor saxmen Ben Webster and Dexter Gordon, the drummer Joe Harris, and pianist Horace Parlan.

Now Getz was in Copenhagen again, and just the night I was walking the streets, the blood caked on my scalp. It was simple: I couldn't be the man she wanted, and she couldn't be the woman I wanted, not Miltonian "fit conversing mates" for each other. Maybe there wasn't a fit conversing mate for me.

The interior of the new Montmartre on Nørregade was like a cave. Concrete stalactites were formed on the ceiling and rough gray stucco hung on the walls—as I remember it. Neither was it large. The entry fee was like fifty or a hundred kroner, and I took a bottle of beer at the bar—

another twenty kroner, and talked sweetly to the barmaid, but she wasn't having any of it. I took a seat on the end of one of the benches—no room at the long wooden table to place my bottle. I held it.

My head hurt. The back-up group came out first—Kenny Baron on piano, Rufus Reid on bass, and Victor Lewis on drums. I didn't know their names—only knew they were players by the applause that greeted each one of them. They were more or less my age, forty-three, but Getz was sixty that year and rumored to have cancer. Seventeen years, when you're younger, can seem an interminably long time, but it's not. Four years can seem a long time, too—enough for a college education—but it goes fast. This was how long Getz had to live, but I couldn't know it then.

Stan Getz came out last with his horn, and the applause was a roar and whistles. I don't remember if people stood up—or for that matter if they genuflected, but his light blue eyes were both warm and humor-filled and bright, and they were the only thing in the room, boring through the smoke and applause, and I could feel it was good that I'd come.

Despite everything, despite the rages against his family, despite the prison time, Getz was a master, and he was a star, and everyone in the room knew it, could see it from his eyes in the moon-face. Measuring the applause to his group, to his right and left, he concluded the sweep with a sign to stop. The crowd fell slowly silent, and he spoke. "I left my heart in Copenhagen...," and the applause flared up, the audience being very sentimental about Getz and Montmartre and Copenhagen. But he delivered the punch line: "I said the same thing about Stockholm last night." There was a smattering of laughter throughout the crowd, but people knew that Getz had supported this jazz club from the start, play-ing regularly four days a week from the start of the club by Dyrup—at less money than he could command, trying and failing to find peace and serenity in Copenhagen. Now he was back for his sixtieth birthday year. Born on the birthday of James Joyce, forty-five years later; when Joyce had only fourteen years left to live, Getz saw life for the first time in 1927. It's arbitrary, but it's not arbitrary to me; these are two of my heroes, a literary and a jazz master.

Getz could have been named Gazetakis if his grandfather hadn't changed it when he came to America to flee the pogroms of the Ukraine. The eyes of Getz were not hindered by cataracts as Joyce's were; on the other hand, Stanley's ear had to be re-attached by sutures at birth—ears are important to a musician, Beethoven notwithstanding, and many blind jazz musicians have conquered their lack of sight and played (Roland Kirk, Ray Charles, George Shearing, Horace Parlan). Nevertheless, Joyce chose to make Leopold Bloom a Jew, which Getz was—at one of the worst times; anti-semitism was flourishing, considered incidental by the best people, and when Getz was only a child and teenager, Adolph Hitler had many millions of Jews interred in death camps.

Getz's hair was blond at birth, his eyes luminous blue. You could see genius in his gaze. I saw it that night.

The quartet played two sets, twelve numbers: a Johnny Mandel, two Cole Porters, one Victor Feldman, one Kenny Baron (whom Getz described as "the other half of my heart"), two Johnny Mercers, two Ned Washingtons, one Vernon Duke and Ira Gershwin, one Gigi Gryce ("Stan's Blues"), and one Billy Strayhorn. But the author of the lyricism, cool, hard-bop, west coast jazz of upbeat and downbeat tempos, melodious screaming and elegiac interpretation, was Stan Getz in the middle register of his tenor.

One particular movingly deep elegy stayed with me. I had heard it played by Duke Ellington with Johnny Hodges playing alto sax and for the last time and continuingly, Getz owned that tune while he played it, and after he played, it was etched in my synapses: Billy Strayhorn's "Blood Count."

Getz said, "I think about Strayhorn when I play this song. You can hear him dying. When it's in a minor key, you can hear him talking to God."

Strayhorn wrote it for Duke Ellington for Carnegie Hall in 1967, when Billy was in a hospital dying of cancer. Billy would never attend that concert, and Getz was now dying of cancer, though not yet, playing it once again, and Strayhorn was with him in his tenor.

Getz's intense blue eyes were calm within his round face, as he played the incredible, flowing, lyrical improvisations, deep trembling notes, a scream, a yell, mellow line disappearing into a deep register—contemplative with surges of emotion, lyrical with melodious metallic screams, he talks with, pleads with God, and on and over the bridge, halfway through the short melody, supported by Barron's notes and explosions of chords and Reid's and Lewis' work, then it wails up and down the scales leading to the melody, getting weaker, stronger, weakens, then resolved to his mortality, to our mortality, but it must be the mortality of one man, then proceeds to a sudden, explosive ending of all the instruments. This is not a resolution; this is the *end*.

Followed by the surprised, startled applause.

It was a short number, perhaps four minutes, and it was like life itself, the fluttering out of life, but not fluttering, screaming at times, and then it was over, short and strong and over.

At the end of the concert, Getz says, "Thank you. Thank you very much..." and shares the accolades with his quartet, "...Kenny Baron, Rufus Reid, Victor Lewis. Thank you. Beautiful audience."

"Blood Count" came at the conclusion of the concert, I think. It *must* have. Because as so often with live jazz, it left me feeling it was personal. My scalp bleeding onto the beige carpet. My blood. From my head. Vibeke had been violent before. Kneed me in the testicles. She was violent in the car, too—knocked a worker off a ladder, made for pedestrians by accelerating so they had to leap out of the way. Jumped on my back and pulled my hair, and I smacked her in the face, thinking it would be an end to all the violence between us if I spoke her language, but it just made me feel that I was losing all sense of control, that I was *losing* all civilized behavior.

That must be the end.

The end of "Blood Count," the entire span of it had made me conscious of the stakes of my life, what I must do. I remembered once when Vibeke had thrown our son on the bed, and she hurried out of his room, blurting, "I think I just did something to his back!" I went in and comforted my 6-year-old son, made sure he was not hurt.

I thought now, in the club, *You can't leave them alone with her. You have to stay. Until the kids are old enough to protect themselves.*

You're not innocent. You have done some things you're ashamed of, some things far less than civil. And I continued for twelve months in Vermont, debauching myself for ten days in January and August, but I longed for a warm body to hold close. It was not my fault or hers. It was a myriad of reasons, starting with my uncertainty about whether I loved her when I married, was integrated with her way of being and my wanting to get out of my "nice" Catholic schoolboy manners, and my reverence that she was a doctor and her violence.

It was simple: It was all based on a misunderstanding. I could not be the man she wanted, and she could not be the woman I wanted. Fit conversing mates.

But I had to be a buffer for the children. My kids made excuses for her, liked her, loved her, but I could not leave them alone with her. From that night, we slept in separate beds, in separate rooms. And I lived two lives: A life with my kids and my work, and my jazz and my readings and writing and my trips. I was teaching then and I had frequent business trips and reading tours.

And a life with Vibeke. Which was civil—and distant.

PART FOUR

Tenor Madness

THE YEAR 1994 WAS A COMPLICATED ONE for me. I turned fifty in March, was writing well—I had a reputation (such as it was) as a small press fiction writer and literary critic and translator—and was at the height of my business career (the height it could reach anyway). The failure consisted of my two decades old marriage, and it colored everything.

When I wasn't drinking—a couple of glasses of red wine with dinner, a double vodka or whiskey on the rocks before and a cognac afterward—I was traveling a lot, day trips to Brussels and once a month for a three-four day conference to a variety of other places. This was the period when you could get duty-free liquor, and I always brought back VSOP cognac and a bottle of Johnny Walker Black or Jack Daniels, cigarettes for Vibeke (I had quit smoking when my son was born and started cigars years later, not inhaling them; if I survived to seventy I would start inhaling), and toys for the children. And Christmas decorations—Vibeke would make a Christmas village with houses and figures from everywhere and a make-up mirror of a lake, surrounded by cotton, upon which skaters with their hands behind their backs skated. My daughter had a collection of Barbies with national dress from all over Europe, and my son had troops of soldiers from every capital and a miniature of every kind of car that was manufactured.

Then the couple of glasses of red wine became a bottle or two. Vibeke was having trouble at the hospital, and she would join me in the wine and cognac. "Join me" is probably a misnomer. We rarely spoke to each other. We spoke to the children and tried to keep our arguments in abeyance, and it wasn't difficult under the anesthesia of fine liquors.

I had the job—*hell*, privilege—of singing and reading to the kids at bedtime. I had a whole repertoire that I tailored to them ("Sloop John B," "Mr. Blue," "Twinkle, Twinkle," "Lonely Girl," and nursery rhymes—"Dr. Foster," "Anna Lisa she jumped with surprise..."). It was a pleasure until they were ten or eleven—and then I switched over to reading children's classics (*Moby Dick* for children and James Fenimore Cooper, *Alice i Eventyrland*, *Alice in Wonderland*, though the translation was awful, and *Skatteøjn*, *Treasure Island*). When they were asleep, I took another deep cognac and listened to Bird or Webster or Getz or Mulligan and wrote in my office/bedroom, while Vibeke watched TV or read.

On weekend mornings, when I wasn't traveling, I ran writer's workshops for the kids. I had bought a couple of books by Kenneth Koch about writing poetry with children. My daughter, who was younger, didn't have trouble, but my son had difficulties. He always wanted to write poems about fast, sleek cars and, Chuck Berry notwithstanding, they were all about speed and none about language. But he finally broke through with an imaginative poem:

> The Lonely Feather
> Terribly sad to be a feather
> That falls from a bird.
> You lose your friends
> and your home.
> It is cold to be alone
> In the snow.

My eyes got damp when I heard that poem—because it was beautiful, and it was true of our lives.

And my daughter wrote:

> Crazy Poem
> I am a bird.
> I fly in water.
> I am a fish
> that swims on land.
> I am seaweed
> growing on a roof.
> I am a garden
> of pink moss.
> I am a tree

that grows on the sea
with blue penguins
for fruit.

The Louisville Review devoted a section to "The Children's Corner," and I submitted them, and they were published.

I picked wild strawberries, which grew on our lawn in summer, just tiny things, and we had them for breakfast on cornflakes. In the early fall, dust ball mushrooms appeared on our grounds, 'round the back. They grew large as soccer balls, but they were better when you picked them only the size of baseballs or softballs. I sliced and fried them in cream sauce in a skillet and served them on toast with a glass of dry Alsatian white—half glasses mixed with water for the kids.

Vibeke, who was very handy, made a witch for midsummer night—a hideously beautiful little thing with a hat, a pair of the old, little kids' shoes and a robe which, before she stitched it up, we put papers in with secret things written on them that we wanted to be free of and, when the night was turning dusk at 10 p.m., burnt it in the garden in a little bonfire and toasted marshmallows on a stick or made "snow bread," and I made martinis for Vibeke and me.

A guy I knew came from Lolland and used to have a pumpkin patch on his property—large, oblong *græskar* —(this was before Danes celebrated Halloween), and Vibeke scooped the pulp and the seeds out of them and carved intricate faces. We put them in the front windows with candles in them, and the neighbors grew interested. We threw a Halloween party for the kids and parents, a costume party. There were only three kids on our street, but with ours they made five, and four parents. I bought from Dublin, where they celebrated Halloween, paper pumpkins and strings of black cats and little profiles of cardboard witches flying against a moon.

In April, the forsythia bush would flower yellow, and I still have a photo, where I can see it, of my two-year-old daughter in a pink jogging suit, smiling. In May, the magnolia tree would flower first white, then a blue, almost purple with strains of pink, and I have a photo, right next to the picture of my daughter, of my three-year-old son, running on his short legs down our long driveway beneath the magnolia blooms, smiling.

In Amsterdam, I bought Queen of the Night tulip bulbs, and Vibeke planted them with other tulips—yellow, orange, pink, red—in a large patch with yellow daffodils at the front of the house where we could see them from the elevated patio. She had a green thumb.

These were happy times, focused on the children, until they were eleven or twelve, and they began to let go of our hands, never to take them again. My son had a habit from when he was twelve or thirteen of placing his hand on my shoulder and walking a little behind me, like he was a blind man, and I would lead him everywhere. Until he stopped doing that. Then my daughter was twelve or thirteen, and she started placing her hand on my shoulder. It only lasted for one or two years—maybe it lasted for one or two months or seasons—but I loved it, leading them, like my son and I or my daughter and I were a unit. Until they stopped doing that.

Still, Vibeke and I argued, bickered over little things (like whether the Christmas tree was plumb straight) and larger things (like my traveling). She could not be the woman I wanted, and I could not be the man she wanted.

I had ended the previous year drinking a lot. At the company Christmas banquet, the height of the year 1993, the men all had tuxedos on as we drank the welcome champagne, and the CEO and her husband came 'round, greeting everyone. Vibeke had worn the same dress, a silver material that glittered, as the CEO, bought in Paris on Montmartre—I don't know where the CEO bought the dress, but it must have cost plenty whereas Vibeke's had cost only a few hundred francs. Everyone was looking but not looking, in the Danish way, with a curl to their lips. I thought it was funny, the way the CEO uttered, "Oh!" and didn't mention the dresses. Vibeke didn't mention them either, but I could see she was embarrassed, which made her furious.

I said, "Good taste!"

Vibeke turned sour in the cab home in the small hours due to some imagined slight. The woman who was my *bord dame* (table lady), the wife of a younger colleague whom I hadn't met before, after we had had a pleasant conversation during dinner, had said, when Vibeke came over, "Is this your wife?" Vibeke heard it disparagingly as, "*Oh, is this your wife!*" Vibeke had not been satisfied with her tablemate, who ignored her all evening.

214

When we got home, as we were undressing, she whipped the white suspenders of my tuxedo pants across my head, and the clasp hit my scalp, which bled on my ruffled shirt. I retired to my room and my own bed to fall into an unrestful sleep. Next morning, when I woke, I put on Getz, "Here's That Rainy Day." It quieted my thoughts, was so beautiful with Gary Burton shimmering the vibes and Getz improvising on the tenor, screaming, followed by sadly lyrical lines. As soon as I recalled the events of the night before, I started thinking about my liquor intake and Vibeke's violence.

I resolved to stop drinking and start exercising. After all, I was turning fifty this year. I saw it as my last chance. Vibeke and I had a tradition when we weren't arguing that on January 1st, we watched the New Year's concert from Vienna on TV and had brunch with champagne. I thought to make an exception for just a day, start my new year's resolution on January 2nd, but she wasn't having any of it this year.

The gym was thirty minutes from my home, forty-five minutes from my office, by bicycle, and I biked there every morning at six a.m. and started with a half hour, but soon graduated to an hour, then two hours on the machines and with the weights. They played music to get into the rhythm of the motion—real music, not muzak—and one morning I heard jazz, a tenor sax. I asked the bored woman at the desk what the name of that song was. It sounded so happily intricate and energetic. She looked at the play list and said it was something called "Tenor Madness." I wrote it down on my note pad—I always kept a note pad and pen by me when I was exercising.

I enquired of David at the Jazz Cellar on Gray Friars Square.

"Don't you know it?" He asked. He wouldn't consider his stock complete without it. It was composed by Sonny Rollins—only record that had Rollins and Coltrane playing together. Coltrane should not have been in the studio, but he had his sax and was ready. On May 24th, 1956, in New York: It is a simple swing blues line, but Rollins and Coltrane exchange a very high level of language.

I biked into the gym next morning with it on my Walkman. Then I biked to work, with Rollins and Coltrane exploding in my brain, and took a shower. I was eating less and drinking not at all, and in a matter of months I lost thirty pounds.

215

Vibeke sobered, too. She seemed to try to make amends. For my fiftieth birthday, she bought a painting—an oil of a sad angel seated at a table with an empty bottle of wine, post festum, by Teodor Bok, a Polish artist resident in Denmark and whom Greg and Birgit Stephenson used on the cover of *Pearl*, a magazine they edited and published.

I wondered if Vibeke was trying to tell me something with the sad, post-fest angel, but it was too convoluted and too late.

She had quit the medical profession seven years earlier, in 1987, a year short of completing her pathology specialty, explaining that it was too grueling going into the hospital every day to abduct corpses. That was still when the hospital system automatically performed an abduction if the family didn't fill out a form requesting not to be autopsied. Not all the families of the deceased were familiar with the rules. That was also the period of the AIDS epidemic, and sufficient precautions were not in force. Vibeke was concerned about that, not knowing if the corpse she was slicing up had died of AIDS.

We had just bought a new Volvo, a cream-colored hatchback, and we had to sell it back to the dealer, at book value, with a fifty thousand kroner reduction on the price we paid. We still owed a lot on the house and with private school fees (we didn't want to make the kids change schools) and heating bills on our big house and clothing bills for our growing kids and our income reduced by a quarter million kroner a year. We were still five thousand kroner short a month.

My company salary was enhanced by a private income from my small side business of translation and editing, but it was not enough. The quantity of work was potentially there. I had to increase my translation to bridge the gap. Vibeke agreed to do rough translations which I could fine-polish, and it lasted a while, but we soon had complaints that our translations were faulty. I was too tired at night to do the fine-polishing sufficiently, and Vibeke made mistakes. She was excellent at English, but she translated too literally, and I couldn't catch all the literals. We had complaints about "howlers," which didn't alleviate our arguing.

Then I hit upon some lucrative business: A British publishing house proposed it, and my company approved. The Brits suggested a series of handbooks for which I could solicit articles from my contacts—I had contacts all through Europe who were hungry for publication, would do it for free to acquire publications to fatten their CVs and bibliographies—to acquire prestige and steep-up their professional fees, and my company had the prestige of the handbooks in its name. The handbooks were free; they were financed by advertising. I would be editor, and the Brits would sell advertising with advertorials that the advertisers would provide. The advertorials were clearly marked as ads with the other articles, solicited from my contacts. I could earn an extra twenty-five thousand twice a year.

I wasn't especially proud of the advertorials, but I had the prestige of the glossy, thick magazines twice a year. I had the money, which we sorely needed.

Soon, the advertising money proved so profitable that my fee was increased to fifty thousand twice a year. I dropped translating except for poetry—I was a fiction writer and low-grade literary critic, but the translation of poetry made me feel like a poet. I was traveling to London for a day two times a year. It would take two hours to fly into Heathrow (one hour with the time difference) and I would take the tube to Blackfriars Bridge and because I was perennially early, to kill time, I used to buy a bacon sandwich at a hash house right at the beginning of the Bridge and smoke a cigarillo from a metal case.

One morning, a fruit vendor in for a coffee and a count of his coins was attracted by my metal cigarillo box and asked, "Whatever is that?" I told him Dutch cigarillos and asked if he would like one. He looked from beneath his smudged bowler and said, "Well, I wouldn't say no-oo."

After the bacon sandwich, I would walk over Blackfriars Bridge, deliver the manuscript on a flash drive and be invited out to a sumptuous lunch, and fly back in the evening to Kastrup with a carton of duty-free Prince cigarettes for Vibeke.

Everybody was happy: the publishing firm, the advertisers, the authors, my company, and me. Vibeke was not happy about my increased traveling, but she couldn't argue with the money. She said, "You have your ass full of money." Which I took as a compliment.

The publishing firm was taken over by a conglomerate and increased my fee to seventy-five thousand kroner, thrice a year. My prestige increased, too, and soon I was being called in as a consultant by companies in Dublin, Brussels, and Geneva, and by the European Union Commission—for a fee every time. I paid off as much as I could of our house and car (by this time we had a new car, a used blue hatchback Toyota—I was expecting the bottom to drop out of this business). Meanwhile I salted money in my private pension. I didn't know what Vibeke was going to do (inherit from her parents), but I planned on retiring at sixty and getting divorced and becoming a full-time writer. She would make it on alimony.

Then Vibeke started getting dizzy spells—it was 1992—and she was scheduled for an MRI scan and, a couple weeks later, for the results, and she came out of the office into the hospital waiting room, and said glumly, "Let's get out of here."

Downstairs in the car, she said, "*Shit!* I've got MS." She tightened her lips. "The doctor said it just like that. 'Well, you're a colleague so no sense beating around the bush. You've got MS.'"

I could see she was very affected, but I didn't understand. "Uh... What's MS again?"

She looked at me, and I could see in her eyes, her lips, she was focusing all her disdain on me, but I didn't understand. My mother had taught me that there was no such thing as a stupid question, but Vibeke disagreed: She considered some questions utterly stupid. And I felt stupid for not knowing. I was forty-seven and should have known.

Finally, she said, "Multiple Sclerosis. Disseminated sclerosis. Encephalo myetitis disseminate."

"Shit," I said like I understood, but I didn't. I needed to look in the medical dictionary at home.

She looked at me, then away. She was behind the steering wheel because she didn't like how I drove.

"Want me to drive?"

"No." She put the transmission in drive and pulled out of the hospital parking lot without speaking. I could tell she was furious. I recall the buds were on the tree branches, light green and furry. At the first red light, she told me, looking over the wheel through the windshield, that it begins between twenty and fifty and is twice as a common in women than men.

She was forty-three. Our children were twelve and eleven.

We drove home in silence. She went in to lay on her bed on top of the spread. I lay beside her, although it had been a long time since we were sleeping together. I put my palm on the nub of her shoulder, but she was taut and shook it off. I remembered that we had bought that bedspread fifteen years before for eight hundred kroner. It was the first "nice" thing we bought in relatively happier times—Finnish, with dark brown and beige squares, a checkerboard of squares. I recall thinking it was like a chess board, like the Rubyait: *one by one, moves and checks and slays. And one by one, back in the closet lays.*

"Do you want me to make some tea?"

She didn't answer. I got up and put the kettle on and went for the medical encyclopedia.

Multiple sclerosis: Disrupts the ability of parts of the nervous system to communicate, resulting in a range of signs and symptoms including physical, mental, and sometimes psychological problems. Specific symptoms can include double vision, blindness in one eye, muscle weakness, trouble with sensation or trouble with coordination. Between attacks, symptoms may disappear completely. However, permanent neurological problems often remain as the disease advances. The long-term outcome is difficult to predict—often seen in women, life expectancy is on average five to ten years lower. Fatigue, depression, anxiety, unstable mood, weakness, spasms, ataxia, diarrhea or constipation, frequency of urination or retention, visual, motor and sensory problems, tingling, pins-and-needles or numbness, muscle weakness, difficulty in moving and with coordination and balance, a worsening of symptoms due to exposure to higher than usual temperatures....

I had been planning on retiring as soon as I was sixty and divorcing Vibeke; but *this.*

We took an annual vacation to Norway in July. I invited Vibeke and the kids to accompany me on my business trips whenever I could. With this combination, we had gone to Venice, Dublin, Killarney, Waterford, Rhodes, Crete, Lesbos, the U.S., Rome, Malta, Madeira. And we had planned to take a long vacation in two years, rent a car and drive through the Mojave desert, as Vibeke and I had done in 1978 just before we had kids, motor through southern California, Arizona, New Mexico, and Nevada, and Los Angeles, to Salinas, Monterey, Carmel, Big Sur and San Francisco. But in Vibeke's condition, it was a question that we danced around.

Two years passed, and the condition of her health didn't get any worse. She didn't show any signs of the illness, but she said that it was an invisible handicap. She got breathless and dizzy. She couldn't walk for any long periods; she grew dizzy and had to lay down.

She insisted we carry through our plans for the U.S. tour without her. The kids were counting on it. She said she couldn't take the heat of the desert, couldn't take all the walking, and anyway she would have a long rest at her parents' summer house. My mother- and father-in-law were retired now. They had turned seventy, and they couldn't get up to the country house all summer, and they had offered it to Vibeke while we were gone for the whole month of July. She insisted the kids and I go to the U.S. as planned. I was impressed. It was the single most selfless thing she did.

We flew on Icelandair from Kastrup via Reykjavik. We had enough of a layover to swim in the Blue Lagoon; the air was cold, even in the summer, but the water was heated by a hot spring: Floating on your back, your nose and toes were cold, your body warm. We flew into Las Vegas and there, after a couple of nights in a room at the Sands Hotel and prime rib with cola ad libitum for $3.95 and the sights on the strip—it was like Disneyland with all the oddly-shaped and neon lighted hotels—and we sent the first of a postcard a day to Vibeke, signed by all three. This was before cell phones—at least, I didn't have one.

We rented a white Pontiac Sunbird, four-door sedan with air-conditioning and loaded our luggage in the trunk and locked it and purchased a Styrofoam cooler which we stocked with bags of ice and pop-top cans of Coke and Diet Coke and orange and club soda that we kept in the vacant place in the back seat. There was a cassette player in the Sunbird, and I stopped in a record shop in Vegas and bought some tapes for the kids and a copy of Rollins' *Tenor Madness*, but my daughter said, "Oh, Dad: *Jazz*?" They were into rock and punk.

"Do you realize that is the only cut of Rollins playing with John Coltrane in *existence*?"

To appease her, I added a *Getz À GoGo*, featuring Astrud Gilberto. And I bought a Prince for her and a Rage Against the Machine for my son. My son could tolerate jazz, and my daughter liked romantic songs, but I didn't tell her that Getz and Burton played a set without Astrud, mainly "Here's That Rainy Day."

We made a deal that we would play the jazz twice a day, morning and evening, and they negotiated that I play the Getz in the morning and the Rollins when the sun went down. Otherwise I would play their tapes, the radio, or nothing.

They soon got so enraptured by the Mojave scenery that they let me play the Getz/Gilberto tape twice. Then I forgot about the music with the high desert so flat and yellow and the rock formations majestic in the morning sun and the big sky.

We drove across Boulder Dam and reached Lake Mead by late afternoon and found a motel. The motel was so high on the mountain wall that the Mojave stretched out before us as far as we could see. We ended the day swimming in the motel pool and dined on Big Macs for a buck—everything cost less than in Copenhagen, mainly because of the 25% value added tax.

In the morning, we drove further southeast to Grand Canyon, and the kids were duly impressed. We saw an eagle gliding in the sky over the Canyon, and the three of us looked up at it, silent.

My son said, "Don't you get envious? Of that big bird, just hanging in the sky? Over that beautiful landscape?" It was majestic, walls and depth and walls and depth, stretching out as far as you could see. Ineffable was the word that occurred to me, and I saw it through my kids' eyes and the eagle's, hanging in the canopy of the sky.

I was impressed, too, but I had seen it sixteen years before, Vibeke and I dangling our legs over the edge when we drank our postprandial cognac at sundown on the dramatic cliffs and sheer walls. We were happier then—in our unhappiness.

A rail extended around the edge everywhere now, and you couldn't do that anymore, sit on the edge—which I was happy for, with the kids. My son and I pressed my daughter to give up the idea of joining a tour to ride a horse on a trail into the canyon, a mile below. We were no equestrians, but my daughter was, riding since she was eight. I almost gave in to her, but when I heard that it was an overnighter, I was certain.

Early the morning after the Canyon, we drove further east and didn't reach Tuba City until noon, but we saw the desert which was stark and beautiful and made my daughter forget her ride on a horse into the canyon. We passed a motel called Whispering Winds in Tuba City. My son joked that the Whispering Winds was a luke-warm fart.

We found a place to park the Sunbird in the shade from noon to four p.m., as we had been advised by the rental car company, while we ate lunch in a diner and went sightseeing in the late afternoon, then booked a motel. We drove through the Hopi and Navajo lands and the Painted Desert. We saw Shiprock or "winged rock," as it was called in Navajo, massive in the sun, and Camel Rock off in the distance—it looked unmistakably like a camel—and crisscrossed over the Mojave and the high desert. We saw saguro and barrel cactus and a roadrunner and tumbleweed.

We visited the Taos Pueblo and the Teseque Pueblo—members of the eight northern tribes of Pueblo, who speak the Tewa language. Chief Dan came out of the pueblo and danced and sang for us and sold us an LP in a paper case with his picture on it, dancing in full regalia. For a dollar. We took turns standing in the four corners which were shaped by the northeast corners of Utah and the northwest corner. of Colorado and the southeast corner of Arizona and the northwest corner of New Mexico, all straight lines. My son didn't like to have his picture taken, and he operated the camera, which Signe had given me, fourteen years before. I bought color film, 35 mm, and thought of Signe and the love I had for her, until she showed herself to be mad. I imagined telling my kids about Signe, but thought better of it.

Driving west again, we stopped in a sports lounge in Sante Fe because my son wanted to see a soccer (*fødball*) match between Denmark and the U.S. My son, who was only fifteen, had a full red beard, so he didn't have any trouble ordering a Corona with a wedge of lime in the neck of the bottle (this was the time when a song was popular on Danish radio where the refrain was something like, "Comachucka, gimme a cool Corona!" and we drank only Corona beers). We stayed in the bar until the match began on TV, and I cautioned my son about rooting visibly for Denmark before my daughter and I went out shopping for jewelry.

Vibeke had bought a thick silver bracelet last time we were in Sante Fe with a large turquoise of blue and white and beige, broad as her wrist, but it was stolen in a hotel. Vibeke had asked, if we could, to buy a piece of jewelry with a turquoise thunderbird.

We went into a store that specialized in Zuni jewelry and were assisted by a young, pretty Zuni woman with long, straight, black hair. She showed me a silver thunderbird bracelet, arranged of tiny pieces of turquoise made by a Zuni silversmith. When I was looking at it, the sales-woman leaned in to polish the stones with a buffer cloth, and her long, straight black hair whisked across the bare arm of the hand that I was holding the bracelet in. I don't know where it came from, but I got the idea that she bewitched me. I must have been under a spell, the bracelet was so shining and beautiful.

"How much is it?"

"Only four hundred fifty. I'll give it to you for four hundred."

My daughter said in Danish, "It's beautiful. Buy it."

I still imagined I was under the spell of the Zuni woman. Sensing my resistance, the woman asked how long I would be in Sante Fe, and I told her we left at noon tomorrow.

"Until noon tomorrow this bracelet is not for sale; it's yours. You think about it tonight and come in tomorrow and look at it again. But at noon tomorrow, I will put it back on display."

"*Køb den!*" my daughter whispered. (Buy it!)

Thinking about that bracelet of silver and deep-blue turquoise all through our Mexican dinner, it shone in my imagination and grew more and more beautiful.

In the morning, we packed the car trunk and bought a bag of ice from the machine at the motel and more pull-tab cans of soda. It was over a hundred degrees F. I settled the motel bill, and the three of us walked over to the jewelry store.

The Zuni woman smiled when we came into the shop, her white teeth flashing, her angular cheekbones exquisite in her lean, tan face. Without a word, she retrieved the bracelet from under the counter. "I knew this was for you," she said softly.

The bracelet was tooled silver, delicate, a solid piece of silver with many tiny blue, sparkling stones of the purest deep-blue turquoise shaping the thunderbird The wings were striped in silver and the same arrangement of tiny turquoise stones and a yellow turquoise beak on the bird, more beautiful than I had imagined it. "It is fitting to be owned by someone who sees its beauty."

My daughter was at one of my ears, whispering in Danish, "Buy it. Mom will love it," my son at the other, "Mom will think it's too expensive, and it is!"

Again, the woman leaned in to polish the tiny stones with her cloth—apparently she always had it in her left hand, and again, her long, straight, fine, black hair brushed my arm.

We took U.S. 40 south out of Sante Fe, intending to skirt Albuquerque to drive through the Laguna reservation and head for Gallup. Gallup was about a hundred miles north of the Zuni reservation on a very bad, perhaps unpaved, road so we didn't go there. My daughter was in the back seat, eating a devil's food cupcake and repeating, "You should have bought it!"

When the Sunbird got about a hundred miles west, I realized that I should have. But it was too late to turn back. We drove on to Gallup on the main highway and overnighted and, next morning, headed southwest for Petrified Forest on a two-lane highway and reached the national park by eleven and left the Sunbird on a cliff over the mini-badlands. It was isolated, white-ash dunes, and we imagined what the pioneers and the Indians thought of such a desolate place, where you couldn't even see the big country.

The Petrified Forest was other than the kids thought. I had seen it. They had expected a forest, but it was all fallen redwoods, stone-like, and scattered pieces of petrified wood, glittering in the sunlight. It was like thrown jewels across the desert floor.

We drove on to a cliff over the forest and could see for miles and miles over the desert to the horizon and the big sky to the distant cliffs. It was isolated and beautiful, and I watched a hawk, circling in the sky above us, just circling, hanging in the sky.

Next was Flagstaff, Arizona, and I kept hearing the song "Route 66" and thinking how many times I crossed the U.S.A. in the '60s on that route, a road that ran through towns from Chicago to L.A. just like the song said, and had been replaced by U.S. 40 and bypassed the towns. U.S. 40 was more efficient, but 66 drove through the middle of towns where people lived and diners were one of a kind, not a chain emporium that all looked alike. Route 66 was not there anymore, only in scattered patches.

I remembered a diner in Joplin, Mo., when I was in my early twenties where I hitched through on the eponymous highway, and I was taking notes of all I had seen over a cup of coffee, and a guy at the counter asked me if I was writing a book.

"Trying to."

"Well, goll-ee! I just read the first book in my life. Sarah," he said to the waitress, "give this man anything he wants! On me." To me, he said, "And you know what? I own the bowling alley right across 66. Come on over when you're done eating and bowl a couple of lines—on me! Never thought I would meet an actual writer!"

That was over twenty-five years ago, and I regretted for the first time not asking what book he'd read. I decided it was better a mystery.

We drove up thirty-seven miles of north 9 Flagstaff and saw Meteor Crater, formed of an iron meteor, which fell to the earth fifty thousand years ago, and walked on the parapet over. It was a huge depression. In the shop, we bought petrified dinosaur dung because it delighted the kids. "Ew! They said, "Ew!" with delight.

My back and arms and right ankle ached when the Sunbird reached Kingman, Arizona. We took the first decent motel that showed itself. I needed a rest, and the only thing in my mind was a six-pack of cold bottles of Corona. I hadn't been drinking for six or seven months. I asked the motel clerk for the nearest liquor store. The kids were tired, too, and I left them sprawling out on the motel room beds. We would have to split the one before bedtime. We took turns, sleeping on the full bed and mattress and box spring of the other. I left them sacking out on the two full beds while I went to follow the clerk's directions to the liquor store.

The store was a long, narrow place, just a mile east. A long liquor counter had all the spirit that the spirit could desire: several different brands of whiskey, vodka, gin, cognac, American and French and Italian and Australian and Chilean red wines, white wines and champagnes. I had that image in my mind. I bought a six-pack of Corona bottles in a cardboard carrying case, a pack of cigarillos, and bags of chips.

When I swiveled to leave, I saw the opposite counter was a long glass display case of guns and ammunition: handguns—a nickel-plated .45 called a hardballer, .32s, .22s, snub noses, Colt .45s and magnums half the size of a rifle, automatics of every size which had a clip that fitted into the butt, revolvers with hatched wooden and pearl hand-plates, shoulder holsters and belt holsters and ammunition belts. Rifles, lever action, double-barreled shotguns, semi-automatic rifles and automatic rifles which had banana clips and extender clips.

They were beautiful and sexy, all those guns, powerful, with hatched or pearl butt plates. The snub-noses particularly appealed to me—no! the hardballer, nickle-plated .45. I almost bought it until I saw, at the nadir of the long, narrow shop, which I hadn't noticed before, was a large, framed photograph of the president of the United States, William Jefferson (Bill) Clinton—who had brought Chuck Berry and Little Richard to the White House inaugural party—with a bull's eye target superimposed over his face.

I shuddered.

When I got back to the motel, sans hardballer, the kids were in the pool, and I changed into my bathing suit and took a Corona from the cooler and sliced a lime with my Swiss Army knife (which I bought in Geneva and served me for twenty years and would serve me for another twenty until I lost it to an airport security check).

A corpulent family came out to the pool—a mother and two sons and the father, and they started cannon-balling. I got splashed so that my Corona and lime tasted of chlorine until the mother reprimanded them. But I wondered if they had hardballers in their car trunks, three of them, so the three men could shoot all three of us, while the mother reprimanded them.

The three men didn't want to refrain from cannon-balling, and they retreated to the motel room. The mother came over to us, and I wondered whether to thank her when she said that the bottle was glass.

"I don't follow you."

"Could slip out of wet fingers and break on the pool patio. Wouldn't be nice on bare feet."

"Just going to my room, ma'am."

That night, we found a good French restaurant and ate entrecôtes, and I drank a split of Pinot Noir and a post-prandial XO cognac. The corpulent family left next morning; I saw that they had Arizona plates on their car. We stayed in the motel another night—because of the French restaurant and because I was weary of driving and from swimming in the pool, drinking Corona in glass bottles. My Swiss army knife has a bottle opener among its myriad blades.

The direct route was partially unpaved, so we took U.S 40 south the next morning through Yucca and Needles and through the Fort Mojave Indian Reservation to Bullhead City. I was excited because Vibeke and I had swum, sixteen years ago, in the Colorado River at Blythe, about 250 miles lower on the state line. It was a happy memory. We took a motel on the river, visible out the window behind the hotel desk when we checked in. I asked the clerk, "Can you swim in the Colorado here?"

The red-mustached, three-piece-suited man looked at me for a moment, apparently composing his response: "If you want to drown freezing!"

Bullhead City was a casino town, so we dined on big $3.95 prime rib with cola ad libitum. In keeping with the days before, I had a full bottle of red wine and a large cognac after, and reminisced to my kids about the trip with Vibeke nearly two decades before. Then I remembered we had written a postcard to her parents on that trip. She wrote a PS that "Edward speaks Danish as well as he drives (awful!)." I didn't tell my kids about that.

In the morning, we snaked NW through a hatch-work of two lanes and one lanes to Death Valley National Park. I wanted to see Zabriskie Point. We saw the valley, but my daughter wouldn't get out of the car. She was suffering with the heat.

"Do you know that point is noted for its erosional landscape. It is composed of sediments from Furnace Creek Lake, which dried up five million years ago. Long before Death Valley came into existence." Trying to cheer her up, I read ironically as though it was of great interest— which, in fact, it was—from the fact box on the map. The Point was beautiful. It looked like an alien landscape.

My son and I liked the heat. My daughter was like her mother, couldn't tolerate it. Which made me think of years ago, whether she had the MS already in her system, when she spent the summer in New York with me in my un-airconditioned apartment. I hadn't taken it seriously that she was hypersensitive to heat. I thought she was being a prima donna, but here was evidence of it in the genetic make-up of my son versus my daughter. She had her mother's brown eyes, while my son and I had blue. She had her mother's genes. After sixteen years, I felt retrospective guilt. I hadn't taken Vibeke seriously; I tried to take my daughter's genetic response to the heat more seriously. My daughter had been tested whether she had the MS gene in her system and it came up negative, but here was the heat gene, or whatever it was.

I started the engine and the A/C. I said we were leaving Death Valley, but she protested, said that if we got to Furnace Creek and into an air-conditioned restaurant, she would be able to eat lunch and drink a big Coca Cola with plenty of ice cubes.

"You sure?"

"I'm sure," she said. "We came all this way. It's insane not to go the Furnace Creek."

"Sure? I'll turn the car around and get out of this heat." It was 120 F. Still hot, but ten degrees cooler than where we had come from.

"Sure."

My son and I left her in the car with the A/C running and made a quick visit to Zabriskie Point and then drove the fifty miles to town. It was hotter in Furnace Creek. 131 F. We stopped in an airconditioned restaurant and ordered cold chicken and Coke floating with quickly melting ice cubes. Even in the A/C, it was 88 degrees.

"You okay?" I asked my daughter. She said that she only wanted to get to an air-conditioned motel with a swimming pool.

"After we stop in the P.O. to buy an airmail stamp for Europe and postcard from Death Valley for your mother." The car was parked in the shade to cool off until four p.m., when we would start to Vegas. It was noon.

At the Post Office, the metal doorknob burned my palm. I wrapped my hand in my shirt tail to turn the door latch, and we found a motel with a pool where they would rent us a room for a few hours at a day rate.

We settled on loungers in the shade under a canvas canopy with the cooler close by: cans of soda and bottled corona. Sweat was running down our faces, dripping from our chins, pooling in our armpits, staining our shirts. I made the mistake of stepping on the concrete apron of the pool in the sun, and the callus on my heel split.

"Wear your flip-flops if you want to swim!" I called to the kids. I resolved to smile over my split heel. Just wanted to get into the water. It was warm as tepid tea.

By four p.m., it was cooler by ten or fifteen degrees, and we ate watermelon and iced Cokes in the 88 F restaurant, mailed the postcard with the Furnace Creek postcard to prove that we had been to Death Valley.

On the way back to Las Vegas, we heard an ad on the radio that rooms at the Sands were going for thirty dollars. We secured a room at the hotel for three days and ate $3.95 prime rib and Big Macs every day, and swam in the pool every afternoon until our flight back to Copenhagen.

No Mean City

VIBEKE AND I HADN'T SLEPT in the same bed since the night she bashed me on the skull seven years before. I remembered it as the night of "Blood Count." I only had to listen to that cut from Getz's CD *Anniversary*, which I bought in '89 soon as it was out, five years before, to clarify my intentions: I was living with her for my children, for the sake of her disease.

I wanted to check into John Milton, took out my *Norton Anthology of British Literature* from the beginning of the '70s. "The Doctrine and Discipline of Divorce, Restored to the Good of Both Sexes from the Bondage of Canon Law," published in 1643, three and a half centuries before. I had underlined and written in ballpoint beside it, "marriage is so sacred that if it is disturbed it must be ended. A marriage must be between 'fit conversing mates—or souls.'"

This pamphlet was condemned by the state. I had underlined a footnote, "Cf. Erasmus' Commentary—the state obliges incompatible mates to 'live miserably and ungodly together with the great peril and danger to both their souls' healths.' (The Censure of Erasmus, 1550, CVIII, v.)"

I remembered that I did not go into this marriage with seriousness. "Marriage is so sacred..." Sacredness was far from my mind when I married. To say the least, I had doubts about my love. Was that fair to the "health of her soul"? Written in pencil—I could hardly read it—was, "1659: Milton was arrested & in prison for 2 months." The seriousness of Milton highlighted the un-seriousness with which I had entered this marriage. But serious was the fact that I was standing by my children. I could not leave my children—for a couple of years more.

Meanwhile, my life was separate from Vibeke's. I traveled, worked, wrote, read, and enjoyed my children and tried to raise them. I observed the birthdays, the holidays with the family, to Brønshøj, to Slagelse, to Hundested. I lived two—no three, no four—lives: one with myself, one with my children, one with the family, but my life with Vibeke was dis-

229

tant, chilled. I lived falsely with her, manufactured enthusiasm, manufactured a false persona, a mask. I manufactured a character, as surely as in a fiction. I used to test her: If she was in a bickering mood, I retired to my study, to my bedroom.

It was not a healthy way to live, but I felt I had no choice. She made it so difficult for me to relax, to be myself. When I was learning Danish, she refused to speak slowly, to enunciate, so that I could learn, but she got exasperated when I didn't understand—or sarcastic.

I remembered the time we were at her parent's house with guests, after dinner, and her mother asked if I would like more coffee, and I said in Danish, "I'm fine," *Jeg er fin.*

Sarcastically, Vibeke imitated me: "*Jeg er fin!*" And I realized "*fin*" means something else in Danish, "high class." I was embarrassed in front of all the guests. Her mother told me she'd understood me, but I was concerned with Vibeke's embarrassing me and hurting my feelings. I expressed it with coldness. I learned to bite in the hurt.

It was tiresome. I abhorred these exchanges. Eventually, I put on my Walkman or Discman or went into my study and put jazz on. After that time, I wrote a story about a woman who was a witch and turned a man into a dwarf, and it got published; "I got my money back," as Hans Christian Andersen used to say.

Looking at the albums of family snapshots, I began to notice that she always had the same expression on her face: disappointment, depression. She didn't seem to remember our happy times together. She didn't remember the past. If you don't remember the past, you only live in the present, and the present melts to the future and is more of the same. If you could not remember the past, you lived in only one dimension, and you can't remember the reasons for aging, you don't live in an ever-increasing time where you have experiences deepening as you live the years.

Did she even recall hitting me on the head that day that put a gash in my scalp? Did she recall our American vacation, the day we drove from morning to night in the Mojave Desert and took a motel on the highway, stretching flat in every direction, with big trucks—semis—rumbling past, and we swam in the pool on the fringe of the highway at sunset and were happy with our bodies and came into the room and made love and watched B&W television, some situation comedy with John Travolta before he got famous, and he said, "*Drugs!*" and we laughed hysterically.

Because we were happy. She was off the pill then, and that could have been the day that we made our first child, though we didn't know it.

Then I remembered a shameful fact. It was the day that she had been diagnosed with MS, and I took notes. When she was drinking tea, I took notes in the living room. I was without feeling. To take notes while she was faced with her mortality. *It was my job! Writing!*

Unfortunately, I fell in the water and started drinking in earnest that October, but the furor around it was based on a misunderstanding and my saving some seemingly damning evidence.

I'd gone to a conference at Castile e Leòn in northwestern Spain. This was celebrated by the Spanish hosts on the Friday after the conference with a 45-minute bus ride out in the countryside outside of Segovia for a meal. Adelina, the woman who was my Spanish counterpart, sat next to me on the bus and entertained me with the fact that the restaurant we were going to eat in, for *cochinella*, was the best inn for suckling pig in Spain. Adelina told me that it was also one of the places where they raised bulls for the bullring. Young ones. She said that she was looking forward to me fighting one. Merely wrestle it down. A young one, not bigger than a very large dog.

"I have an Army wound that precludes me from wrestling a bull. Even a small one." I didn't go into detail, that a sergeant in basic training at Fort Dix ordered me to lift a garbage pail filled with water, and my back cracked. Every time I was overweight and moved in a certain way, the injury recurred.

Adelina said, "Where is your *machismo*?"

Maybe that was the problem with Vibeke and me: I lacked machismo, and she wanted it.

When we got there, we filed into the bullring and a bunch of small bulls (looked full- grown to me, they were skinny, but they had growing horns) were released from the pen. The Spanish hosts actually expected us to wrestle them! A line of younger, northern and central European men were standing in the entry gate to the ring, the place that the bull-fights were staged, and I was witness to the first one being knocked on his ass. I took the exit and made a direct line to the bar.

"A gin and tonic," I asked the white-coated barman. The first drink I'd had practically all year—except for the wine and cognac and Corona

I'd had on my vacation with the kids in the States. He poured a tall glass of gin and spritzed a little tonic in. "You don't want to wrestle with thee bulls?"

"Later."

He laughed.

I sat in one of the carved armchairs, and Fiona, a young Scottish woman, came over to me. Fiona was my counterpart in the London office, had ragged, multi-colored punk hair. She was about twenty-five years younger than me. She was small and slender and had a Glaswegian accent.

I said, "You remind me of Jim Taggert. On TV. I love that Maggie Bell theme song. *Blues!* Like a drink?"

"Well, I wouldn't say no."

She asked for the same thing as me, and the white-coated barman poured liberally. "Please," I said. "Give me another, too."

People were straggling in from the bullring, and Adelina popped up and said she was looking all over for me. "To wrestle thee bulls."

I steered Fiona by the elbow, saying over my shoulder, "Bad back." When we got out of hearing, I said that I hoped Fiona didn't mind, but I was trying to avoid Adelina. I didn't say why. She seemed determined to embarrass me: Maybe that was how certain Spanish girls showed she liked a man.

Fiona told me she was trying to avoid a couple of young bulls, too— Leif and Dennis, the men from the office in Stockholm and in Dublin. "I'd like you to take me under your wing. Mature men make good conversation," she said in her Glaswegian patter.

"How charmingly you rolls your 'r's," I said, trying not to imitate her.

Leif and Dennis appeared at our table. "May vi join you?" Leif asked. He was a tall Swede with kinky brown hair and full lips and big eyeglasses. They sat, and a tall Danish woman joined them, and a German girl. The table was complete now.

The dinner was served with white, red, port, and brandy with the coffee, and afterward, the buses came to take us home.

The bus was blue. I sang, "The blue bus/Is calling us!" and sneaked two full snifters of brandy onto the coach for Fiona and me. We were quite tipsy and sat beside each other. The little hours were upon us. They dimmed the cabin lights on the bus so that people could sleep, but Leif had brought an opened bottle of wine and two glasses and, apparently, he had found another female—a Turkish one with blue eyes—because we heard his voice all along the bus to where Fiona and I were sitting: "I vant to kees your feet."

Somehow—I think it was after we finished the brandy—we got to the point of my asking if I could kiss her.

She started. "You ask? Well, the answer is *yes*."

In the dark, we began to kiss in earnest and feel each other up.

I should have left it at that, the kisses on the bus, the feeling up, but I was drunk and whispered in the pink shell of her ear as we were pulling into the carousel of the hotel, and the light blinked on, "Your room or mine?" I was trying to be flip, or worldly, or both. After all, we were both married, though my marriage was a shadow play, and I assumed hers was more than that. She was only 26 to my 50. I should have known better.

"Mine," she said. She said the room number—it was on the same floor as mine—and just give her five minutes. That was five minutes pause. I could have changed my mind. Just left it with the making out in the bus. But my pride was too much invested in it: a young, pretty woman desiring me, young woman with a Ph.D., who was already my counterpart on the organizational chart, though I had nearly twenty-five years on her. She was slender and her muscle tone was delicious. She had told me during the dinner that she ran five miles every day and had done so for ten years.

I had said something like, "That's why you're delightfully slender," and her eye lit, and mine lit at imagining her in gym shorts and a little middy blouse and further imagining her wearing only her bird's nest. I wondered what the color was. Maybe she had it shaved. I think I did say something like—in the fog of the third glass of white—or maybe it was the fourth glass of red; it takes a lot of wine to open my mouth to what I'm thinking: "Like to see you in all the splendor of your nakedness," and under the table, she squeezed my hand.

In short, I did knock softly on her door in ten minutes. She had been into the minibar for two splits of cava, and we didn't forget where we left off on the bus. I actually said that I would like to go down on her, and she replied, "Oh, my!"

But then I got cold feet. Feet, it was. My desire freed me of care as I undressed her in the opulent uniformity of her hotel room—I had precisely the twin of it—but her feet brought me back to sobriety. Or maybe it made me leave my sense behind. The slender firmness of her body dazzled my palms as they slid down her flanks, her legs to the bottom of her feet.

She was lying on her back on the bed in the dark, and I was about to go down, final abandon, hovering like a bee-mouth above her beige bloom, as my palms caressed the bottoms of her feet and felt there a thick, hard sheet of callus.

Oh, yes, she jogs, I thought. Runs to keep trim. An image of her running along a sidewalk to burn away the fat of oral pleasure stopped me from my orality, turned poisonous as I was about to descend on her. My erection went soft as cotton. It made no sense but it woke me from abandon, before the first taste with a question: *Can you get AIDS from doing this*? And another, more vulgar statement: *You don't shit where you eat*. And: *She's only twenty-six, almost a quarter century younger*. It occurred to me what people would think, what *I* would think. Tongues wagged in that business, and when a tongue wagged it wagged other tongues: *A family father! Seemed like a nice man, a gentleman he's not*. What would I think after it was over. *Th'expense of spirit in a waste of shame is lust in action*.

Raising my mouth to her ear again, I said, "I'm sorry. I can't do this." And heard the breath of her gentle snores. Saved! Both she and I! I still had my pants and briefs on, my shirt, too, unbuttoned and the tails flapped out.

Then, as now, a second voice cursing me—for perhaps the last time in my life, such a pretty young woman would, just like that, want me. *Sin boldly*. While the first voice urged, *Go! Don't look back, cut your losses, burn this bridge now while you still have enough sense left, knowing you almost fell, stumbled, but regained your balance*.

In the hall, in my sock feet, shirt tails flapping, shoes in my hand and suit jacket over my arm, silk necktie god knows where, as only could have been ordained, I met the kinky-haired, thick-lipped, horn-spectacled Leif; he was apparently on the same floor. Startled, we paused.

Apparently, Leif had struck out with the Turkish woman. Or made short business of her. I met his eye and winced. "This is not what it seems," I whispered. "Nothing happened."

Leif puckered his thick lips, grinning, enjoying my predicament.

"Some evidence is undeniable. As vhen von finds a trout in the meelk. Want to have a drink and recount your adventures in the Scottish lowlands?"

"Nothing happened," I whispered and dog-trotted to my room before some other curious soul would come to his or her door.

In the morning, I rose at seven and hoped I would not meet anyone from the conference—I didn't—and paid my room bill, prepared to roll my bag out to the taxi queue. The desk clerk gave me a message in a sealed envelope.

> Dearest,
> Sorry, I fell asleep. I wish to have more of the same!
> I don't take a plane until late, and I have secured the room
> until five pm. Want to have (French) breakfast in my room?
>
> Love and kisses,

In place of her name, she had kissed the notepaper with a surfeit of lipstick. I put it in my inner pocket as a souvenir and proceeded to the taxi queue.

On the plane, I drank champagne with a breakfast of scrambled eggs, a fried tomato, mushrooms, and a sausage: business-class (instead of French) breakfast. I vacillated between congratulating myself on my escape, congratulating myself on igniting the desire of a sexy, pretty young woman, admiring the note from Fiona, and having cold sweats about Leif, who was ten years younger and more powerful than me, who was elected president of practically every honorary organization and was rich.

He would surely get tongues wagging, would surely tell everyone, one at a time. With horror, I recalled one time on the Greek island of Crete, a woman at a conference had said to me, "Want to have a laugh, Leif asked me to meet him on the roof of the hotel. He's always after me. Want to show up with me and watch his smile fade." And she linked her arm to mine, and we took the elevator up to the roof restaurant. Leif was waiting in the shadows—the restaurant was closed—and his smile did fade.

Afterward, we had a party in my room, six or seven of us, Leif included, and five—including me—passed out on my bed, fully clothed, but Leif was not among them. He stole away and was up early next morning and told everyone, the ones who would listen. I was greeted at the meeting by a woman, saying, "Five on a bed!" and another man said, "You had a busy night!" and Leif sat behind the Swedish flag, smiling like a razor. My retort that, "Nothing happened!" was met by knowing smiles of all in the vicinity. "Ah," a third man intoned, "yes, nothing."

Because she was a sexy, pretty, young woman, and he had struck out with the Turkish woman and hadn't had Fiona and god knew why she wanted me. Maybe because I had asked before I kissed her, and a more powerful man like Leif didn't ask. He just took. Took revenge, too. What could he do to me?

Danes didn't butt into your private life like Americans or Brits or Swedes did. Maybe Leif could speak to the British delegation, complain, and upset my lucrative deal. *A trout in the meelk!*

At the CD shop at Kastrup airport, I bought a Bob Dylan CD for my son, a Prince for my daughter. I thought: Maggie Bell—*No Mean City*. I took them to the cash register.

I was still of two minds about Fiona—flattered that she wanted to be with me in that way and relieved that I chose not to, although the fact that Leif had seen me in the hall was damning. Men were the worst gossips. I could not help taking the note from Fiona out of my inside jacket pocket in the taxi. It tickled me.

The champagne was still operative in my blood. "I fell in the water," I said to Vibeke when I got home, handing her the carton of filtered Prince.

"You're *stinko*!"

It was no use. She wanted to argue. The kids were already in their rooms, listening to music, talking on the telephone, reading. My son was fifteen, my daughter thirteen. I tapped on their doors, one by one, gave them their presents. They seemed pleased, expressed pleasure that I was home but not like when they were little kids, whooping. We chatted. To my son, I said, "Want to have a *pivo* with your old man?" I noted the echo of what my father had asked me so often. To my daughter, I proposed a Coke. They said they had homework.

I hung my raincoat and suit jacket in the hall closet, went into my study to listen to the Maggie Bell CD with ear buds. I lay on the bed, listened to "No Mean City," enjoying the way the electric notes of the blues guitar joined the hoarseness of Maggie Bell's voice, the Glaswegian accent.

Drifting off, listening to the accent, I wondered that my life should be so strange, to be in northwestern Spain and fly to this northern capital to be with my children and the enemy who was my wife of twenty years.

Waking to the sounds of my son and daughter eating breakfast, I focused on the dropped, knotty pine ceiling which met my gaze, the eyes of wood, drifted off, woke some time later to silence. I wanted only to pee, brush my teeth, and have black coffee. I put my pants on and bare-footed out of my study.

Vibeke was waiting in the hallway, a sarcastic grin on her face.

"I don't want to bicker."

She stepped close, her face in mine. "You smell foul from your mouth."

"Let me brush my teeth."

"Dearest," she said. "Want to have French breakfast in my room?" She kneed me in the balls. Direct hit. I gasped, couldn't stand, went down on one knee, choking for air, pain radiating up from my groin. Vibeke stood over me.

"Nothing," I gasped, "happened," and she spun and stomped up the stairs, slammed her bedroom door and turned the lock.

It served me right. Keeping the souvenir.

Traneing In

WE HAD ANOTHER SUMMER VACATION two summers later. To Normandy. We flew down to Brussels, stayed in the Radisson on my frequent flyer points, ate Belgian waffles and *moule* in white wine sauce and French fries with mayo, went to Á la Mort Subite and enjoyed strawberry beer on Rue Montagne aux Herbs (*la Mort Subite* means sudden death). Next day we picked up a rented Mitsubishi and drove to Cabourg, outside of which we had rented a "villa" which turned out more to be a prefabricated shack in a village of prefabricated shacks. There was no warm water, about which I complained and got a hundred-fifty euros off the total price, but no hot water.

Driving distance to the seaside beach town Cabourg, we visited often and had afternoon coffee and a madeleine at Le Grand Hôtel. We visited Omaha Beach and Bayeux and bought plastic rulers imprinted with the tapestry and saw ex-pat American friends in Honfleur: Ben Hawthorne, a short-story writer, was minus one hand from birth and could do far more with his one hand than I could do with my two; and Carol, an economist from an international NGO who had taught me that I had to file taxes in Denmark and in the U.S. If the IRS came after me, they would eat my lunch, but if I went to them, they would only require me to file for the last six years with no penalties if I didn't owe anything. I didn't owe anything.

They had a rented apartment in Paris on the Seine in the 16th arondissement, across the river from the Eiffel Tower. Their apartment was around the corner from where *Last Tango in Paris* was filmed, beneath the bridge where Marlon Brando throws back his head, pinching his ears, and roars, "Fucking god!" underneath the hammering of the elevated Metro. And they had an 18th century farm house in Honfleur, on the Seine, too. Ben was slowly refurbishing it t the period the house was built. When he heard about a house from that period that was in the process of being torn down, he would drive out to it in a borrowed truck and salvage all the doors and beams and even cast-iron nails that he could and build an extension on their own house.

We brought flowers for Carol and a bottle of Carte Noir cognac for Ben. "*Merci beaucoup!*" he said in his deep bass voice.

Ben and I did some damage to the cognac on the deck outside their house until four in the morning, catching up. We had a tradition that when we met we drank by a body of water. We had so far done it by the River Maas at a writers conference in the Netherlands, the Kattegat in Denmark and the street lakes in Copenhagen, the Atlantic in the south of Portugal, and the Seine, two times, in Paris and Honfleur, out on his deck which had a view of the river where it bends in its mouth at Le Havre.

I was not getting much rest anyway. Vibeke was not allowing me to sleep in "her" bed, neither in Brussels nor in Cabourg. I slept on a two-man sofa at the Radisson, near the Grande Place in Brussels, and in an armchair in our "villa" in Normandy. It was a relief to sit up with Ben, gazing at the Seine glistening in the summer night and listening to Ben's *Traneing In* with the Coltrane Quartet—Red Garland on piano, Paul Chambers on bass, and Art Taylor on drums, recorded in Hacksensack, NJ, in 1957.

"I have to make a pilgrimage to Hackensack," I said. "It's not far from the Hudson River. All those great cuts recorded there."

"Hear, hear!" Ben said and stood to top our snifters of cognac. He was a tall man, maybe 6'4".

It was past midnight. The others were asleep, and we were into the third playing of Coltrane's tenor entering the shush of the Seine and the black sky.

I said, "I'm not long for this marriage. I gave it twenty-two years, but I'm ready." It was the first time I spoke of it to anybody.

"You'll feel differently in the a.m."

Trane came on, his tenor screaming softly into the Vieux Port night over the river, toward the black twinkling sky. I *knew*. "It's only a matter of time."

"Cliché," Ben said. "You shouldn't use so many clichés. Makes you sloppy when you write." He was a splendid writer of short fiction.

"Clichés are time tested."

"Another cliché."

"Clichés are old as the hills. There's truth in clichés. That's why they became clichés."

"As in the cliché, My wife doesn't understand me. They never do."

"I'm a battered husband." I said it like a joke, but I meant it.

"Some men like that," he said, "and I'm not putting it down." Apparently he wanted to make it go away, but I didn't wish it to go away. I had never admitted it to anyone, and now that I had, it wouldn't go away.

"I don't like it."

He looked for a long moment into my eyes, then dropped his gaze to my chin. "Serious?"

I nodded.

"Belt her back."

"You speaking from experience?"

"No."

"I tried that. It only led to more violence."

In the morning, I woke up on a three-man sofa in their living room, the remnants of the Carte Noir bottle on the coffee table—about two snifters worth. Ben came in from the kitchen, bearing a large mug of black coffee for me. Picking up the Carte Noir, he said, "A monument to our shame. Want a little eye opener?"

"I've had quite enough eye-openings."

Kind of Blue

IN AUGUST, THE NEXT MONTH after we returned to Copenhagen from Normandy, I had plans to fly, after I taught in New Jersey, on a book tour for four of my small press books to Kansas City, MO, Portland, La Grande, San Francisco, and San Diego. I would do interviews and readings, sign off on the third and fourth books, which were due to be published early in the next year.

People you meet, they say, "What do you do?"

"Writer."

"Books?"

"Yeah."

"*Oh!*"

They figure you have a big New York publisher and an agent, and you make lots of money.

I didn't make a lot of money, but still you had to master your craft, you had to learn how to write, and sometimes it took years, decades. Less than five percent of what got written got published, even for free, and even what got published is not necessarily serious. That year, with two books out and two books on the way, I had a taxable income from fiction writing of $4,479, and that was because I had an O. Henry Prize story which came out in hardback and paperback, and my share of the royalties was $1,248.

You got $9 for a story from *Glimmer Train* plus ten copies (those sisters! Susan Burmeister-Brown and Linda Swanson-Davies who'd made their fortune in computers), about $400 to $1,000 from *Missouri Review*, about $400 from *Epoch*, $300 from *Southern Review* and *Boston Review,* $50 to $100 from *New Letters* (depending on their grants), $50 from *Cimarron Review*, $20 from *Confrontation*, and one or two contributor's copies and *no* honorarium from many other literary journals. Then, for readings, I got $200 to $1,500, workshops and talks another $300 or $1,000. The good thing is you sell the stories, one by one to magazines and then sell them as a collection for which you get a royalty and, if you're lucky, an advance on royalties.

I'm not complaining; the whole thing goes around in a big picture. You got tax deductions. When you start, you don't know if you'll be a small press writer. You start because you want to write, the only thing you want is to write. It becomes a spiritual discipline. You got good after some years and along the way, you acquired an agent or agents who believed in you, and when you got an agent you thought you would get rich, but the agent didn't sell anything for you, and you wanted to quit. After 20 years, you try to quit, but you couldn't. So you continued writing on the terms that you started. And if you dissolved your marriage—and more writers than don't got divorced, most people, too (slightly over fifty percent of "highly educated" persons are slated to get divorced at the twenty-year mark)—there was an economic bite that came. A couple split in two, but their economy does more than split in two. A house is more expensive than expensive than two little apartments, and a couple can live more cheaply than two singles.

I don't want to be misleading about my writing and publications. I'm not complaining or bragging about it. These four books that I was publishing this and next year were from small- to micro-press publishers. Three of the four of them are still in print more than two decades later, only because the initial thousand or two-thousand copy press-run were not sold out. The fourth was not in print because the publisher had gone under in his tenth year of business; the press would offer to sell me the last eighty-seven copies of the five hundred press-run for a dollar a copy before they went out of business. This was before print-on-demand was possible; otherwise, they would have been POD, no press run at all to speak of.

The 1996 editions were a collection of stories which was being issued in Oregon, a short novel that was being published in Prairie Village, KS, just across the state line from Kansas City, MO, by a retired lawyer in his mid-seventies. He had vowed to put all his savings in a publishing company that would have contests for book publication and would issue a bi-monthly magazine and have writers conferences. I had won the contest for a short novel that I had written 27 years before, for which I had won a T. B. Goodman Prize in 1970 for $2,350 and never got published, dusted it off and entered the retired lawyer's fiction book contest. He would publish worthy fiction that no one else wanted to print because they couldn't make money on it—not even the publishing costs. Of course, people were so desperate to get published, they will enter multiple contests for publication for a $20 or $25 entry fee.

The wife of the publisher, of about seventy, a slender, natural beauty named Polly, met me at the KC airport mid-afternoon. Polly told me the short novel had not been published yet—it would—but her husband was in the hospital, dying. Would I consent to meet him? Only he thought my book had been published, and I mustn't tell him it was not. He had lung cancer at seventy-four. He had quit smoking thirty years before, but he still had lung cancer. It had spread to his brain. She was so soft-spoken, telling these facts so that I couldn't say no if I wanted, and I didn't want. I looked in her pretty face and said, "Of course, I'll visit Herman!"

Polly drove me over to see Herman in the hospice. She led me into a large room that had the lights low. She called out to Herman that I was there, and she whispered to me that she would leave me alone with him.

I approached the bed in the big, dim room. He was lying on his back with his eyes closed and the covers up to his chin, a tall man who had shrunk.

I couldn't think of anything else to say but, "Hi, Herman." I whispered it, then said, in a firmer tone, "Hello."

Without opening his eyes, he said in a gravelly voice, "Are you satisfied with your book?"

"It's beautiful. It has the cover art, Bok's *Angel in a Well*, and the blurbs. And it has the shade of corn-flower blue I wanted. It's perfect."

"I haven't seen it yet. But is the title, *The Weather of the Eye* or *A Weather of the Eye*?"

"It's *A Weather of the Eye*. Just like you advised. From the Dylan Thomas poem, *A darkness in the weather of the eye is half its light*. I wanted it to be *The Weather of the Eye*, but I wasn't satisfied until you suggested collapsing the line, using the indefinite article."

"Maybe use no article at all? *Weather of the Eye*."

I thought he was confused. The fiction was that my book had been published. "It's published already. And I'm happy with it."

He didn't speak, nor open his eyes for long enough that I feared he had expired. Then: "The concept of voice in fiction. I would like to discuss that with you. Do you think that's just syntax?"

"Mainly syntax. And vocabulary. All I know is when you have it, you have it. It's a mystery to me—that I don't want to solve."

A slow clicking erupted from his throat that at first startled me, then I recognized it as laughter. I smiled.

"It's a beautiful book—*Weather*. My family, my siblings, I thought they should have a preview of it. It was related to them anyway. I sent the galleys to them, and wrote in a cover letter to all three that they might recognize the characters, but I took some liberties with the plot to consolidate it. I added that it was all written with love for the family. My sister telephoned me and said, 'Is that *really* us?' She'd read it before, but she hadn't recognized our family. 'It's *fiction!*' I said, and she said, 'Well, Jos., he said, It's posthumous character assassination of our parents, and James, Jr.'"—he's the boxer—"'is gonna kick your ass,' but James claims he didn't receive it.

"So, next time I was in Queens, I visited James. Face the music and all that. He let me in with his mean boxer's face on, the flattened nose. Just about everything I'd published was piled on the coffee table and all available surfaces. I spotted the galleys of *Weather*, too, among them, and I said, 'James, you really have great taste in literature!' and he said, 'I want you to know how proud we are of you, brother.'"

More clicking erupted from Herman's throat.

"And I want you to know, Herman, how proud I am of that book. It's beautiful. And it took me twenty-seven years to publish it, but now it's published, and it's a definitive statement about my late father. At least from my point of view. I have you to thank for that, Herman." I hoped it hadn't been awkward, what I'd said, but I had to thank him.

"Thank you for saying that." Herman cleared his gravelly throat. "My butt hurts." He asked if I could help him to sit up. With difficulty, I helped him to sit on the edge of the bed, his long legs dangling down beneath his white smock. I was surprised to see no machines or tubes attached to him and how meager he was.

He shook my hand and held it. His grip was strong, and his eyes seemed deep in his skull, dark and hollow. I met his gaze. It was as though he was staring at me from the threshold of death, from behind it, with his dark, unblinking eyes. I understood that this was the last time I would see him. He knew it was the last time and communicated that knowledge to me with his eyes and his strong hand, gripping mine.

Polly dropped me off at the University House on Rockhill Road which housed the other publisher, BkMk Press and *New Letters*, a quarterly journal that had been issued for eighty years, and some solid writers were in it.

The associate editor rose. I didn't remember her name and I'd asked it so many times that I couldn't ask again. She showed me a mock-up of the cover of *Drive, Dive, Dance & Fight*, eight stories, five of which had been in *New Letters*, published by the University of Missouri Kansas City. I'd earned $250 for the five and the O. Henry Prize royalties of $1,248. The other had been in *Glimmer Train* (for $700) and two excellent but non-paying markets. That was $2,199, and *New Letters*, in lieu of an advance from BkMk, invited me to judge their fiction contest for $1,000. So, I would make on this collection, in all, $3,199, plus royalties of 10%. It was selling for $14.95. So $1.49 on royalties, per copy sold. Every little bit helps. Every little bit as an author—it was indifferent to me how much I earned on my NGO work. That was what kept me and my family alive, but that was not important. The important thing was how much I made on my authorship; that was how I kept my soul alive.

I wished I could remember the associate editor's name. She was a young girl with a 6-month-old baby. She labored so much on the cover, simulating the white letters in typescript on a varied blue background, like the depths of the sea, and hunting out a photo of a diver, which depicted the title story but not too closely. If it was too close, the cover would appear amateurish.

"Like the picture?"

"I *love* the picture. And the cover."

"I doctored the photo of the diver. It's a woman."

"Can't tell. I love the way the title and my name are big enough to see, in typescript—the letters clogged by the make-believe ribbon, but clear enough. Not too cluttered."

I should have given her a credit in the book. The three blurbs on the back cover were by Andre Dubus, James Carroll, and Duff Brenna, against an underwater background, a photo of me (one of the only ones I liked, by Mel Buffington), and the cover seemed to hint of the mystery in the final diving scene in the title story.

Bob Stewart, the editor of *New Letters* and of BkMk, stepped in the door, a tall, broad man with a receding hairline. "Were you picked up at the airport okay?"

I've known Bob since the end of the '80s. He has always been supportive, nurturing. He's published seven of my stories and now this book and would publish countless essays, stories, translations, and photographs. Mention of the airport reminded me of Herman, his dark stare. "Herman's dying."

"Yes, I know."

We glanced in each other's eyes, a glance that said he and I were only in our early fifties, Herman was in his mid-seventies. Twenty years away. Herman's dark stare.

"Let me get you over to the place you're staying."

In his Cherokee half-back, he explained that if I had something against it, he would put me up in a hotel, but he had another idea. "You'll stay in Sabrina's apartment. Alone. She's fixed something up for you."

Sabrina was Bob's girlfriend, a beautiful Korean woman in her late twenties, a classical concert pianist and a poet, who was shopping around for an MFA program, being courted by two leading poets in the U.S. She had sent me a couple of letters, handwritten in painstaking calligraphy, on profound philosophical matters. When the second letter arrived, I called Bob with a pretense about a manuscript I had sent him. I added, "I got a letter from Sabrina the other day."

"She told me she was going to write you," he said. "Asked for your address."

They were works of art, her letters, as gorgeous as she was.

Bob dropped me off at the apartment. Sabrina was not there. Bob showed me around, the refrigerator, bathroom, bedroom, living room. It was just as slender and neat and pretty as she. He handed me a letter in an unfastened envelope with something thick in it. He said he had to go, but he'd be back tomorrow afternoon to take me to my class and reading at Barnes & Noble and in between we'd get a bite and a martini. He gave me another envelope with a check in it for $500.

"It feels like Christmas!"

Like all Midwesterners west of the Mississippi he was soft-spoken with the few words he spoke. "You okay now?"

I opened the second envelope of fine parchment paper. It contained a letter, lovely as Sabrina, and a CD. It started, "Dearest Sweet Edward," and I have to recall what she wrote in her inimitable way because I don't have any of her letters. They were lost in a move, in a carton of cherished letters. She enumerated her suggestions in perfect calligraphy, shaded just so, never a mistake, or she used wite-out so expertly that it couldn't be detected.

She said in the first line that I had agreed to stay in her apartment, and she was glad because I could have chosen a hotel, and it was a sign of confidence in her and that these were only suggestions:

First, she had put some sandwiches and chocolates filled with vodka that she had prepared. I was welcome to eat or drink anything in the refrigerator, but if I opened the freezing compartment, she had put a bottle of black label Stolichnaya on the ice, like they served it in Denmark.

Second, feel free—she *insisted*—to rummage in her books (she would consider it an honor if I read any of her books) and hear the CDs (if I would listen to any of them, feel free to play them on the disc player—she had included instructions in case I didn't know how to work it).

Third, feel free to open any drawers and rummage in them.

Four, if I am not familiar with the CD of Miles Davis' *Kind of Blue*—I may well be—it is (in her opinion) the *best* set of cuts in the history of jazz, and she had enclosed it here, a gift for me.

I was baffled why she was so nice to me—and remembered the line in Hemingway about Robert Cohn, that he had married the first woman who was nice to him. Was it because Bob had respect for my writing? Or was she trying to win me over with her "niceness," to collect me? Was she a victim of OCD? Or was she just as nice as she seemed, admired me as a writer and as a person. Was her beauty beside the point, perhaps a burden to her? Or was I calculating unclearly? Regardless, I would accept her as being nice, perfectly nice.

I looked at the CD. It was recorded in 1959 and consisted of all Miles Davis' compositions. In addition to Miles himself on trumpet, Cannonball was on alto, Trane on tenor, Wynton Kelly and Bill Evans on piano,

Paul Chambers on bass, Jimmy Cobb on drums.

I had heard about it—perhaps heard a couple of cuts from it out of context, but was not familiar with it. How had thirty-seven years passed without my having heard it all the way through, repeatedly? I was fifteen years old when it was recorded, and it remained available, one of the best-selling albums of all time.

First, I had to feed my stomach. I looked in the refrigerator. There was a platter of mini-sandwiches on mini-rolls with a yellow mini-stick-it label on each—eel and egg, smoked salmon, shark meat, crab, boar-liver pâté—each lettered calligraphically. With a black-label Stoli rocks, I wandered around munching the rolls, looking at her book shelves. They were arranged perfectly, with the edges of the spines flush in alphabetical order—I looked sporadically: Dylan Thomas, Simic, Kowit, Rios, Myers, Sappho, Neruda, Emily Dickinson, Whitman, Rukeyser, May Swenson, Stewart, Eliot, Cummings, Horace, Brecht, Mary Oliver, Cavafy, Plath, Gilgamesh, Heaney, Hughes, Jean Valentine, Rilke, Delmore Schwartz, Eavan Boland, Patchen, Tess Gallagher, Frank O'Hara, Yeats, Ferlinghetti, Ginsberg, Sexton, Atwood, Marianne Moore, Kumin, William Carlos Williams.

There were even a couple of mine. I chose another sandwich and topped up my Stoli and wandered further. In the bedroom, I saw a chest of drawers. *No, I would never do that—even if she insisted.*

I opened the widest, deepest drawer, the lowest one. Stacks of skinny dungarees, the same cut for her long legs, blue, red, pink, copper, yellow, black, all ironed neatly, folded so they were the same dimensions and impeccably stacked. Ashamed, I slumped the drawer shut. It rolled smoothly. I got out of the bedroom, feeling like a Peeping Ed.

How's the peeping, Tommy?

I poured another Stoli and had some dark vodka-filled chocolates, so dark they must have been 95% cacao, and sat in an easy chair by the CD player and took up *Kind of Blue*, discovered a booklet in the jewel case with liner notes by Bill Evans, the legendary jazz pianist who died in 1980 at fifty-one.

Evans compared improvisation in jazz with Japanese painting in which spontaneity is forced upon the artist, such that changes are impossible, "allowing the idea to express itself in communication with the hands in such a direct way that deliberation cannot interfere, but that those who see will find something captured that escapes explanation."

That must have been what Beckett meant when he said that it all happens between the hand and the page.

Evans goes on to say that Miles presents in this "framework melodies that are exquisite in their simplicity and yet contain all that is necessary to stimulate performance with a sure reference to the primary conception. Miles conceived these settings only hours before the recording dates and arrived at the studio with sketches which indicated to the group what was to be played. Therefore, you will hear something close to pure spontaneity in these performances. The group had never played these pieces prior to the recordings and I think without exception the first complete performance of each was a 'take.'"

I started the CD. As the first scattered piano notes of "So What?" came on—played by Bill Evans, the man who had explained the ideas that had been foggily obsessing me ever since fifteen years ago when I had my leg in a cast and I met that Danish general on my street. I looked out the window and saw in the dim light, across Brush Creek, on a wide expanse of yellow grass, an enormous shuttlecock as if fallen to earth from the Badminton Game of the Gods. The giant shuttlecock, I knew, was a work of art by a Swedish sculptor, Claes Oldenburg, and the building behind it was the Nelson Atkins Gallery.

I was seized by an intense sense of synchronicity—that I should be looking out this window of Sabrina's apartment which Bob Stewart had driven me to, and Sabrina had given me the CD by Miles, and I'd happened to read the liner notes by Bill Evans which explained the thought that had been informing me vaguely all these years, that I could not articulate it clearly, that serendipitous coincidence of these moments had conspired to solve a central problem of my life.

It was so severely simple and required discipline as Cannonball blew runs on his alto and Trane responded with the tenor and Miles' trumpet played among a smattering of such exquisitely simple notes and the plucking bass and tapped drum snares and ringing clear as hammers striking the strings of the piano notes. This was recorded a week before my fifteenth birthday, on 30th Street in Manhattan, across the East River from my home in Queens, and I didn't know I would meet it thirty-seven years later in Kansas City—the Swedish sculptor reminding of my new home in Scandinavia and the game of the gods, this music from my old home, and Evans explaining it clearly, concisely, effortlessly as only one who *knew* the matter—it was complexly simple—and the calligraphic skills of Sabrina mediating all these elements together.

It was a severe and unique discipline. You had to follow the words in such a way that an unnatural or forced deliberation could not interfere. You have to let it bubble up, and you cannot scratch out and wait for the right word to occur to you, the right image, the right line to create something coherent but inexplicable—as in the short-story "Drive Dive Dance & Fight," when you were diving down in your mind, your imagination, as the character Twomey was diving down into the ocean at Far Rockaway—you should see it then, a yard from your face, grinning with a white jaw and teeth, flesh eaten from the bone, an eel supping on its glistening eyeball.

Death.

I saw death, the black mass of death. At that moment of my writing of the story. And fitted it into—as the best of art always is—a coherent natural whole, built of hand-mastered skill.

It took until now that you saw what you were driving toward, trying to comprehend: How you write. You had to keep going until it was revealed.

I left Kansas City, god-awful early in the morning to catch my flight to Seattle at 6:05 a.m., which meant getting a taxi for the airport at 4:30 a.m. The cab driver was a woman of perhaps sixty-three, unremarkable in appearance, but talkative, and in the course of our conversation, *her* conversation rather, as the taxi rolled along the highway through the pure dawn darkness toward the airport, she said, "Well, I live in town now so I can't keep the kind of cats I'd like to anymore."

Still half asleep, I felt the phrase reach into some private areas of my mind, prodding gently. "What, uh, *kind* of cats did you mean?"

"Well at one time I had four mountain lions, a leopard, a cheetah and three bobcats. But all I'd have now would be mountain lion. Now your mountain lion is a *sweet* animal by nature, but she does smell, I'll tell you that, and you need room out in the country for her. My leopard was also a dear animal, but she took a liking to my little Bobby, and I'll tell you, she'd go right after my knees, slash 'em, if I said a bad word to that boy. She followed him around wherever he went. She was a one-boy cat, she was. Bobcats are honeys, too, but they have a temper."

I peered out of the window of the taxi into the darkness rushing past, and the moment posed unanswerable questions. Did I have the enlightenment two nights ago so that I could be intercepted by this bizarre monologue at an ungodly hour in a dark vehicle in this city I heard sung about by Willard Harrison in my youth? Or is it all chance? Flash without meaning?

The plane for Seattle was cancelled. As I stood on the security line, wanting to get through to question the woman at the dias of my cancelled flight, a young man in uniform who I can only describe as runty— shorter than me—stepped up and said, "Are you having a good day so far, sir?"

"Well, my flight has been cancelled, so I didn't have to get out to the airport so god-awful early, but then I wouldn't have heard the cab-driver's bizarre monologue, so I guess it's a win-lose situation, but I'd like to get through security to ask the woman at the desk whether there's another flight, maybe a connecting flight."

"You're out of luck, sir."

"Luck?"

"You have been chosen at random to be investigated further, so I'll just have to ask you to step out of the security line, sir, and be wanded."

I stepped out. "I'll have to ask you to take off your shoes and put your arms out straight, and you can flap them and make a noise like an airplane, sir. Vroom-vroom."

At the moment my anger was about to reach the pinpoint of rage, it occurred to me what inconvenience this young runt in uniform could subject me to, so I flapped my arms and said "vroom vroom" and felt like a ridiculous person. So this was the succession of events that ended in ridicule.

Flamenco Sketches

I CAME BACK FROM THE TOUR knowing I had some painful things to do. These had dominated my thoughts throughout the remainder of the tour.

In Oregon, I was to visit La Grande to read publicly from *Unreal City*, stories that were, each in its own way, surreal, involving, e.g., good and bad angels and angels in a well-like contraption, stories about a man who eats excessively and gets mistaken for a "Great Master," about a child who manipulates his parents by acting like he's insane and he winds up insane, a man to whom God appears and he makes the mistake of asking for money, and as they say, *other stories*. I had gone through a period of surrealism, which is fun, making preposterous shapes and unreal situations come to happen, hopefully startling, even shocking me—and readers—out of our normal expectations of reality, only to coax us back in again by manipulating our senses, informing us against our skepticism. Or as Chekov's "Black Monk" says, "I exist in your imagination, and your imagination is part of nature which means that I exist in nature, too."

Until I recognized that everything in a fiction was surreal—a lamp, a door, a dead horse—and perhaps reality was surreal, too, incorporating such bizarre shapes that everything is possible. But it was fun to read the surreal stories. I had won a Pushcart Prize for one story, "Murphy's Angel," and several had been cited for honorable mention. The Pushcart Prize is something you can put on your CV, you don't get any money for it.

I didn't know the extent I would take my surrealism to realism that was informed by surrealism, but five years later, I would publish a book of essays on the craft of fiction, titled *Realism & Other Illusions*. Vibeke, of all my writings, admired the title of that—I had conceived it years before, when writing my Ph.D. thesis, *The Uses of Verisimilitude*, which I described as "The Uses of Bullshit."

Too late now to repair, the marriage was ending.

In Portland, Oregon, I read at Powell's Book Store, and my roommate in grad school who lived just across the Columbia River, Paul Casey, drove me the some hundred miles to La Grande, where I was signing off on the cover of *The Book of Angels*. My New York agent contacted me to ask if I had anything to sell. I did have, and he racked up thirty-six rave rejections for the novel. The publishers couldn't find out how to sell it: Was it a literary book or a thriller or even a ghost story? What genre was it? I sold it myself, but for the price of a hundred copies and royalties of 10%. No agent had yet sold anything for me. I accepted that I was a small press writer.

On the way into La Grande, Paul and I stopped at Prescott on the

251

Columbia River to organize my papers for the reading at the University of Eastern Oregon. We sat in a booth of a bar where they served only cans of Olympia, no glass, and American Indians were sitting along the bar, their backs to us, unspeaking—at noon! I proceeded to organize my manuscripts on the table, and Paul whispered, "Uh-oh!" as two more cans of Olympia appeared at our booth from the bartender, who was also a big Indian. "Gentleman down the bar wants to buy you a drink."

I raised one of the two cans, but no one wanted to acknowledge the generosity. Their backs were still to us. So I gathered my manuscripts in a plastic folder, preparing to exit. We quaffed our beers, two of them, but I had to cast my water before I left.

In the men's room at a urinal, the door opened behind me, and a very large man looking like the obverse of the Indian on a Buffalo nickel took the urinal beside me and asked, "You a lawyer?"

I didn't think that to be a lawyer was necessarily a good thing in that Indian bar at noon. "No," I said, "I'm a writer. Going to read at the University in La Grande."

Without moving his lips or a muscle in his face, he said, "Thought you were a lawyer."

So, he was paying the legal fee in advance—two cans of Olympia beer. I shook and zipped and left.

Paul Casey drove me back to Portland where I flew to San Francisco to read at City Lights. I was excited to meet Lawrence Ferlinghetti before the reading. That I should meet the beatnik poet whom I had heard on record with the Cellar Jazz Quintet thirty years before in Ocean Beach, San Diego, while I was with Toni June and Lori May. I told Ferlinghetti that recording had bowled me over. I exaggerated that I had gone out and bought all of his books. I had bought *Coney Island of the Mind* and *Her* (which I found unreadable—it might have been my fault), but *Coney Island* was a tremendous influence on my writing, especially the record, on which you could hear his oral interpretation. "But Frank Heller borrowed it and drilled a hole in it. Didn't even apologize or tell me why he did it." I was gushing.

He said, "You still can get it on CD. It'll cost you about fifty bucks, but at the exchange rate between the kroner and the dollar, it'll be a bargain for you."

I gave him copies of *Coney Island* and *Pictures from a Gone World*, which I had purchased from the stock of City Lights, for him to sign. He was seventy-seven—twenty-five years older than I. Ferlinghetti was an old man. He couldn't live so much more, and the autographed books would be keepsakes. (Today, he has lived to ninety-nine years and is clear as a bell, has an alley in San Francisco named after him—Via Ferlinghetti.) While he was autographing the books, I said that it was an honor that he had my story collection among his stock and to read at City Lights. I was still gushing, and it probably set me up for what he said next.

"What's the title of your book?" he asked in that same New York accent with which he spoke on the record.

"*Unreal City*," I said.

"Is that from Eliot?" he asked suspiciously.

"Among others." At the moment, I couldn't remember that there were three epigraphs in the book the title related to—Rilke, Eliot, and Baudelaire's *Fleurs du Mal*.

"Isn't that a little *overused*?"

He didn't come to the reading, but I had a deprecating—for me and him—bittersweet anecdote to tell about lost illusions. And illusions, I decided, should always be lost.

When I got home, I laid in my office for three days and listened to "Flamenco Sketches," take 1 and take 2. It was a soothing and profound nineteen minutes.

Vibeke confronted me in the hallway on my way to pee and told me I could accept that international job which had been dangled before me. The company I worked for was a member of the international NGO I had been employed by twenty-two years ago in Ferney-Voltaire, and the CEO of the headquarters in Ferney was retiring, and there was talk of my being the front-runner for the job. My company was encouraging me to apply for it. Rather, the elements who wanted to be rid of me were encouraging me. I had grown, according to some power sectors of the company, too long in the tooth. I had a policy of being not plugged into the grapevine; that way I could be nice to everybody and avoid playing politics. That had worked out well for me. But that Vibeke was encouraging me to take the job in Ferney made me wonder if somebody of those elements were manipulating her. Besides, I liked Copenhagen and didn't want to relocate again, but maybe this was a last-ditch effort by Vibeke to save our marriage.

"Could you just tear up roots and move to Ferney? What about the children's high school?" My son and daughter were in their first year and next to last year of high school. To relocate them would be brutal.

Calmly, she said, "I didn't say anything about me or the children leaving. I meant you could take the job and have an honorable way out of this marriage."

We were standing in the long, narrow hallway outside my office. It seemed as though we had all our important conversations there, though I had to watch her knee or kept my hip turned to her.

That job was not me, I told her; besides, my retirement was in eight years.

"Oh?"

"Yes, I told you I'll be retiring at sixty. And I depend on my capital pension to be able to."

After a moment of considering, I couldn't say what I wanted to add, standing in the hall, like an afterthought. "In fact, wouldn't you like to sit down and have a cup of coffee? Glass of wine?"

"I don't want to sit down with you. Tell me standing."

"We're not happy together. I can't be the man you want, and you can't be the woman for me."

"You certainly can't be the man I want."

"So, why don't we split?" So, I was saying it. "You can keep the house. I'll keep paying for it and give you enough money in addition to your disability pension and your doctor's pension."

"If you want to do this, do it fast."

"And if the kids want to stay with you, I'll pay extra child support."

"Of course the kids will stay with me."

"They're old enough now to choose."

"If you want to do this, do it fast. But the kids stay with me."

The kids can decide for themselves, I thought. But they had to be confronted with it.

My son had overtaken the apartment in the basement. One room was nicely finished and one room was less nice, but it was finished and large. He had a kind of battery of computers, our old B&O television and our old console stereo set up there. My daughter had the finished room with the two windows, which was almost at the level of the ground floor and a staircase up to the driveway. It was large, and she had a stereo. She seemed happy there. They had their own bathroom with a bathtub, but the other two rooms of the basement were not finished. I was not handy, and trade workers charged the white out of your eyes, as the Danes said.

Because I thought my daughter would take more time, I went down to my son first. He was at the computer screen, playing a game in which he negotiated the future of Denmark.

"Who do you negotiate with?"

"Stalin," he said, not looking from the screen, continuing to play.

I told him I had something important for us to talk about and could he sit down with me.

"Busy."

All at once, I could sense that he had listened in on his mother's and my conversation in the hallway upstairs. I asked him repeatedly to sit down with me or at least to turn away from the screen, but he didn't move away from staring at the game. This could not wait. So, I told him to his back what he probably already knew.

"Fuck you, Dad."

I told him I realized that he was angry, but I would continue to provide for him and his sister and his mother, and they could stay in this house. However, I was not getting along with his mom and I could not stay. I considered making a scene, to force him to come to the present, but I remembered that I was not so good with scenes.

"You'll see. It's a difficult time to come, but it will be better." Tensions would ease. "I can't stand her sarcasm. After twenty-two years, it's wearing away on me."

Still with his back to me, he said, "Oh, yeah, you're gonna leave me alone with her sarcastic remarks."

I asked if he wanted to come with me. He could decide.

"I'm not the one who abandons the family, Dad."

He was better at negotiating than me.

I left him with assurances, spoken to his back. He continued to negotiate over the fate of Denmark with Stalin, it had something to do with Bornholm at the end of the Second World War, but I was aware of what demons he was dealing with. I remembered the Updike "Maple" fiction where the father told the son that his mother and he were divorcing. The son asks tremulously, "*Why?*" and the father thinks, "I didn't remember why," and knew it for a stronger story than mine. I could remember the reasons why, but I had dreaded the day when my golden son, who had looked at the world with blue eyes of wonder and fear at birth, might say *fuck you* to me. With those words, I felt the connection between us was broken, and I had to assure myself that it was not.

Despite what I'd thought, my daughter was easier with it. "I see that you and Mom don't get along. Do it. Don't do it and then come back, and I'll get used to the idea, only to have you come back. I can't live like this."

So, she was aware of the past attempt to split up, even if it was only three or four weeks.

We hugged, and I repeated what I'd told my son, that she could always come with me. She told me if it got bad, it was good to know.

The day the movers came, the kids were in school. My son was seventeen, my daughter fifteen. Vibeke kept watch over the movers that they didn't take too much. We had disagreements over books, over spiritual volumes and, of all things, over Norman Mailer's *The Prisoner of Sex*. But she apportioned some kitchen things and bedding to me and I took the ashtray with which she had hit me. It was a gift from her—cutglass and with a map of the EU carved in the well—a gift when I got my first promotion.

When they had born the last cartons (mostly of books and manuscripts and clothes, cassettes and CDs), she looked around the spaces where the cartons had sat for three days and said wistfully, "We could have been happy here."

I felt hollow, stepped close to hug her, and she stiffened and stepped back. "You'll regret this." In parting, she said, "May you die a slow and painful death."

Safari Redux

I HAD A PLAN.

The first apartment I looked at was ideal, but I thought I couldn't take the first apartment I looked at, so I looked at ten more, the one more dismal than the other. Except for the tenth, which was good—it had two balconies and 90 square meters and two extra bedrooms, but it was a fifth-floor walk-up. I thought, *What about when I get older?* It cost eight hundred thousand kroner compared to the first, seven hundred thousand—about fifteen thousand dollars cheaper.

The apartment had six windows facing out on Sortedamsø, one of the street lakes, and it was on the first floor of a three-story, three-apartment building with a basement, divided up into three storage rooms and a laundry room.

I bought it, and both my children loved it with its three-block view over the lake dead-ahead and to the left and right as far as you could see. It had only three rooms, two front rooms—the wall had been removed, made into one room—and a bedroom and kitchen with a shower in it, and a WC. It was 80 square meters.

So, on moving day, I transported my cartons and tried not to be happy.

I had a plan to patch things up with my children. I had to go to a conference in Cape Town, South Africa, and I did some research with the head of the Cape Town office what was the best safari camp. I found it was outside of Kreuger Park, the Honeyguide Camp, and it was offering four days in a "luxurious" tent in the headquarters camp and three days in a walking camp in the field.

My CEO knew I was very recently divorced so he smiled at me from behind his big desk in his big office. He had initiated his CEO-ship at the Christmas party for all the two hundred employees. We had a tradition of Christmas parties which were lavish. He took the floor at the party—which was usually reserved for the CEO to tell the mass of employees that they had done a good job, but he looked out over the mass of staff, pausing for a full two minutes after which he said, "You're all spoiled rotten." And he left.

I made my pitch: business class from Copenhagen to Cape Town would cost so-and-so much and tourist class for three to Honeyguide, outside of Kruger National Park and Pretoria, and a tourist ticket down to Cape Town and two tourist tickets back to Copenhagen would cost less than one business class ticket from Copenhagen to Cape Town. Would it be okay if I took my children? After all, I hadn't taken my family on a conference trip for a couple of years.

257

He looked at me and firmed up his lips and briskly nodded his head.

After two hours in a sweaty, dusty, banged-up SUV from Won-derboom airport, Pretoria to the Honeyguide camp, I snickered when the woman in the check-in tent had us sign disclaimers that we would take no legal action against the camp in the event that we were mauled, killed, or in any way injured by wild animals. It was my idea that this area outside of Kruger National Park—in the northeastern part of South Africa—would be a kind of variant of Disneyland, a realistic one, but not to include mauling animals.

We were instructed sternly never to return alone in the dark from mess to our sleeping tent without being accompanied by one of the rangers—there was danger of encountering an angry dugger boy buf-falo. I began to wonder whether I had been wise inviting my teenaged daughter and son along. Settled in my tent a few minutes later, I heard my son holler in alarm that an elephant had stuck its trunk into his tent flap—and I ran into him, but the elephant was gone. Nonetheless, I be-gan to suspect this was not a good idea at all.

We would be two days here in the main camp, Khola Moya, touring in a jeep, three days in a bush camp, Mantobeni, tracking on foot, then the final days back in the main camp to celebrate—perhaps to celebrate that we were still alive, if indeed we were.

The remainder of our first afternoon there was spent relaxing in the sun on the edge of the little ornamental pool, our bare feet dangling in the cool water—my son and I—drinking bottles of Castle beer. We watched half a dozen elephants busy at something or other just outside the camp in a clearing some sixty meters away. One of the elephants was leading the others in some sort of game of tear up the earth with your trunk. My daughter wisely decided it was too hot in the sun and chose the shade of a little lounge lean-to alongside the bar, drinking iced tea. Early afternoon by the pool was thirsty work. We took turns, my son and I, fetching fresh rounds of cold Castles from the bar. After a couple of rounds, we figured out why the elephants were digging into the loose earth with their trunks. One of them got hold of something and stepped backward, tearing it from the ground. A plastic water pipe. Who said elephants were dumb? These ones had figured out that water flowed into our camp through buried pipes. Apparently they had decided that if they got hold of the pipe and brought it home with them, they would have a ready steady supply of the wet stuff. They went running off, following their clever leader who had a couple of yards of water pipe tucked into his trunk.

"Think they'll elect a new leader when they get back and find out the water didn't travel with the pipe?" I wondered aloud.

"Want another Castle?" my son asked. A neat row of empties along the edge of the pool informed me this would be our sixth. My son was 17-years old and appeared to be perfectly sober. I felt like a bad Dad.

"Son," I said. "How in the world can you drink that much beer?"

He tilted his head quizzically. "Am I not your son, Father?"

We slept well that night after a succulent meal of antelope stew washed back with South African cab, each of us alone on crisp clean sheets in his or her tent, listening to the sounds of the jungle night. Bird cries, the *WA-hoo! WA-hoo!* of a baboon followed by the silencing grunt of a dog leader, the almost sub-audible crunch of elephant and buffalo and hippos, stepping quietly through the bush around the camp.

In the morning we woke up early—at 5:30 a.m.—for a breakfast of eggs and warthog bacon and go out in the jeeps. Our ranger was a 21-year-old named Brendan from Johannesburg, working for the summer to earn money for his education. He was equipped with a rifle, and aided by a tracker named Alfus. If he fires the rifle, he told us, he would lose his job because that would mean he had led us into danger. This sounded to me like text-book logic; I would prefer to know that he would not hesitate to use the rifle if necessary.

We set out in the 4 x 4 jeep—an open truck really with a roll bar (no doubt in case of being turned over by a mad rhino) and a seat mounted on the left fender in which Alfus sat to watch for game. Soon—much more quickly than I expected—the tracker's hand shot up, the signal that he had spotted game, and he said, "*N'goni.*" *N'goni*, I learned, was Xitsonga for lion. And I saw that we were already closer to a pair of lion than I ever expected or wanted to be. It occurred to me that if I had been on a safari with Ernest Hemingway, and if he heard me thinking such things, he would have considered me beneath contempt, not even worth mocking in fiction. Of course, I carefully concealed any sign of fear from my children, lest I surrendered my tentative hold on patriarchal authority. The lion seemed unimpressed by us. The lioness rolled onto her back, exposing her belly, as if to invite a scratch.

"We're fine in the jeep," said Brendan. "In the jeep, we're a large, dangerous animal to them. They respect us. But if you separate from the truck, even stand up or stick your hand out, the lion will see you for what you are."

Indeed, I thought, remembering "The Short Happy Life of Francis Macomber," when the point of view shifts to the lion's, who saw Macomber clearly only when he was out of the jeep. The way I felt at the moment Macomber, despite his cowardice, was a pillar of courage by comparison to me.

Next there were grazing rhinos, curious tall giraffe, thirsty lions sipping from a dam. I grew bolder, seeing that the animals would glance curiously at us but seemed basically unaggressive, disinterested mostly. Brendan parked the jeep by the dam so we could stretch our legs. My son stepped into the tracks left by an elephant that had been there before us for a drink—the print was thigh-high on him.

Brendan enquired about my constant note-taking as he related about the vegetation and animals and insects. I explained that I was a writer, and he beamed.

"I was named for a writer. An Irish one. My parents didn't have a name for me because I was unexpected, you know. Not planned. They were going to take me home from the hospital without a name but there was an Irish nurse there who said that was bad luck. She suggested 'Brendan'. The name of a great Irish writer, she said, who had died just ten years before."

"Brendan Behan," I said, touched by his openness and trust.

"Yes! That's who! And *you're* a writer. I'll do my best to make the safari as interesting as I can for you!"

Not too interesting, please, I thought, as he led me to a magic guarri tree, explaining what a good friend this tree is: sprigs of magic guarri, placed close to the food, kept the flies away and could also be used to swat them off in case that didn't work. The wood was perfect for a cattie—a catapult, or slingshot—and the ragged edge of a magic guarri twig was perfect for brushing your teeth in the bush.

"Trees are the kindest of the earth's creatures," Brendan told me. "They stand and wait for your need and let you take without complaint. They feed the elephants and impala, the waterbuck, kudu, giraffe, and give a place for the leopard to drag her prey." He pointed to the chipped bark of a tree. "See cher, a leopard climbed up with her kill. See how the bark is chipped away by her claws." Then he turned and gestured toward a rocky rise, a weeping werbie tree, explaining how it provided seats for the baboons among the rocks and how the baboon ate the werbie fruit and in turn scattered the seeds in their droppings.

His eye caught something and he turned to the dam where a hippo floated, face just above water while an ox picker bird cleaned its snout. "That cher hippo is called Sapo," he said. "He comes up and wanders about at night for vegetables to eat. One time a woman—a nurse, a white woman—tried to beat Sapo on the nose with a broom because he kept stealing her carrots, and just as quick as that, Sapo jumped forward and bit off her arm. Hippo look slow but they're fast."

I gauged Sapo to be about 150 meters out on the dam and wondered *how* fast.

Halfway into the meadow alongside the dam, Brendan showed me a dead leadwood tree—it looked like a short, ashen-faced man standing stiffly, one rotted up-thrusting branch like an arm raised to get our attention. Even dead, he explained, it provided perches where the buzzards could sleep while they waited for an updraft because the buzzards were so big they had trouble lifting their own weight with muscle. "And what the trees do for men!" he went on. "Wood for your fire, leaves to heal you—silver cluster leaf to stop you vomiting, common spice leaves for a runny tummy, acacia thorns to pick your teeth and leadwood leaves for toothpaste, boiled knob thorn for a toothache, sour plum tree after too much wine or gin and the soft leaves...," Brendan lowered his voice so my daughter did not hear, "...to wipe your bum."

Brendan had only begun. He proceeded to tell of the many things he could do with the buffalo thorn: the leaf stops a wound's bleeding and a branch, the natives said, would catch the spirit of the dead if brushed across the place a person fell so you could bring the spirit home to rest in peace. Impala ate buffalo thorn leaves, and an impala buck had to keep many she's happy. Brendan smiled. "Help a man with that, too." The Tamboti tree, though, never cook meat over it in a campfire. Its sap is poisonous to humans, but animals can eat the bark and leaves.

By now the notebook I had thought would last me all week was already half full. I could hardly write fast enough to keep up with young

Brendan's enthusiasm and knowledge. While I was still recording the last details, he was onto another idea. He was telling Alfus that we would proceed from here on foot because Mr. Fitzgerald was a writer and they must give me good experiences to write about.

Before I could protest, we were many meters from the dam, wading through thigh-high yellow grass, solemnly instructed that we were to walk in single file, that we were to stay together, that we were not to chatter, and that we were to obey the ranger's instructions without hesitation. The file was structured thus: first the tracker, next the rifle-bearing ranger, behind him the guests—my son was placed in front of my daughter to protect her from the front, and I was to cover the rear. If we happened upon something dangerous, the tracker would signal by repeatedly flapping the palms of his hands backward at waist level toward the flank, which meant we must step backward rapidly. Under no circumstances were we to turn our backs on a wild animal and absolutely never were we to run away: That was an invitation for the chase.

I was wondering what we did if an animal sneaked up behind *me*, last in the flank, wondered whether that was a dumb question, remembered African movies—*King Solomon's Mines*—where the last bearer in a flank was suddenly picked off by a hungry cat and went down yelling, "Aieee…!" One of the cast's expendable characters, good for a shudder of blood lust.

But Brendan was too far ahead, second in the flank, for me to shout out my question with dignity. Anyway, shouting was forbidden. We moved forward in file through the grass at a brisk pace toward a tangle of small trees and bush when suddenly we stopped. I saw palms flapping backward, just glimpsed a young lean lion male lying within the trees and grass, another female on her feet to the left of the clearing, eyes burning at us like Blake's Tyger. I managed to snap two pictures before the backward jog reached me. Although I was last in the flank, I also flapped my palms backward. We were jogging quite swiftly backward toward the dam, and the two lions were creeping toward us, one off to the left, the other to the right.

Brendan called back in a whisper over his shoulder to me, "Mr. Fitzgerald, just keep an eye open for any hippo in the dam! Don't get close to them!"

Oh, I thought, you can be certain I will not.

In the clearing again, we huddled. The jeep was perhaps 200 meters off to our right. I was thinking how nice it would be to have my children and myself safely back in that big-animal-looking vehicle, but Brendan said, "Here's the thing. The one has cut us off and the other is flanking us. He knows we want the jeep, and he's not going to let us."

I glanced at my son. His eyes seemed to reflect my thoughts: *We're meat!*

"I don't like that they're crawling," Brendan whispered. "They're stalking us. They're hungry. They're too young to know it's best to stay away from humans."

"I may have to fire the rifle," said Brendan.

"Can you kill them both?" I asked.

"That would mean my job, and Alfus' job, too," Brendan whispered. "I'd just hope to scare 'em off."

We all exchanged stoic glances as I regretted having chosen South Africa over Casablanca for our vacation, and Brendan began to make noise with his rifle, cranking the bolt and slamming it shut, smacking his palm hard against the wood of the stock. Alfus was doing a kind of dance in the grass which I very much hoped was the right magic. Then Brendan said, "Now they've regrouped behind us, see?"

I didn't see.

"We have a clear path to the jeep."

Across the spongy dam bank and soon we were piling into the beautiful, sturdy, olive-green jeep—truck really, big as a double-rhino, big enough to draw respect from a lion, two lions, even hungry ones. Brendan didn't start the ignition. He sat there for a moment behind the wheel and Alfus turned back in his tracker's chair and began to laugh. Brendan laughed, too, and soon we all began to chortle, belly laugh, and that was when I realized how real the danger was.

As we pulled away, Brendan pointed across to the tree line where a herd of bachelor impala leaped off into a run—two hungry lions close behind, no doubt.

"They taste better than us," said Brendan. "You'll see."

For lunch there was impala pie in hot onion sauce, and after lunch we learned that Brendan had been reprimanded by the camp director for putting us in harm's way. The story spread, and no one was taken out that afternoon, we stayed in the main camp. At dinner—zebra steaks in mushroom gravy—the other guests enquired with ill-concealed envy if it was true we were stalked by two lions today. Clearly, they were disgruntled, felt they were not getting their money's worth. *They* did not get to go out on foot. *They* were not stalked by lion.

The leader of the camp, a short, lean man with a neat brown moustache, asked if we would like a new ranger. I consulted with my children, who instantly agreed we were perfectly happy with Brendan. We definitely wanted to continue with him. My daughter's apparent great relief was my first clue that other factors were at play here than Brendan's merely wanting to help me gather material for my writing. I was not oblivious to my daughter's beauty.

Next day we stayed in or very near the jeep from morning to evening, which suited me fine. It seemed we were concentrating on less dangerous game. We saw a cut-throat finch, blood red feathers topping its breast, and a brown snake eagle circling overhead and a yellow-faced little bee eater, green coat iridescent in the sun. Brendan spotted the hole of a baboon spider, big around as a fat plum and sheer as a polished pipe opening; Brendan poured water down the hole, but the spider did not emerge. We hunkered down in whispering silence by a jackal pup asleep in a drain pipe which Brendan asked us not to tell about—otherwise the others would come to see it and might frighten it into running off from its mother who was out hunting for her pup's food. We saw bush babies and vervid monkeys, waterbuck and zebra, a wild dog with spotted hide and big ears sticking up from the grass.

Across the dam, a lone wildebeest, abandoned by the herd, danced madly, whipping its head in agony from the maggots planted in its brain. In the distance, we heard the bark of a dog baboon and a blacksmith plover clicking overhead, and a giggling lady flew near with a shiver of wings. Brendan showed us where a herd of elephant had passed, dragging their trunks through the dust.

When Brendan saw another tree, this one with leopard claw marks in the bark, he parked and gave Alfus his rifle and told him to go off to see where the leopard had gone. He wanted us to see leopard. While Alfus was gone, we lounged alongside the jeep, waiting, and Brendan said, "You mustn't tell I let Alfus take the rifle. I could lose my job for that, giving the rifle to a black." I was concerned—not because Brendan gave the rifle to a black, but because we were sitting here without a rifle to defend ourselves. I began to wonder about Brendan's judgement. Still, we had the jeep. Up above the crest of a hill, we saw a giraffe running and an ostrich.

"There are not many ostrich any more," said Brendan. "The lion eat them." Then he led us from the jeep a little way out into the field. "See here," he said, "these are zebra tracks. Running. And see here. A leopard overtook her. The leopard are shy but they are here."

Alfus came back shaking his head and handed the rifle back to Brendan. I noticed that Brendan was very tall, six-three or -four, though very slim, and Alfus was shorter than I and had a younger face than I had thought at first. Early thirties perhaps. Brendan checked the chamber of the rifle and slung it on his shoulder.

"It's soon time for a sundowner," he said. "Then back to the camp for dinner. Tomorrow we camp in the bush." He drove the jeep to a water hole the size of a small pond in a clearing that sloped gently like a shallow bowl from all sides. We parked on the crest of the hill. He and Alfus broke out the chest with the cool drinks and snacks.

We stood around the jeep, chatting and sipping G&Ts in the gathering dusk, sun stripes pale and low to the ground across the yellow grass and the darkening water of the drinking hole. Abruptly Brendan raised his arm for silence. "Listen," he whispered.

At first I heard nothing, then an almost sub-audible slow crunching sound. Brendan gestured with slow caution across the water hole just as the animals stepped out of the trees—tens, scores of them, hundreds of buffalo. They kept appearing. Brendan whispered, "This herd has about four hundred—I saw them on the Roebuck Plains the other day. They drink in order of rank—the bulls first. Look, you can see the last of the sunlight lighting up their eyes as they look across at us."

"Will they charge?" my son asked.

"No. They feel safe in a herd. It's only the strays that are dangerous, the dugger boys. In a herd they feel safe and would run from a sneeze back into the safety and comfort of the herd, powerful as they are. The dugger boys will charge without warning, and they don't mock charge either like most big animals. They won't tolerate anything getting too close. See that bull there, how he raises his nose to smell us. Stay close to the jeep."

When the first wave of the bulls had drunk their fill, the next took their places in the water, and the lead animals headed slowly for the trees again but turned around, to protect the herd. How lightly they stepped for an animal that weighed fifteen hundred pounds. Awed, we watched the quiet, orderly procession of enormous animals disappear back into the trees, leaving the empty landscape behind them, as though they had never been there, had been an illusion, a dream of buffalo in the dusk.

Next day, we were in the bush in the Mantobeni camp, in a grove of hardwood Tamboti tress, with narrow straight trunks.

There conditions were more primitive than the main camp—no roomy tents with private sinks and toilets and crisply folded sheets. Here was more like the Army, though the tents were mounted on foot-high platforms to discourage crawling intruders. The shower consisted of a suspended bucket with a watering can spout mounted in the bottom, and the toilet was porcelain but didn't flush and was out in the open, behind the tents. Sitting on the bowl, you looked down to the dry pit of the river bed below, dotted with fresh elephant droppings, bright brown and orange, melon-shaped balls and hyena spoor, white from the bones they ate, crushing them with their powerful jaws.

The bush staff consisted of cooks and trackers and, of course, ranger Brendan. We dined in a mess tent, a canvas overhead mounted on four poles, a wood platform for a floor beneath our canvas chairs. We were served by Moses, who had cooked on an open campfire off behind us. Brendan ate with us beneath the canvas ceiling. After he had served, Moses joined the black staff to eat seated on rocks and vehicle running boards around the cooking fire. I asked about that, and Brendan told me, "They prefer to. Sometimes they invite me to join them and laugh because I use a fork instead of my fingers."

We sat long after dinner, drinking gin or bottles of beer, talking by the flickering kerosene lamp, watching shadowy elephants circle by, snapping trees for night snacks, huge black shadows against the blue and green darkness of the jungle night.

Brendan told us that the name the trackers had given him in Xitsonga was *Mariband*, which meant one too cool to lose his temper. But that was close to another word, *maraband*, which meant one who eats too much, so he had to listen carefully to be sure he was not being teased.

Lowering his voice so my daughter could not hear, he said to me,

"Tell me about the name Brendan, about the writer. I have heard two stories about him. One that he had many women, another that he was for boys. What is true?"

This brave young man had such concern in his eyes that I was touched. "I only know that he was a great writer and was well loved and that he had many women," I said. Brendan smiled happily.

It was very dark, nearly ten. We had to rise early next morning. My son and I were sharing a tent, and I suggested we turn in.

"I'll stay up a little longer, Dad," said my daughter. Brendan said nothing, nor did he move or look at me.

"Okay. Ten minutes, right?"

"Fifteen."

"I'll be sure she reaches her tent safely, Mr. Fitzgerald," Brendan said.

We lighted our way back to the tent by flashlight, alert to the possibility of dugger boys. My son retired and was soon snoring away in whatever dreams this day had inspired. I sat at the little table on the wooden platform outside the tent, shining the beam of the flashlight onto my watch from time to time. I could see the flickering kerosene lamp in the mess tent, perhaps seventy-five meters away, concealed behind trees. I heard the burbling of a zebra off in the distance, the bark of a dog baboon. Brendan had trained our ears well. At ten-thirty, I stepped out to the path and followed my flashlight beam down to the mess tent where Brendan and my daughter sat alone on either side of the table, speaking softly.

"Better come to bed now, daughter," I said, weary of my Dad role, but unwilling to give it up. "It's late." And to Brendan, "Thanks for a terrific day, Brendan."

"My pleasure, Mr. Fitzgerald," he piped, and I followed my child back to her tent, wishing I could be less of a stereotype.

Our last day in the bush, we drove to the Roebuck Plains. On the way we saw two bull giraffe square off to fight for leadership of the herd, swinging their necks at one another's belly, gouging with skull horns. Much of the fight passed in stillness and glaring. I was unable to determine which of them, if either, was winning.

"Could take hours," Brendan said.

We reached the Roebuck Plains about noon and set out on foot, single file through the trees. Brendan explained that we would follow an animal path which was a truer path, did not take turns forward around thorn bushes as a human path would. When we had hiked for fifteen or twenty minutes we came to the edge of a broad yellow clearing. The sun was high overhead. Sweat rolled from beneath my cap, down my back. There was nothing in the clearing other than a broad, round, chin-high bush about a third way across. The tree line on the other side was maybe two hundred meters away. Brendan signaled that we should follow him across. I was hoping that we would see no *n'goni* here.

When we had made our way nearly a third across, almost at the bush, two white rhino stepped out of the tree line on the other side and paused perhaps seventy meters away. Brendan signaled us to stop.

"Should we move back?" I whispered.

"They're too fast for us," he whispered back. "And if we start moving they'll know we're here and might go for us. A rhino hits full speed in three strides and full speed is forty miles an hour. But they can't see us. They *look* like they can, but they can't. They're almost blind. But if the wind changes, we're in trouble. They'll smell us." He looked at me. "If that happens, you all get down on your bellies under the edge of that bush. They'll smell you but they won't know what you are."

This sounded dubious, but I could think of no alternative. "Son," I whispered. "I'll cover your sister. Can you manage yourself?"

"Yeah."

I was thinking of protecting my daughter with my own body. She was hale and hearty, had never been bullied by girls or boys, but such is a father's protective instinct over a fifteen-year-old-daughter. And against rhinos.

Then we were silent. We watched the two big animals. I could feel a light breeze on my forehead. Then suddenly it riffled my hair, and the two rhino heads swung toward us in one swift movement.

None of us spoke but my daughter whispered, "*Shit!*"

They started forward in a side by side charge. I was poised to scoop my daughter under the bush, too frightened to feel my fear, thinking, Why didn't Brendan shoot? But he was only making noise with the rifle, rattling the bolt, smacking the stock as Alfus danced about like a wasp on a doughnut. But the rhino were on stride, maybe thirty meters away and moving fast as an automobile. The ground rumbled with their charge. Alfus had his cattie out and was firing stones now. The rhino were about twenty meters from the bush when one of Alfus' stones struck the underbelly of the bull. In unison they changed direction in a ninety-degree turn and headed for the trees to our right.

Brendan smiled at me. "You know that thing about hiding under the bush? I never actually tried it, but I heard it works."

That night in camp there was much laughter. Alfus had his cattie out to show it, and he was laughing, too.

"Can I try that?" Brendan asked and took the slingshot, loaded it with a stone and drew back the rubber sling. Suddenly he turned, aiming it at Alfus' leg. Alfus chuckled. At the last moment, Brendan swung away and fired his stone at the wooden water tank. He hit it but the rubber sling recoiled, smacking his hand so he yelped and dropped the cattie. Alfus chuckled again and retrieved the weapon as the ranger cooled his stung fingers, shaking them up and down in the air. Alfus loaded and fired at the trunk of a tall, slender Tamboti tree. The stone whacked the bark, chipping it. He quickly loaded and fired again, slicing off a cluster of ticking seeds that fell and lay twitching on the earth, eager to release their larvae of grey moths—jumping bean trees.

"That's how to operate a cattie!" Brendan said.

I wanted Alfus to join us for drinks that evening, but he stayed with his own while the four of us celebrated with gin and whisky and beer the continuing fact of our existence.

Next day we tipped Alfus and Brendan well, and we told Brendan if there was any trouble at all about the rhino to lay the blame on us, that we insisted. We exchanged addresses and sat up long into the night. Brendan asked me to send him a copy of what I wrote.

In Wonderboom lounge next day, my son stocked up on Castle beer. He stowed, one by one, seventeen bottles in his rucksack for his friends. My son and daughter had one flight to Copenhagen, I another to Cape Town. Their flight was taking off first, and I escorted them to the gate. My daughter and son hugged me before they proceeded to the boarding corridor that snaked onto the plane. They hugged me in a bunch, at once, and we stood there in a tangle. No one said anything.

269

On the airplane to Cape Town, lifting up over the yellow landscape below, patches of green, mountain, river, blue lake and dam, I wondered if I really experienced the days I was leaving behind there. A zoo would never again do it for me. I flipped through my note pad, completely filled with my scribble and augmented by many extra sheets folded into quarters so they could fit in my back pocket. The stewardess came with drinks. I let down my table as a writing desk and took out a legal pad. I began to write a short story.

The story was about a hero, the hero of our safari, Alfus. I had plenty of local color from Brendan to fill in the background. I tried to catch my viewpoint—the point of view of a brain surgeon about my age who drank too much—through Alfus' viewpoint; I made Alfus very old, puzzling over the consciousness of the brain surgeon. It was an interesting exercise, and it must have worked because it was published on the first time out. Ten years later when Brendan wrote to me, I wrote a short story titled "Alfus Revisited," and it was published by the same editor. The editor must have believed it.

A Love Supreme

THE LAWYERS REPRESENTING US through the divorce were women, and the judge at the divorce hearing was a woman. I had faith in the fairness of women—be it not that it was Judge Judy, who reminded me of Vibeke with her sarcasm, quick, pithy responses.

The way a divorce worked in Denmark—the way my divorce worked—was that you have a trial separation for six months and then the divorce is effectuated; you split everything you have accumulated since the wedding. If one party had more income—in this case, me—I paid alimony for six years, the sum of the alimony being according to the difference of income. And the one ex-partner paid child support at an astonishingly low rate for every minor child until that child was twenty-one.

Weighing the relative incomes, the court figured the alimony was to be three thousand kroner per month and 733 kroner child support per child. I offered to pay double the alimony and triple the child support.

However, our pensions were different in nature—Vibeke had a monthly disability pension plus the partial pension that was figured on her time as a physician, that would be paid to her until she died, whereas

I had a capital pension: My company paid 20% of my salary, over and above that salary, into a rate-pension fund, without income tax until I was retired; then it would be paid to me in annual or monthly portions until the fund was used up. I would pay income tax on it annually, according to my annual pension income. Roughly, the rate of that annual tax was calculated at 40%, far less than the rate would be if I paid it straight when the income was credited to me. At the time of the divorce, I had about a million and a half kroner in my pension fund; that equaled 60% of that total, after taxes (about 900,000 kroner).

The difference between our pensions was that mine was figured into the sum of what we had accumulated since our wedding; Vibeke's was not. It was complicated. That meant I owed her 450,000 kroner from my pension, and she owed me, in addition to the amount I was paying on the house and the alimony and child support, not a crown.

I wanted my pension. I was dependent on it from the year I turned sixty, if I was to retire from my job and if I would be a full-time writer. The salary from my writing was negligible and not constant. I *needed* my pension. I was willing to give the house to Vibeke, if I could keep my pension.

Vibeke countered that I would pay triple child support and pay off the house (there was only a little left in debt), give her seven thousand kroner a month for six years in alimony—that was over and above the 216,000, I was required to give her by 288,000 if I was to keep my pension. In the end, I figured that was fair. The house was worth over a million kroner, so that was a half million or six hundred thousand I was giving her, instead of 450,000. As I said, it was complicated. I wanted to keep her and the kids in the house in Hellerup as long as she wanted to, and at least until the kids were twenty-one, when she would get over a million kroner from the sale of the house. When her parents died, she would split the inheritance with her brother on the both houses they owned and any capital they had—which they had plenty of at present.

However, she added some things on the settlement at the court room hearing for the divorce: that I would pay a thousand more in alimony per month, and make her the beneficiary of my capital pension and my insurance policy. My lawyer said I had to do that if I wanted the divorce, so I capitulated.

The judge pronounced that the financial settlement was skewered against me, and did I understand and want to contest that? I did and did not. She further pronounced that if I were to return to the U.S. or settle in another country, this settlement, having been adjudicated under the laws of Denmark, would not be legally binding upon me. What that judge did not understand was that I wanted to stay in Copenhagen, where my children were and where I thought the Danish way of life was humane, being that it provided full health care to every member of the population and free education up through graduate degrees, and if you needed a hand financially, you would get it. As Oliver Wendell Holmes and my ex-father-in-law said, "With taxes, you build civilization" (and Bernie Sanders, supported by a sizeable portion of younger people, would say in the 2016 American election).

Vibeke offered me a ride home—the car having been given to her. I didn't want a car. I had ridden my bicycle to the court, and I would ride home.

The first few Christmases are difficult to divorced people without a family. I was not invited to my in-laws for First Sunday in Advent or Christmas Eve and not invited to my brother-in-law's on Christmas Day—rightly so. The only thing was that I had spent those feasts for twenty-one years at the house of my in-laws for home-baked cookies and coffee with avecs on First Sunday in Advent to watch from the top of the hill the sun going down over the bog at 3 p.m., for roast goose after the church on Christmas Eve, and to my brother-in-law's for Christmas lunch of twenty-six courses on First Christmas Day. The second Day of Christmas, turkey being provided by Vibeke and me was a non-starter.

My children visited me for Little Christmas Eve, the 23rd of December, the evening which is generally devoted to decorating the tree, and for Second Christmas Day, December 26th. This was Boxing Day in England and Ireland, the day that gifts are exchanged. It was spent by my kids and me in a restaurant.

My kids exchanged gifts with me that day. My son gave me a gift-wrapped bottle of black label Stolichnaya, and my daughter a shiny red CD-wrapping tied around with a bow, a John Coltrane CD—*A Love Supreme*. In turn, I gave them each a Christmas card with a crisp new five hundred-kroner note in it.

I reminded myself of the bickering between Vibeke and me, even on the Christmas holidays—of whether the tree was straight and her repositioning every ornament I placed on the tree, and a few dozen other things, not to mention violence upon my person.

On those short days of the week between Christmas and New Year's that my office was closed, I made good use of the gifts with which my children presented me. I listened to the Coltrane in my new apartment drinking the Stoli on the rocks, looking out over the frozen lake.

From my windows, I skåled to the twin Christmas trees on the twin roofs of Riget, gazing at the Peace sculpture over on the other side of the Peace Bridge. The Peace sculpture was a tall monolith, set in the earth askew like a structure about to fall but never quite falling—perhaps symbolic of the peace process of any war or modern civilization.

I watched a lone skater on the ice of the lake, hands behind his back, tilting into the curves he made as he built up speed—perhaps the skater was a divorcée, too—listening to the formal introduction of the Coltrane and then to the bass line and a little later to *a love supreme a love supreme*, deep chanting voices of the band like a Gregorian chant but more certain, as I became more certain of my daughter's and my son's love, I would never stop loving them, as Trane screamed the tenor and Elvin Jones beat the skins and McCoy Tyner played chords underneath it as a foundation and Jimmy Garrison plucked the bass preparatory to Trane screaming melodiously. I sipped the Stoli and lit a cigar and then the candles on my little, pygmy tree.

We could have been happy here. May you die a slow and painful death. You'll regret this.

Already did.

Round Midnight

AFTER NEARLY TWENTY-TWO YEARS, I had to rebuild my domicile, from the few scraps of furniture I had taken with me—a captain's bed which my father-in-law had built for Vibeke of oak, a single-bed, with two roomy drawers underneath, that could serve as a sofa; the trunk from Mrs. Vesterberg via my Jackson Heights superintendant's wife; a floor lamp; some kitchenware; an end table. Slowly, over four months, I bought a double bed with a feather mattress, a three-man and two-man sofa and matching chair in blue-green material with oak armrests and legs, three Iranian area rugs, two faux Tiffany floor lamps and one table lamp with marbleized beige glass shades, two antique chandeliers (one a cast-iron church lamp, one a faux art deco), two blue half globe bathroom lights and had them installed by Knud Brun, an electric shop on Sølvtorvet, two stereo speakers with amplifier, cassette and CD player, one TV and video player on rolling stand, a picnic-style table and four straw-seated chairs with blond wooden arms; ABC bookcases for two walls; cutlery plates, varied glasses, cocktail shaker, ice bucket and tongs, ice-cube trays which made ice-cubes in the shape of elephants; B&O telephone plus installation; vacuum cleaner, toaster, coffee machine, assorted brooms, mops and buckets, and a feather duster.

Last, pictures for walls in addition to the Teodor Bok angel at an empty table with empty wine bottle and Bok "Angel in the Well." Slowly, I bought six pictures—two oils, two aquarelles, two lithographs; two colorist Viliam Skotte Olsen oils of smiling and leering abstract faces; two colorist aquarelles by Savino of semi-realistic weird eyes and shapes; two lithographs, one by Wilhelm Freddie and one by Teodor Bok of a contraption looking like a man—all arranged in Beidemier style like the Næstved art dealer in addition to the masks I had bought in Cape Town, Bangkok, Japan, and a street market in Brussels.

Total, about kr 91,250, give or take a couple of thousand, which seriously depleted my savings.

On February 1st, 1997, I bought a cassette from David in the Jazz Cellar by Miles Davis,'*Round About Midnight,* recorded in 1956 in New York City, because I read that the Hale-Bopp comet would be visible over the lake in early morning February 9th at 1:30 a.m. I had a plan. February 8th was a Saturday, and I looked up the phone number of Alexandria Holme and telephoned her on Saturday morning at 10:30 a.m., which is the earliest time I figured I could call her.

Alexandria—Dria, for short—was a girl I was chatting up in the office, a secretary who painted barefoot (she told me once) and wrote in the evening and on weekends She was a sweet, mild, and lovely girl, divorced, with a pretty face, slim with large breasts, and often she touched my hand and arm and chest, when we chatted, with her delicate sculpted hands. I wanted to kiss those fingers and had done so and various other parts of her at various office Christmas parties over the years—when the little hours came and the staff was inebriated.

She touched everyone's hand often, man or woman, but I felt she touched my hand in a special way, cupping it under her palm. She had three grown sons—and thus no commitments from her or me. I call her a girl—she was five years older than I, but she looked five years younger. Occasionally, she had a braid in her long blond hair (no doubt colored, but it looked delicious) which hung down like a plumb-line to her lovely backside. And she was kind and mild as she was fair and free—of her husband (divorced) and I fancied free of her sons.

When she answered the telephone, I asked her straight-off if she was barefoot. She recognized my voice which I thought was a good sign.

"Are you painting?"

"Yes."

We chatted on, and it turned out she was painting a red toad. I had come back from Reykjavik recently, raving about a sculpture of a red toad I had seen in a restaurant and asked the waiter if I could buy. "Of course," the waiter responded "For only a million kroner." I didn't ask whether that was Icelandic, which was considerably less than the Danish kroner because, Icelandic or Danish, it was out of my financial reach. But if she was painting a red toad indicated that the way in which she touched my hand was indeed special.

I told her that the Hale-Bopp would be visible over the lake outside my windows at 1:30 a.m. and would she like to come by 'round about midnight for a night meal of some champagne and caviar and to see it.

"But that's after midnight!"

"So? You can bring your tooth brush."

She was silent for a moment. Then she said, "Okay."

The Hale-Bopp was not a disappointment. Nor was Dria. She brought the red toad, an apartment-warming gift for me. It was the precise red toad sculpture, though painted in acrylic rather than sculpted in stone, I had seen in Reykjavik, about which I told her in detail. Made me feel she had access to my mind. *And* she had brought her toothbrush.

We danced slow to "'Round Midnight," which was written by Thelonius Monk and played by Miles with the mute on his trumpet and Trane making some small, unnoticeable, but telling sketches on his tenor, and Paul Chambers and Philly Joe Jones making unnoticeable but telling strokes on their instruments, and at about three minutes, it changes tempo for two heartbeats and Red Garland comes in with piano chords.

This was the birth of the cool four years before the cool was born.

My body welded against Dria's, one hand on her back and the other lower, her hands clasped at the small of my back were heaven in the dark apartment, and we made love on the wall-to-wall.

What life was made for.

We sat it out for Parker's upbeat "Au, Lew-Cha" and took another look at the comet. Which appeared in the sky directly over the lake as a fire ball and a curved tail of blue. The last appearance of the great comet of the late '90s had been about 4,200 years before, and it wouldn't return for thousands of years.

We began to dance again fast, briefly, to "Bye-Bye Blackbird," everything flopping and twisting as we did our approximation of the music before I collapsed in the armchair, but she kept dancing. She circled around the carpet, unashamed in her nakedness like some Eve in paradise, dancing for me.

I wanted it to be light and cheerful. Twenty-two years of marriage was enough; I didn't get out of one to have another sprung on me. I wanted to be free with all that meant of solitude, both good and bad, and the temporary alleviation of loneliness. I wanted to explore the areas of Copenhagen which had been barred to me by dint of my marital expectations. I wanted my life to begin and continue. At fifty-two, on the cusp of fifty-three. I had seen the Hale-Bopp. It was a ball of fire with a tail.

I had always wanted to try something.

Something Dria showed me—by way of a carved, wooden African flute in the shape of a phallus which she allowed me to insert in the dimple between her thighs and via the act of fellatio she entertained me with until I exploded in her mouth and then, exhibiting to me that she had held it in her mouth, lips closed firmly until she kissed me and let it flow into *my* mouth; it tasted like liquified oyster but more salty—made me remember a deed I had experienced thirty years ago, just before I met Toni June. A woman who had picked me up hitchhiking asked me if I liked to swim and took me back to her pool in Santa Barbara. I will call her Deidre because I don't remember her name. At one point she was standing on the edge of the swimming pool, and I was in the water below her, clutching the concrete border of the pool. She had just been in, and water cascaded down her shoulders in her two-piece and rested in running beads down her legs and to her bare feet, with which she stepped on my fingers, stepped harder, and her green gaze fixed my eyes, and she said, "I feel sadistic." It was a hot day.

"Want to go in?" I asked.

We did that.

I never told that to anyone.

One day, in a serving house in Østerbro, Dria spoke low about a man she knew—who was two meters tall—about 6'7"—named Kjeld, whom she met in this café and he told her he was experimenting in sadism on a masochistic woman he had left in his apartment, tied to the bed, with a crocodile clip on her labia and plastic clothes pins on her nipples. She set her teeth together in horror or mock horror as she told this. "Kjeld invited me to return to his place."

Dria didn't say whether she went, and I was too embarrassed to ask her.

I don't know if I proposed it or she did. I think I did, because it made me curious—in an immediate, erotic way. We visited an introductory meeting of SMil—Sadomasochism in love—on Nørrebrogade. I had seen it in the classifieds of Politiken when we ate Sunday brunch at a café on Østerfarimagsgade. I passed the ad to her, and she zeroed in on it immediately.

We told the taxi driver to pass it by one block and walked back. SMil was on the second floor above a ground floor shop. There was no signage of any sort. You had to know it was there and what went on in the shop and the upstairs rooms. The shop was some kind of porn shop. It was shut, and a sign was on the window ONLY OPEN FOR MEETINGS OF THE ASSOCIATION. You obviously had to know when the meetings were. You couldn't see in the window. We pushed open a door on the side of the shop and took the stairs up. A tall man wearing a black T-shirt and black leather trousers said, in Danish, "Welcome. I'm Mads. You're here for the introductory meeting? Come in."

He opened a door to a bar and some sort of a check-in desk where a man dressed in a similar fashion to Mads, only he had a black leather vest over his T-shirt, told us, "Welcome. My name is Jes. Take a seat in living room. We'll just wait five or ten minutes for more people to come, then we'll get started with giving information." He took our coats.

"Please, is that bar functional? I'd like two glasses of red wine."

"The bar is closed during introductory meeting," Jes said.

My heart sank. If I knew her, so did Dria's.

We filed into the living room, past the closed bar, and there were two long sofas—also black leather—and two leather easy chairs and a scattering of straight-backed chairs, and we introduced ourselves, with only first names, to the other people. There were a couple lounging on the sofa, and a young woman, sitting in a straight-back chair. The young woman was non-communicative, didn't say even her first name, but the couple, especially the man named Jan, was easy and conversational, particularly to me, as though he wanted to assure me that he wasn't after Dria—who introduced herself as Alex. "Alex" had dressed the part, with beige leather pants and a black pullover with gauze on the top above her breasts and over her delicate shoulders, asserted by a simple large silver pendant, hung round her neck and nestling in her bosom. She looked smashing.

The woman looked nervous or embarrassed. She introduced herself as Lisbeth. Her complexion was ruddy. I didn't know if she was blushing, or had a skin condition. I thought she was an M, Jan was an S. I wondered what I was. Too proud to be an M, I opined that I was a switchhitter, although I had only come there out of curiosity—but it was heady, the closeness of the possibility.

There was something I hadn't noticed before: A room with a wide entryway that had a velvet-covered chain—like something you would see in a theater—I wondered if there were any ticket-takers in SMil. There was a large black X-shaped cross in the nadir of the room, with a bucket of whips and canes in it, of varying thicknesses, beside it. And next to that was a darkened hallway. I touched Dria / "Alex" on the wrist to look. She was interested. I could see from her reaction. "Looks like a movie, stretched across a ticket-taker," I said softer so that no-one could hear and join in the conversation. But Jan joined in with, "It does."

A few other people came into the living room. They didn't introduce themselves. Jes came in after with his leather vest and said, "Let's get started."

He said that we might have noticed the chain stretched across the cross room. That was meant as nobody could come closer and join in. People could sit in the living room and be voyeurs and drink a glass of wine, but if that chain was down, people could come closer and possible join the fun. That room was for exhibitionists. If you want a more private scene you were welcome to enter the hallway, where there were more rooms with implements which were self-explanatory. You would be free to look around within the next hour. There was also a locker room with a locker for every dues-paying member. He asked were there any questions so far?

Someone asked how much were the dues? Jes said a figure, which I can't remember, but it seemed reasonable.

Jan asked if we had to give our real names—could we give a code name? The answer was that since 1979, when SMil was founded and, a year before that, when S/M was legalized, the registry law would have to be followed. On the member registry, every dues-paying member—there were not any non-dues-paying members—had to include his or her full name and address on the registry. That was true of any club, society, or association; you were required to use your full name, address, and telephone number.

You could give a code name in everyday use, but for the registry you had to include your legal name and address. This was partially because of our right to have a supplementary grant in accordance with the number of members we have registered and partially due to the registry law stipulating that it is legally required that we have the full names and addresses of every member registered.

"There is currently no one who has a code name in everyday use. Every member has his or her legal first and often last name in everyday use. We have respect for one another and don't reveal our membership in SMil. The list is confidential and secret." There was respect also in that a no is a no. If anyone says no, that is final.

"How much is a glass of wine?" I asked.

"The bar is closed now," Jes said, "but the red or white wine is 20 kroner, and we buy 100 kroner bottles, and a bottle of beer is 10 kroner."

We were released from the information with Jes setting up the desk to anyone who wanted to join.

I wanted to see down the darkened corridor; the switch had been turned on and lighted the hallway now. There were three dimly-lighted rooms with no doorways. The one was a large one with an X cross in it and adjustable manacles and ankle loops. Along one wall were an array of what looked like leather helmets, one with a zipper on the mouth and one with a large zipper over the eyes, and some latex suits and skirts. The other wall had a display of canes and whips and leather belts and straps.

Dria grasped my arm and whispered, "Think of all the bacteria on those!"

"I hadn't thought of that."

"What did you think of the implements?"

"I don't like whips and belts and canes."

"You could bring your broad belt and whip my back."

"Your back?" I asked incredulously.

"Yes!"

In the second room, which was even more dimly lighted, there was an enormous mattress, suitable for ten or twenty people, according to how close they wanted to get. There was a plywood wall with holes at different heights and of different sizes cut in it with a jig-saw and smoothed edges.

"What's that for?" Dria asked.

"I never saw one before, but I think they're glory holes."

"What are they for?"

"People in the adjoining room put one or another organ through and people on this side put the organs in their mouths or lick or torture them. Torture in a glorious way."

"Oh!"

"I heard of that in San Francisco. Before the AIDS epidemic."

In the third room was a gynecological bench—and, on the other side, a flat table—on the third side was a leather-padded kneeler with the kneeling slats elevated and a stock and pillory.

The GYN bench, I didn't know whether Dria or me would sit on. Maybe take turns. I had butterflies in my stomach, while we gazed upon it.

"I know what *that* is," Dria whispered, indicated the GYN bench. "Your turn!"

The butterflies in my stomach started to move their wings faster.

Another couple—Lisbeth and Jan—started to come into the room, and Dria and I stepped into the hallway. Jes was still at the desk enrolling members who had decided.

"Should we enroll?" I asked. "Or not?"

"You have to give your real name. And address. I'm not that liberated. I've seen what confidential secret lists do."

We still had the shop on the ground floor to look at. There was a staircase down to the shop right alongside of the other stairs. There were a few dues-paying members in the store, mostly men, which sold clips and clamps and chastity belts for men and women, poppers, electrical devices, butt plugs and dildos and double-dildos and intricately belted dildos for lesbians, and whips, canes and belts. Dria looked through a supply of canes and whips. A patron in a leather vest and motocycle hat, wearing an "S" black T-shirt, asked "Want me to try one on you?"

Quick as that, Dria asked him, "Want me to try one on your face? Which one do you want?"

The S-man actually blushed and shut up. I had never seen Dria like that before. Yes, I had, but it was non-sexual repartee. I was impressed. She continued to look through the whips and bought a penis-pussy-whip and a jar of poppers.

"Do you intend me or you to use them?"

"Maybe both."

We ate in Shezan closer in on Nørrebrogade to my place in Østerbrogade. I could never figure out Copenhagen, could not get a sense of the city. The city was not big, but it was coiled and twisted. I was continually surprised to learn that two points I had thought distant from each other were, in fact, back to back. This was a city built by start and stop over a millennium. Still, I was learning. By the time when I died, I should almost know the city. Only the dead know Copenhagen. And you forget—if you're not in practice.

Shezan was a Pakistani restaurant, one on the north side, one in the center, one on the west side. The one on the north side was darker, the lights were dimmer, which suited my mood, as I sat across from Dria, eating my lamb curry. A bottle of wine stood on the table, half empty or half full. She had surprised me in the SMil shop, and I half wanted to get the upper hand, and half wanted to dissolve in the moment. I chose the latter. Or the latter chose me. Or Dria chose me.

She reached across the table and enclosed my wrist in her hand, her small hand with delicate sculpted fingers.

We asked the waiter to call a cab—she asked. I paid.

She was mild in every way, but she was a vixen in bed.

Paradise

ALONE, ONE NIGHT I WAS IN THE PALÆ BAR just off the King's New Square on Ny Adel Street, and I took a seat at the table with two women who were dolled up to go out on the town. The Palæ Bar is like that. Everyone sits with everyone. The woman opposite me said that they were meeting a couple of men later. She was pretty, tastefully dressed and was endowed with very thick lips, and I said, "I have to kiss you."

For whatever reason, she showed every intention of complying and I said, "Stand up. I want a full-bodied kiss." She did that—maybe it was the sense of my urgency, and I laid a long slow smacker on her. I messed up her lipstick with the rotation of my lips with the lovely pillow of hers, grinding my middle into hers, enjoying her breasts against my chest. My hands took liberties. It was just a kiss. After all, she was meeting some gentlemen later. She stood there, the deep red lipstick smudged around her mouth and thick lips.

She said, "I have to repair my make-up," and went into the ladies room, the *dame toileten*. She took a long time there and came back with the deep red lipstick repaired. She had on a waist-length, beige leather jacket and a beige mini-skirt, the same shade as her jacket, and I looked at her very thick lips. I said, "I *have* to kiss you, *again*."

"But I just repaired my lipstick."

"Again."

"All right," she said reluctantly. Maybe it was her thick lips that made her comply. Maybe the possessing of such pillowing lips was a sacred trust that any man who demanded a kiss she felt she had to let him. Or maybe it was the urgency of my demand that made her comply, that I overpowered her will. The pleasure of man and woman together on earth.

After the kiss, she went into the *dame toileten*, and I walked into the night. I was planning to pay a visit to Andy's Bar on Gothersgade, but I came to a curious brass sign on the far corner of Ny Adelsgade. The sign said,

VELVET ROOM
10 PM to 4 AM
RING BELL

Such was my desire, so to speak, of knowing Copenhagen: It was a quarter past ten so I pressed the brass button, and waited. A woman opened the door, smiling skeptically. "Yes?" she asked.

She was young and not young, late forties perhaps. She wore a low-cut blouse, but her face was ordinary, the little make-up she had on was tastefully applied.

"May I come in?"

I followed her through a foyer, glimpsed a bar through the curtain at the other end. I headed for it.

"Hey," she called to me. "It costs two hundred kroner to go in there."

"Can I pay with a card?"

"Of course. Let me take your coat."

I pulled off my Burberry. The bar was dark and not crowded. A few men sat at tables or on stools around the oval bar. Colored lights flashed on the dance floor, and one whole wall was a series of nine large TV screens on which a variety of pornographic scenes flickered. I took a stool, at the end of the bar, facing directly on to the abandoned dance floor. Music was playing, which I recognized as Sadé's "Paradise," about the secrets of the soul, about giving it all up, letting it all go, about surrendering, surrendering love. A young woman came out in the center of the dance floor, right opposite me.

The woman who let me in apparently doubled as the bartender. I asked how much was a beer. "Sixty," she answered.

"Kroner?"

"Yes."

"Would you like me to hold your card?"

"Sure. Are you the manager?"

She put the card in a glass where I could see it and nodded.

"That is a very beautiful woman." She was wearing a gray miniskirt and a black silk blouse which showed generous cleavage and black, sheer stockings. Her hair was long and black and straight, and her face was very white and beautiful, even featured, full-lipped, dark eyed.

"Yes and a very talented dancer."

"They just dance?"

"It's up to the customers if they want to buy them a drink and talk. If you want to go upstairs and talk, you buy them a bottle of champagne, and then you *talk*. What happens then is between the two of you."

She glanced at me, my silk tie, my sports jacket that did not have hand-stitching in the lapel. "The champagne costs a thousand kroner. Then what happens is between you and her."

"A full bottle of champagne? That is not cava?"

"Two splits. Prices start at fifteen-hundred."

This was just for fun. I filled my mouth with beer. The young woman started to dance as Prince came on singing "Sexy Mother Fucker."

Sexy, sexy, sexy. Then her blouse was on the floor, and I saw a tattoo at the top of her shoulder. She danced near to where I sat, my back to the bar, a yard away, meeting my eyes, as she unhooked her bra and flung it away, danced left, right directly in front of me, turned abruptly, and pressed up against the wall of TV screens, which I began to notice.

Each screen featured a different act or body part, and the real woman's flat outstretched palms glided down those she could reach as she pressed up against the wall. On one screen was a naked woman going down on a naked woman, on another a woman going down on a naked man with a big erection, on yet another a woman in nothing else but stiletto heels whipping a naked man…

Then the dancing woman reached down and removed her skirt, and there was another tattoo of a flower just above her buttock, and now she danced wearing nothing but one stocking. She danced well, keeping from the borders of vulgarity. Finally, she was naked. She rolled on the floor, looking beautiful in nakedness, sprung up and, staring full at me, she walked briskly in time to the music across the length of the dance floor toward me, her long black hair swaying across her breasts.

She stopped in front of me, not a foot away, staring into my eyes. My breath caught. Her body was flawless, so beautiful, so *fucking* sexy. And what was behind her eyes? In her mind? What was she thinking? Or was she pure instinct, the hypnotist collector?

Then she turned her face away and abruptly whipped her head so her hair slashed across the distance between us. It lashed my cheek lightly, just as the music ended with the intricate tenor saxophone and Prince saying repeatedly "Sexy MF," and she was retreating without a glance back, gathering her clothes, behind the disco booth, to disappear.

I turned back to the bar, dry in the mouth, breathless. The bar-maid-hostess stood there at a discreet distance, but close enough to contact.

"Some dancer," I said, though I barely had breath enough to speak. I felt the pressure between my legs as some alien pressure.

"Another beer?" the hostess asked. "A split of champagne? Two splits?"

"Beer."

The woman lingered when she had brought the schooner.

"Can I bring my girlfriend here?" I asked.

She knitted her brow. "What for?"

"Inspiration."

"How old is your girlfriend?"

"Fifty-seven."

She wrinkled her brow; that was apparently the sign for disapproval and for affirmation.

The fat-lipped girl was long gone from the Palæ Bar. I called Dria from the pay phone.

"It's almost eleven!"

I told her to meet me. "I want to show you someplace special."

I nursed a beer, two beers, until Dria came about an hour later. I had told her we had plenty of time.

When the Velvet Room door opened, the now-familiar hostess let me in without comment, but she obviously looked over Dria with approval. People usually approved of Dria.

I paid the two hundred kroner for her. "Is it all right?"

"I paid for myself once before."

She wrinkled her brow. "It's okay."

We filed into the bar. A group of dancers-escorts from behind the disco desk looked at Dria. There were titters of approval. Apparently the hostess had spread the word that the American and his girlfriend wanted inspiration.

The same dancer did the same dance to Prince—*sexy mf shaking that ass*—and when her flawless body was completely undressed she walked directly across the dance floor and whisked her long black hair across Dria's cheek. Her blue eyes turned electric and she kissed her lips at me. I thought of doing a threesome with the flawless dancer—her ass was so perfect!—but I didn't have the money in my account.

We stayed until two and drank two splits of champagne and I tipped the hostess, and the black-haired dancer and some of her colleagues waved from the disco stand to us when we left, and the hostess, opening the door for us when we exited, asked "Do you have inspiration now?"

Unsquare Dance

A LETTER CAME TO ME IN 1997. It was mailed to me at the address of my eleven-years dead mother and successive addresses crossed out, it reached me after two years. It was forwarded to my apartment in Copenhagen. (They would do that back then.)

It was from Toni June, in her loopy handwriting, with the i's dotted with circles:

Dear Eddie-Frank,

I have decided to forgive all of my past. I'm not asking any questions, so you don't have to answer this—if you would anyway.

Love,

Toni June

It was post-dated Evanston, Illinois and had an address on the back flap with her last name not Holland, but Brewer.

I held the letter for weeks and then, seized by some urgency and a couple of double vodkas, I answered it. I told her that I was living in Denmark, had been married for twenty-two years, now divorced, had two children, a son and a daughter, now in the end of their teens, had a job for soon a quarter century, and written several books ("As you predicted, they weren't very good—at least they had not been bestsellers, but I wrote some stories that were good." I crossed out the last phrase.) "How is Lori May faring? She must be in her thirties now!" I invited her to fill me in on her past, since we parted.

I got a letter two weeks later. She had married Greg Bush and had a child with him in Indiana, she was a girl named Stephanie, now twenty-seven. He was violent, and she divorced him. He was like me—not in being violent—but wore only dark socks, too. She met an older man, a widower with three kids, and married him with two kids, and lived happily ever after. We're building houses for less fortunate families (voluntarily).

She added a PS: "I'll bet your books are not so bad!" and a PPS: "Lori May is not doing so well for the moment. She's with a motorcycle group. She is thirty-two, involved with a biker named Frank. I pray for her."

I wrote back that I would be teaching in Spartanberg, South Carolina, for a month in January. "Could we meet?" She said she would drive down to Spartanberg with her husband, Larry, and one or two of her stepchildren ("It's an SUV!") if you have time in between teaching.

Toni June and her husband and her stepson, Larry Jr., showed up at the dorms. Toni June looked worse than me. She was still trim, though wrinkled around her eyes and her face showed the thirty-one years since we last met, and she had a triple chin—not from pudginess but from wrinkles.

She said, "Men age so much more gracefully."

"And women grow more beautiful." *When they are younger*, I didn't say. She didn't say things either—about the weight I had gained, twenty pounds since last we met. Larry was older, but he was ageless; he was the kind of man who didn't age after he turned sixty, and Larry Jr. was barely fifteen, tall and pudgy. Larry must have had him when he was fifty.

We stood in a knot, making small talk. I said that there was a Dave Brubeck concert in Asheville at the UNC, only about eighty miles away. "Unless you've driven enough."

Larry said that they were staying at a motel in Asheville, and that they would like to invite me to dinner and to stay the night. "After the concert. In a separate room."

"I can pay."

"No, you're our guest."

"I think all of you're my guests."

"In our country."

"Well, I'll pay for the concert tickets, then."

On the ride up to Asheville, we didn't talk about Lori May or about San Diego or Ocean Beach at all, but it was on my mind. We talked about contemporary times, how Toni June had gone on and gotten her RN. "Registered Nurse." In fact, that was the way Toni June and Larry met. Mrs. Brewster, Larry's first wife, was in for a heart attack. She hadn't made it, and Toni June was a nurse on her team. "Stephanie is going to be an RN, too."

We stopped for lunch. Of course, there were no cocktails. I ordered a glass of wine.

"Do you drink wine all the time?" Larry Jr. asked.

"Practically."

"I'm going to order a glass of wine, too."

"No, honey," Toni June said. "You're not old enough. When you get as old as Eddie Frank, you can drink wine."

I paid the bill above Larry's objections.

The concert at UNC was not really a concert. Held in a classroom, thirty or forty people were there in folding chairs, and it was not the same without Paul Desmond on alto sax. Dave Brubeck was seventy-eight, Eugene Wright on bass was seventy-five, and Joe Morella was seventy.

Brubeck played "Blue Ronda á la Turk" and "Take Five" with the pounding chords and explained that "Blue Ronda" was influenced by a Turkish street musician—so, it was like a lecture. Finally, he played "Unsquare Dance," which Toni June used to like—she had it on *Time Futher Out* with her boyfriend Steve who used to play pool with her uncle (Packett, a top-ten pool player). But it was not the same without Desmond's alto sax.

Still, it was good to see and hear Brubeck and Wright and Morella.

We ate out in a diner, and they had iced tea with their hamburgers. I asked the waitress if they had a liquor license, and I had a large glass of red wine with liver and onions and planned to have another large glass of wine and cognac afterward. I wasn't making a demonstration; I just liked red wine and cognac.

They talked about Habitat for Humanity and how Toni June didn't have a clue about building houses, but Larry helped and advised her, starting from the most simple tasks. She started by making coffee and sandwiches and graduated to actual building.

"Empower women!" Larry said.

I began to feel guilty. *Empower me!* I thought. What had I ever done for somebody else? Build houses? I pictured myself working with lumber, hammer and nails and unnameable things. That was what stumped me. That "unnameable." I didn't have any skills at building. Houses or anything else. Only writing. I couldn't even move, paid someone to improve my tiny apartment. Paid the super. *Are we friends and neighbors, or aren't we?*

Then we got into the "Under God" in the Pledge of Allegiance. Whether we should require schoolboys and girls to that preposition?

"Shouldn't we?" Toni June demanded.

Larry mumbled something appeasing like, "We don't know where Eddie stands on that question."

"Shouldn't we?" Toni June challenged.

I had the reminder that she was as feisty as ever. Fortunately, I held my mouth.

After breakfast, which I paid, I took the Greyhound back on Sunday, insisting, "You've driven enough yesterday."

I didn't ask any questions either.

Somethin' Else

ONE DAY IN SUMMER '98, Dria telephoned me from Femmeren on Classensgade in Østerbro. She told me a guy named Morten was behind the bar, and he had just played a CD that she thought I should listen to.

It was Saturday, noon of a mild day, the swans and ducks and grebes and seagulls and pigeons gathered on the bank of the lake for some dark foreigner, breaking fingerfuls of bread from a white plastic bag to feed them. I had not seen Dria for a couple of weeks. We had spent the past year seeing each other more or less exclusively, but then something happened, and I wanted to distance myself—as I did when we got overly close. After twenty-two years of marriage, I was free and wanted to keep myself from backing into a trap. That was how I thought of it. I saw other women in addition to Dria, but she didn't want to hear details.

We had a more or less exclusive—I wanted to say "relationship," but I'll say friendship. With benefits. It was dangerous; sometimes affection blurred into something more profound, but the key word there was "blurred," and I didn't want anything blurry. I had a natural redoubt—of my business travel and my book tours. It didn't get too permanent, broken up by my trips.

Because of my traveling for work, I had a goodly stock of bonus miles which I could exchange for free flights and hotels, and I had invited Dria on four-day weekends to Dublin, Paris, and Amsterdam through that first year of our friendship.

In Dublin, we stayed at the Davenport on Merrion Square, just down the street from the house that Oscar Wilde was born in and was commemorated by a gaudy statue, sculpted and painted to resemble Wilde lounging on a rock in Merrion Square and just around another corner from Sweney's Chemist on Lincoln Place where Leopold Bloom in *Ulysses* stopped to buy Bronnley's lemon hand soap. I told Dria the soap was purchased for Molly, who was based on Joyce's wife Nora. The day the novel was set was the day Joyce and Nora had their first date. I didn't reveal to her that Poldy used it to the masturbate in the public baths—it seemed unnecessarily brutal information. She would never read *Ulysses*. What did it matter to her if Molly was unfaithful with Blazes Boylan to Poldy, who masturbated in the baths?

We walked in Stephen's Green and had a full Irish breakfast in Bewley's Oriental Café on Grafton Street and strolled to the left through the flower stalls to McDaid's on Harry Street, off Grafton, and had a mid-morning pint of Guinness at the outside tables where—by god!—we saw bearded J. P. Donleavy, dressed in tweeds right up to his cap, exiting a pub across the street—I think it was called Luxembourg. He hurried away at the sight of me recognizing him, but he didn't know that I wouldn't have disturbed him; I had been a guest in his mansion at Mullingar to interview him half a dozen years before, and he was gracious to me, though he didn't give me one whisky. He gave me tea and scones and cheese.

"That's the author of *The Ginger Man*," I said excitedly to Dria; she didn't know the novel, but she copied it in her notebook, with starfish imprinted on the cover. I made a spontaneous rhyme to that starfish notebook:

> The starfish crawl upon the wall,
> upon the floor and through the door,
> the starfish with their many legs
> and not so many eyes,
> the starfish that can hug and crush,
> never seeing why.

We walked back down Grafton, her arm linked in mine, to Duke Street for a lamb stew lunch at Davy Byrnes. Dria, seated with me at the front tables, peered around and said she felt something that she remembered from her childhood in Copenhagen which had been lost, with all these people from their offices eating lunch. I told her that's what I felt in Copenhagen, an ineffable thing that had to do with the people and the light and the serving houses and the buildings, the cobblestone streets. We looked into one another's eyes—hers electric blue which I called her "blue lamps"—and I think we understood each other. She reached her hand to clasp mine. Her palm was warm and soft and had a quality to the touch that moved me.

I thought Dria would like to see the long hall of the library, and we crossed Nassau on the way to the Book of Kells to see what the Dubliners had nicknamed "The Tart with the Cart"—bronze Molly Malone with her cockles and mussels cart. Across the Liffey, on O'Connell Street, was a more horrendous sculpture of Anna Liffey with a simulation of the river around her, which Dubliners nicknamed, "The Floozy in the Jacuzzi" or "The Whore in the Sewer."

"The Irish are not so fortunate with their sculpture as the Danes," I said.

"Maybe it's that their culture is governed by the ear, while the Danes are governed by the eye," she said. "You're governed by the ear for language. English anyway."

"Wait until you look at the Book of Kells. An illuminated Bible, more than 1,000 years old."

On the day we were to fly home, we sat in the Davenport bar, drinking spicy Bloody Marys complete with celery stalks, at the end of a successful four-day weekend in which I had not succumbed to the romance of the situation by telling her I loved her.

The trip to Dublin was such a success that we followed it up with a trip to Paris at Easter time. We'd had such unseasonably warm weather in Dublin in mid-February that we expected warmth in Paris. Easter was as late as April 12th that year, but it was cold and rainy. We made the mistake of standing in the queue that was waiting to get into Notre Dame for Easter Sunday mass, and we waited so long that we got soaked and had to give it up without seeing the inside of the cathedral. I was wet through all my layers—topcoat, handwoven tweed jacket (which I'd picked up in Dublin—the sleeves were short enough for me), sweater-vest, shirt and undershirt and briefs, even my silk necktie and my Dublin Walking Hat were drenched, and Dria was wet down to her bra and pantyhose and panties. Shivering, we walked across to the left bank, the fifth Arrondissement, to Rue de la Harpe to buy pastries at the corner Tunisian bakery and cold cuts and a bottle of wine at the deli across from the hotel.

Afterward, we went directly to our room at the Hôtel du Levant, a hotel which had been recommended to us by Ben Hawthorne, my friend in Honfleur. We stripped and wrapped in blankets and hung our clothes in the bathroom and on the radiator to dry. We were away for four days; they were the only clothes we had except for changes of shirts, underwear, and socks.

We ate the cold-cuts and drank the wine and munched the Tunisian pastries—they were green and tasted of pistachios—and sent down for another bottle of wine. I took up the hardback of *The Song of Songs*, which I had picked up in Shakespeare & Co., the day before. I opened it at random and read aloud, extemporizing, "And you, my darling, how beautiful you are in your birthday suit…. Hey! This is divided into the girl's and boy's parts. Wanna read it aloud? Get over here beside me nekkid as the day when you were born, I am in the fever of love! Let us make love all day and night long!"

She did as I suggested, and we had a good four-day weekend after all, with the rain splashing down the window panes. We sent down frequently for pâté and cheese and apricots and grapes and bread and wine.

We didn't know what book to bring to Amsterdam in case of inclement weather; the discovery of *Song of Songs* seemed like a one-time shot. We flew to Schipol the last weekend in May, and we stayed in a narrow, tall guest house run by a gay couple on Herengracht near Rembrandt Plein. It rained half the time so we took shelter in the nearest brown bar when it began to drizzle. I developed a taste for genever, which was half as strong as aquavit so you could drink twice as much.

When the sun shone, we walked, though it was chilly; we were glad we'd brought our topcoats. We went to the Rijksmuseum and the Vincent Van Gogh because Dria wanted to see specific works of Van Gogh and Gaugin and Toulouse-Lautrec. I didn't have much patience with museums—there were so many pictures in an artificial setting, but

I liked that Dria did. She looked at the texture and the colors of the oils, studied them closely and at a distance, and her face was serious. I looked at her. She was beautiful. She wore a long, corn-blue woolen coat, and her long blond hair was fanned out against it, and her face was so serious, studying the paintings. She also wore a medallion of a sizable bronze big fish on a heavy chain I'd bought her in an African shop. I resisted the impulse to come up behind her and kiss her on the back of the neck and say—say *what*? *I love you*? That was the kind of impulse that sprung shut traps of affection. Nonetheless, I felt an intense emotion over which I puzzled: I loved her because I didn't have to love her, a complex feeling which I didn't dare try to express or explain to her. I couldn't understand myself or it.

Instead, I walked up behind her and kissed her on the back of the neck and said nothing.

Looking around questioningly, she smiled and shook her head: "What was that for?"

"Because I like you. Very much."

When we were back in Copenhagen, as we were walking along Østerfarimagsgade to dinner at Krut's Karport, she took my hand and held it.

"I don't like that," I told her, and she quickly removed her hand from mine. However, I felt guilty about what I'd said. I thought, *What a sweet gesture*! Couldn't I have reacted less brusquely? It would have been okay if she looped her hand in the crook of my arm or even put an arm around my waist, but holding hands walking along the street made me feel owned. I was sorry, but it was just how it made me feel. I didn't care to be owned, and it seemed as though she owned me like that, holding my hand, that we were one unit, walking the street, like man and wife. I didn't want to a wife. At least, not now. Maybe never. I could have said it more gently, though, or simply made a subterfuge to get my hand free, make a show of trying to search in my pocket and kept my hand there.

At least my statement was clear, but my behavior depressed me, and I excused myself after dinner at Krut's Karport, without finishing my beer, explaining that I had a miserable headache and went home alone and hadn't called her since.

This phone call from Femmeren was an excuse to see each other again, on neutral territory. Which was probably why she telephoned me. I was ready to take up with her again.

I hiked over to Femmeren which was just ten minutes away. The Femmeren—The Fiver—was a brown bar, a serving house, a *værtshus*, which had one of the best collections of jazz CDs in Copenhagen. One was playing. I could hear it at the door. Sounded like Miles Davis.

There were few people in the small, dim bar room. Dria was seated at a minuscule table, only room for two, and she said to the bartender, "Would you start that again, Morten?" and she kissed me on the mouth. Just a peck.

The CD started with rippling piano notes over a plucked bass. The piano notes were simple, but evocative. Then an alto sax came in with a lean line, burgeoning, and a trumpet entered with explosive short lines, blaring to disrupt all that came before, and then the trumpet—it could only be Miles—began to play the melody of "Autumn Leaves."

Dria knew it was one of my favorite songs—I had it on a CD by Eva Cassidy and by Diana Krall, but the only instrumental of it I'd heard was by Roger Williams, kind of a pseudo-classical rendition on piano, which I heard when I was, like, thirteen years old. The melody haunted me, brought up emotions from the well of my young soul that spoke to me of distant cities and a teasing isolation that was sovereign because it was a condition of life. This song appeared as a poem in French by Jacques Prévert, which I'd heard in French class in college, "Les Feuilles Mortes"—"The Dead Leaves," and Joseph Kosma, a French-Hungarian composer, set it to music. I'd heard it in French by Yves Montand and by Edith Piaf; it was rendered in English by Johnny Mercer. Here I was listening to the melody by Miles Davis. Then the alto began to improvise, and Miles stepped back, and the alto sax went up and down the range of notes and took that melody apart and put it back together again. When Miles' trumpet hit a flat or sour note, the note starts out uneasily but rights itself as something choice.

The melody ended with rippling piano notes like blowing fallen leaves, dead leaves, and mirrored what was played on the piano at the start of the tune, with a plucked bass line.

When the song concluded—it must have been ten minutes—all I could say was, "Wow!"

Morten took the CD off—letting me catch my breath—and said,

"Best rendition of that song *ever*, full stop."

I asked who was playing the alto, and he gave me the jewel case. It was Julian "Cannonball" Adderley on alto sax and leading the group, though I was to learn, it was the last record Miles Davis ever played as a sideman (but what a sideman!), recorded in Hackensack, NJ, on March 9, 1958—my fourteenth birthday! I couldn't know what was going on two rivers removed in New Jersey from me while I was celebrating my fourteenth birthday in Queens and that I should hear the product of it forty years later in Copenhagen with a beautiful Danish woman named Dria, the song that haunted me, made me dream of distant places, recorded to perfection. I had to cross a wide ocean to the east and pass forty years before I encountered it once again.

I didn't have a notebook, so I copied down on a napkin all the information from the booklet—that Cannonball was on alto, Miles on trumpet, Hank Jones on piano (the same Hank Jones who had played with Anita O'Day in *Jazz on a Summer's Day*, when Anita said simply, "Mr. Jones?") Sam Jones on bass, and Art Blakey on drums, that the cuts were "Autumn Leaves" (10:55, Kosma-Mercer/Prévert), "Love for Sale" (7:01, Cole Porter), "Somethin' Else" (8:15, Miles Davis), "One for Daddy-O" (8:10, Nat Adderley—Cannonball's brother), "Dancing in the Dark" (4:10, Schwartz-Dietz), and "Alison's Uncle" (a.k.a "Rangoon," 5:03, Hank Jones). I even copied that this was a bonus feature added in 1982, seven years after Cannonball died in the Village, and Nat Adderley, discovering that the title was blank, named it for his daughter who was born that day, with a nod to Cannonball. I vaguely remembered reading in the papers that Cannonball had been evicted from his Greenwich Village apartment by the authorities, before he died, and someone trying to convince the "authority" doing the eviction that Adderley was a great musician and composer, but he put his furniture out on the pavement nonetheless

It was one o'clock. The Jazz Cellar on Gråbrødretorv closed at 2 p.m. on Saturday. I just had time. I asked Morten to call a cab. The proprietor of The Jazz Cellar, David said, "One for the short list." I bought two copies—one copy for me, and one for Dria.

"No need, I can listen to yours."

But I wanted to buy it for her. We bought a bottle of Alsatian champenoise and half a smoked eel at the fish store, and in my apartment, I scrambled some eggs and Dria skinned the eel and cut it in small lengths. We ate it in my front room at the table with chives and black pepper fresh from the mill, looking over the lake and listening to Cannonball and Miles *et al* until the sun went down. We didn't turn on the overhead lights because the yellow sky over the dark water, the chestnut trees bathed in yellow light and the jazz provided enough illumination.

There were no words necessary to add to the moment with Cannonball's alto screaming softly and Miles' sour, muted notes which were perfect, and I could see the dentist's son with his deep brown face, devoting all his sixty-five years to music, now dead these seven years.

These were all dead men, but living in the grooves, cut in wax, like a perfect echo. Cannonball dead at forty-seven in 1975, Sam Jones plucking the thick strings of his bass at fifty-seven in 1981, Art Blakey at seventy-one in 1990. Only Hank alive still. And all the composers and lyricists, composer Kosma and the poet Prévert getting together in France in 1945. These were men who lived on in perfect echoes.

I got up from the table and moved to the sofa, and Dria moved with me, as I hoped she would, and folded into me on the three-man, and no words were necessary, but the lyrics of "Autumn Leaves," vaguely beneath the melody.

Sweet Fire

ON WEDNESDAY, FEBRUARY 24TH, 1999, on my lunch hour, I browsed through a record shop in Østerbro, the east side of Copenhagen. One CD arrested my eye, Rahsaan Roland Kirk. *Sweet Fire*. I picked it from the rack and studied the cover photo; there was Kirk, sporting a black beret, dark glasses wrapped around his unseeing eyes, three reed instruments strung round his neck while he blew into a transverse flute. The jewel case was not wrapped in plastic, and I opened it. Fanke Damsté wrote the liner notes: Saxophonist Roland Kirk (1935-1977) became famous in the sixties. Blind from the age of two, he was playing professionally on tenor sax at fifteen. In 1977, Kirk founded the Vibration School of Music to teach saxophonists black classical music.

I should buy this, I thought, and listen to it, just so I can write to Andre Dubus and tell him I finally heard Roland Kirk. Andre had written about Kirk in perhaps the greatest of many published stories, "Dancing

After Hours," published in '96, the title story of his most recent collection. He printed the story in *Epoch* at Cornell University, the collection by Knopf the same year, 1996, the year he won the Rea Award for the Short Story. Andre had written a memorable scene in that story which featured a performance by Roland Kirk in prose through the point of view of the main character.

But I had to get back to the office from lunch.

Later in the day, I checked my email, and there was a message from Susan Dodd. She informed me that Andre Dubus had, suddenly and unexpectedly, died the night before. He was sixty-two. Although I had not seen him for a dozen years, we were in correspondence and spoke a few times on the phone, and he was not far from my thoughts.

I went home early because I wanted to make a private telephone call. I managed to get his son, Andre Dubus III, on the phone. I had known Andre III at Vermont College in 1988, two years after his father had stopped to aid an accident victim on a Massachusetts highway and got run down himself and—as he put it—was "crippled"; he spent the rest of his short life in a wheelchair. Andre III was a student at Vermont College's Master of Fine Arts program where I taught. I had graduated from being a student in the program to a teacher, as writers occasionally do who were working at their craft for many years. He was in my workshop, and he was too modest to tell me that his own collection of stories—*The Cage Keeper*—was about to come out from E. P. Dutton. Maybe it wasn't modesty so much as delicacy; he was twenty-eight, I forty-four, and while I had published one book of nonfiction and many stories in literary journals, it would be another two years before I published my first novel.

He had submitted a short story for the course. Before the story was workshopped, I asked him privately if he would mind me mentioning the circumstances of that story.

Andre lifted his brows. "Circumstances?"

"They are both excellent stories, but the story is the same one your father published. Only in your father's case, it is from the father's point-of-view, in your story, it is from the son's." The concluding scene had the boy throwing pebbles at his father's car as he drove away; it was a wrenching scene from the father's viewpoint and from the boy's, though both were in the prose style of the author.

He was not aware of the coincidence. I didn't touch on it in the workshop.

He and I went out for a night in Montpelier that summer, a kind of commemoration of the years when I had done the same with his father. We talked, laughed, drank peppered Stoli as I had done with his father a few years before, and ended at a campus party in Nobel Lounge, where Andre III played blues harmonica and invited me to come out with Tim O'Brien after the party. I was scheduled to teach the next day and, much as I wanted to meet O'Brien, I packed it in.

Although I had seen him only a few times since, I still felt I knew him when he answered the phone that evening to allow me to express sorrow at his father's death. Coincidentally, we both just recently had stories and been interviewed in *Glimmer Train*. What Andre III told me on the phone that evening was that his father had a very good last day, had some very good last months. He was happy. His death had come quickly.

He didn't tell me that a group of writers and fans had been chipping in to pay the hospital bills, which were extensive, and funeral expenses; Andre had had no medical coverage. Neither did he tell me about the trouble he was having with a town ordinance; apparently he and his brother Jeb, both trained in carpentry, were going to build their father a coffin and his father's wishes were to be buried on his property. The township had a regulation that he could not.

I apologized that I had no possibility of traveling back to the States for the wake and the funeral.

"Look," he said, "I think he's still here. He's over there, too." He told me about his pleasure at having had a long conversation with his father just the week before he died, and I told him about the Roland Kirk CD that had caught my eye that afternoon. I hesitated to tell that, for he might think I was dishonoring the moment with sentiment, but he seemed to take it in the spirit I meant it. Kirk was born the same month and year as Andre, but lived only thirty-one years whereas Andre lived twice as long. These details floated around in my brain as one of the coincidences of fate.

Afterward, I found out that Andre, before he died, had read his son's novel, *House of Sand and Fog*, and he said, "Do you have a tuxedo? Because that's going to be nominated for the National Book Award." The novel was, in fact, a finalist for the NBA and was selected for Ophrah Book Club on TV and would be made into a movie that would win an Oscar. Andre III was forty years old; his father had died when he was sixty-two. Father and son had had a lot of years together.

When I met the father in the summer of 1984, as a Vermont MFA student, I discovered that he had written a story that had been included in the *Best American Short Stories 1970* that had been so spiritually important to me that I remembered it. I met Andre in Julio's Bar in Montpelier, a burly guy not taller than myself, full-bearded with dark hair the color of his beard. I met him through my roommate in the graduate program, Paul Casey, and somehow, I made the connection between his name and the title of that story I had read fourteen years before. I carried that story in my heart.

It was the month my first story had been published after a two-year wait. I had been writing for twenty years, since I was seventeen, and I knew it would be my first published story. I got twenty dollars for it—which I offered to share on drinks for the table on the night I met Andre. Of course, I was carrying it around with me the night I met Andre Dubus. After two decades of not getting published, I was *desperately* proud of it. Andre asked what the magazine was, "Looks like a literary journal," and I had an opportunity, between peppered Stolis, to tell him. He offered to read it the next day and to meet me here in the evening for a critique.

That night we wound up in Charlie-o's, which stayed open late, eating pickled eggs and drinking beer served by the wife of the president of the Hell's Angels who was a barmaid there, and I bought a Charlie-o's T-shirt for Gladys Swan, my mentor in the program, who just had a contract for her novel *Carnival for the Gods* from Vintage. At closing time, we huddled around Andre under a light pole, singing a June Christy song from the '50s, "Something Cool," imagining Pete Rugolo, who had composed and arranged it.

Next night, Andre was in the bar already when I got to Julio's, a vodka and my copy of *Confrontation* before him. He told me he wanted to publish the story in an anthology of short fiction he was editing. Stories would be included by Gina Berriault ("Stone Boy"), Mark Costello ("Murphy's Xmas"), Susan Dodd ("Public Appearances"), Leonard Gardner (author of *Fat City*), Thomas Williams, Tobias Wolff, and Andre's own "If They Knew Yvonne"—some of my most revered stories and writers. In addition, he gave me the names of his agent and his editor at Godine and introductions. "No guarantees," he said. "But they'll give you a fair read."

They did, and the agent took me on; it didn't do me any good other than that this writer whose story I so admired had enough of a regard for my had administered e a hefty shot of salt water to my blood, as the Danes say.

The anthology was published in 1988—*Into the Silence: American Stories*—by a new imprint that went out of business in a year. Nonetheless, I had been included in a volume edited by Andre Dubus between the sheets with some of the stories by the writers who meant something to me. This was before he'd had his "Genius Award" of half a million dollars from the MacArthur Foundation.

To celebrate my meeting this author, I proposed to undertake an interview with Andre. My appetite for what occurred in a writer's mind was ravenous after I'd read all his books; I asked him 128 questions, which represented a long tutorial with one of my significant influences. He answered my many questions in his own voice, on five cassettes over the next couple of months. The ninety-page interview was published in *Revue Delta* in a special issue devoted to Andre Dubus, and the general editor of the Twayne series of books about short-story writers invited me to do a whole volume on Andre, and it became my first published book—*Andre Dubus: A Study of the Short Fiction*.

Many times, over that and the two summers after, Andre invited me to the house he rented off-campus with his wife, who was a student in the MFA. program for salami sandwiches with raw rings of onion on rye—he had some garlic wild-boar salami—and Dos Equis Mexican lager. He also invited me to go to Mass at St. Augustine's Roman Catholic Church in Montpelier with him and Susan Dodd, a teacher in the program. Susan had recently won the Iowa Award and a contract with Morrow—she gave me a sterling-silver letter-opener which she had in her possession to see if some of her luck would rub off on me. Sundays, Andre and Susan used to go to Mass together, but when I quoted Joyce to Andre—"I will not serve that in which I no longer believe, whether it call myself my home, my fatherland, or my church"—he apparently concluded that I was hopelessly lost to apostasy. Or maybe he considered me in the temporary Augustinian cauldron of temptations. However, he continued to invite me for salami sandwiches and Dos Equis.

After I had hung up the phone, I sat at my writing desk, viewing the fading winter light on the street lake outside my window. It was just five; the shops closed at half-past. I thought about that Kirk CD. I thought about the fact that I had the privilege just a few months before to publish a fiction anthology as a special issue of *The Literary Review*, "Stories and Sources," for which Andre had given me permission to include his story that had so captured me almost thirty years before, "If They Knew Yvonne." He had provided an essay, too, explaining the background upon which he had written it—despite the fact that I had no budget to pay him for the story or the essay other than in copies.

Money had not been his first concern as a writer. This was the man who once had a three-story contract with *Penthouse* for several thousand dollars which he cancelled when they made unauthorized changes in the first of the three. He also withdrew a story from *The New Yorker* ("The Winter Father") when the then editors wanted him to drop the word "fuck" from a sentence that he judged required it; forfeiting the $3,000, he sold it to *The Sewanee Review* for some hundred dollars, and the story was selected by Hortense Calisher for *Best American Short Stories* that year.

"If They Knew Yvonne," he told in the essay in *The Literary Review*'s "Stories and Sources," was inspired by a priest to whom he had once confessed the sins of a dozen years by opening his heart and explaining what he believed sinful and what *not*. The priest exacted a penance which was to chant three times the word *hallelujah*!

I hurried down to my bicycle and rode through the darkening evening to the Østerbro record shop and bought the Roland Kirk CD. Home again, I surveyed the play list:

1. My Little Suede Shoes (Parker)
2. Groovin' High (Gillespie) 6:34
3. Petit Fleur (Becket)
4. When the Saints Go Marchin' In (trad., arranged by Kirk) 8:45
5. Roller Coaster (Kirk)
6. Sweet Fire (Kirk) 2:50
7. Love for Sale (Porter)

8. Bags' Groove (Milt Jackson)

9. My Cherie Amour (Wonder) 13:48

10. Three for the Festival (Kirk) 7:57

11. Boogie Man Song (Kirk) 5:22

It was recorded live in 1970 but didn't say where it was cut. My guess was that it was in the Netherlands or the Dutch part of Belgium. The jacket revealed to me that on the CD Kirk played tenor sax, strick, manzello, siren, transverse flute, nose flute, whistle, and did vocals. The other personnel were Dick Griffen (trombone), Ron Burton (piano), Vernon Martin (bass), Harold White (drums), Joe Texidor (percussion).

I didn't know what a strick, manzello, or nose flute were. With a little research, I learned what Kirk called a "strick" was a Buescher straight—a straight alto sax lacking the instrument's upturned bell; and a manzello was a modified saxello *with* a larger, custom-made, upturned bell; and a nose flute was simply a flute you played with your nose, a South Pacific or African instrument. Kirk could play several instruments simultaneously; using circular breathing, he played the transverse flute at the same time as a nose flute, for example.

With a little more research in my *Jazz: The Rough Guide*, I discovered that his dreams were important to him. He dreamed as a child of transposing two letters in his first name, Ronald, to make Roland, and in 1970, as a result of a dream, he added Rahsaan to his name. This is perhaps why Ron Burton, who plays piano on *Sweet Fire*, wrote a song titled "A Dream for Rahsaan" in 1985, eight years after Kirk was dead.

I put the CD on my stereo and broke out the Stolichnaya vodka and a bucket of ice. While the CD played, for sixty-three minutes and forty-four seconds, amazement captured me. Kirk blew as fast as Bird, and the vocals were so mysterious and evocative on "Sweet Fire" that they made the hair on back of my neck lift.

I lit a cigar and I cracked Andre's last story collection, *Dancing After Hours*—a gift from my friend, Mike Lee of Cape Cod who wrote in it, "What better gift for an exceptional friend than an exceptional book"— opened it to the title story, to the section that had made me think of Kirk in the first place.

The story has many characters, but through the viewpoint of a barmaid called Emily Moore. A crippled man is rolled into a bar in his wheelchair, a black man pushing a white man. Emily believes her face is homely, not pretty, and is listening to a jazz cassette out of the wall speakers—Bill Evans, Chet Baker, John Coltrane. At one point, Roland Kirk is playing tenor sax, and she remembers when she saw him in a club, twenty years before:

The blind black man wore sunglasses and sometimes he played two saxophones at once, improvising, playing fast as I heard him on the CD. He smiled and talked to the crowd, said that it was nice coming here blind. "Not seeing who's fat or skinny. Ugly. Or pretty. You know?" He was dead now, but here was his music, coming through speakers. Then he stepped into the audience, led by his percussionist still beating his tambourine. Kirk followed the sound, playing his horn, walking among the spectators, standing now, moving back their tables and chairs, and he touched some people and hugged others. He embraced Emily, once, very tight, almost toppling her, but she could smell his sweat and feel the sound of the sax, in her body.

Then he was gone, back on the bandstand, led by the percussionist, and she experienced an epiphany, listening to Kirk, that it would come like that, "*something ineffable that comes from outside, something that changes the way we see what we see; something that allows us to see what we don't.*"

I never saw Andre in his wheelchair, saw him only as a whole man, vital, an ex-Marine captain, who had resigned his commission at twenty-eight when he published his first story in *The Sewanee Review* to go to the Iowa Writers Workshop, a runner, a jazz lover, and he lived only a dozen years beyond the car hitting him, helping another person who had been in an accident. He threw her clear when another vehicle came around the curve, taking the full brunt of the speeding car and losing his one leg and the use of the other. He called himself a cripple then and continued to write. He wrote perhaps his best story in the wheelchair, "Dancing After Hours," his last story.

I read the part in the story where Kirk blew his tenor. I smoked the cigar. I listened to Kirk's tenor blowing "Groovin' High." I peppered my vodka and lifted my glass to two men—two artists, an author and a musician.

Sexy Motherfucker Redux

MY DAUGHTER GRADUATED FROM HIGH SCHOOL in 1999 when she

was eighteen with the highest average in her class at Gammel Hellerup Gymnasium, the high school her mother had gone to. Primary school in Denmark runs until fifteen years of age with ninth grade, and the gymnasium runs three years until you are eighteen or nineteen. My son had graduated a year before with the second highest average in his class from Øregaards Gymnasium, a school where everyone was rich—I think that was where he got his left of socialist ideas from.

When the students graduate from gymnasium, there is a tradition in which they wear white caps with glossy beaks and rent a horse-wagon or an open-backed truck and go around to each home of the students in the class, by turn, and have a drink or two and a bite of something.

Vibeke had prepared the three-meter folding table beneath the magnolia tree in the center of the front garden of the Hellerup house, bounded on the street side with tall liguster hedges. On the table she had many bowls of strawberries and Thai prawn tails with every kind of sauce, and I had bought ten bottles of bubbly cremant for the students in my daughter's class.

The day was sun-dappled on the neat, close lawn—it could have been a golf course, so thick and close it was. The truck arrived, and the twenty some-odd, white-capped students spilled out of the back and straggled into the front garden. I greeted them with a bubbly plastic wine glass of cremant, and Vibeke received them at the long table beneath the blooming magnolia.

My son had celebrated his twentieth birthday in Hanoi in a jazz club, drinking champagne and treating his backpacker friends to a meal. It cost all of $50 for everybody, drinks included. While in 1964, when I was twenty, people were wearing "Bomb Hanoi" buttons, thirty-five years later, my son had celebrated his twentieth in Hanoi getting bombed in a jazz club. Some things got better. He had come back from his eight-month backpacking trip through southeast Asia, looking clean-favored and imperially slim in his new, tailor-made silk suit which he'd had made from a Thai tailor. He'd just bought a small apartment on the fashionable north-side with a down payment of the savings I'd salted away for him from the day he was born. With her account, my daughter had bought a horse which she kept in the stables just north of Hellerup.

It was a fair, blissful day. I looked at my son and his friend, Christian, from first grade, in their silk suits, happy, and my daughter beaming beneath her white cap, surrounded by classmates and drank a glass of cremant in the sunlight.

After that day, Vibeke put the house on the market—for 1.7 million kroner, about double what we'd paid for it. She rented an apartment in the north-west quarter of Copenhagen, where rents were cheap, determined to wait out the inflated prices of condos and houses in Copenhagen. Meanwhile, she had a five-room apartment. The inflation never abated. The price of apartments and houses soared, and Copenhagen became an expensive city—like London, Paris, Dublin and lastly, a dozen years later, Berlin. The last I heard, the house in Hellerup was sold for a million—not kroner—but dollars.

Her rental had a room for my daughter. My daughter called me up one day shortly after they had moved into Vibeke's apartment. She said that her mother was napping in the afternoon, repeatedly complaining that our daughter was making noise.

"You know how she is."

I knew how Vibeke was. Immediately, I asked, "Do you want to move in here?"

"Maybe. For a few months."

I gave her the bedroom, slept on the spare couch—a captain's bed which my father-in-law had had made for Vibeke. I had slept on worse beds. Besides, I had all the run of the living room with five of the six windows looking out over the lake.

What followed was a year of our living together. I made dinner for her—porkchops, lambchops, sirloin steak, hamburgers, krebinetter, with a variety of oven-ready potatoes and of vegetables (peas, peas and carrots, broccoli, cauliflower)—anything that could be fried or boiled—and a salad of lettuce and tomato and vinegar-and-oil-mustard-black-pepper dressing. For dessert, we had ice cream or ready-made portions in plastic cups of chocolate mousse, tiramisu, or Irma supermarket's frozen pie—blueberry, apple, pear.

Once a week, she cooked an Italian meal. She made excellent chopmeat gravy with onions, celery, and tomatoes on shells or spaghetti or penne. I had to admit that she was a better cook than me—I could only fry or boil things—and the Italian meal, with a Valpolicella, was a respite from my frying.

After four months in a South Carolina college, where I arranged that, entrusting my daughter to my friends, the poet Rick Mulkey and fiction writer Susan Tekulve—she studied poetry with Julie Faye and two months with my beloved sister, Jenny, in New York, she worked in an alternative pharmacy while she went to university. First, for Tibetan (her mother had taken up Buddhism), then for psychology, then for philosophy, then a course of study for brain-damaged adults. She stuck with that.

She asked me for permission to get a piercing. I refused. "No one will have piercings when they're living with me." I heard my father talking: No one will drive on a vehicle with two wheels and a motor when they're living under my roof. I softened my tone: "Do you want your ears pierced? That's okay."

One day she came home with something shiny on her tongue, a stainless-steel ball. I asked her what that was and then it occurred to me what it was: She had gotten her tongue pierced.

I opened my mouth and heard my own, strangled words, "Are you out of your fucking mind?" I wanted to know who had done the piercing and telephoned him and demanded in English how he could pierce the tongue of a girl who was under twenty-one.

Calmly, he said that a young person had the right to a piercing or a tattoo from when she was fifteen.

"We'll see about that!" I barked and called the police, and the woman who answered the phone told me, sympathetically, that was so. "*Min sympati.*"

Then she began to bring a boy over—a giant with a gentle manner. They would go into her bedroom and shut the door and smoke hashish, play Prince's "Sexy Motherfucker." I had got used to, even liked the music—it was jazz, despite the lyrics, which were all right for me, but not for my daughter—didn't object to the hash, I didn't even object any longer to the pierced tongue. It didn't make sense, even to me, but what I objected to was the closed door. I thought she was out of control.

That summer I had an invitation to a castle in the Netherlands—a ten-day writing seminar. I invited my daughter with me. "You can ride horses all day when I have the writers workshop."

I planned to build up her confidence in me, then I would ask her not to shut the door when her boyfriend was in her bedroom. I realized, in fact, that *I* was out of control when a woman colleague asked me if my daughter would present a demonstration of the pierced tongue to the assembled students, her kissing a boy "of her choice." Automatically, immediately, I grew protective of my daughter and her tongue piercing. I told the colleague that I thought that would be an invasion of privacy, and the subject was dropped.

Slowly, I began to realize that my daughter was old enough to decide what she did. She told me she was moving in with her boyfriend. As a last act of farewell, she said, "Daddo?"—she called me Daddo—and ran her tongue out of her mouth.

"What?" I asked.

She ran her tongue out of her mouth again and said, "No piercing!"

I had been completely inured to it.

She completed her bachelor's degree in caring for brain-damaged adults and invited me to a play that was to be her commencement exercise—*Mama Mia*. With a cast of brain-damaged adults, including people with Down's Syndrome. When I saw the pride they took in that, under my daughter's tutelage, I felt the water in my eyes.

She had found meaningful work.

My son was working as a bartender—I considered it his mode of going in the Army—but soon he would go back to university and complete his master's in the Cold War, as enacted in Latin America and Africa. (I didn't even know that the Cold War had reached Latin America and Africa, but it did with Cuba and Angola.)

In 2008, my daughter called me up and said, "I'm pregnant."

"That's a good thing?" I was confused and asked it mildly, and she answered, "Yes!" She was on the outs with the gentle giant; some time before, she had called me up to borrow money to rent an apartment—*alone.* After her one-year hiatus with me, she had moved in with her boyfriend, and they had suffered some kind of break-up.

Only one way to ask the question, directly. "Who's the father?"

"My boyfriend, of course!" The gentle giant!

I rented the grand hall at my former office. Even though I had retired a year before, in 2004, I still had good relations with the company, though I didn't have good relations with Vibeke. She didn't come to her daughter's wedding, because I would be there, making a speech, but my ex-in-laws did. Vibeke had decided she didn't want to see me when she learned I was dating other women.

I Wished on the Moon

MY FATHER-IN-LAW ONCE ASKED ME, "Don't you like a woman who's soft as butter?" I don't remember the context or whether it was before or after my divorce from his daughter, but I remember it. From vague hostility to affection to naked hostility when first I wasn't doing well; then, when I was doing well, he recognized a few of my good qualities, and I recognized a few of his. Slowly, he became like a father to me. Maybe because of his generosity, maybe because I was doing well in business as well as writing, maybe because I had become like a son to him.

His name was Ib, and we became fonder of one another before and after the divorce. He was twenty years older than me. My father died suddenly in the late summer of of 1964, fifty-eight years old, when I was twenty, and I always regretted that we didn't have a relationship into my adult years. I was definitely *not* adult at twenty—or even at thirty—or maybe *never*. Just living the years into adulthood, not becoming what I thought of as adult. Ib was nothing like my father, who read poetry and even wrote poetry sometimes at night when he came home from the bank—when he wasn't drinking, even published a couple of poems, one in *The New York Times*, a sonnet, even though he had said, "I used to fold the *NY Daily News* into the *NY Times*; now I fold the *Times* into the *News*," and supported Senator Joseph McCarthy. Sometimes, I thought of my father in the current context, that he would have been a dabbler in songs—like the rock songs that were prevalent in my twenties. He was raised in the age of poetry when published poets were like rock stars akin to The Beatles, The Counting Crows, The Doors, or Bob Dylan. Take Robert W. Service, for example.—of whom Paul McCartney wrote a parody of, "Rocky Raccoon." But sometimes I thought, despite being a bank vice president, he was a poet at heart, a frustrated poet.

Ib was nothing like my father. Ib once said, "If you're going to be bored, it might as well be in comfortable surroundings." Ib was generous, and his generosity encouraged me to be generous. He was generous in the parties he hosted and with his gifts. He always gave us half a dozen bottles of vintage wine for Christmas, saying to me, "That can keep for years." I think he wanted me to start a wine cellar, but by mid-January, the wine was gone. As a young guy, I wasn't earning much for some years, and when Vibeke and I were going on our trip to the USA in 1978, before we would have kids, he gave me his surplus dollars from their trip to America two years before—$500. A dollar was a dollar then, before this age of billionaires. He put them in my hand without show.

And when I came back from a business trip in Dublin on which I had been invited to a cruise on Dublin Bay in a seven-meter sailboat and came home raving about it, he actually purchased, within the month, a twelve-meter cruising yacht and invited me out to sail. The yacht was a beautiful thing, with a wood-panel interior, a galley, a head, and two berths and a single foresail and mainsail with twin engines.

As a captain, unfortunately, Ib was a tyrant, kept ordering me to do something I didn't know how to and got short and sarcastic with me at my ignorance. He made me want to get off the yacht within half an hour. When we cruised back to the dock and tried to nose into his berthing slot, while he cut the engines, there were yachts berthed in the slots at either side of us; he ordered me to "fend off" when he cut the engines. I figured out what he wanted me to do—to give a shove with the bottom of my shoe to the boats on either side of our berthing place. I fended off the one, but I was not quick enough on my feet to fend off the other. Unfortunately, it was constructed of fiberglass and there was a crackled dent the size of a large grapefruit well above the waterline, over the hull.

I said to Ib that I was responsible for that and would like to pay for it.

He said, "Let's get out of here."

We didn't speak all the way back in his Amazon Volvo. Thus ended my yachting career. Though I still admired Ib, I had to keep him at arm's length.

Ib asked me once if I didn't like a woman soft as butter. I interpreted that as my wife, his daughter, was hard as steel—or maybe hard as fiberglass. Vibeke used to say to me, "You're not married to a goose!" Which, in Danish, meant a young pretty bird of a woman who was, well, soft as butter—and who talked a lot, but was dumb.

I used to wonder, though not aloud, when Vibeke was bickering, how it would be to have a goose for a girlfriend. The woman I took up with after my divorce was soft as butter and she was pretty and sexy and hot—though not dumb as a goose. She was malleable, flexible, though not in bed, and loved me (at first). With Dria, I was determined not to be owned.

In October 1998, though I'd been going out off and on with Dria—mostly on—I took a business trip to Ottawa, which is in Ontario, about twenty miles northeast of Toronto, which is also in Ontario, and about a hundred miles southwest of Montreal, Quebec. On the last day of my trip to Ottawa, my plane didn't take off to Copenhagen until four p.m., and I opted to spend the morning in my hotel room over breakfast and *The Sunday Toronto Star*, which was delivered with my Sunday breakfast: two poached eggs and thick Canadian bacon, a grapefruit, toast (halved, in a toast caddy), and a pot of coffee. I sat by the window. True to myself, I turned back to the classifieds and scanned the ads and saw:

The rub of love:

"If I were tickled by the rub of love...."

Vancouver woman, professional, late forties, seeking?

Francesca da Rimini

Immediately, I recognized title and first line of the Dylan Thomas poem and was charmed by the ad. Vancouver is in British Columbia, on the western border of Canada, about a hundred miles north of Seattle, Washington, where I had an open invitation to give a return reading at Elliott Bay Bookstore, a giant Seattle emporium, which didn't pay, but always advertised for an audience. The last time, two years ago, there were fifty people attending the event for my *Drive, Dive, Dance & Fight* reading, published by BkMk press in Kansas City, Mo., a small press that was fitting for a small press writer. I had recently published a couple of stories in *Glimmer Train* in Portland, Oregon—some two hundred miles south of Seattle—and had a standing invitation to sit for an interview by one of the *GT*'s editors. A reading could be piggy-backed on that at Powell's, a giant independent bookshop in Portland, and Eastern Oregon University in La Grande, about 350 miles east, then southeast of Portland along the Columbia River, the home of another of my small presses, Wordcraft, run by David Memmott; he had published two of my books, a novel and a story collection. David had me also working on an essay collection about the writing of fiction. The subject of that book was my Ph.D. thesis, *The Uses of Verisimilitude*. Instead of a raise in salary, I had negotiated, when I got my doctorate in 1988, two paid weeks per year to do my "research" and a ten-thousand kroner budget to travel on. And

Portland was only six-hundred-plus miles north of San Francisco with its City Lights Bookshop.

So, this personal advertisement would be, if it all worked out, an advertisement for myself. You had to be self-serving; no one else would serve you. And as the Danes say, If it works, it works, and if it doesn't work, maybe it will work anyway. "It" was all because of a singles ad in a Toronto newspaper by a woman who was tickled by the rub of love and was seeking whatever.

I took a few sheets of Marriott Hotel stationery and drafted a response. It had to be concise, filling only part of one page, since Francesca's was so concise, and it had to involve both Dylan Thomas and Dante—because Francesca da Rimini was in hell, suffering for her adultery with Paolo in the cyclone of souls in *The Inferno* by Dante Alighieri.

Thus, I arrived at:

Dearest Vancouver Woman,
"If I were tickled by the urchin hungers
Rehearsing heat upon a raw-edged nerve,
I would not fear the devil in the loin
Nor the outspoken grave."
In a hotel in Ottawa this Sunday before flying back
to Copenhagen from a conference, I chanced to read in
The Toronto Star, your words, Francesca. When reading of
Dylan Thomas' *smile long-awaited for*, your call kissed
me upon the mouth, and I was tickled by the rub of love.
Not believing in the cyclone of souls, I grew faint nonetheless.
The two-year divorced,
Paolo.

If I reckoned right, the Vancouver woman was just looking for a tryst with poetic lyricism—thus, I added *the smile long-awaited for*, being a hint of *the little crooked smile*.

I added my email and addressed it on the hotel envelope to the post box number and bought a couple of stamps while checking out, mailed it in the postbox at the side of the desk clerk and promptly forgot about it amidst the stewardesses' rattling trolleys on the flight home and the play list of the jazz track of the jumbo jet.

When I arrived in Copenhagen, I was focused on getting back to my apartment on the street lakes. It was sunny October, which was unheard of in Denmark, a second Indian summer. I biked around Copenhagen, taking photos. Composing the pictures in balance, I had read somewhere, helped you to *see* the subjects. I took photographs of disappearing aspects of the Danish capital: Some shops—cheese shops, *mejeris* (dairy shops), facades of buildings that had cement medallions of various fish and birds over their doors, old brown bars in Frederiksberg and "the mine field" between Nikolaj Street and the King's New Square, about a kilometer comprising some twelve bars, starting from Nick's Café and bounded by Hviids Vinstue. And fields of abandoned city trains on abandoned city tracks, midway to the airport. I wanted to take pictures of the interior of the trains—all with broken windows and punched-out doors and covered with ornate graffiti—but I discovered that homeless people lived in them, and I got out fast. It wouldn't do to invade the living rooms and bedrooms of the homeless.

All around I biked with my Walkman, hearing jazz cassettes while venturing into unknown (to me) parts of the city. For more than twenty years, when I was married, Vibeke's and mine and the kids' years were structured around family birthdays and holidays. In February and March, we invited Vibeke's parents and brother and sister-in-law and their kids for my daughter's and my birthdays. On different days in April we got invited for my father-in-law's and sister-in-law's birthdays. For Easter, we had a standing invitation to my parents'-in-law summer house with the whole extended family—my aunts- and uncles- and nieces- and nephews-in-law. In June, we invited and got invited for my son's and nephew-in-law's birthdays. In July, we were invited for my brother-in-law's and my other nephew-in-law's birthdays. In October, we got invited for my mother-in-law's birthday. In November, we invited the family for Vibeke's birthday. In December, we got invited to my parents-in-law for the first Sunday in Advent and Christmas Eve. On Christmas Day, we were invited to my brother- and sister-in-law's for lunch, and on Second Xmas Day, we invited the family for a roasted turkey. On New Year's Eve, we were invited to our neighbors', who also had two kids. On Halloween, we held a costume party for the family and the parents and three kids on our street in Hellerup.

We nearly exclusively drove from Hellerup to Slagslunde and to Brønshøj to my in-laws' or stayed in Hellerup or took a cab to my office for the Xmas Gala. I hungered to see other parts of Copenhagen and, frankly, be free of the calendar which was agendaed for birthdays and holidays.

Then, for Christmas, Dria gave me a guide to *The Humble Establishments* by Allan Mylius Thomsen to a hundred of the traditional restaurants and pubs of Copenhagen and Frederiksberg. We decided first to sample them, then to visit all of them—and then more of the 1,525 værtshuse (serving houses) in Copenhagen and environs.

It gave Dria and me a purpose other than birthdays and holidays on which to suspend the skeleton of our calendar, and it soon turned into a novel that I didn't want to complete. I just wanted it to go on. We were having too much fun. Dria developed into the Research Associate and Kerrigan, the main character of the novel, with whom he was resisting falling in love. The novel became a metaphor for my existence. *To love: that is the ultimate development of a man*, proctored by some psychiatrist or other. I wished I could remember which psychiatrist.

I kept assuring Dria that "the Research Associate"—or "the Associate"—was *not* her, was a fictional character that happened to share some characteristics with her. It gave me a character on whom to hang the features of the Associate. The research dragged—glided—on boozily for two years.

There was jazz, too: sometimes bebop at the Christiania Jazz Club (just around the corner from Pusher Street) or the Jazz Cup or Det Hvide Lam, sometimes R&B at Long John's or Mojo's, sometimes Big Band at the Copenhagen Jazz House, and sometimes standards with Asger Rosenberg at Krut's Karport or Cykelstalden. Montmartre was closed at its second location and was yet to open at its third location. We sometimes heard Asger and Co. at Krut's Karport while the snow fell lightly outside the windows.

Just after New Year's I was embarking on a reading tour and to meet, at long last, Francesca. Meanwhile I had been carrying on an email correspondence with Francesca da Rimini. I had received a response from her two weeks later, and she proved to be not only a poetry and a jazz aficionado, divorced with a fourteen-year-old son. As for being a professional, she was a psychiatrist.

By email, she turned me on to *The Rough Guide to Jazz*, written by three jazz musicians and broadcasters—Ian Carr (the definitive biographer of Miles Davis), Digby Fairweather, and Brian Priestley. I don't know how I ever lived without it!

Also, she turned me on to Billie Holiday's *The Silver Collection* from 1956-57. The record was Lady Day in the perfect company of Ben Webster (tenor), Harry "Sweets" Edison (trumpet), Jimmy Rowles (piano), Barney Kessel (guitar), et alia. And Frank O'Hara's 1959 *Lunch Poem* "The Day Lady Died"—"in the 5 SPOT/while she whispered a song along the keyboard/to Mal Waldron and everyone and I stopped breathing."

Lady Day died when I was fifteen and Ben Webster died when I was twenty-nine and Frank O'Hara died in an auto accident at the age of forty when I was twenty-two in 1966. I knew about Ben Webster, but knew only vaguely about Billie Holiday and only more vaguely about Frank O'Hara. To learn of the existence of these people by a 48-year-old psychiatrist from Canada in my mid-fifties—they had died in my native New York City (Queens)—intrigued me. Would I ever have learned about them or about the fact that Ben Webster was Lady Day's favorite accompanying tenor saxophonist, had I not chanced to come upon that personal ad in *The Toronto Star* when I was in Ottawa in 1998, and Francesca had answered me, and we proceeded to become email-pals? I'm no stickler for jazz, my tastes are eclectic, and I happened not to consider Lady Day until Francesca told me and turned me on to *The Silver Collection*, on which is one of my favorite songs and that "The Day Lady Died" is one of my favorite poems.

Now I loved the voice, the tenor, the lyric, the poem by five dead people, but what bothered me was that the day Lady died, two days after Bastille Day in 1959, forty years before, I would know about it. Even if I would be living in the city she died in the city O'Hara describes in his poem, where he buys *The New York Post* and sees her fateful picture and thinks of Lady Day in the 5 SPOT, whispering a song along the keyboard to Mal Waldron. I didn't know who Mal Waldron was until I looked him up in *The Rough Guide* and learned he had played with Coltrane and Mingus and Eric Dolphy.

I loved the lyric, too, "I Wished on the Moon," written by Dorothy Parker whose death I vaguely recalled in 1967 when I was twenty-three and lived on East 3rd Street between Avenues A and B in alphabet city.

But now I knew, when I was living in Copenhagen, she was a *New Yorker* writer and a poet and a blacklisted screenwriter—Senator Joseph McCarthy did so much harm with his false accusations.

Billie's voice so sweet and wistful, lilting and strong, when she says, "April day...that will not...dance away," the heart is filled with the accepted sadness of its retreating dance, and Webster's tenor softens it all with a reedy, mellow, cool nod. I knew now that the songs on this album were recorded in August 1956 and I was twelve, and Dorothy Parker wrote that line.

I never made a systematic study of jazz, didn't have a systematic knowledge. I trust that there are great musicians being recorded, and I'll happen to hear the great performers when I'm ready. If I'm still alive. I don't need to take a scholar's attitude to the whole of jazz. I usually picked one cut and immersed myself in it, listened to it repeatedly over a long period, and the track cuts itself into my brain, and my memory can reproduce whole sections of it.

That a chance occurrence on a business conference could impart this pleasure and information, this knowledge of something that I'd never known, through a woman that happened to start a personal ad with a Dylan Thomas poem that I knew and loved, gradually over the year made me eager to meet Francesca. Dria had requested me not to tell her about my involvements with other women.

Not that I had much involvement. I was coming out of a twenty-two year captivity, and I was wary of stepping in a snare, made it clear that I was getting over my marriage. When Dria, with whom I took vacations and spent most weekends, said, "I am not just for fun"—she repeated this periodically—I answered, "Well, aren't we having fun? I'm not ready for an exclusive relationship."

I hated using words like that, "relationship" and "love." It made me think of a story by somebody or other—Jonathan Baumbach—that was in The O. Henry Prize collection: "I'm Having Trouble with My Relationship" or maybe it was titled, "Passion"? I would not call Dria for a couple of weeks, go out by myself or with another woman. I rarely slept with anyone, kissed and cuddled and spooned and petted. There was a young American professor with long wavy light brown hair with whom I used to go to the movies. She had a warm sense of humor, used to tell me I was "a bad boy," because I drank and smoked. She sent me a letter once that said my novels and stories were "seductive," and she realized that there was an age gap between us—she was about twenty years younger—but she was interested in "more" from me. I tried sleeping with her, but it didn't work out, and I wound up not having anyone to go to the movies with.

There was a married woman with whom I used to teach at a ten-day summer seminar which shifted venue—some years it was in Amsterdam, some summers in Paris or Geneva or London. We carried on some nights—kissing, cuddling, spooning, petting—but it was usually when we were drinking, and half the times I couldn't get it up. And there were others—a divorced Finn who was little and blond, with blue, icy eyes, a very tall Dane whose long, shapely legs turned me on. But usually, Dria or I would call one another after a few weeks and say that she or I missed one another, and we fell into the "relationship" once again, though we would veer away from the word "love," settling on "passion." It seemed we were destined to be together.

But Francesca.

I listened to "I Wished on the Moon" by Lady Day and Webster, looked out at the lake, surrounded by chestnut trees—in spring, summer, and early fall, blooming with buds, and then small candle-like flowers, and then with horse chestnuts. I gathered them because as a boy I used to carve rings and make animals of them with toothpicks. Then, in late fall and winter, the trees would have black bones and the lake would freeze over, and when the ice thickened, there would be iceskaters and young Danish couples walking baby carriages on the solid surface of the water.

I made a pilgrimage to Ben Webster's apartment, on Nørresøgade, a half mile from my apartment on Østersøgade. On the second floor in the building, facing the lake, where Webster lived from 1965 until his death in Amsterdam in 1973, sixty-four years old. There he would sit, as Bent Kauling tells it, on the balcony with the superintendent of the building, drinking beer in green bottles and staring out the window over the lake. The superintendent, Olsen, could not speak English—he called Webster, "Vesper"—and Webster spoke virtually no Danish so they sat in silence, saying no more than *Skål!*, raising their bottles, enjoying what Webster called, "The world's luckiest conversation." Two silent men drinking their bottles of beer, watching the lake.

A friend of mine, Dale Smith, the African-American bluesman from St. Louis who had lived in Copenhagen for decades, had a couple of stories about Webster. He tells of Webster getting fed up one night in the Club Montmartre with the tootling of some very post-bop avant-garde saxophonists, and barking, "Practice at home, motherfuckers!"

Dale also tells of Webster playing a gig somewhere, getting paid, and Dale—very tall and muscular—carrying him home and putting him to bed, only to have Webster phone him next early afternoon and demand to know how he'd got home last night.

"I carried you."

"Where's my wallet," he grumbled, "Where's my money?"

"I put it under your pillow."

There was a silence while Webster checked, and he murmured, "Oh. Okay. Thanks."

I listened to *The Silver Collection*, staring out over the water, hearing Billie's exquisite phrasing and "Sweets'" hot trumpet and Ben's reedy tenor, and Kessel's electric guitar, Red Mitchell's thick plucked bass strings or played with a bow, and Stoller who sticked the skins—not only for Lady Day, but Frank Sinatra or Ella Fitz, Art Tatum, Coleman Hawkins, Erroll Garner...

I thought about Francesca, with whom my mails were first occasional, then every week and two or three times a week. I planned a reading tour for mid-January 2000, Seattle-Portland-La Grande-San Francisco-San Diego and home from Los Angeles to Copenhagen. I mentioned in a mail to Francesca in December, I would be in Seattle for three days. Did she want to meet?

She didn't answer for two days. Then I got a mail from her that she hoped I wouldn't be angry, but she had booked a room in the Elliott Hotel, which was near my reading venue. Not only had she booked a room, but she had booked two rooms with an adjoining sitting room to both rooms. If there wasn't chemistry between us, we would have our own bedrooms and could continue our friendship. She added a confession: her real name wasn't Francesca da Rimini, but Louise de France, but I could call her Francesca if it pleased me. She signed, "Love, Louise (a.k.a., Francesca)." Included was a P.S.: "I specified a smoking room. I know how you like your cigars. In fact, I have a fantasy where I undress and you smoke a cigar, straight-faced, evaluating my naked body."

So, there was the "L-word." We hadn't used it before in closing. However, there was the fantasy, too, and my mention of "chemistry."

Since I was not welcome at Vibeke's parents' for Christmas Eve—I was only welcome for a couple of years until Vibeke learned I was dating other women—I didn't celebrate Christmas Eve. I had the kids over on the 23rd to decorate my dwarf tree, and on the 26th, Second Xmas Day, to celebrate the giving of gifts and to light the tree and dance around it, singing Christmas Carols, which is a Danish tradition (the Danes say that it isn't a real tree until it's been "danced"), and then had them out to the restaurant at Hotel D'Angleterre for a fancy meal. Vibeke had a standing invitation to the restaurant on December 26th, but she didn't answer the invitation. The one time she came, she made a point of announcing beforehand that the kids could order anything they wanted, "Your father's paying." The kids and Vibeke could indeed order anything they wanted, but I would have preferred to announce that invitation. She made it sound like a taunt.

Dria invited me for Xmas Eve for a dinner of duck and roast pork with crackling and all the trimmings, including her three sons and their wives and children, but I didn't want to start another Xmas Eve tradition with another family. Besides, her middle son, Lars, discovered the penis-pussy whip under a pillow on the sofa and asked, "Is there S-M in the house?"

After he was gone, Dria opined, "That was a sweet way Lars said it," but I didn't think it was sweet—rather prying. So I went out to the restaurant at the Copenhagen Plaza Hotel by the Central Station, where they had a Christmas tree hung upside down from the ceiling of the Library Bar—it seemed fitting, a negation of Christmas that was still Chrismas-y. I had coffee and cognac after my fixed menu in the restaurant with three wines. I dressed up in a suit and tie for my Christmas Eve alone, making observations about the other diners in my notebook.

There was a quiet camaraderie in the dining room. One year a Swedish couple recognized me (that's the first time that happened—before or since) and sent a glass of wine over, and we wound up sharing a table in the Library Bar over coffee and an avec. Another year the husband of an Australian couple came to my table and invited me to join them for Xmas Eve dinner. I thanked him, but said no. I was okay alone. One

Xmas, a New Zealand woman, there with her daughters, asked me to dance around the Xmas tree with her family. And one year, I thought I was getting lucky; a young, beautiful, tall, dark-haired woman with a ruby dangling in her cavalier passage was shown to the table beside mine. I asked if she was alone, and she said she was waiting for someone. Yes, of course, I thought. Then a shorter woman sat down, not more than twenty years older than her tablemate—which made the second woman about twenty years younger than me. They began to eat and converse in a language that was not familiar to me.

Tentatively, I asked them what language they were speaking: Slovakian.

"Actually, we were talking about you," the older woman said. "How noble it is of you to get dressed up in your suit and tie to eat alone even if you don't have a woman."

We had a pleasant Xmas Eve and ended in the Library Bar over coffee and parted at the train, after exchanging email addresses. I wrote a story about it for *Broad Street,* "Prix Fixe—The Table Next to Yours."

The next year I came with a woman, but the Slovakian mother and daughter showed up again, and the daughter intercepted me on the way to the gents, saying a bit accusingly, "My mother was talking about Edward, all the year." I invited them to join us in the bar, but fortunately they refused.

Dria came over to my apartment at midnight on Christmas Eve with a duck leg and a thick slab of roast pork with crackling, and sometimes she stayed for the lighting of the tree, and I put a jazz CD on, and the only lights were the candles, burning on the tree.

I didn't play *The Silver Collection.*

I Can't Give You Anything But Love

BUTTERFLIES WERE IN MY STOMACH when I knocked on the room door of the Elliott in Seattle. Francesca had already arrived. I had decided to call her Francesca, though I had confessed that my name was not Paolo. I thought it condemning that we had the names of the couple that dwelt in the cyclones of passion of Dante's second circle of hell: *Ye who enter here surrender all hope,* inscribed on the gates. I might have found myself on a dark road in the middle of my life—more than the middle, I would have had to live over a hundred years to make this in media res. Not to take the metaphor too literally.

Francesca opened the door. "Edward?"

The chemistry of her voice was right. We had avoided exchanging photographs or describing our looks. Self-descriptions were of necessity deceptive. You either over- or under-described. With a photo, you captured the living body or face in a static moment, flattering or unflattering. We had let it go at height and weight—she seemed the right measure, and I assumed that I was right (I only added a half inch to my height and dropped five pounds from my weight)—and added that we exercised every other day. She admitted that she had read some of my books so she must have seen the jacket photo. I don't photograph well—or maybe I really look like that.

She was more than I bargained for, in a good way—the readiness to rent a hotel room, that she was a doctor, a physician, and eight years younger than I and had friends (she described white-water rafting with a circle of women), and that she liked jazz and poetry. That she had to resort to placing a personal ad, albeit a charming one, made me suspicious that she had an—there is no other way to put it—ugly face or grotesque body. But I had responded to the ad, and I was okay—*wasn't* I? Unless all those bad jacket photos were accurate.

She was attractive, sexy, dressed in a black leather mini-skirt and cream-colored, off-the-shoulder silk blouse with low décolletage. I had told her the word for cleavage in Danish—cavalier passage—mentioning, as an aside, that it turned me on. She had not only dressed in an off-the-shoulder blouse (which I also said turned me on)—with cleavage, she wore open-toed shoes that showed a hint of toe-cleavage. I had mentioned, in passing, that feet turned me on, too.

When we hugged and looked at each other's face and, surreptitiously, at one another's bodies to see, and I had poured a champagne for us, I produced my stiff leather three-cigar humidor from the inner pocket of my hand-woven tweed jacket and pulled out a Cohiba Exquisito which I'd bought in the cigar department of the duty-free in Copenhagen Airport. You could buy Cuban cigars in Denmark. I cut the cap and roasted the end with a long cedar match, rotating it in my hand, blowing gently on the charred end until it glowed and put the cap to my lips and drew. I filled my mouth with rich smoke, let it tease my throat and blew it through pursed lips. Then I looked at her.

She was sitting on the ege of a chair opposite the sofa, looking questioningly at me.

"Well?" I said. "Undress. Slowly."

After we made love, which made us hungry, we ordered room service: white-wine poached salmon and another bottle of champagne and made love again.

The one room was a mess of rumpled sheets, bedspreads and duvets dangling toward and on the floor and the six or so mashed pillows, all stained with champagne and other fluids, and we were head to foot. I was embracing and kissing her feet, and she was fiddling with some other thing. That made me extremely ardent with her toes (which, I had to admit, but not in complaint, were rather stubby), arches and her heels and insteps.

We got an idea to start with the bed in the other room that had not been used except for the room-maid's turn-down. She set up her lap top on the glass-topped desk in the living room and did something with it. She got jazz—Sonny Stitt, doing "I Can't Give You Anything But Love, Baby" with his alto, and we were both naked, and I was so tipsy on champagne that I went down on her where she stood.

We woke in the second bed—late morning. My reading was at four p.m. After room-service breakfast, we took a cab to Elliott Bay Bookshop—only five minutes away, but we didn't know which direction. I read to about thirty people a shortened version of a story called "Bonner's Women," which had been published in *Glimmer Train*. It was about a man visiting his senile mother, the man glimpsing his ex-mistress on the way while he was speaking to his wife on a pay phone, and he was filled with the deceit of his ex-mistress and him, perpetrated on his wife Jenny, who was trusting and trustworthy. Or was she? He suddenly didn't know.

"A full life well-lived," a woman in the first row said authoritatively, followed by a long moment of silence before another woman asked, "Why does he *drink* so much?"

"He doesn't," I said. "He only gets drunk for the length of the story," longing to get back to the hotel room for some more champagne and carnal love. After autographing three or four purchased books and the organizer asking me to sign ten more—signed books cannot be returned!—we walked back to the hotel for a room-service meal and more champagne.

I would be flying out of Seattle for Portland tomorrow and wanted to get as much time with Francesca as I could. But after eating and more champagne and making love yet again, I perforce, despite myself, fell asleep. I had wanted to get as much conversation in with Francesca as I could, but she craved more love-making.

In the wee hours, I woke to find Francesca sitting on a chair, the bedspread wrapped around her. At first, I thought she had a cold, but realized she was weeping. I've never been good with crying. I hadn't cried since I was a child other than wet eyes at a sentimental movie or when my father died or certain times with my kids.

Of course, I went to her. I squatted and reached out, whispering, "Hey? What's the matter?"

She pulled away from me, tugged the bedspread closer around her. She sipped from a flute of champagne. It must have been from the mini-bar because it still had bubbles in it and was chill. *Was she drunk?*

I looked at my watch: 3:29, repeated sleepily, stroking her arm, "What's the matter?"

She asked between sobs, "Don't you know?"

I felt a familiar coldness chilling me from within. It was a reflex, the way crying affected me. I tried to check it by making my whisper softer, traced my palms over her shoulders, along her arms.

"You're so…cold," she muttered and blew her nose in some tissues that she pulled from a box on the table beside her chair, which was where she had the split of champagne.

"Hey," I whispered, "You shouldn't drink so much. Clouds the emotions," I added, attempting lightness in my tone. Was she expecting me to say I loved her? I *didn't* "love" her at that moment. When she was crying and flinging questions and accusations at me.

"What, precisely, is the matter?"

"Don't you understand that I'm crying because our time together is almost over. And who knows when we'll be together again."

"I can arrange for a reading anytime."

She was silent for a moment. "Why does there have to be a reading? Can't you come to just see *me*?"

"I don't have unlimited funds. It has to be a tax write-off."

Which started her crying harder. "You're so…calculating. You didn't even ask about my son!"

"You didn't ask about my children either. Rightly so," I said softly, not accusingly—"This meeting was only for us to get to know each other."

"And for your *reading!*"

What had happened to the woman who quoted Dylan Thomas and Dante, who was a jazz aficionado, who turned me on to aspects of jazz I'd never heard of, who fantasized about my smoking a cigar and looking with evaluation upon her body as she undressed, the woman who would dream up the scheme of our meeting like this, renting two hotel rooms en suite?

We patched it up before we parted—although I said things I didn't want to say, not the L-word, but things I didn't automatically think, like we would write every day to each other and that we knew each other so much better now. She drove me to Seattle-Tacoma International, and we embraced and kissed in her SUV. I taught her something a girl decades before had taught me: to look at one another's face for a full minute, memorizing the features. That way you let a portrait of the features of the face into your consciousness. Then we kissed again, and I memorized her lips and tongue and eyes and cheeks and forehead and nose and ears. I thought of her stubby toes and banned them from my memory, but they were already in there.

I stood on the pavement outside the terminal, and she fluttered her fingers at me from the SUV, and I watched as the vehicle disappeared. There was a CD/cassette shop in the airport, beyond security, and they had an amazing collection of jazz. I had my Discman in my shoulder bag and a CD of *Milestones* with Miles Davis, Julian "Cannonball" Adderley, John Coltrane, Red Garland, Paul Chambers, and "Philly" Joe Jones. I bought two CDs—Cannonball Adderley's *Mercy, Mercy* and *The Best of Horace Silver*.

Relieved a little to be without Francesca—without her crying anyway and her stubby toes—women's feet did, indeed, turn me on, and stubby toes and weeping turned me off. I threw myself into the rest of the tour, listening to "Miles" and Cannonball Adderley and Horace Silver.

Straight, No Chaser

I LISTENED FROM SEATTLE TO PORTLAND to San Francisco to San Diego and via Los Angeles back to Copenhagen on the SAS jumbo jet to *Milestones*: "Miles," "Straight, No Chaser," "Sid's Ahead," and "Two Base Hit." But mostly to Monk's "Straight, No Chaser," and to "Miles." The two numbers were almost sixteen minutes, and I must have heard them forty times. Until it colonized my brain and produced a sound cocoon across the U.S. and Canada and the Arctic and to Greenland and Iceland and Scandinavia to Kastrup.

Back in my apartment, I listened to *Milestones* at my windows over the lakes as far as you could see, to the left and right and about two hundred meters across the water to a tree-line, black now in winter night and a wall of apartment buildings and of lighted windows behind which anything could be happening. Over the roofs, the State Hospital—Riget—loomed in two massive buildings that were connected by a hallway and extended into the sky. It was the tallest building, above the five-floor apartment buildings, but you had a view of the black sky infinitely in the January night. They put lighted Xmas trees on the rooves of either building of Riget, just the outline of trees, defined by lights. Sometimes you could hear a helicopter landing at the heliport on the roof behind the Xmas trees to bring a donor organ to the hospital and then you knew someone was opened on the operating table waiting for a heart or liver or kidney.

It was a majestic view. If I didn't have trouble with my upstairs and downstairs neighbors. They were friends with one another, and the upper ones had three kids who rollerskated on the bare wood floors. The downstairs ones, who had just moved in and who were trying to get me to sell so they could devise a commune of the building.

However, now, it was peaceful, with "Miles." I could look out at the black velvet night, sprinkled with brilliant stars and hear the simplicity of the refrain—dat dat dat dat dat/daaaa—over and over, harmony of horns and underlying the plucking of Chamber's bass, evolving into mad improvisations, sometimes a muted blue mood of Miles' trumpet, getting more complex with Trane's tenor or Cannonball's alto or

Chamber's bass and Philly's drum kit.

I hadn't written to Francesca yet, was still trying to digest her sudden appearance and the love-making and her unexpected weeping in the wee hours—when suddenly I was consumed by a yen to be with Dria. It was a sudden yearning of the type I was prone to. The yearning was irresistible, woven into the music, and I was powerless against it. I had to call her immediately.

It was about six p.m., and I abandoned the view, and the music fell into the background and I telephoned Dria and asked her if she, like me, had a yen to be in Copenhagen Jazz House or one of the humble establishments. If she was, I would call a cab and take it over to her apartment. Meanwhile, she offered to phone around and hear where there was jazz and what genre it was.

She was like that, was prone to yens. Maybe she was prone to my yens, or maybe she matched my yens. Maybe we were wired similarly. "Straight, No Chaser" was playing currently, and I had to get out and be with Dria, drink and hear live jazz. It didn't matter what kind—bebop or modal or Dixieland or standard vocals. It had to be live and sipping a drink and with Dria sitting next to me, her blue eyes, lit like lamps, and her delicate fingers twined in mine, and her lips and face near my mouth. I was a leaf in the wind of my yearning, seeking Dria. I had to be with her. Francesca was far from my mind now.

I dismissed the cab at the door to her building and rang the bell. She buzzed me in. Dria's apartment was on the ground floor, so everyone could look in when the shades were drawn up. In fact, a person could, and did, lean in an open window, and address us when we were sitting, watching TV on a warm night.

However, the apartment was large—unlike mine, which was only a double living room and a little bedroom and kitchen. The front room of her place was stunning, converted from two big rooms, with three-meter ceilings. Always when I hadn't been to her place for weeks, the sight of the front room arrested me in the doorway, and I had to just *look*. It wasn't the furniture, but the pictures—Dria's day job paid the bills, but she was an artist—and the tall triptych windows and expanse of wide-plank floor, scattered with Afghan and Chinese and Tibetan carpets.

Somethin' Else was on, Cannonball and Miles playing "Autumn Leaves." She made a drink for me—a double Stoli on the rocks—and took another red wine for herself, and as we sat on the sofa—her delicate face and desirable body right down to her bare, sculpted, long-toed feet, I realized I was fortunate to have her. She began to rattle off what serving houses were playing jazz: The Copenhagen Jazz House was closed for refurbishment; Det Hvide Lam had "happy jazz"; Krut's Karport had Asger Rosenblum singing and playing bass; Long John's had R&B.

She stopped in mid-sentence and said quietly, "You've been with someone." She was staring at me with her electric blue eyes.

"How did you know?"

"I can just *see* it on you."

"You said you didn't want to hear."

"I'm not just for fun."

Usually that statement was my cue to leave, but there was something else in this: The long-time emails exchanged with Francesca, the burgeoning feeling for her, that she had stubby toes, that she had wept (Dria never cried except over a death or a sentimental film). She had pegged it just right. She had *known* I was with someone. How had she known? Either some feeling she had had, or my aura. I didn't feel guilty, but she knew me in some profound manner. This impressed me, made me want to be with her. Exclusively.

I said, "I only want to be with you."

"How do you know?" she asked. She wasn't accusing or sarcastic. Just a question.

"I didn't know it until now. But all of a sudden, I know it. By what you said to me. You know me, understand me. On a profound level. I *love* you."

She looked at my eyes and my lips and back to my eyes. "Well, *I* love *you*."

We went out to Krut's Karport and heard Asger sing, spanking the bass with a piano and drums behind him. Asger knew the introduction to every song and who had written it and who had made it popular, and he had a deep, crooning voice. We came in on the introduction to a song. Asger was saying that the song was a hit for the Ames Brothers and Louis Armstrong and Ella Fitzgerald from the 1950s and was composed by Bennie Benjamin and George and David Weiss, and he started singing, "Can anyone explain the thrill of a kiss/No! No!" The arrangement was original.

Dria and I looked into one another's eyes, the memory of saying the "L" word fresh in our minds—or at least *my* mind, and we were inspired by the song and our mutual smiles to kiss. I thought it would be a peck, but we fueled each other, so it became a lengthy, wet tongue-kiss. A middle-aged woman seated alone at the table beside ours, muttered, "Get a room."

We waited until the break, which came at the end of the song. Asger said, "Now we're going to take a very short and intense beer pause. I always feel like a new man when I take a beer. Trouble is, that new man wants a beer, too. And on it goes."

We left without having a drink, walked quickly to my place, just a block toward the lakes, through the streets of attached houses, all laid out in rows. Mine was on an end, which had a coveted view of the lake. Still there was something moving inside me. I wanted a change, to do something drastic, and I needed to know if my emotions were not based on my desire for Dria. I wanted not to say something rash because of my desire for her body. No, it was not her body I desired, but her. I had to be certain that I was not confusing lust, hunger, with love. I had to disentwine, if I could, the moment of passion from the more elemental, long-term things.

I looked at Dria in the entryway to the building, and we were drawn together and kissed. I started undressing her on the dark stairway, and we tossed our coats on the floor and headed straight for the bed. I was fifty-five years old and she fifty-nine, but we made love like 20-year-olds—*with* experience.

Afterward we were breathless and held each other close, our hearts going like mad. I put on *Somethin' Else* because Dria was a new-comer to jazz; we both liked "Autumn Leaves."

In a moment, she went into the WC and came out and joined me, still naked with the lights off. There was enough light from the street outside my window; it highlighted her breasts and her bird's nest, silver among the blonde, and her slim thighs and trim belly and bottom. I was getting hard again. We sat on the sofa and looked at the lake and cuddled. She asked if I wanted a drink.

"If you do."

I turned up the heat. She came out with a double Stoli on the rocks for me, a red wine for herself and black olives in a jar.

"I love your apartment," she said.

"I like yours better. I don't like my neighbors."

"I'm surprised. You used to have the kids in for Halloween."

"That was before they got roller skates. And before the upstairs and downstairs were in league to build a commune and to make me want to move."

Cannonball was doing an alto run on "Dancing in the Dark," and Miles picked up where he left off. "Oh, that trumpet! Wanna dance?"

We started doing a lindy hop, but she tried to lead until I held her close and forced her to twirl overhand, then caught her hand at the small of my back and twirled her again.

"You can *dance*!"

"Only the lindy hop. And only with you."

"I hope so—totally nude."

I twirled her again and watched her breasts.

"I'm getting dizzy."

"I like the way your melons quiver. In that light from the streetlamp."

"I used to hate being big-breasted. Until you started calling them my melons," she said, sitting again on the sofa. I cupped her face in my palms and kissed her on the mouth.

She lit a Prince Light with her Bic and inhaled slowly and blew perfect smoke rings. Then she said, "You know you can move in with me? If you want."

I didn't want to accept too fast. "I could double my money on this place. In only three years."

"Don't you want to rent it? In case...."

"It doesn't work out? If it doesn't work out, I'll buy a new place. Besides, it *will* work out. What kind of thing is it to go in thinking it won't work out. I want a change."

"And if you want a change again?"

I looked into her blue-blue eyes, thinking how different it was when I decided to marry Vibeke—a woman colleague, Dominque, had corrected me when I said that once, "Vibeke decided to marry *you*!"

I said, "I won't."

Portions of this novel appeared previously in altered form in:

Absinthe: New European Writing, Agni, The American Poetry Review, Arts & Letters, Best American Magazine Writing, Boston Review, Booktrader Christmas Album / Julehefte, Broad Street, Confrontation, Ducts, Ecotone, Epoch, Esquire Weekly, Frank: A Journal of Contemporary Writing and Art, The Gettysburg Review, Glimmer Train, The Independent, Kenyon Review, The Literary Review, The Literary Traveler (for legal reasons, later called *The Literary Explorer*), *Main Street Rag, McNeese Review, New Letters, The New Yorker, Oh Sandy, Poet Lore, Prism International, The Pushcart Prize XV* and *XLI, Ronde Dance, Serving House Journal, The Southern Review, The South Carolina Review, Vintage 13,* and *The Writers Chronicle of AWP.*

Books by Thomas E. Kennedy

Novels

Crossing Borders (1990)

A Weather of the Eye (1996)

The Book of Angels (1997)

Kerrigan's Copenhagen: A Love Story (2002)

Bluett's Blue Hours (2003)

Greene's Summer (2004)

Danish Fall (2005)

A Passion in the Desert (2007)

In the Company of Angels (2010)

Falling Sideways (2011)

Kerrigan in Copenhagen: A Love Story (2013)

Beneath the Neon Egg (2014)

Novel-in-essays

Last Night My Bed a Boat of Whiskey Going Down (2010)

Short-story collections

Unreal City (1996)

Drive Dive Dance & Fight (1997)

Cast Upon the Day (2008)

Getting Lucky: New & Selected Stories, 1982-2012 (2013)

Essay collections

Realism & Other Illusions: Essays on the Craft of Fiction (2002)

Riding the Dog: A Look Back at America (2008)

Literary criticism

Andre Dubus: A Study of the Short Fiction (1988)

Robert Coover: A Study of the Short Fiction (1992)

Translations

Last Walk Through the City: Poems by Dan Turèll (2010)

Four poems by Henrik Nordbrandt, translated by Thomas E. Kennedy in *American Poetry Review,* Volume 42, Issue 3 (May/June 2013): 40-41

Spoken-word recording

an INTRODUCTION: Dan Turèll+Halfdan E Meet Thomas E. Kennedy, a CD on which Kennedy reads his translations of 12 poems by Turèll, with music by Danish film composer Halfdan E and background vocals by Sanne Graulund. Text and sample audio clip of one of those poems, "Last Walk Through the City," appear online in *Serving House Journal.*

Anthologies

New Danish Fiction, co-edited with Frank Hugus (1995)

Small Gifts of Knowing: New Irish Poetry and Prose (1997)

Stories and Sources (1998)

Poems and Sources (2000)

The Secret Life of Writers, co-edited with Walter Cummins (2002)

The Girl with the Red Hair: Musings on a Theme, co-edited with Walter Cummins (2011)

THOMAS E. KENNEDY published the Copenhagen Quartet through Bloomsbury—IN THE COMPANY OF ANGELS (2010), FALLING SIDEWAYS (2011), KERRIGAN IN COPENHAGEN (2013), BENEATH THE NEON EGG (2014). His stories, essays and and translations from the Danish appear regularly in many periodicals. He has won an O. Henry Award, the silver medal given by the Dan Turèll Society once a year, two EUROPEAN awards, and the NATIONAL MAGAZINE AWARD for the essay. He has published 41 books over the years, including novels, story and essay collections, and anthologies.

www.ingramcontent.com/pod-product-compliance
Lightning Source LLC
Chambersburg PA
CBHW030415180626
46812CB00005B/2025